# THE COST OF IT

# IT

## THE ETHAN CALDWELL STORIES - BOOK TWO

## TREY NANTZ

CAROLOPOLIS
PRESS

CAROLOPOLIS PRESS

Published by Carolopolis Press, South Carolina, United States.

www.carolopolispress.com

This is a work of fiction. Names, characters, places, and incidents are products of the author's imagination or are used fictitiously. Any resemblance to actual persons, living or dead, events, or locales is entirely coincidental.

ISBN: 979-8-9935380-2-0

First Edition

# CONTENTS

# EPIGRAPH

*"There is no trap so deadly as the trap you set for yourself."*
*Raymond Chandler*

# 1

## CHAPTER 1: THE CALL

C HAPTER 1: THE CALL

*Greenville, South Carolina — October 2015*

Ethan's phone rings at 2:47 AM on a Tuesday.

He knows it's bad before he answers. Nothing good happens at 2:47 AM. Not phone calls, not knocks on the door, not the sound of boots on a compound wall.

The phone says UNKNOWN NUMBER.

He answers anyway.

"Ethan." The voice is familiar but wrong. Strained. "It's Yousef."

Ethan sits up. Yousef al-Tamimi. Literature professor from Baghdad University who spent 2008 translating for American contractors because literature professors didn't get paid enough to feed a family. Who fell in a sewage ditch outside Baqubah and never lived it down. Who made it to the US in 2011, with his wife and two daughters soon after, settling in Rochester a few years later where there was a small Iraqi community and winter that reminded no one of home.

"Yousef. It's three in the morning."

"I know. I'm sorry. I'm in Kurdistan."

Kurdistan. Not Rochester.

"You're supposed to be in New York."

"I came back. Temporary work. Cultural liaison for an NGO. Or that's what they said." Yousef's English is perfect, Oxford-inflected from his PhD work, but right now it's ragged. "It wasn't temporary. It wasn't an NGO. And now I can't leave."

Ethan gets out of bed. Walks to the kitchen in the dark. Doesn't turn on lights because the conversation feels like something that should happen in darkness.

"Can't leave how?"

"My passport. They have it. Security review, they say. Routine." Pause. "It's not routine."

"Who's they?"

"CIA. A man named David Chen. You know him?"

That's the point, Ethan realizes.

Chen. Yale-educated, preppy, six years in Kurdistan running sources and mapping networks. Last time Ethan saw him was January 2009. Green Zone, Baghdad. Drinking beer that tasted like aluminum and talking about slightly more good than harm like it was an ethical framework instead of an excuse for doing questionable things in an impossible situation.

"Yeah," Ethan says. "I know him."

"He said you would. He said you'd understand."

Ethan opens his refrigerator. Light spills out. Empty except for beer, leftover Chinese food, condiments that expired in 2014. The refrigerator of a man who eats dinner standing over the sink.

"Understand what?"

"I've been working for him. Four years. Since 2011."

The refrigerator hums. Ethan stares at expired mustard.

"Say that again."

"2011. He approached me in Baghdad. Said they needed help with refugee resettlement. Identifying people for SIV program. Good money. Help my community. I thought—" Yousef's voice breaks. "I thought I was doing refugee work."

"But you weren't."

"No."

Ethan closes the refrigerator. Opens the freezer. Pulls out a bottle of vodka he keeps there for emergencies. This qualifies.

"What were you doing?"

"Intelligence work. Mapping networks. Kurdish political parties, Iranian operatives, Turkish intelligence. He'd send me to meetings. Cultural events. Ask me to talk to people. Report back. At first it seemed harmless. Then—" Pause. "Then it wasn't harmless anymore. And by then I'd taken money, signed things, met people. I was in."

"How deep in?"

"Deep enough that Chen says I can't leave until the mission is complete. Deep enough that my passport is in a safe at the US Consulate. Deep enough that when I asked to go home last month, he reminded me that my green card status is contingent on cooperation with US government entities during ongoing security matters." The bitterness comes through. "I'm trapped, Ethan."

Ethan pours vodka. Doesn't bother with a glass. Drinks from the bottle because some conversations require that.

"Why are you calling me?"

"Because you're a lawyer. Because Chen said you'd understand. Because—" Yousef's breathing gets unsteady. "Because I'm scared. My family is safe in Rochester. But I'm here and ISIS is twenty kilometers away and Chen keeps pushing for one more meeting, one more contact, and I think he's going to get me killed."

The vodka burns going down. Ethan welcomes it.

"When did he recruit you?"

"February 2011. I was teaching at Baghdad University. He came to a lecture I gave on medieval Arabic poetry. Approached me after. Said he admired my work. We had coffee. Talked about literature, about Iraq, about the situation." Pause. "He was very good. Made me feel seen. Understood. Said there were ways I could help people. Refugee work. Just identifying candidates for resettlement programs."

"How long does Chen say you need to stay?"

"Until I complete the Kamal recruitment. But Ethan—" Yousef's voice drops. "Chen's rotation ends in January. Sixty days. If I haven't delivered Kamal by then, his replacement inherits the operation and starts from zero. That could mean another year. Two years. Chen's the only one who knows me, who trusts me. A new handler won't. They'll want to rebuild everything."

The timeline crystallizes. Two months. After that, Yousef resets to square one with an unknown officer who has no investment in letting him go.

February 2011. Ethan had been helping Yousef with his SIV application then. Forwarding letters of recommendation. Connecting him with an immigration lawyer. Thinking he was helping a friend.

While Chen was cultivating him.

"Did he know you and I were in contact?"

"Yes. He asked about you. Said you'd worked together. Said you were a good man trying to do good work in bad circumstances." Another pause. "I think that's why he recruited me. Because you'd vouched for me. Because I had connection to someone he trusted."

The vodka bottle is suddenly very heavy.

"I helped him recruit you."

"You didn't know."

"I wrote letters saying you were reliable. Trustworthy. Good under pressure. Had worked with US forces in dangerous conditions." Ethan sets the bottle down before he throws it. "I gave him your résumé."

"Ethan—"

"Four years. He had you for four years and I never knew."

"How could you know? I couldn't tell you. The agreements I signed—classified programs, security protocols. I couldn't tell anyone."

"Your wife knows?"

"She knows I work for Americans. Thinks it's State Department cultural exchange. I couldn't even tell her." The shame in Yousef's voice is thick. "Four years lying to my wife about what I do. Four years taking money to introduce people to Chen, to report on meetings, to—"

He stops. Ethan waits.

"To help Chen recruit others. Like he recruited me. That's the mission now. There's someone he wants. Kurdish intelligence officer. Lost family to Iranian proxies and AQI. Perfect profile. And Chen thinks I can introduce them. Vouch for the work. Explain how it helps people."

"And you don't want to do it."

"I can't do it anymore. I can't look at this person and lie and know I'm pulling them into the same trap. I want out. I want to go home to Rochester and teach my daughters English and forget any of this happened."

"But Chen won't let you leave."

"Not until I complete this recruitment. Not until he has someone else to do the work I'm doing. That's how it works. You know that. You were a contractor."

"Chen's rotation review is in three weeks. If Kamal isn't recruited by then, Chen loses the operation—and I stay until his replacement starts the process over. That could be years."

Ethan does know that. Contractors don't quit mid-deployment. You finish the rotation or you get blacklisted. And intelligence assets don't quit mid-operation. You finish the mission or you become a security risk.

"What do you want me to do?"

"Tell me if I have legal recourse. If there's something—anything—I can use to force them to give me my passport back. If—" Yousef's voice drops. "If you can help me get out."

Ethan picks up the vodka bottle again. Looks at it. Sets it back down.

"Send me everything you have. Employment documents, correspondence with Chen, anything that shows the arrangement."

"I will. Thank you, Ethan."

"Don't thank me yet. I don't know if I can do anything."

"But you'll try."

"I'll look at what you have. See if there's any legal angle."

They both know there isn't. But Yousef needs to hear it anyway.

"One more thing, Ethan—" Yousef's voice becoming empty, hopeless. "Chen. There's a KRG cultural conference next week. Seven days. He wants me to introduce him to Kamal there. Says it's perfect venue—diplomatic event, natural context for meeting. If I don't make the introduction then, he's moving me to Sulaymaniyah. Different city. Different surveillance patterns. Harder for—" Yousef stops. "Harder for anyone to find me."

Seven days. The window is closing faster than Ethan thought.

After they hang up, Ethan sits in his dark kitchen with a bottle of vodka and tries to process what just happened.

Chen recruited Yousef. Used their shared connection—Ethan's connection—as leverage. Spent four years cultivating him from refugee liaison to intelligence asset. And now won't let him leave because the mission isn't complete.

And Ethan never knew. Spent those four years thinking he'd helped a friend escape Iraq. Thinking the letters he wrote, the contacts he made, the legal advice he gave—all of it was helping.

Instead he'd been part of Chen's recruitment package. Proof that working with Americans was safe. Productive. That people like Ethan vouched for people like Chen.

The deception sits heavy. Not Yousef's deception—he understands that. Chen's. Using their friendship as tradecraft. Weaponizing trust.

It's smart. It's effective. It's exactly what Chen would do.

And it makes Ethan complicit in trapping someone who fell in a sewage ditch in Baqubah and never complained, who translated under fire, who helped them understand a country that made no sense to outsiders.

The scar on Ethan's left arm itches. Shrapnel from Baqubah, November 2008. Seven years ago but it might as well be yesterday.

He touches it unconsciously. Raised tissue. The reminder.

Then he opens his laptop.


***


The emails arrive at 3:47 AM. Three attachments.

First: Employment contract with International Cultural Exchange Foundation. Position: Regional Cultural Liaison. Salary: $85,000 annually. Duration: Six months, renewable.

Ethan searches for the foundation. Nothing. No website, no tax filings, no registered corporate officers. Standard CIA front company. Competently done but obvious once you know what to look for.

Second attachment: Email chain with Chen. Starts April 2015—right after Yousef's deportation case began. Which means Chen reached out exactly when Yousef was most vulnerable. Six months of documented correspondence about the "Kurdistan opportunity." Before that, presumably, was verbal. Meetings. Phone calls. The careful cultivation phase where nothing gets written down.

Ethan reads through the emails. Professional. Polite. Chen asking for meeting reports. Yousef providing summaries. References to "developmental targets" and "network mapping" and "situational awareness."

Intelligence work dressed up in bureaucratic language.

Buried in a September 2015 email: *Yousef—understand your concerns about timeline. However, completion of current developmental cycle is essential to mission success. Appreciate your patience. —DC*

Translation: You're not leaving until I say so.

Third attachment: Visa documents. Entry to Kurdistan Region, July 2015. Original six-month contract through January 2016. No extension stamps—just a handwritten note in Kurdish and English: "Departure authorization required from sponsoring organization."

Extensions granted by Kurdish authorities at request of US Consulate. Which means Chen has the relationship to keep Yousef stuck there indefinitely.

Ethan stares at these documents and tries to find any legal recourse. There isn't one.

Employment contract with a fake company. Visa extensions from a regional government that doesn't fully control its own immigration policy. Verbal promises of temporary work that became permanent.

No court has jurisdiction. No lawyer can help. This is internal agency business happening in a semi-autonomous region during a war.

The legal answer is: Yousef is fucked.

But Ethan already knew that. Yousef knew it too. That's why he called at 2:47 AM asking for help instead of asking for a lawyer.

The question isn't whether there's legal recourse. The question is whether Ethan is willing to fly to Kurdistan and try to fix this anyway.

He opens a new browser tab. Searches for flights to Erbil.

One stop in Istanbul. Total travel time twenty-two hours. $1,847 round trip. Next available: Thursday night, arriving Friday morning.

He stares at the screen for ten minutes.

Then he opens his contacts and scrolls to P.

Peterson, Derek. Petey. Last contacted March 2012. They'd exchanged messages when Ramos got married. Brief updates. The kind of contact that passes for friendship when people move on with their lives.

Before that: daily contact for six months. Living in each other's pockets. The kind of proximity that comes from sharing CHUs and MRAPs and operations where one mistake gets everyone killed.

Ethan types: *Petey. Need to talk. You still in the game? —Ethan*

He stares at the message. Considers not sending it. Considers trying to handle this alone. Considers letting Yousef figure it out because it's not Ethan's responsibility.

Then he thinks about the sewage ditch. About Yousef climbing out covered in filth while everyone laughed. About him translating through all of it, never complaining, showing up the next night for the next mission.

We don't leave team behind.

He hits send.

The reply comes forty-seven seconds later: *Always. Call me.*

*** 

Ethan calls at 4:23 AM. Petey answers on the second ring.

"Counselor. Been a minute."

The voice is the same. Relaxed. Confident. The voice of someone who's been in enough bad situations to know panic doesn't help.

"Three years."

"Not that long. Ramos's wedding in '13."

"That was a shitshow."

"That was Ramos getting married in Vegas at a drive-through chapel with Elvis officiating. What'd you expect?" Petey laughs. Same laugh from 2008. "So. Yousef's in trouble."

"You know already?"

"You texted me about 'the game' at 3:15 AM. I made calls. Yousef al-Tamimi, our old terp, working in Kurdistan for a company that doesn't exist. Passport held by Kurdish authorities at CIA request. Been there since July 2015. They're using him to map networks."

"Jesus. You got all that in an hour?"

"I got all that in thirty minutes. Spent the other thirty finding out who's running him." Pause. "It's Chen."

"I know."

"You know Chen's in Kurdistan?"

"Yousef told me."

"Did he tell you Chen's been there since 2010? Five years building networks. Running sources. He's not just an officer. He's THE officer. You want to operate in Kurdistan, you coordinate with Chen or you get shut down."

Ethan hadn't known that. Thought Chen was just another case officer. Turns out he's the entire operation.

"So getting Yousef out means going through Chen."

"Going through Chen or around him. Neither option is good." Petey's voice goes serious. "Talk to me. What happened?"

"Yousef called at 2:47 this morning. Says Chen recruited him in 2011. Started as refugee liaison work. Became intelligence work. Now Chen wants him to recruit someone else and Yousef wants out. Chen says not until the mission's complete."

"And you're thinking about going there."

"I'm past thinking about it. I'm looking at flights."

Silence on the line. Long enough that Ethan checks to see if they're still connected.

"Petey?"

"I'm thinking." More silence. "You remember the grain field?"

Baqubah. November 2008. The compound outside the village. Ethan spotting the fighters before anyone else did. Making the call to engage. The man dropping. His first kill. Ramos getting hit. The village surviving.

"I remember."

"You've been carrying that for seven years."

"Not carrying it. Just living with it."

"Bullshit. You're carrying it like a fucking rucksack. And now Yousef calls and suddenly you've got a chance to save someone, make up for That first kill, balance the books." Petey's voice is gentle. "It doesn't work that way."

"I know that."

"Do you? Because from here it looks like you're flying into a situation you can't fix because you need to prove you can save people."

"Yousef was my terp."

"Yousef was our terp. I was there too. So was Ramos and Torres and Kozlowski. We all feel the obligation. But that doesn't mean you can fix this with righteous indignation and a plane ticket."

"So I should do nothing?"

"I didn't say that." Pause. "Tell me about Chen. When did you meet him?"

"January 2009. Green Zone. Some coordination meeting about contractor intelligence products. We got drinks after. Talked about the war, about whether any of it mattered. He had this phrase—slightly more good than harm. Like it was an ethical framework."

"And you think he's still using that framework?"

"I think he's spent five years in Kurdistan convincing himself anything he does is justified by the mission."

"Probably right." Another pause. "Here's what you need to understand. Chen's smart. Really smart. And he's been in Kurdistan long enough to know every player, every angle. You show up trying to extract one of his assets, he's going to see you coming."

"I'm not trying to extract him. I'm trying to see if there's any legal recourse."

"Ethan. Come on. You're not flying to Kurdistan to file paperwork. You're going there because you think you can convince Chen to let Yousef go. Or because you think you can get him out without Chen's permission. Either way, you're fucking with an intelligence operation in an active war zone."

"So what's my alternative? Tell Yousef I can't help?"

"Your alternative is to think about what you're actually trying to accomplish and whether it's possible."

Ethan drinks more vodka. Petey waits.

"He fell in a ditch," Ethan says finally. "Baqubah. That sewage ditch outside the village. Remember?"

"Of course I remember. We gave him so much shit."

"He climbed out and kept working. Covered in sewage, smelling like death, and he kept translating. Didn't complain. Didn't ask to go back. Just did the job." Ethan sets the bottle down. "We don't leave team behind."

"Yousef left the team in 2009."

"Because we left. We pulled out, cut contracts, told terps good luck. He got out because I helped with his SIV. Then Chen recruited him using me as leverage. That makes it my responsibility."

More silence. Then Petey sighs.

"You're going no matter what I say."

"Yeah."

"Thursday night?"

"Yeah."

"You're going to need help. I'm in Virginia, but I've got a friend in Erbil. Lars Petersen. Norwegian. Volunteered with the Pesh in 2014 when ISIS was at the gates. Stayed on doing security work. Knows everyone, speaks Kurdish, can move around without attracting attention."

"Another westerner doing security work isn't going to attract attention?"

"In Kurdistan right now? No. Place is full of foreign volunteers, contractors, journalists, spooks. Everyone's there mapping the same networks. One more American asking questions won't register unless you're stupid about it."

"I won't be stupid."

"You're already being stupid. You're flying into a war zone to fuck with a CIA operation." Petey's voice softens. "But I get it. So here's what I'll do. I'll call Lars, tell him you're coming. I'll make more calls, see what else I can learn about Chen's operation. And I'll keep my phone on."

"In case I need extraction."

"In case you need extraction from Kurdistan during an active ISIS offensive while you're interfering with US intelligence operations. Yeah."

"You'd come?"

"We don't leave team behind. Even when team is being a dumbass."

***

After they hang up, Ethan books the flight. Thursday night, 11:47 PM. Istanbul layover. Arrive Erbil Friday 2:15 PM local time.

$1,847 on his credit card. Nonrefundable.

He closes the laptop. Looks at his kitchen. Clean counters. Empty sink. The refrigerator with expired mustard. His life for six years. Quiet. Safe. Boring.

He'd thought he was done with Iraq. Thought he'd left that life behind. Came home, passed the bar, started practicing law. Estate planning. Wills and trusts. Problems that could be solved with paperwork.

It was exactly what he'd wanted after Baqubah.

But sitting in his kitchen at 5 AM with a bottle of vodka and a plane ticket to Kurdistan, Ethan realizes he'd been fooling himself. You don't leave that world. You just pretend you did until someone calls asking for help.

The scar on his arm itches.

He touches it. Raised tissue. Permanent reminder of the night he stopped being an observer and became a participant. The night he killed someone. The night the math became personal instead of theoretical.

Seven years ago he thought that night would define him. Turns out it was just the beginning.

\*\*\*

At 7:30 AM his alarm goes off. Tuesday. Client meetings. Paperwork. His normal life.

Except now he's flying to Kurdistan in three days.

He showers. Shaves. Looks at his reflection and sees someone who looks older than thirty-two. The years since Iraq haven't been hard, but they've accumulated. Small changes. Lines around the eyes. Gray in his beard if he doesn't trim it.

He puts on a suit because Margaret insists on professional appearance even though Greenville lawyers show up in khakis.

The office is fifteen minutes away. Margaret's door is open when he arrives.

"You look terrible," she says without looking up.

"Didn't sleep."

"The Iraq situation."

She knows. Of course she knows. Margaret knows everything about everyone in the firm because she pays attention.

"Yeah."

"And you're going."

"Friday."

Now she looks up. Takes inventory with that expression that suggests she's finding his soul wanting.

"How long?"

"Week. Maybe less if I can't do anything."

"Which you probably can't."

"Probably not."

"But you're going anyway because seven years ago he was your interpreter and you think that creates permanent obligation."

It's not a question. Margaret understands him too well. Hired him in 2009 knowing he'd done things in Iraq that didn't fit neat categories. Kept him on through the first year when nightmares made morning meetings difficult.

"Take the time you need," she says. "I'll cover your clients. But Ethan? Come back."


                              ***


That afternoon Ethan researches Kurdistan.

Not the Kurdistan from 2008—that's buried under six years of change. Kurdistan in October 2015.

The articles paint a picture:

ISIS took Mosul in June 2014. Swept through northern Iraq. Got within thirty kilometers of Erbil before Peshmerga and US airstrikes stopped them. Now there's a front line. Trenches and berms. Peshmerga on one side, ISIS on the other. Sometimes close enough to shout insults.

The siege changed Erbil. Turned it from regional capital to front-line city. Every intelligence service operating there. CIA, MI6,

German BND, French DGSE, Iranian Quds Force, Turkish MIT. All mapping the same networks, recruiting the same sources, trying to figure out what happens after ISIS.

And the western volunteers. Showed up after seeing beheading videos. Ex-military mostly. Some wannabes. A few idealists. Funded equipment via Instagram and GoFundMe. Fought with Peshmerga units on the front. Some died. Some went home. Some stayed, got into security consulting, never left.

Kurdistan united for first time in decades. KDP and PUK working together against common enemy. The dream of independence feeling possible if they can just hold the line.

All this happening twenty kilometers from where Yousef is trapped translating for Chen.

Ethan reads accounts from journalists embedded with Peshmerga. Descriptions of the front lines. Fighters drinking chai in fighting positions. No light discipline because everyone knows where everyone is. Occasional exchanges of fire. Mostly watching. The boredom of war punctuated by moments of chaos.

One article mentions western volunteers. Norwegian, British, American. Fighting because they believed in something or couldn't stay home or thought they could make a difference. Raised money online for equipment. Showed up with gear bought on Amazon. Peshmerga commanders simultaneously grateful and bemused by these foreigners.

Lars Petersen is mentioned. Norwegian. Former military. Arrived November 2014. Fought at Gwer. Stayed on doing security consulting. Described as "competent and low-key, with better Kurdish than most foreigners."

That's who Petey's sending him to.

Ethan keeps reading. Tries to understand what he's walking into.

Kurdistan isn't Iraq. Functionally independent since 1991. Different government, different flags, different currency. But technically still part of Iraq. The autonomy is negotiated, contingent, always at risk of Baghdad deciding to reassert control.

The politics are Byzantine. KDP controls Erbil and Dohuk. PUK controls Sulaymaniyah and much of the east. Both have their own Peshmerga forces. Rivalries go back decades. Civil war in the '90s. But right now they're unified against ISIS. Question is what happens after.

Iran has relationships with both. Turkey watches nervously. Baghdad resents the autonomy. The US needs Kurdistan as ally against ISIS but doesn't want to support independence.

Chen's been mapping this for five years. Every party, every relationship, every leverage point. Using assets like Yousef to understand who's connected to who, who can be turned, who can be pressured.

And now Yousef wants out.

Ethan closes his laptop.

He's flying into the most complex political situation in the Middle East, to a city full of intelligence services, to extract an asset from someone who's spent five years building networks.

This is going to go great.

***

Wednesday evening he starts packing.

One bag. Light. Jeans, t-shirts, light jacket for cool evenings. Kurdistan in October is warm days, cool nights. Nothing fancy. Doesn't want to look like businessman or contractor or anything that draws attention.

His passport is still valid. The Q clearance from 2007 DOE work expired in 2009. Not that it matters. This isn't official business.

He packs the cash from the bank. $3,000 in small bills. The kind of money that opens doors in places where official channels don't work.

His phone buzzes. Text from unknown number:

*Landing tomorrow 2:15 PM. I'll be at arrivals. Lars*

Followed immediately by:

*Petey says you're friend. Good enough for me. Be ready to move fast. —L*

Ethan replies: *Thanks. See you Friday.*

Another text, this one from Yousef:

*Thank you for coming. I know what you're risking. —Y*

Ethan doesn't reply to that one. Because he doesn't fully know what he's risking. And he's not sure he wants to articulate it.

***

Thursday morning he goes to the office one more time. Briefs Margaret on his active cases. Pemberton trust documents are ready for signature. Morrison estate is in probate. The Jenkins business formation can wait until he's back.

"Anything else I should know?" Margaret asks.

"If I'm not back in two weeks, call Petey. Number's in my phone."

"Ethan."

"Just covering contingencies."

She studies him for a long moment. "You're a good lawyer. Better than you give yourself credit for. You could have a real career here."

"I know."

"And you're throwing it away to fix something that probably can't be fixed."

"Maybe."

"Why?"

Ethan thinks about how to answer that. About the math that never works. About Yousef in the sewage ditch. About Chen weaponizing trust. About seven years of trying to be normal and realizing normal doesn't erase what you did, what you saw, who you were.

"Because I was there," he says finally. "And being there creates obligations that don't expire."

Margaret nods. "Then go. Do what you have to do. Come back when you can."

***

Thursday night, 11:47 PM, Ethan boards a plane to Istanbul.

The flight is half empty. Late night departure. Mix of business travelers and people visiting family. Nobody asks why he's going to Erbil.

He doesn't sleep. Sits in the dark cabin and thinks about Kurdistan. About Chen. About Yousef working for four years while Ethan thought he was helping a friend.

The deception still tastes bitter. Not Yousef's deception—he understands that. Chen's. Using their friendship as leverage. Weaponizing the letters Ethan wrote, the contacts he made, the trust he extended.

It's smart tradecraft. It's effective recruitment.

It makes Ethan complicit.

The math never works. But you do it anyway because the alternative is doing nothing.

That's what Chen believes. What he's believed for five years. The mission matters more than the people running it. Yousef's discomfort is acceptable cost for mapping networks that could prevent attacks. One asset's freedom is less important than mission success.

It's logical. It's cold. It's probably right.

But Ethan's flying to Kurdistan anyway.

The plane banks east toward Istanbul. Toward Erbil. Toward whatever's waiting.

He touches the scar on his arm.

Here we go again.

# 2

## CHAPTER 2: ERBIL

*Erbil, Kurdistan Region — October 2015*

The approach to Erbil is all dust and distance.

Ethan watches through the plane window as the landscape resolves below. Brown and tan and occasional green where irrigation reaches. The Zagros mountains to the north—jagged peaks separating Kurdistan from Iran, snow-topped even in October. To the west, somewhere beyond the haze, Mosul. Thirty kilometers. Close enough that on clear days you can see the minarets from Peshmerga berms.

ISIS territory. The caliphate at its peak.

The plane banks hard. Erbil International appears below. Single runway, modern terminal building that looked ambitious when they built it during the boom years. Now it's a lifeline. Military cargo planes mixed with civilian flights. C-130s and Turkish Airlines. Royal Jordanian and German Luftwaffe. The coalition and the commerce side by side.

The descent is aggressive. Steep approach, hard landing. Standard procedure for conflict zones. Minimize time in the approach corridor where you're vulnerable. Not that ISIS has surface-to-air capability this far north—their technical expertise tops out at truck-mounted machine guns and improvised explosives—but procedures are procedures. Pilots don't get paid enough to take chances.

They hit the runway like the pilot's angry at it. No apology over the intercom. Welcome to Kurdistan.

The terminal is chaos pretending to be order.

Modern architecture, bullet-resistant glass, air conditioning that works most of the time. But the infrastructure can't quite handle the volume. Every intelligence service in the Middle East operates through Erbil now. Every NGO working the refugee crisis. Every journalist covering ISIS. Every arms dealer, contractor, diplomat, and adventurer who thinks they can make a difference or a profit.

Security checkpoints every twenty meters. Kurdish Asayish in olive uniforms, serious and professional. They check passports, ask questions, watch everyone. Looking for ISIS infiltrators, Turkish agents, Iranian operatives, or just the general chaos that follows when a city becomes this important this fast.

Kurdish flags everywhere. Red, white, green with the yellow sun in the center. Not Iraq's flag—Kurdistan's flag. The distinction matters. On the walls, photos of Masoud Barzani looking stern and paternal. Father of the nation. President of the Kurdistan Regional Government. The man who's held this region together through civil war, sanctions, ISIS, and Baghdad's constant attempts to reassert control.

More photos: martyrs. Young men in Peshmerga uniform who died holding the line against ISIS. Fresh faces, most of them. Died at Gwer, at Makhmour, at Kirkuk. Places that used to be names on maps and are now graveyards.

The passengers disperse into different lines. Ethan follows signs for visa on arrival. Tourist visas, business visas, journalist visas—each line moves at different speeds depending on how much scrutiny your category receives. Tourists move fastest because nobody believes you're actually here for tourism, which means you must be something else, and figuring out what else takes time nobody has.

The man in front of Ethan is German. Journalist credentials visible on a lanyard. The immigration officer asks him questions in English, German, then Kurdish, testing to see which language gets the most honest answers. The journalist responds carefully in English. Says he's covering the humanitarian crisis. The officer stamps his passport, writes something in Kurdish on the entry form, waves him through.

When it's Ethan's turn, the officer looks at his passport for a long time.

American. South Carolina address. No previous stamps for Iraq or Kurdistan. Arriving alone. No visible press credentials, no NGO affiliation, no business documents.

"Purpose of visit?"

"Tourism."

The officer looks at him like he just claimed to be Santa Claus.

"Tourism." Not a question. A statement of disbelief.

"Historical sites. The citadel. I understand it's being renovated."

"The citadel is closed. Has been closed for two years."

"Then I'll see what's open."

The officer sets down the passport. Studies Ethan's face. Comparing it to the photo, to some mental database of people who shouldn't be here, to the general category of Americans Who Show Up In War Zones For Unclear Reasons.

"How long you stay?"

"One week. Maybe less."

"Where you stay?"

"Guest house. I have an address." Ethan shows him the paper Lars texted. Handwritten Kurdish with English translation below.

The officer copies the address into his computer. Types something else. Waits for the screen to refresh. Whatever database he's checking takes thirty seconds to load. Finally he nods. Stamps the passport. Writes something in Kurdish on the entry form—probably "suspicious American, notify Asayish if he does anything stupid."

"Welcome to Kurdistan. Stay in Erbil. Do not go west of city."

"Understood."

"Do not go to checkpoints. Do not photograph military positions. Do not—" The officer pauses, choosing words. "Do not cause problems."

"I won't."

"Good. Enjoy citadel." Sarcasm without quite breaking protocol.

Ethan takes his passport and moves through.

Baggage claim is organized chaos. Three flights landed in the last hour. Passengers from Istanbul, Vienna, Amman. The luggage carousel moves like it's tired. Bags emerge slowly, covered in dust from the cargo hold. Everyone watches their bags like hawks because theft is rare but not impossible and replacing anything in Erbil takes weeks.

Ethan's duffel appears. He grabs it, clears customs without being stopped—they wave him through after seeing the entry stamp—and emerges into the arrivals hall.

It's like walking into a bazaar that someone tried to make look professional.

Drivers holding signs in Arabic, Kurdish, English. Family members crowding barriers trying to spot arriving relatives. Aid workers with NGO badges clustering near the exit. Journalists with too many cameras. Contractors in 5.11 tactical pants and polo shirts, trying to look inconspicuous and failing because they all look exactly the same.

And the spooks.

Ethan can spot them. Seven years gone but the pattern recognition remains. Too aware of their surroundings without obviously scanning. Moving with purpose but not hurry. Positioned where they can see exits and entrances. The body language of people who know they're being watched and don't care because everyone here is being watched by someone.

He counts at least five possibles. American, British, maybe German, definitely at least one who's either Turkish or Iranian. All pretending not to notice each other. All cataloging who's arriving and who's meeting them and whether any of it matters.

Welcome to Casablanca.

A man separates from the crowd of drivers. Tall, six-two, lean like someone who runs or doesn't eat enough. Blonde hair going gray, cut military short. Scandinavian features—high cheekbones, blue eyes, the kind of face that looks carved rather than grown. Maybe forty but could be younger. War ages people.

Cargo pants, hiking boots, loose shirt hanging over his belt line. Covering something. Sunglasses despite the sun being past its peak. The casual preparedness of someone who's been in enough bad situations to always assume the next one's coming.

"Ethan Caldwell?"

"That's me."

"Lars Petersen." They shake hands. His grip is firm but not performative. Working hands. "Petey says you need help with a situation."

"Something like that."

"We'll talk in the car. Not here."

The parking lot is chaos. No marked spaces, just cars parked wherever they fit. Toyota Land Cruisers dominate. Kurdistan's fleet vehicle of choice. Reliable, parts available, anonymous. You can't drive through Erbil without passing fifty of them.

Lars's is ten years old, white paint turned gray from dust, dents and scratches telling stories about roads that don't forgive mistakes. He unlocks it manually—no key fob. Ethan throws his bag in the back seat and climbs in front.

The interior smells like dust, cigarettes, and gun oil. A bottle of water in the cup holder, half-empty. Kurdish-language newspaper on the dash. Prayer beads hanging from the rearview mirror—not Lars's, probably came with the car from the previous owner. In the door pocket, a map of Kurdistan marked with pen, circles and notes in Norwegian.

Lars starts the engine. It turns over rough, settles into an idle that sounds like it's considering quitting but decides to keep going.

"First time in Kurdistan?" he asks, pulling out of the parking lot.

"First time in Erbil. I was in Iraq in 2008. Baqubah. Different war."

"Very different. Kurdistan wasn't Kurdistan then. Just northern Iraq under Saddam's shadow. Now it's its own thing. Government, parliament, military, borders, flag. Still technically part of Iraq but nobody believes that anymore. Especially not after ISIS."

They merge onto the main road heading toward Erbil. Traffic is chaotic but functional. Mix of cars, trucks, minibuses packed with passengers. Mercedes next to beat-up sedans from the '80s. Peshmerga vehicles with mounted machine guns. Everyone honking like it's a form of communication.

The first checkpoint appears two kilometers from the airport.

Concrete barriers form a chicane. Peshmerga in olive uniforms, mismatched equipment. Some have M16s, some AK-47s, one has what looks like a Yugoslav-era M70. Their gear doesn't match but their discipline does. They wave through the cars they know, stop the ones they don't. Watching.

Lars slows but doesn't stop. The Peshmerga recognize his vehicle, wave him through.

"They know you," Ethan observes.

"I've been here almost a year. You show up often enough, fight alongside them, they learn your face." Lars lights a cigarette, doesn't offer one. "Plus I pay attention. Learn names. Bring cigarettes sometimes. Tea. Small things that build rapport."

"Petey said you fought at Gwer."

"November 2014. ISIS pushed hard after taking Mosul. Thought they could roll through Kurdistan. Peshmerga held them at Gwer. Barely." Lars takes a drag, exhales through his nose. "That's when I learned what this war actually is."

"What is it?"

"Static front. Trenches and berms. World War One with smartphones. Both sides dug in, watching each other through binoculars. Occasional exchanges of fire. Lots of talking on radios. Lots of sitting around drinking chai. Then suddenly mortars or a truck bomb or a push and it's chaos for thirty minutes before it settles back into watching."

They pass another checkpoint. This one smaller. Two Peshmerga, one smoking, one talking on a radio. Photos of martyrs on the barrier. Young faces staring out.

"You see those photos everywhere," Lars says. "Every checkpoint, every government building, every Peshmerga base. The martyrs. Boys who died fighting ISIS. Some of them eighteen, nineteen. Too young. But that's who holds the line."

"How many have they lost?"

"Officially? Maybe fifteen hundred since 2014. Unofficially? More. Peshmerga doesn't always report casualties accurately. Bad for morale.

Bad for international support. Better to say we're winning than admit how much it costs."

The landscape starts changing. Open ground giving way to construction. Half-finished buildings. Boom-era projects from when oil prices were high and Kurdistan thought it might become the next Dubai. Now they stand empty, rebar rusting, concrete exposed. Dreams on hold.

"All this was supposed to be new Erbil," Lars says. "Shopping malls, office towers, luxury apartments. Then oil prices crashed and ISIS came and suddenly nobody wanted to invest in Kurdistan. So it sits."

They pass a billboard advertising luxury condos. The rendering shows glass towers and happy families. The reality behind it is bare concrete and empty lots. The cognitive dissonance is complete.

"How long have you been here?" Ethan asks.

"Since November 2014. Ten months, give or take." Lars flicks ash out the window. "I was in Oslo. Software developer. Good job, good money, boring life. Then ISIS took Mosul. Started posting videos of executions. Yazidis being massacred. Women enslaved. I watched it on my phone while eating breakfast and thought—" He pauses. "Thought I couldn't just watch. Couldn't pretend it wasn't happening. So I bought a plane ticket."

"Just like that?"

"Just like that. Romantic bullshit. Thought I'd make a difference. Fight evil. Save people." A bitter laugh. "Found out war is mostly boredom and bureaucracy with occasional moments of absolute chaos. But I stayed."

"Why?"

Lars doesn't answer immediately. They drive past another checkpoint. More martyrs. More Peshmerga watching traffic.

"Because leaving felt like quitting," he says finally. "And because it matters here. ISIS is real evil. Not theoretical geopolitical abstraction. Not governments doing questionable things for strategic reasons. Just pure fucking evil. They'd crucify me for being Christian and you for being American and not think twice. So fighting them matters. It's one of the few wars where you can point at one side and say definitively—those are the bad guys."

They enter Erbil proper.

The city sprawls in all directions. Mix of old and new, traditional and modern, trying to be both ancient capital and contemporary metropolis simultaneously. The citadel rises in the center—massive mud-brick structure on a tell, inhabited continuously for 6,000 years, now surrounded by scaffolding and tarps for renovations that probably won't finish in Ethan's lifetime.

Kurdish flags everywhere. On government buildings, on lamp posts, flying from apartments. The yellow sun on red, white, and green. Not Iraq's flag. Kurdistan's flag. The difference matters.

Peshmerga checkpoints at major intersections. More photo displays of martyrs. More barriers directing traffic. The infrastructure of a city that knows it's thirty kilometers from enemy lines.

"Security's heavy," Ethan says.

"Three layers," Lars explains. "Peshmerga controls outer perimeter. Anything coming into the city goes through them. Asayish handles internal security—intelligence, counter-espionage, making sure ISIS sympathizers don't blow things up. Then there's everyone else."

"Everyone else?"

"Every intelligence service in the Middle East operates here. American, British, German, French. Iranian Quds Force. Turkish MIT. Even Russians, though they keep low profile. All mapping the same networks. Sometimes cooperating. Mostly competing."

They pass a compound with American flags. High walls, guard towers, blast barriers. The US Consulate.

"That's where Chen works when he's not in the field," Lars says. "Officially he's political officer. Actually he runs northern Iraq intelligence operations. Been here since 2010. Knows everyone. Has relationships with KDP, PUK, probably Iranian contacts too. If you want to operate in Kurdistan, you coordinate with Chen or you don't operate."

The compound disappears behind them. Ethan files it away. He'll need to know where Chen works. Where he lives. Where he can be found.

They drive through a neighborhood that's clearly wealthy. New construction, satellite dishes, good cars parked behind walls. The homes of people who profited from the boom years and haven't lost everything yet.

"This is Gulan," Lars says. "Where the money lives. KDP officials, successful businessmen, people connected to the right families. Rent here costs what a Peshmerga fighter makes in a year."

Next to Gulan, separated by less than a kilometer, a park full of refugees. Tents and makeshift shelters. Laundry hanging on lines. Children playing in the dirt. Families from Mosul and Sinjar and villages ISIS overran. Living in Erbil because it's safe. Because the Peshmerga held the line and they didn't.

"Half a million refugees in Kurdistan now," Lars says. "Maybe more. Nobody knows exactly. They keep coming. Walking from Mosul with whatever they can carry. Getting smuggled through ISIS territory. Paying everything they have for passage. Then they end up here."

The contrast is stark. Wealth and desperation separated by a chain-link fence.

"The Kurds take them in," Lars continues. "Feed them, shelter them. Not because they have the resources—they don't. But because not taking them in means leaving them to ISIS. So they take them in and figure out how to make it work."

They drive past the citadel. Up close it's even more impressive. Ancient mud-brick walls rising thirty meters from the tell. The structure is organic, like it grew from the earth rather than being built. Parts of it are 5,000 years old. Other parts are from Abbasid period, Ottoman period, modern renovations layered on top of older foundations.

Scaffolding covers the southern wall. Tarps hanging. Workers visible but moving slowly. The UNESCO World Heritage Site restoration, stalled when ISIS came and budget evaporated.

"They've been renovating for five years," Lars says. "Probably take another five at this pace. Maybe longer. Hard to prioritize cultural heritage when you're fighting existential war thirty kilometers away."

They turn down narrower streets. Less traffic. Residential areas. Concrete walls around compounds. Satellite dishes on every roof. The smell of cooking—lamb grilling, spices, bread baking. Life continuing despite everything.

More checkpoints. Smaller ones. Local security rather than official Peshmerga. Neighborhood watch armed with AKs. They wave Lars through without stopping.

"This is Ankawa," Lars says. "Christian quarter. Mostly Assyrian and Chaldean. They've been here longer than Islam. Longer than Christianity technically—some of these families trace back to Assyrian Empire. Now they're protected minority in Muslim-majority region because Kurds actually practice the tolerance they preach."

Churches visible between buildings. Crosses on roofs. In a region where ISIS is crucifying Christians thirty kilometers away, Ankawa exists as counterpoint. Proof that different approach is possible.

"How many Christians?" Ethan asks.

"Maybe thirty thousand in Erbil. More came as refugees from Mosul and Nineveh. ISIS gave them choice—convert, pay jizya tax, or die. Most fled. Kurds took them in. Now Ankawa is overcrowded but everyone's alive. Could be worse."

They pass a church with people gathering outside. Evening service. Families in modest dress, children running around. Normalcy in the middle of chaos.

Lars turns down an alley, parks in front of a compound with high walls and metal gate. He honks twice in a pattern. The gate opens. They drive through into a courtyard.

The guest house is two-story building, beat-up but functional. Cars parked haphazardly. Laundry hanging from balconies. Garden that's more dust than green but trying. Generator in the corner, already running for evening power.

"Home," Lars says.

***

The room is basic. Bed with thin mattress, desk with chair, window with bars. Bathroom down the hall—shared, Lars explains, but hot water in the evenings if the generator holds. The walls are concrete, painted white years ago, now yellowing. Electricity runs through visible conduit. No air conditioning but a fan that might work.

Ethan drops his bag and looks out the window. View of the street below. Checkpoint visible two blocks away. Peshmerga smoking cigarettes. Car passing through. Life.

Lars appears in the doorway. "You hungry?"

"Yeah."

"Kurdish food or western?"

"Kurdish."

"Good answer. Western food here is terrible. Come on."

They walk three blocks to a restaurant. Small place, plastic chairs and tables, menu in Kurdish and English written on a whiteboard. The owner greets Lars in Kurdish—clearly regulars have been established. They sit in the back corner where Lars can see the door and the street.

The place is maybe a quarter full. Peshmerga fighters off duty. Family having dinner. Two men who might be Asayish, might be something else, sitting separately and watching everyone.

The owner brings chai without being asked. Strong and sweet. Then menus, though Lars clearly doesn't need one.

"Kebab is good," he says. "Rice with almonds and raisins. Yogurt. Keep it simple."

They order. The food arrives fast. Ethan eats because he hasn't eaten since Istanbul seventeen hours ago. Lars eats slower, watching the room.

The kebab is excellent. Lamb grilled with spices, tender and smoky. The rice is fragrant. The yogurt cuts the richness. Simple food done right.

"So," Lars says, setting down his fork. "Petey said you need to extract someone. Interpreter from 2008. Stuck here working for CIA. Wants out. Chen won't let him leave."

"That's the situation."

"And you think you can fix it."

"I think I can try."

Lars tears bread, dips it in yogurt. "You know who you're fucking with?"

"I know Chen. Knew him in 2008. Baghdad. We had drinks. Talked about the war."

"Six years ago. Different Chen. He's been here five years. That changes people. Makes them certain." Lars eats the bread. "I've heard about him. Never met him. Don't particularly want to. But everyone who operates here knows the name. David Chen. The American who runs Kurdistan. If you want to do intelligence work, run sources, recruit assets—you coordinate with Chen or you get shut down. Americans shut you down. Kurds shut you down on American request. Even other services defer to him because he's that embedded."

"So getting Yousef out means going through Chen."

"Going through Chen or around him. Either option is bad. Through him means negotiating from position of no leverage. Around him means operating without permission in city where he controls access and information." Lars drinks his chai. "What's your plan?"

"Talk to him first. See if there's any give. Any angle."

"And if there isn't?"

"Then I figure out plan B."

"That's not a plan. That's hope."

"It's what I have."

Lars signals for more chai. The owner brings it, along with baklava nobody ordered. Hospitality.

"Tell me about Yousef," Lars says. "What's his situation?"

Ethan explains. The 2008 interpreter relationship. The sewage ditch everyone joked about. How Yousef got his family to America. How Chen recruited him starting in 2011, slow cultivation from refugee liaison to intelligence asset. How Yousef came to Kurdistan in July 2015 thinking it was six months of cultural liaison work. How

Chen won't let him leave until he completes recruitment of Kurdish intelligence officer.

Lars listens without interrupting. When Ethan finishes, he's quiet for a long moment.

"Four years," he says finally. "Chen worked him for four years before bringing him here. That's patient. That's professional. And now Yousef wants out before completing the mission. Chen's not going to accept that."

"I know."

"You need leverage. Something Chen wants more than he wants Yousef's cooperation. Or something that makes keeping Yousef more expensive than letting him go."

"Like what?"

"That's what we need to figure out." Lars eats the baklava. "But first you should talk to Yousef. Understand exactly what Chen's trying to accomplish. What the mission is. Who this Kurdish intelligence officer is and why Chen wants him so badly."

"Can you set that up?"

"Already did. He's expecting you tonight. Eight PM. Different restaurant. I'll take you."

***

They spend the rest of the afternoon driving around Erbil. Lars playing tour guide and intelligence briefer combined.

He shows Ethan the markets. Traditional bazaars selling everything from spices to satellite dishes. Modern shopping malls built during the boom, half-empty now. The contrast between aspiration and reality.

He points out Peshmerga headquarters. Asayish buildings. Political party offices for KDP and PUK. The architecture of governance in a place that's inventing itself.

They drive to Dream City. Shopping mall complex that opened in 2013, immediately became symbol of Kurdistan's ambitions. Massive parking lots, western stores, food courts with American franchises. Now it's still operational but struggling. Too expensive for most locals. The dream receding.

"This is what Kurdistan wanted to be," Lars says. "Modern. Prosperous. International. Then reality intervened."

They drive past the university. Salahuddin University. Students visible between classes. Young people trying to get educated in the middle of a war. The library is open. The cafeterias serving food. Life insisting on continuing.

More martyrs photos. On campus bulletin boards. Students who joined Peshmerga, died at the front, won't graduate. Their friends walking past their faces every day.

They drive to the edge of the city where construction gives way to empty lots and then to countryside. In the distance, haze obscuring the horizon.

"Thirty kilometers that way," Lars points west. "Gwer. Front lines. You can't see it from here but it's there. The berm. Peshmerga on one side. ISIS on the other. Static positions. Sometimes they shoot at each other. Mostly they watch. Wait. Drink chai. The most boring war in history until suddenly it isn't."

"You said you fought there."

"November 2014. ISIS tried to push through. Massive assault. Truck bombs, mortars, infantry assault. They wanted Erbil. Would've taken it if Peshmerga broke." Lars lights another cigarette. "But Peshmerga didn't break. Held the line. American air strikes helped. But mostly it was Kurdish fighters saying no further. They die here or ISIS dies here. ISIS died."

"And you were there."

"I was there. With Peshmerga 2nd Division. Norwegian with an AK-47 and more balls than sense." He smiles without humor. "Fired maybe a thousand rounds. Killed maybe five ISIS fighters. Maybe. Hard to know in chaos. But I was there. That matters."

"Did it change you?"

Lars doesn't answer immediately. They watch the haze in the distance.

"It showed me who I actually am," he says finally. "Not who I thought I was in Oslo. Not who I pretended to be. Who I actually am when everything's chaos and people are trying to kill me. Turns out I'm someone who can function in that. Maybe even someone who's good at it. Not sure if that's good or bad. But it's true."

They turn around. Drive back toward the city.

"The western volunteers," Ethan says. "How many are there?"

"Maybe two hundred. Americans, British, Germans, Scandinavians. Few Australians. Mix of ex-military and people who just showed up. Some are competent. Some are disasters. Some are glory-seekers who post on Instagram. Some are true believers who think they're saving civilization."

"Which are you?"

"All of the above probably." Lars flicks ash. "I came for the fight. Stayed because leaving felt like quitting. Now I'm here because Kurdistan matters. It's the one place in the Middle East that might actually work. Democratic enough. Tolerant enough. Women fight in Peshmerga alongside men. Christians and Muslims coexist. It's not perfect but it's trying. That's worth fighting for."

They drive past another checkpoint. The Peshmerga recognize Lars's vehicle, wave him through without stopping.

"Plus they treat us well," Lars continues. "The Pesh. We're curiosities. Foreign volunteers who came to fight ISIS when their own governments hesitated. They respect that. Give us positions on the line. Let us fight. Some commanders are skeptical—see us as liability. But most appreciate the help. And the western presence helps with funding, equipment, international attention. So they tolerate us. Sometimes more than tolerate."

"You like them."

"I respect them. They're fighting for their home. Their families. Their right to exist as Kurds. That's real. Not abstract geopolitics. Not oil or influence. Just survival and identity. You can't fake that kind of motivation."

***

At 7:45 PM they leave the guest house. Walk four blocks through cooling evening. The sun is setting, painting the dust orange and gold. The call to prayer echoes from mosques. People heading home from work. Shops closing. The city transitioning to night mode.

They pass checkpoints. Peshmerga lighting cigarettes. Starting night shifts. Generator sounds rising as evening power demand kicks in. Satellite dishes all pointed the same direction, pulling in the world.

The restaurant is smaller than the lunch place. Family-run. The owner nods to Lars like they've discussed this already. There's a back room, private. They go there.

Yousef is already sitting. Waiting.

He looks older. That's Ethan's first thought. Four years should age someone from thirty-three to thirty-seven but Yousef looks fifty. Gray in his beard that wasn't there in 2008. Lines around his eyes. The look of someone who hasn't slept well in months. Maybe years.

He stands when he sees Ethan. They embrace. Middle Eastern style, three times, right cheek left cheek right cheek. The physical language of friendship.

"Thank you for coming," Yousef says. His voice cracks. "God, thank you for coming."

"Sit down. Let's talk."

They sit. Lars positions himself facing the door. Always watching.

The owner brings chai and water. Asks if they want food. Lars orders for everyone—meze, kebab, rice. Something to do with their hands while they talk.

Yousef looks at Ethan and something breaks behind his eyes.

"I didn't know," he says. "When it started. February 2011. I didn't know what I was agreeing to."

"Tell me everything."

# 3

## CHAPTER 3: THE LECTURE

*Erbil, Kurdistan Region — October 2015*

Yousef talks for ninety minutes.

He starts with Baghdad in February 2011. Teaching medieval Arabic poetry to twenty students who'd rather be anywhere else. Making $300 a month. Barely feeding his family. Then Chen appeared at a lecture on Abbasid-era verse. Sat in the back. Asked intelligent questions afterward. They had coffee.

"He knew poetry," Yousef says. "Actually knew it. Could quote Al-Mutanabbi. Discussed metaphor and meter. I thought—finally, an American who understands Iraqi culture beyond oil and insurgency."

They met six more times over three weeks. Always in public. Cafes, bookstores, the university. Chen asked about Yousef's life, his family, his hopes for Iraq's future. Expressed concern about brain drain—intellectuals leaving, taking culture with them. Asked if Yousef had considered emigrating.

"I told him about your help with my SIV application," Yousef says. "How you'd written letters, connected me with immigration lawyers. He was very interested in that. Asked about you. How we'd worked together. What kind of person you were."

That's when Ethan realizes. Chen had been researching him through Yousef. Using their friendship as data point.

"What did you tell him?"

"That you were fair. Competent. That you'd treated Iraqi staff with respect when other Americans didn't. That you'd kept your word about helping after you left." Yousef drinks water. His hand shakes. "I thought I was explaining why Americans could be trusted. I didn't realize I was providing recruitment intelligence."

After three weeks, Chen made the offer. Cultural advisor for refugee resettlement. $500 per successfully placed case. Help identify SIV candidates. Provide cultural context on applicants. Nothing classified, just informed opinion from someone who understood Iraqi society.

"It seemed legitimate," Yousef says. "He had official position at embassy. Business cards. The money came through proper channels. I thought—this is real work helping real people."

For six months, that's all it was. Yousef would attend community meetings, identify families who might qualify for SIV, provide assessments to Chen. The money was good. His family ate better. He could afford books for his daughters.

Then Chen asked him to attend a political meeting. Just observe, he said. Report on who attended, what was discussed, general atmosphere. Still nothing classified. Still just cultural context.

"That's when it changed," Yousef says. "Not all at once. Gradually. Each request slightly beyond the previous one. Attend this meeting. Talk to this person. Ask about this topic. Each time I'd think—this is still helping. Still gathering information that protects people. Then one day I looked at what I was doing and realized I was an intelligence asset."

By then he'd been working for Chen for eighteen months. Had taken thousands of dollars. Had signed papers he should have read more carefully—nondisclosure agreements disguised as employment contracts, security protocols he'd agreed to without understanding implications.

"I tried to quit," Yousef says. "August 2012. Told Chen I wanted to stop. He was very understanding. Said of course, I could stop anytime. Then he explained what would happen. My visa status would be reviewed. Questions might arise about my activities. The SIV application would face additional scrutiny. Nothing threatening. Just explaining reality."

The leverage was implicit but total. Yousef kept working.

In 2011, his SIV came through. Family moved to Rochester. Yousef thought—finally, this ends. I'm in America. Chen can't reach me here.

He was wrong.

Chen visited Rochester in December 2013. Friendly visit. Checking on the family's adjustment. Brought gifts for the daughters. Mentioned that some refugees needed help understanding American systems. Would Yousef be willing to provide occasional consultation? Just phone calls. Just advice. Good money for minimal work.

Yousef said yes because saying no meant explaining to his wife why an American diplomat was visiting and what their actual relationship had been. Said yes because $500 for a phone call seemed easy. Said yes because Chen made it seem like saying no would complicate things that should remain simple.

"He came to my home," Yousef says. The bitterness is thick now. "Met my wife. Played with my daughters. Made himself part of our lives. So refusing him felt like betraying a family friend."

For a year, Yousef did phone consultations. Talking to refugees, providing cultural guidance, reporting back to Chen. Nothing that seemed dangerous. Nothing that felt like intelligence work. Just helping his community.

Then in July 2015, Chen called with an opportunity. Six months in Kurdistan. Cultural liaison for International Cultural Exchange Foundation. $85,000. Help coordinate refugee services while Kurdistan dealt with ISIS crisis. His family would stay in Rochester—schools, stability, safety. He'd send money home. Return by January 2016 with enough savings to help his daughters attend good colleges.

"I thought it was temporary," Yousef says. "I thought—six months, help people, make good money, come home. I didn't know the foundation was CIA front. Didn't know Chen had been positioning me for five years for this deployment. Didn't know I was walking into trap I couldn't escape."

He arrived in Erbil in July 2015. ISIS was at the gates. The city was chaos—refugees flooding in, Peshmerga mobilizing, every intelligence service scrambling to understand what happened after ISIS took Mosul.

Chen met him at the airport. Explained the real job.

Network mapping. Attend cultural events, political meetings, academic conferences. Talk to Kurdish intellectuals, party officials, businessmen. Report on relationships, allegiances, who's connected to who. Help Chen understand Kurdish political landscape for post-ISIS planning.

"I said no," Yousef remembers. "Said I came for refugee work, not intelligence. Chen was very calm. Explained my visa was contingent on employment. My passport was held by US Consulate for safekeeping. My green card status could be reviewed if questions arose about my work history. Nothing threatening. Just explaining reality."

For the past year, Yousef has been Chen's primary cultural access. He attends lectures, seminars, poetry readings, political discussions. He talks to people Chen can't approach directly—intellectuals suspicious of Americans, party officials who prefer indirect contact, businessmen hedging bets across multiple patrons.

He reports on conversations, relationships, intentions. Helps Chen understand who's loyal to KDP, who's secretly PUK, who has Iranian contacts, who's talking to Turkish intelligence. Helps Chen map the network of allegiances and interests that will determine Kurdistan's future after ISIS.

"And now he wants me to recruit someone," Yousef says.

"Kamal," Ethan says.

"Kamal Barzani. Asayish officer. Counter-intelligence. Lost his brother to Iranian proxies in the '90s. Lost his cousin to Al-Qaeda in Iraq. Chen thinks he's perfect recruit. Anti-Iranian, anti-Baghdad, loyal to Kurdistan. Exactly the kind of asset CIA wants for post-ISIS operations."

"And Chen wants you to make the introduction."

"More than introduction. Vouch for the work. Explain how intelligence cooperation helps Kurdistan. Make it seem patriotic rather than collaboration. Chen's tried approaching Kamal directly. Didn't work. Kamal's too smart, too cautious. But I can approach him culturally. Academic contexts. Poetry discussions. Build relationship before revealing purpose."

"And you don't want to do it."

"I can't do it." Yousef's voice breaks. "I can't look at this man and lie. Can't pull him into the same trap. Can't become the next link in Chen's chain. I'm already compromised—I accepted that. But I won't compromise others."

"So you called me."

"So I called you because you're a lawyer and I'm desperate and Chen said you'd understand." Yousef looks at Ethan. "Will you understand? Or will you tell me to finish the mission and go home?"

The food has arrived. Nobody's touched it. Lars sits watching the door. The restaurant continues around them—other diners, conversation in Kurdish, the smell of grilling meat and chai.

"I'll talk to Chen," Ethan says.

"He won't listen."

"I'll talk to him anyway."

"What will you say?"

"That you're done. That this ends. That he lets you go home to your family."

"And when he says no?"

"Then I figure out what leverage works."

Yousef laughs. Bitter sound. "Leverage on CIA? You'll be gone in a week and I'll still be here. Trapped. That's reality."

Maybe. But Ethan flew six thousand miles, so he's going to try anyway.

***

They eat in silence. The food is good but nobody appreciates it. Yousef picks at his plate. Lars eats mechanically, still watching the room.

Ethan's mind works through the problem. Chen has all the leverage—passport, visa, green card status, five years of documented collaboration. Yousef has nothing except moral objection, which doesn't count for much in intelligence work.

Standard legal approaches won't work. No court has jurisdiction. No law protects intelligence assets who decide they're done. The relationship is extralegal by design.

Which means Ethan needs something Chen wants or something Chen fears. And he has twenty-four hours to figure out what that is before the lecture tomorrow night.

His phone buzzes. Text from unknown number. Kurdish country code.

*Be careful with Chen. He watches everyone. —A friend*

Ethan shows it to Lars. "You recognize the number?"

Lars looks. Shakes his head. "Kurdish mobile. Could be anyone."

"Who knew I was coming?"

"Petey. Me. Yousef." Lars glances at Yousef. "Who have you told?"

"No one. I've been careful. Chen has people watching me. I can't—" He stops. "My cousin. I told my cousin I'd contacted American friend for legal advice. But I didn't say you were coming here."

"Your cousin is who?"

"Asayish. Low level. Administrative work. He's been helping me. Sending warnings when Chen's people are around. Trying to protect me."

Lars and Ethan exchange looks. That's the point, Ethan realizes. The anonymous warnings aren't random. They're from someone inside Kurdish intelligence. Someone with access to information about Chen's operations.

"Is your cousin the one trying to recruit?" Lars asks. "Kamal?"

"No. Different person. My cousin works in records. Kamal is senior officer. But they know each other. Kurdish intelligence is small world."

The phone buzzes again. Same number.

*Chen knows you're here. Knows why you came. Don't trust obvious answers. —Friend*

"Kamal," Ethan says. "Does he know Chen's trying to recruit him?"

"I don't know. I've made approaches. Cultural contexts. Building relationship. But I haven't revealed purpose. Chen says Kamal is smart enough to suspect. Says that's good—means he's right person for the work."

"What do you know about him?"

"PhD from Istanbul. Counter-intelligence specialist. Survived Iraqi civil war, Kurdish civil war, ISIS offensive. Lost family to everyone—Baghdad, Tehran, Al-Qaeda. He's careful. Plays all sides. Maintains relationships with Americans, Iranians, Turks, Baghdad. Survives by making himself useful to everyone and committed to no one."

The Old Man. Sophisticated operator playing multiple games simultaneously. Never fully committing. Always hedging.

Which means Kamal already knows Chen's trying to recruit him. Already knows Yousef is the approach vector. And he's letting it play out because it gives him information about American intentions.

"He's playing Chen," Ethan says.

"What?" Yousef looks confused.

"Kamal. He knows you're approaching him for Chen. He's letting it happen because watching how Chen operates tells him things he needs to know. He's gathering intelligence while pretending to be target."

Lars nods slowly. "Makes sense. If he's as good as Yousef says, he'd see through the approach. But refusing directly creates problem. Better to appear receptive. String it along. Learn what Americans want."

"Which means Chen doesn't have leverage over Kamal," Ethan continues. "He has information flow he thinks is going one direction but might actually be going both directions."

"How does that help me?" Yousef asks.

"I'm not sure yet. But it means Chen's operation isn't as secure as he thinks. There's a crack. Maybe we can use it."

The phone buzzes again.

*Lecture tomorrow night. Kurdistan Studies Center. Chen will be there. Good place to talk. Public. Witnesses. —Friend*

"That's tomorrow," Ethan says to Lars. "Can you get me in?"

"Kurdistan Studies Center hosts events for diplomats and academics. I'm neither. But I know someone who is." Lars pulls out his own phone. Types in Norwegian. Gets response thirty seconds later. "Norwegian consul will bring me as guest. I'll bring you as mine. Security won't question it."

"What time?"

"Seven PM. Topic is post-ISIS governance. Every diplomat in Erbil will be there. Including Chen."

Perfect.

***

They walk back through dark streets. Generator sounds rising. Checkpoints glowing under lights. The city settling into night rhythm.

Back at the guest house, Lars and Ethan sit in the courtyard smoking cigarettes Lars pulled from somewhere. They don't talk for a while. Just smoke and watch the gate.

"You have a plan?" Lars asks finally.

"Talk to Chen. See if he'll negotiate."

"He won't."

"Probably not. But I have to try."

"And when he says no?"

"Then I figure out what pressure works. Who he answers to. What makes keeping Yousef more trouble than letting him go."

Lars flicks ash. "You're thinking about going around him."

"I'm thinking about options."

"Going around him means contacting Langley. Means filing complaints about case officer conduct. Means bureaucratic warfare you can't win from Greenville."

"Maybe."

"Or you're thinking about something more direct."

Ethan doesn't answer. Because he's not sure what he's thinking. Just that Yousef is trapped and Chen won't release him voluntarily and legal channels don't exist.

Which leaves options that aren't legal.

"I'm not asking you to help with anything that gets you in trouble," Ethan says.

"I know. But you should know—if you need help, if it gets complicated—" Lars pauses. "I'm in. Whatever you decide."

"Why? You don't know Yousef. Don't owe me anything."

"I'm in Kurdistan because I think some things matter more than following rules. ISIS matters. Freedom matters. People getting trapped by their own side matters too." Lars stubs out his cigarette. "Plus Petey vouched for you. That counts for something."

They sit in the dark. The generator hums. Somewhere in the distance, a dog barks. Normal city sounds.

Except this city is thirty kilometers from ISIS and full of intelligence officers and one of them has Ethan's former interpreter trapped in an operation he can't escape.

Tomorrow night, Ethan confronts Chen.

Tomorrow night, he finds out if six years and five thousand miles have changed the man who drank beer in the Green Zone and talked about dancing in the gray like it was a philosophy instead of an excuse.

***

The next day passes slowly.

Ethan tries to plan what he'll say to Chen. Different arguments, different approaches, different ways to frame the request. They all sound weak. Chen has the leverage, the authority, the institutional support. Ethan has moral objection and a friendship from 2008.

Not a fair fight.

Lars spends the day making calls, gathering information. In the afternoon he comes back with intelligence.

"Chen's been in Kurdistan since 2010," Lars says. "Started as political officer. Became chief of station by 2012. He's run every major Kurdish asset we have. KDP officials, PUK intelligence, Asayish officers, businessmen with Iranian contacts. He knows everyone. Has files on everyone. If you operate in Kurdistan, Chen knows about it."

"Reputation?"

"Smart. Professional. True believer. People who've worked with him say he's mission-focused to the point of obsession. Doesn't socialize. Doesn't waste time. Everything is advancing the operation. He's been here five years without rotation because nobody else can do what he does."

"What about his bosses? Who's he report to?"

"Division Chief for Near East, based in Langley. But Chen's in the field. Has operational discretion. Unless someone files formal complaint or operation goes sideways, Langley doesn't interfere. And nothing's gone sideways. Chen runs clean operations. No scandals, no exposures, no blown covers. By CIA metrics, he's model officer."

Which means going around Chen to Langley won't work. He's successful, effective, professional. Langley loves him.

"What about the Kurds?" Ethan asks. "Do they trust him?"

"Mixed. KDP works with him because he's been useful. Provided intelligence on ISIS, Iranian activities, Turkish operations. But they know he's CIA. Know he's gathering intelligence on them too. It's transactional relationship. He helps them, they help him, everyone understands the limits."

"And Kamal?"

"Kamal's different. He's counter-intelligence. His job is catching foreign agents. Which means his job is catching people like Chen. So approaching him is high risk. If Kamal refuses and reports the attempt, it could damage US-Kurdish intelligence relationship. That's probably why Chen's been so careful. Why he's using Yousef instead of direct approach."

The afternoon drags. Ethan reads articles about Kurdistan. Studies maps. Tries to understand the terrain he's operating in.

His phone buzzes. The anonymous friend again.

*Chen will agree to meet. But not tonight. He'll suggest tomorrow. Private location. Be careful about accepting. —Friend*

Ethan shows it to Lars. "Your thoughts?"

"Someone with access to Chen's schedule. Someone who knows his patterns. Could be Kamal. Could be someone in Asayish watching American operations. Could be someone in Chen's own orbit."

"Or it could be Chen's people testing me."

"That too."

Which means the warnings might be manipulation. Might be steering Ethan toward choices that benefit Chen's operation rather than helping Yousef.

Welcome to the fog.

\*\*\*

At 6:45 PM they dress for the lecture. Lars in the one sport coat he owns. Ethan in the blazer he packed. Trying to look like academics or diplomats instead of what they are.

They walk six blocks to Kurdistan Studies Center. Modern building, marble facade, Kurdish and American flags. Security at the entrance checking invitations and IDs.

The Norwegian consul is waiting. Mid-fifties, gray hair, the comfortable confidence of someone who's spent thirty years in foreign service. He greets Lars in Norwegian, switches to English for Ethan.

"Lars says you're researcher. American politics?"

"Legal policy. Immigration and security issues."

"Timely topic. Lots of both here." The consul hands them name tags. Guest credentials. "Stay with me. Don't wander. Security is serious about protocol."

They pass through security. Metal detectors, bag searches, Kurdish Asayish checking faces against lists. The building is full. Diplomats, academics, journalists, NGO workers. Every intelligence service represented. Everyone watching everyone else.

The lecture hall is upstairs. Two hundred seats, half filled already. The crowd is mix of Kurds and foreigners. Conversations in Kurdish, English, Arabic, German. The atmosphere is university seminar crossed with diplomatic reception.

Ethan scans the room. Looking for Chen.

Doesn't see him yet.

They find seats near the back. Good vantage. Ethan can see everyone entering.

The room continues filling. Kurdish officials in suits. Peshmerga officers in dress uniforms. American diplomats in business casual. British, German, French representatives. Everyone who matters in Kurdistan's political future.

Then Chen enters.

Ethan recognizes him immediately despite six years. Same preppy look—khakis, blue Oxford shirt, wire-rimmed glasses. Hair a little grayer. Face a little more weathered. But same confident bearing. Same way of moving through a room like he knows everyone and everything.

He's talking to a Kurdish official. Animated conversation. Chen laughs at something. The official laughs back. Easy rapport. The relationship of people who've worked together long enough to develop genuine comfort.

Chen finds a seat in the third row. Center section. Where he can see and be seen.

Ethan watches him. Trying to reconcile this version with the man who drank beer in Baghdad and talked about moral ambiguity.

Six years. Five years in Kurdistan. A lifetime in intelligence work.

The lecture begins.

Kurdish Studies director welcomes everyone. Introduces the speaker—American professor, expert on federalism and ethnic governance. Topic is post-ISIS political structures. How Kurdistan can maintain autonomy while managing relationships with Baghdad, Ankara, Tehran.

The professor is competent but boring. Speaks in academic abstractions. Federalism models. Power-sharing arrangements. Constitutional frameworks. The audience listens politely.

Ethan doesn't pay attention. He watches Chen.

Chen takes notes. Nods at certain points. Makes small annotations. The performance of engaged academic. But every few minutes his eyes scan the room. Taking inventory. Noting who's here, who's sitting with who, who's paying attention and who's distracted.

Mapping the room like he maps everything else.

Halfway through the lecture, Ethan sees Kamal.

He enters late. Moves to the back row opposite side. Kurdish man, mid-forties, close-cropped hair, civilian clothes but military bearing. Asayish, definitely. He doesn't sit immediately. Stands for a moment scanning the room.

His eyes pass over Chen. No reaction. Then over Yousef, who's sitting in the middle section looking uncomfortable. Brief eye contact. Kamal nods slightly. Yousef doesn't respond.

Then Kamal sits. Pulls out a phone. Takes notes on it. Or pretends to take notes while actually doing something else.

Chen hasn't turned around. Hasn't looked at Kamal. But Ethan would bet money he knows Kamal arrived. Knows where he's sitting. Is calculating what his presence means.

The lecture continues. Post-ISIS economic reconstruction. International investment. Security sector reform. Important topics delivered in soporific monotone.

Finally it ends. Polite applause. The director thanks everyone. Announces reception in the atrium. Please help yourselves to refreshments.

The room empties slowly. People clustering in conversations. Chen is immediately surrounded—Kurdish officials wanting his attention, diplomats comparing notes, academics seeking insights.

Ethan waits. Watches. Lets the crowd thin.

Chen finishes his conversations. Starts toward the atrium. Ethan intercepts him at the door.

"David."

Chen stops. Turns. Studies Ethan's face. The recognition takes three seconds.

"Ethan Caldwell." Genuine surprise. "Jesus. What are you doing in Erbil?"

"Need to talk to you. About Yousef."

The surprise vanishes. Chen's face becomes professional mask. "I see. Let's talk outside."

***

They find a balcony. Empty. Overlooking the city. Lights spreading to the horizon. Checkpoint glow. The dark beyond marking where Erbil ends and the war zone begins.

Chen lights a cigarette. Offers one to Ethan. Ethan accepts. They smoke in silence for thirty seconds.

"You came a long way," Chen says finally.

"Yousef called me. Said he needs help."

"And you thought you'd fly to Kurdistan and—what? File a legal brief?"

"I thought I'd ask you to let him go home."

Chen smokes. Looks at the city. "You know I can't do that."

"Why not?"

"Because the mission isn't complete."

"The mission is never complete. That's how intelligence operations work. There's always one more source, one more recruitment, one more network to map. If you wait for complete, Yousef dies here."

"Dramatic." Chen flicks ash. "He's not in danger. He's doing cultural liaison work. Meeting people. Attending lectures. Nothing risky."

"He's doing intelligence work he didn't agree to. You recruited him under false pretenses. Leveraged his SIV status and his family's safety. That's coercion."

"That's recruitment." Chen turns to face Ethan. "You were a contractor. You know how this works. We identify people with access, capabilities, motivation. We offer opportunities. They accept or decline. Yousef accepted. Multiple times over four years. Nobody forced him."

"You threatened his visa status. His green card. His family's security."

"I explained consequences. That's different than threatening. Yousef made informed decisions. If he'd said no at any point—really said no—we would have accepted it. Might have been complicated, but we would have accepted it."

"Bullshit."

"It's not bullshit. It's reality. Yes, we have leverage. Yes, we use it. But we don't operate at gunpoint. Yousef chose to take the money. Chose to do the work. Chose to come to Kurdistan. Those were his decisions."

The logic is airtight. The morality is ambiguous. Chen's right that Yousef chose. But he's wrong that the choices were free.

"He wants out," Ethan says. "Now. Not after completing your operation. Now."

"And I want successful recruitment of a key Kurdish intelligence asset. We both want things." Chen smokes. "Here's what I'll offer. Yousef completes the Kamal recruitment. Does it professionally. Helps establish the relationship. Then he goes home. Full honors. Recommendation letter. Continued compensation for consultation work. We maintain good relationship and he goes home to his family."

"And if he can't complete the recruitment?"

"Then he stays until he can. Or until we find alternative approach. That could take time."

"How much time?"

"Months. Maybe longer. Depends on how Kamal responds."

"That's not acceptable."

"It's not your decision." Chen's voice goes cold. "You don't have standing here, Ethan. You're not Yousef's lawyer. Not his representative. You're a friend who flew here thinking you could fix things with righteous indignation. But this is intelligence work in an active theater. Your personal sense of justice doesn't override operational necessity."

"What about your personal sense of ethics? You talked about making hard calls. About living with ambiguity."

"I still believe that."

"Then let him go. The harm you're causing—keeping a man from his family, making him compromise others, trapping him in work he doesn't want to do—that's not slightly more good than harm. That's just harm."

Chen finishes his cigarette. Drops it. Grinds it under his shoe. "Here's what you don't understand. Yousef's discomfort is acceptable cost for intelligence that prevents attacks. Mapping Kurdish networks means we understand who's loyal, who's compromised, who can be trusted post-ISIS. That intelligence saves lives. Lots of lives. More lives than Yousef's temporary inconvenience costs."

"Temporary. You've had him for a year."

"And we're close to completion. Kamal is almost ready. Another month, maybe two. Then Yousef goes home and we have access to Kurdish counter-intelligence. That's worth waiting for."

The calculus is clear. Chen's not being cruel. He's being rational. One asset's suffering versus intelligence advantage. The math works.

Except the math never works when you're the one being calculated.

"What if I complicate things?" Ethan asks. "What if I make keeping Yousef more trouble than it's worth?"

Chen looks at him. Really looks. Evaluating threat level.

"How would you do that?"

"File complaints with Langley. State Department. Congress. Kurdish authorities. Make noise about coercive recruitment practices. Create attention you don't want."

"You don't have proof. Yousef signed agreements. Took money. Came here voluntarily. His word against official documentation. Who do you think Langley believes?"

"Maybe I go public. Journalists. Human rights organizations. Make it story about CIA coercing intelligence assets."

"Nobody cares. Intelligence services recruit people. Everyone knows this. It's not scandal. And you'd burn Yousef in the process. His name becomes public. His cooperation becomes known. He loses everything."

Chen's right. Every angle Ethan considers, Chen's already mapped. Every threat has countermeasure. Every move has counter-move.

"So I have no leverage," Ethan says.

"You have friendship. Which matters. But it doesn't override operational necessity." Chen pulls out another cigarette. Doesn't light it yet. "Here's what I'll do. Because we did work together. Because I respect what you're trying to do. I'll expedite the Kamal operation.

Push harder. Take more risks. Try to complete it in three weeks instead of two months. Yousef goes home by early November. That's the best I can offer."

"And if something goes wrong? If Kamal refuses? If the operation fails?"

"Then Yousef stays until we succeed. That's reality."

Ethan looks at the city. At the lights and darkness. At the border between safety and chaos.

"I'm not leaving without him."

"Yes, you are. Your visa is good for two weeks. After that, Kurdish authorities revoke it and you leave. Whether Yousef comes with you depends on him completing his work."

Chen lights the cigarette. Smokes. They stand in silence.

"I remember Baghdad," Chen says finally. "That conversation in the Green Zone. You asked if any of it mattered. If we were making a difference or just prolonging chaos. I said slightly more good than harm was the only honest metric."

"I remember."

"I still believe that. Everything I do here—recruiting Yousef, pushing him on Kamal, running operations—I believe it produces good. Maybe not for Yousef individually. But for Kurdistan. For regional stability. For preventing worse outcomes. The math works."

"What if you're wrong?"

"Then I'm wrong and I'll answer for it. But I'm not wrong. Five years here. Hundreds of sources. Intelligence that's prevented attacks, identified threats, shaped policy. It works. Yousef's contribution is part of that. His suffering has purpose."

The certainty is complete. That's what five years in Kurdistan did to Chen. Made him sure. Made him believe his framework justifies anything.

"Will you let me talk to him?" Ethan asks. "Yousef. Will you let us meet without surveillance?"

Chen considers. "One meeting. Tomorrow afternoon. I'll make sure you're not followed. After that, no more unsupervised contact. He's operational asset. Access is controlled."

"That's generous."

"That's professional courtesy because we have history. Don't mistake it for weakness." Chen finishes his cigarette. "Go home, Ethan. You can't fix this. Yousef made choices. Now he lives with them. We all do."

Chen walks back inside. Leaves Ethan on the balcony alone.

Below, the city continues. Generators humming. Checkpoints glowing. Life proceeding while the war sits thirty kilometers away waiting to resume.

Ethan's phone buzzes.

*Chen won't negotiate. You'll need leverage. Real leverage. We can help. —Friend*

Ethan looks at the message for a long time.

Then he goes back inside to find Lars.

# 4

## CHAPTER 4: LAYERS

*Erbil, Kurdistan Region — October 2015*

Ethan doesn't sleep. Lies on the thin mattress staring at the ceiling while the generator hums and checkpoint sounds drift through the barred window. Reconstructing the conversation with Chen. Looking for openings he missed. Finding none.

Chen's logic was airtight. The leverage was real. The calculus worked—one asset's discomfort versus intelligence that prevents attacks. Yousef's suffering had purpose in Chen's framework. The math balanced.

Except Ethan had watched Yousef's hands shake. Had seen four years of accumulation—the weight of lies, the compromise of integrity, the trap closing so slowly you don't realize you're inside it until trying to leave becomes impossible.

The math never accounts for that.

At 5:30 AM Ethan gives up on sleep. Showers in the communal bathroom. Water pressure is weak but it's hot. Small mercy. He stands under it trying to wash away the feeling that he flew six thousand miles to accomplish nothing.

In the courtyard, Lars is already up. Smoking. Watching the gate. He looks like he didn't sleep either.

"Coffee?" Lars asks.

"Please."

They walk two blocks to a bakery that opens before dawn. Kurdish workers, Peshmerga coming off night shifts, taxi drivers starting their day. The smell of fresh bread cuts through diesel exhaust and dust.

They sit at a small table. Drink thick Turkish coffee. Eat bread still warm from the oven.

"How did it go?" Lars asks.

Ethan tells him. The conversation with Chen. The offer—complete the mission, go home. The threat—stay until completion however long that takes. The leverage Chen has and Ethan doesn't.

Lars listens without interrupting. When Ethan finishes, he lights another cigarette.

"So legal approaches don't work."

"Legal approaches don't exist. This is extralegal by design."

"And Chen won't negotiate."

"Chen thinks he's being generous. Three weeks instead of two months. He thinks that's compromise."

Lars drinks his coffee. "What did the anonymous messages say?"

"That I'd need real leverage. That they could help."

"You trust them?"

"I don't know who they are."

"Exactly." Lars taps ash. "Could be Kamal's people. Could be someone in Asayish watching American operations. Could be Chen's own people testing you. Could be Iranian intelligence fucking with everyone. Welcome to Casablanca."

The sun is rising. Orange light cutting through dust. The city waking up. Shops opening. Traffic building. Another day in a city thirty kilometers from ISIS.

"I'm meeting Yousef this afternoon," Ethan says. "Chen's allowing one unsupervised meeting. After that, access is controlled."

"He's being generous."

"He's being strategic. One meeting to let me see the situation is hopeless. Then he expects me to leave."

"Will you?"

Ethan drinks more coffee. Bitter and thick. "No."

"Then you need different approach. Something Chen doesn't expect. Something that changes his calculus."

"Like what?"

"I don't know yet. But conventional won't work. He's mapped all the conventional angles. You need something unconventional."

They finish eating. Walk back through streets getting crowded. Peshmerga changing shifts at checkpoints. Refugees emerging from shelters in the parks. The city's daily rhythm.

Back at the guest house, Ethan's phone rings. Unknown number. US country code.

"This is Ethan."

"Counselor. It's Petey."

Relief floods through him. Petey's voice—solid, competent, the sound of someone who knows what they're doing.

"Good timing. I need advice."

"I know. Lars texted me last night. Said the Chen meeting didn't go well." Pause. "I've been making calls. Talked to some people who know people. Got intelligence on what's actually happening in Kurdistan. It's layered."

"Layered how?"

"Not on the phone. Can you get somewhere secure? Somewhere you can talk for thirty minutes without being overheard?"

Ethan looks at Lars. "Can you get us somewhere private?"

Lars nods. "I know a place. Twenty minutes."

"Twenty minutes," Ethan tells Petey. "I'll call you back."

***

Lars drives them out of the city. East toward Sulaymaniyah. The road is good—paved, maintained, evidence of oil money before prices crashed. Traffic thins as they leave Erbil proper.

They pass through a checkpoint. The Peshmerga recognize Lars's vehicle, wave them through. Then countryside. Brown hills, occasional villages, the landscape opening up.

After fifteen minutes Lars turns onto a dirt road. Follows it two kilometers to an abandoned construction site. Half-built houses, empty lots, the boom-era dreams that died when ISIS came.

"No one comes here," Lars says. "No surveillance. No neighbors. You can talk."

Ethan calls Petey back.

"Where are you?" Petey asks.

"Outside the city. Abandoned construction site. Just me and Lars."

"Good. Because this gets complicated." Papers rustling. "I talked to a friend at DIA. Defense Intelligence Agency. They run parallel operations to CIA in Iraq. Different channels, different methods, sometimes different objectives. My friend says DIA has been watching Chen's Kurdistan operations with concern."

"What kind of concern?"

"The kind where one agency thinks another agency is compromising shared objectives. Chen's been in Kurdistan five years. Very successful by CIA metrics—good sources, solid intelligence, no blown operations. But DIA thinks he's gone native."

"Native how?"

"Chen's primary loyalty has shifted from US interests to Kurdistan interests. He sees Kurdistan as the good guys. The democratic Muslims. The secular success story. The regional partner worth investing in. So his intelligence gathering and his operational choices favor Kurdish interests even when they conflict with broader US strategy."

Ethan remembers the lecture. Chen talking with Kurdish officials. The easy rapport. The genuine respect.

"Is that a problem?"

"Depends on perspective. State Department wants good relations with Baghdad. Chen undermines that by strengthening Kurdistan. Defense Department wants Turkey stable. Chen pisses off Turkish intelligence by protecting Kurdish assets. Iran wants to maintain influence through Shia networks. Chen's mapping those networks to disrupt them."

"So he's doing his job."

"He's doing A job. Whether it's THE job is debatable. The concern is that Chen has stopped reporting intelligence that contradicts his worldview. He's selecting facts that support Kurdistan autonomy and suppressing facts that complicate it. That's not intelligence work. That's advocacy."

The wind blows dust across the construction site. Ethan watches it swirl.

"How does this help Yousef?"

"I'm getting there. DIA has been running their own sources in Kurdistan. Parallel networks. Independent verification. One of their sources is Asayish officer. High-level counter-intelligence. Lost family to everyone—Iran, Baghdad, Al-Qaeda. Plays all sides. Maintains relationships with multiple intelligence services."

"Kamal."

"You know him?"

"Know of him. He's Chen's recruitment target. That's why Yousef can't leave. Chen needs Yousef to complete the Kamal recruitment."

Silence on the line. Then: "Fuck."

"What?"

"Kamal isn't recruitable. He's already working with DIA. Has been for two years. He's their primary source on Kurdish internal politics, Iranian operations, Turkish activities. DIA considers him one of their most valuable assets in Iraq."

That's the point, Ethan realizes.

"Chen doesn't know."

"And he won't know. Not from official channels. But here's your problem—Chen's filing his operational success report in twelve days. November 22nd. Once that report goes to Langley showing Kamal as successfully recruited asset, it becomes official record. After that, the Agency owns Yousef's continued cooperation. Chen couldn't release him even if he wanted to without admitting operational failure. Which he won't do. Ever."

"So I have twelve days before Yousef becomes permanently locked in."

"You have twelve days before bureaucracy makes this impossible. After November 22nd, you're not fighting Chen's judgment anymore. You're fighting institutional policy. Good luck with that."

"Different agencies, different channels, limited sharing. DIA doesn't advertise their sources. CIA doesn't check before recruiting. So Chen's been trying to recruit someone who's already recruited. And Kamal's been playing along to see what CIA wants."

"Jesus."

"It gets better. Or worse. Depends on perspective." More papers rustling. "Kamal reported the recruitment attempt to his DIA handler. Handler told him to string it along. See what Chen offers. Learn what CIA's priorities are. Use it to understand how different US agencies are positioning for post-ISIS Kurdistan."

"So Kamal's gathering intelligence on Chen while Chen thinks he's recruiting Kamal."

"Exactly. And Yousef is trapped in the middle. Trying to complete recruitment that's actually counter-intelligence operation against his own side."

The fog thickens.

Ethan looks at the empty construction site. The abandoned dreams. The houses that will never be finished.

"Does DIA know Chen's using Yousef?"

"They know Chen has Kurdish cultural advisor. Didn't know it was your terp until I told them. Now they're concerned because if Yousef completes the recruitment—if Kamal accepts Chen's offer—it creates problem. Kamal would be double agent working for DIA and pretending to work for CIA. That's sustainable short-term but dangerous long-term. Someone figures it out, both operations collapse."

"So DIA wants the recruitment to fail."

"DIA wants the recruitment to never happen. They want Chen to give up and move on. Which means they want Yousef to fail. Which means Yousef stays trapped until Chen accepts failure. That could take—"

"Months. Years maybe."

"Yeah."

Ethan closes his eyes. The trap is more complete than he realized. Chen won't let Yousef leave until recruitment succeeds. DIA won't let recruitment succeed because Kamal's already theirs. Yousef is stuck between two operations neither side wants to expose.

"There's more," Petey says. His voice goes careful. "The anonymous warnings you've been getting. Phone messages. Kurdish number. Kamal's people, right?"

"That's what we figured."

"My DIA friend says Kamal hasn't authorized contact with you. Says if Kamal wanted to communicate, he'd do it through official channels. Through his DIA handler to approved personnel."

"Then who's sending the messages?"

"Don't know. Could be someone in Kamal's network acting independently. Could be someone watching the situation. Could be—" Petey stops.

"Could be what?"

"Could be Iranian intelligence. They've got Kurdish assets. They monitor American operations. They'd benefit from Chen's operation failing. From CIA and DIA conflict. From Americans fighting each other while Iran consolidates influence."

"So the friendly warnings might be hostile manipulation."

"Might be. Might not be. That's the problem. You can't know. Multiple players, multiple agendas, everyone using everyone else. That's why they call it the fog of war."

Lars lights another cigarette. Offers one to Ethan. Ethan takes it even though he quit smoking in 2011.

"What should I do?" Ethan asks.

"Officially? Go home. This is above your pay grade. Let agencies sort it out."

"And unofficially?"

"Unofficially?" Petey's voice goes quiet. "If you want to get Yousef out, you need to make both Chen and DIA want the same thing.

Either both want the recruitment to succeed—which won't happen because DIA won't give up Kamal. Or both want it to fail publicly enough that Chen has to move on."

"How do I make it fail publicly?"

"That's the question. If Kamal just refuses, Chen will try different approach. Different timeline. Yousef stays trapped. But if something happens that makes the recruitment impossible—if the operation gets exposed, compromised, burned—then Chen has to accept failure and move on."

"You're talking about burning Chen's operation."

"I'm talking about creating situation where keeping Yousef costs more than letting him go. Where operational security is compromised enough that Chen has to shut it down."

"That would end Chen's career."

"Maybe. Or maybe he survives it. He's good at his job. Langley likes him. Might weather it." Pause. "But that's the calculation. Yousef's freedom versus Chen's operation. You have to decide which matters more."

Ethan smokes. Watches the dust blow.

"I'll call you back," he says.

"Be careful. Multiple players means multiple ways to fuck up. Trust no one. Verify everything. And remember—in Kurdistan right now, everyone's playing multiple games. The side someone's on depends on which game you're watching."

They hang up.

Ethan sits in the car. Lars smokes beside him. Neither talks for five minutes.

"You heard?" Ethan asks finally.

"Enough. Kamal's already recruited. By different agency. Chen doesn't know. Yousef's trapped between operations."

"Yeah."

"And the anonymous warnings might be Iranian intelligence steering us toward choices that benefit them."

"Yeah."

"Casablanca."

"Casablanca."

Lars finishes his cigarette. "What are you going to do?"

"I don't know yet. Meet with Yousef this afternoon. See what he knows. See if there's angle I'm missing."

"And if there isn't?"

Ethan doesn't answer. Because he's starting to realize there might not be an angle. There might just be impossible choices and people caught in the middle and calculations about acceptable costs.

Just like Baqubah.

*\*\**

They drive back to the city. The checkpoint Peshmerga wave them through. Traffic is heavy now. Midday rush. Cars honking. Minibuses packed with passengers. The city functioning despite everything.

Ethan's phone buzzes. The anonymous friend.

*Meet at Khan Restaurant. 2 PM. Yousef will be there. So will others. Be aware. —Friend*

He shows it to Lars. "Others?"

"Could mean Asayish surveillance. Could mean Chen's people. Could mean Iranian watchers. Could mean someone wants you to think you're being watched when you're not."

"Everything's manipulation."

"Everything's information. Whether it's manipulation depends on who's providing it and why."

They park near the guest house. Walk the remaining blocks. The heat is building. Mid-eighties and climbing. Ethan's shirt sticks to his back.

Inside the courtyard, another western volunteer is cleaning weapons. British accent when he greets Lars. They exchange words in Arabic. The Brit looks at Ethan, nods, goes back to his work.

"Most volunteers are at the front," Lars explains. "We rotate. Two weeks on, one week off. That's off week for him. He'll go back Sunday."

"What's it like? The front?"

"Want to see?"

"Now?"

"We have two hours before the Yousef meeting. I can show you Gwer. The berm. What this war actually looks like. Might help you understand what's at stake."

Ethan considers. Then: "Yeah. Let's go."

***

They drive west. Through checkpoints that get more serious the closer they get to the front. Peshmerga checking IDs, cargo, asking questions. They recognize Lars's vehicle but still check. Procedure.

The landscape changes. Fewer villages. More military positions. Berms visible in the distance. Defensive earthworks. The infrastructure of static warfare.

Twenty-five kilometers from Erbil, they reach the outer defensive line. Major checkpoint. Multiple guard posts. Peshmerga in full combat gear. Machine gun positions. The atmosphere shifts from cautious to ready.

Lars speaks Kurdish to the checkpoint commander. Shows ID. Gestures to Ethan. The commander looks skeptical. Makes a phone call. Waits. Finally nods.

They pass through.

"What did you tell him?" Ethan asks.

"That you're American researcher studying Peshmerga defensive operations. That I'm your translator. That we have permission from Norwegian consul."

"Do we have permission?"

"We have my reputation and the consul's phone number. Good enough."

Five kilometers further, the road ends at a berm. Twenty feet high, bulldozed earth and fill. Behind it, Peshmerga positions. Trenches, fighting positions, sandbagged emplacements. The architecture of World War One brought forward a century.

Lars parks. They get out. Climb the berm.

At the top, Ethan sees it.

The front line.

Peshmerga positions on this side. Then no-man's land—four hundred meters of empty ground. Then the ISIS berm. Mirror image. Two armies dug in, watching each other across kill zone.

Through binoculars you can see ISIS fighters. Movement on their berm. Someone smoking. Someone on a radio. The mundane reality of warfare between the dramatic moments.

"This is Gwer," Lars says. "Where they stopped. June 2014, ISIS took Mosul, rolled east. Peshmerga fell back, set up here. ISIS pushed hard. Peshmerga pushed back. It's been static ever since."

A Peshmerga fighter approaches. Young, maybe twenty. He greets Lars in Kurdish. They talk. He offers chai. They accept.

The chai is sweet and strong. They drink it watching the other berm.

"How often do they shoot at each other?" Ethan asks.

"Depends. Sometimes daily. Sometimes not for weeks. Depends on temperature, morale, whether commanders on either side are feeling aggressive." Lars points. "See that?"

A flag on the ISIS berm. Black. The shahada in white. The ISIS banner.

"Sometimes we shoot at the flag. Sometimes they shoot at ours. It's communication. Saying we're still here. Still watching. Still ready."

The young fighter says something in Kurdish. Laughs. Lars translates.

"He says ISIS plays music sometimes. Anasheed. Religious chants. Trying to intimidate. Peshmerga plays Kurdish music back. Whose music is louder becomes psychological warfare."

The absurdity is complete. Two armies with music battles while waiting for the next actual battle.

"This is the war," Lars says. "Not explosions and heroics. Just waiting. Watching. Occasional shooting. Lots of chai. Lots of boredom. Then suddenly chaos. Then back to waiting."

They sit on the berm drinking chai. The young fighter points out positions. Explains the defensive structure in Kurdish while Lars translates. Machine gun positions, mortar pits, fallback routes. The math of holding ground.

Ethan thinks about Chen. Five years mapping Kurdistan networks while this line held. While Peshmerga sat in positions drinking chai and watching ISIS drink chai four hundred meters away. The intelligence work happening behind the static front. The operations that matter more than the shooting.

"Why did you bring me here?" Ethan asks.

"Because you needed to see what's at stake. Chen's not keeping Yousef trapped for career advancement. He's doing it because this—" Lars gestures at the front—"this matters. Kurds held the line. Beat ISIS. Now they're building something. Democratic Kurdistan. Tolerant. Modern. Chen believes in that. He's willing to sacrifice Yousef's comfort for Kurdistan's success."

"You agree with him?"

"I understand him. Whether I agree—" Lars drinks more chai. "That's harder question."

They finish the chai. Thank the young fighter. Climb down the berm.

Driving back, Ethan's phone buzzes. The anonymous friend again.

*What you saw at Gwer is one war. What Chen fights is another. Both matter. Both require sacrifice. Question is whose sacrifice and for whose benefit. —Friend*

Lars reads it. "They're watching. Following your movements."

"Chen's people?"

"Maybe. Or Asayish. Or Iranian. Or someone else. Everyone watches in Casablanca."

***

They reach Khan Restaurant at 1:55 PM. Traditional place. Older building, courtyard with fountain that doesn't work, rooms arranged around central space. The kind of restaurant where business gets done. Where conversations happen that don't happen in offices.

Yousef is already there. Back room. Sitting at a table looking like he's waiting for execution.

He stands when Ethan enters. They embrace. Yousef is shaking.

"Chen said one meeting," Yousef says. "Unsupervised. Then no more."

"I know."

They sit. Order chai and food neither will eat. The room is empty except for them. The door stays open. The restaurant continues around them.

"I talked to Petey," Ethan says. "Got intelligence on the situation."

"What situation? I know the situation. I'm trapped. Chen won't release me. There's no legal recourse. You came here and confirmed what I already knew—I'm fucked."

The bitterness is sharp. Ethan doesn't blame him.

"There's more. Kamal—the recruitment target. He's already working with Americans. Different agency. Defense Intelligence. Has been for two years. Chen doesn't know."

Yousef stares. Processing. "He's already recruited?"

"By DIA. Different operation. Different channels. Chen thinks he's recruiting fresh asset. Actually he's trying to recruit someone who's already an asset."

"And Kamal is playing along."

"Gathering intelligence on CIA while pretending to be recruitment target. Using me—using you—to understand what CIA wants in Kurdistan."

Yousef laughs. Bitter sound. "So I'm being used to recruit someone who's using me to gather intelligence."

"Yeah."

"And when Chen learns this—when someone tells him Kamal's already recruited—what happens?"

"DIA won't tell him. They don't share sources across agencies. And Kamal won't reveal it because that ends his access to both operations. So Chen will keep trying. Keep pushing you. Keep Yousef trapped until recruitment either succeeds or fails publicly enough that he has to move on."

"How long?"

"Months. Maybe longer."

Yousef puts his head in his hands. "I can't do months. I'm barely holding on now. My wife asks when I'm coming home and I lie. My daughters ask if I'm okay and I lie. I lie to everyone about everything and I'm—" His voice breaks. "I'm disappearing. The person I was is disappearing and I don't know how to get him back."

The food arrives. They don't touch it.

"There might be a way," Ethan says.

"What way?"

"Make the operation fail. Publicly. So Chen has to shut it down and move on."

"How?"

"I don't know yet. But if the recruitment gets exposed. If Kamal publicly refuses. If Chen's operation becomes known enough that continuing it compromises security. Then he'd have to let you go."

"That would destroy Chen's career."

"Maybe."

"And you'd do that? You know him. You worked with him. You'd burn his operation to free me?"

Ethan thinks about the decisions that cost things you can't take back.

"If that's what it takes."

Yousef looks at him for a long time. "You've changed."

"Six years of estate planning."

"No. You're harder. More willing to—" He searches for words. "More willing to make the calculation. Cost versus benefit. Acceptable sacrifice. You sound like Chen."

"I sound like someone who understands sometimes there aren't good options."

"Slightly more good than harm?"

"Something like that."

They sit in silence. The restaurant noise continues. Voices. Cooking sounds. Life.

Yousef's phone buzzes. He checks it. Face goes pale.

"Chen. He wants report on this meeting. What we discussed."

"What will you tell him?"

"That you tried to convince me to leave anyway. That I explained I'm committed to completing the mission. That you're frustrated but understand." Yousef looks at Ethan. "I lie to everyone now. Even you. Even myself."

He stands. Walks out without eating. Leaves Ethan alone in the room with cold food and the burden of what needs to happen.

Lars appears in the doorway.

"Asayish followed him here. Three cars. They're watching. Chen's not trusting his generous one meeting."

"Did you expect him to?"

"No. But it confirms what Petey said. Chen's serious. He's not letting Yousef go."

Ethan's phone buzzes. The anonymous friend.

*Chen lies. There will be no three weeks. Kamal refuses. Operation fails. Yousef stays. Forever. This is designed. —Friend*

"Designed how?" Ethan types back.

*Yousef is not asset. He is test. Kamal is test. You are test. Chen tests loyalty. Tests commitment. Tests who breaks. This is not operation. This is selection. —Friend*

Ethan shows it to Lars. "What does that mean?"

"I don't know. Could mean Chen's using this whole situation to evaluate people. Who stays loyal under pressure. Who breaks. Who can be trusted with harder missions."

"That's fucking sociopathic."

"That's intelligence work."

"No. Intelligence work is gathering information. This is torturing your own people to see who survives."

Lars doesn't argue. Because maybe it's both.

They leave the restaurant. Walk through afternoon heat back to the guest house. The city continues around them. Normal life. People going about their day while three intelligence services run operations through the same space using the same people without telling each other.

At the guest house, Lars makes coffee. They sit in the courtyard.

"What now?" Lars asks.

"I think—" Ethan stops. Starts again. "I think I need to talk to Kamal directly."

"That's dangerous."

"Everything's dangerous. But he's the key. If Kamal refuses Chen publicly. If he exposes the recruitment attempt. If he makes it impossible for Chen to continue—then Chen has to let Yousef go."

"And if Kamal doesn't want to expose it? If his DIA operation depends on staying quiet?"

"Then I convince him his interests align with Yousef's freedom."

"How?"

"I don't know yet."

Lars drinks coffee. "You need introduction. Can't just approach Asayish officer on the street. That gets you arrested."

"Can you introduce me?"

"I'm Norwegian volunteer. I don't have access to Kurdish intelligence."

"But you know people."

"I know Peshmerga fighters. Low level. Not intelligence officers."

Ethan's phone buzzes.

*We can arrange meeting. Kamal interested. Tonight. Location TBD. Come alone. —Friend*

He shows it to Lars. "Thoughts?"

"Could be trap. Could be Iranian intelligence setting you up. Could be legitimate. Could be Chen's people testing you."

"Or it could be Kamal actually wanting to talk."

"That too."

Ethan types back: *How do I know this is legitimate?*

The response comes thirty seconds later: *You don't. You trust or you don't. Clock is running. Yousef stays or goes. Your choice. —Friend*

Ethan looks at the message. At the ultimatum. At the choice that isn't really a choice because doing nothing means Yousef stays trapped forever.

Just like Baqubah. The decision gets made because not deciding is deciding.

"I'll go," Ethan says.

"Then I'm coming with you."

"They said alone."

"And I'm saying I don't care. You walk into unknown meeting with unknown people in city full of hostile intelligence services, you bring backup. That's not negotiable."

Ethan looks at Lars. Sees the determination. Realizes arguing is pointless.

"Okay. We both go."

The phone buzzes again.

*10 PM. Christian cemetery. Ankawa. East gate. Come armed if you want. Won't matter. —Friend*

A cemetery. At night. In the Christian quarter. The symbolic weight is almost funny.

"At least they have sense of humor," Lars says.

"Or they know what plays in Western minds. Cemetery meeting. Mysterious warnings. The whole thing feels staged."

"Everything here is staged. That's the point. Multiple audiences. Multiple messages. You just have to figure out which audience matters and what message they're actually sending."

Six hours until the meeting. Six hours to decide if he's walking into legitimate contact or elaborate trap or manipulation by hostile intelligence or test by Chen or something else entirely.

Six hours to decide whose sacrifice is acceptable and whose benefit matters more.

The scar on Ethan's arm itches.

He touches it unconsciously. The decision that took another life. The math that never works.

Here we go again.

# 5

## CHAPTER 5: THE CEMETERY

*Erbil, Kurdistan Region — October 2015*

The hours between afternoon and night crawl.

Ethan tries to rest. Can't. Lies on the thin mattress listening to the city. Generator hum. Traffic sounds. The call to prayer echoing from mosques. Normal sounds in an abnormal situation.

At 7 PM he gives up. Finds Lars in the courtyard cleaning a pistol. Glock 19. Standard contractor sidearm. Lars reassembles it without looking. Muscle memory.

"You carrying tonight?" Lars asks.

"I don't have a weapon."

"You want one?"

Ethan thinks about it. Armed American meeting unknown contact in cemetery at night in city full of intelligence services. That could go wrong in multiple ways.

"No. If it's legitimate, weapon creates suspicion. If it's trap, weapon won't help."

"Agreed. I'll carry. Stay back. Close enough to help if needed. Far enough to not spook them."

"They said come alone."

"And I said I don't care." Lars slides the magazine in. Chambers a round. "You're walking into unknown meeting. I'm backup. That's how this works."

They eat dinner at the guest house. Rice, vegetables, flatbread. The British volunteer joins them. Talks about the front. About incoming DShK fire yesterday. About Peshmerga fighter who got hit. Through and through, shoulder. Survived. Back on the line in a week probably.

"That's the war," the Brit says. "Nobody dies clean. Machine gun rounds don't kill instantly like movies. You get hit, you bleed, medics work on you, maybe you make it. War's messy."

After dinner Ethan showers again. Puts on dark clothes. Jeans, dark shirt, light jacket despite the warmth. Trying to look like someone who belongs in a cemetery at night. Failing probably.

At 9:30 they leave.

The city at night is different. Fewer cars. Checkpoints more serious. Generators louder without traffic to cover them. The sense of a place that knows danger sits close but pretends otherwise.

They drive to Ankawa. The Christian quarter. Churches visible in the dark. Crosses lit on rooftops. The architecture of minority survival.

The cemetery is on the eastern edge. Old. Christian burials going back centuries. Chaldean, Assyrian, Armenian. The communities that predated Islam, survived it, thrived under it when Kurdistan allowed them to.

Lars parks two blocks away. They walk. The streets are empty. Ankawa at night is quiet. Residents stay home. Businesses closed. The Christian communities learned long ago not to draw attention after dark.

The cemetery wall is old stone. Eight feet high. Weathered. The east gate is wrought iron. Locked but the lock is old. Would be easy to climb over.

Ethan checks his phone. 9:54 PM.

"I'll wait here," Lars says. "Outside the wall. You go in. I hear anything wrong—shooting, shouting, struggle—I'm coming in."

"Understood."

"And Ethan? If this goes bad, run toward me. Not away. Toward."

"Why?"

"Because if you run away, I can't cover you. If you run toward me, I can lay down suppressing fire and we both get out."

The tactical logic is sound. Ethan nods.

At 9:58 he approaches the gate. It's unlocked. Opens smoothly despite appearance of neglect. Someone oiled the hinges recently.

He steps inside.

The cemetery spreads before him. Headstones and crosses. Some old, some new. Maintained but not manicured. The dead of Ankawa's Christian communities going back two hundred years.

Moonlight provides some illumination. Quarter moon. Enough to see shapes but not details. The shadows are deep.

Ethan walks the main path. Gravel crunching under his feet. Too loud in the silence. He moves to the grass. Quieter.

At the center of the cemetery, a small chapel. Stone building. Empty. Door open. Dark inside.

His phone buzzes.

*Chapel. Inside. Alone. —Friend*

Ethan looks around. Sees no one. Feels watched. Probably is watched from multiple directions.

He walks to the chapel. Pauses at the door. Listens. Hears nothing.

Steps inside.

The interior is small. Maybe twenty feet square. Stone walls. Altar at the front. Benches. Smell of old incense and dust. Moonlight through the windows provides enough light to see shapes.

A man stands near the altar. Dark clothes. Medium build. Face in shadow.

"Ethan Caldwell." Not a question. Kurdish accent. Good English.

"That's me."

"I'm Kamal."

So the meeting is real. Or it's someone claiming to be Kamal. In a cemetery at night. With unknown backup positions. This could still go very wrong.

"You wanted to meet," Kamal says.

"Your people suggested it."

"I have many people. Some know they work for me. Some don't. The ones who sent you messages—they work for me without knowing it. Better that way."

"Why?"

"Because if they knew, they'd be assets. Assets get caught. Get turned. Get killed. Better they think they're helping friend or serving Kurdistan or whatever story makes them useful. They stay clean. I stay safe."

The logic is cold but sound. Kamal's been in intelligence long enough to understand that the best sources don't know they're sources.

"You're DIA," Ethan says.

Kamal doesn't confirm or deny. Just: "You've been talking to people. Learned things. Good. Saves time explaining."

"Chen's trying to recruit you."

"Chen's been trying to recruit me for eight months. Very patient. Very professional. Uses Yousef as approach vector. Cultural contexts. Building relationship. Standard tradecraft."

"And you're playing along."

"Of course. Chen's operation tells me what CIA prioritizes in Kurdistan. What they fear. What they want. That information helps me protect Kurdistan's interests."

"Kurdistan's interests or your interests?"

A smile in the darkness. "Sometimes same thing."

Kamal moves slightly. Into moonlight through the window. Ethan sees his face properly for the first time.

Mid-forties. Close-cropped hair. Hard features. Eyes that watch everything. The face of someone who's survived multiple wars by being smarter than his enemies.

"You came here to help Yousef," Kamal says. "Free him from Chen's operation. That's admirable. Stupid, but admirable."

"Can you help?"

"Can I? Yes. Will I? That's more complicated question."

"What do you want?"

"I want Kurdistan to survive. To become independent. To not get crushed between Baghdad, Ankara, Tehran. I want my people—the Kurds—to have what we've been denied for century. Self-determination. Safety. Future."

"And how does helping Yousef achieve that?"

"It doesn't. Helping Yousef is tactical. Small move. But sometimes small moves matter." Kamal sits on a bench. Gestures for Ethan to sit. "You understand chess?"

"Basics."

"In chess, sometimes you sacrifice piece to improve position. Sometimes you protect piece because losing it costs more than gaining advantage. Yousef is piece. Question is—does sacrificing him improve my position or weaken it?"

"I'm not asking you to sacrifice him. I'm asking you to refuse Chen's recruitment publicly. Make it impossible for Chen to continue operation. Force him to let Yousef go."

"And if I do that, Chen knows his operation is compromised. Knows someone fed you information. Knows his security isn't as tight as he thought. He investigates. Maybe figures out I'm already recruited by different agency. Maybe doesn't. But I lose value either way because Chen becomes cautious."

"So you won't help."

"I didn't say that." Kamal leans forward. "I said it's complicated. Everything in Kurdistan is complicated. Multiple players. Multiple interests. Multiple games happening simultaneously. You're playing one game. I'm playing three. Chen's playing five. The question is whether our games align."

Footsteps outside. Multiple people. Ethan tenses.

Kamal doesn't move. "My security. Don't worry. If Chen's people were here, you'd already be detained."

Three men enter the chapel. Kurdish. Armed. Not pointing weapons but carrying them ready. They position themselves. One at the door. One near the window. One behind Ethan.

Professional positions. Covering angles. Making sure if something goes wrong, they control the situation.

"You don't trust me?" Ethan asks.

"I don't trust anyone. That's how I've survived this long." Kamal lights a cigarette. Offers one to Ethan. Ethan accepts. "Tell me about Chen. What kind of man is he?"

"Smart. Professional. True believer. He thinks Kurdistan is future. Democratic Muslims. Regional success story. He wants to help you succeed."

"And that makes him dangerous. Because true believers don't question. Don't doubt. They're certain their cause justifies their methods." Kamal smokes. "I've dealt with many intelligence officers. American, British, German, Iranian, Turkish. The cynical ones are easier. They're transactional. Offer them something valuable, they deal. But true believers—they won't compromise because compromise means betraying the cause."

"Chen thinks keeping Yousef trapped serves Kurdistan's interests."

"Maybe it does. Intelligence Chen gathers helps Kurdistan. Helps us understand threats. Helps us navigate between Baghdad and Tehran and Ankara. That intelligence costs something. Yousef's freedom is the cost. From Chen's perspective, that's acceptable math."

"From yours?"

"From mine—" Kamal pauses. "I have nephew. Twenty-three. Peshmerga. Sits in trench at Gwer watching ISIS. He drinks chai with friends. Plays cards. Waits for something to happen. He's been there sixteen months. Might be there sixteen more. That's his sacrifice for Kurdistan. Everyone sacrifices something. The question is whether the sacrifice is voluntary or coerced."

"Yousef's is coerced."

"Yes. Which makes it wrong. Not strategically wrong—strategically it works. Morally wrong. And Kurdistan's future depends not just on winning wars but on being better than our enemies. If we coerce our allies, betray our friends, sacrifice our principles for tactical advantage—then even if we win, we lose what makes us worth defending."

The philosophical argument from intelligence officer in a cemetery at night. The cognitive dissonance is complete.

"So you'll help?"

"I'll consider it. But I need something from you first."

"What?"

"Information. About Chen's broader operation. Who else he's running. What other networks he's mapping. What his priorities are beyond recruiting me."

"I don't have that information."

"But you can get it. Yousef has access. He reports to Chen. He knows who else Chen meets with. What other operations are running. That information helps me protect Kurdistan from American interference we don't want while accepting American help we do want."

"You want me to spy on Chen."

"I want you to gather information that helps Kurdistan. Same thing Chen does. Just for different patron." Kamal smokes. "You came here to help Yousef. I'm telling you the price. Information about Chen's operations. In exchange, I refuse his recruitment publicly enough that he must stop. Yousef goes home. Everyone gets what they want except Chen."

Ethan processes this. To free Yousef, he needs to burn Chen's operation. To burn Chen's operation, he needs intelligence Yousef can provide. Which means using Yousef to gather intelligence on Chen while Chen thinks Yousef is working for him.

The layers multiply.

"How do I know you'll keep your word?" Ethan asks.

"You don't. But consider my incentives. If I help you and Yousef goes home, Chen's operation fails. That weakens CIA position in Kurdistan slightly. Strengthens my position slightly. Benefits me. If I don't help, Chen continues operation, maybe succeeds, maybe fails, I continue gathering intelligence on him either way. Neutral outcome.

So helping you costs me little and gains me something. That's good deal."

"What about DIA? Your actual employers. They want you stringing Chen along. Gathering intelligence on CIA operations. If you refuse Chen publicly, you lose that access."

Kamal smiles. "You've done your research. Yes, I work with DIA. Yes, they want me maintaining access to Chen. But they don't control me. I work with Americans because it benefits Kurdistan. When it stops benefiting Kurdistan, I stop working with Americans. That's my leverage. They need me more than I need them."

One of the security men says something in Kurdish. Kamal responds. The man nods. Leaves.

"Your friend outside," Kamal says. "The Norwegian. Lars Petersen. He's good man. Fought at Gwer. Peshmerga respect him. Tell him to stay where he is. This meeting is almost over."

"How do you know about Lars?"

"Because I'm counter-intelligence. Because knowing who operates in my city is my job. Because foreign volunteers are either assets or threats and I track both." Kamal stands. "Here's what happens next. You talk to Yousef. Get information about Chen's other operations. Who he's meeting. What he's prioritizing. You have three days. Send information to number that's been texting you. When I have what I need, I refuse Chen publicly. Make it impossible for him to continue. He lets Yousef go or I create diplomatic incident. Either way, Yousef goes home."

"And if I can't get the information?"

"Then Yousef stays trapped. Chen keeps trying. You go home empty-handed. That's reality."

Kamal walks toward the door. Pauses.

"One more thing. The warnings you've been receiving. About Chen. About trust. Some were from my people. Some were not."

"Who else?"

"Iranian intelligence has assets in Kurdistan. They monitor American operations. They benefit from Americans fighting each other. From CIA and DIA not coordinating. From chaos we create for ourselves. Some of your warnings came from them. Trying to steer you toward choices that benefit Tehran."

"How do I know which warnings were yours and which were Iranian?"

"You don't. That's the point. Multiple players. Multiple messages. You can't know who's helping and who's manipulating. You just make best choice with imperfect information." Kamal reaches the door. "Welcome to Kurdistan, Mr. Caldwell. Where everyone lies to everyone and sometimes the lies are truer than the truth."

He leaves. His security follows.

Ethan sits in the empty chapel. Alone. Processing.

The meeting was real. Kamal wants to help. But the price is intelligence on Chen that requires using Yousef as witting source against his handler. Which makes Yousef a double agent. Which is exactly what Chen would execute someone for doing.

The stakes just got higher.


***


Outside, Lars is waiting. Alert. Weapon not drawn but ready.

"How'd it go?"

"Complicated."

They walk back to the car. The streets are still empty. Ankawa sleeping or pretending to sleep.

In the car, Ethan explains. The meeting with Kamal. The offer—information about Chen's operations in exchange for public refusal that forces Chen to release Yousef. The warning about Iranian intelligence steering him.

Lars drives. Thinks. Finally: "He's playing his own game."

"Obviously."

"No, I mean—he's not just gathering intelligence on Chen. He's positioning himself as indispensable to everyone. Americans need him. Kurds need him. He's making himself the pivot point. The guy everyone has to deal with. That's long-term play. Post-ISIS Kurdistan, Kamal will be powerful because everyone owes him."

"Does that change anything?"

"Changes whether you trust him. He'll honor the deal because it benefits him. But he won't honor it because he's moral or principled or cares about Yousef. He'll do it because helping you strengthens his position."

"I can work with that."

"Can you? Because getting the information he wants means turning Yousef into active spy against Chen. That's dangerous. If Chen finds out—and Chen's good at finding out—Yousef doesn't just stay trapped. He gets arrested. Prosecuted. Maybe disappears."

Ethan looks out the window. The city passing. Checkpoints. Generators. Normal life on top of secret wars.

"What choice do we have?"

"Walk away. Go home. Let Yousef figure it out himself."

"That's not happening."

"Then you're committed. No turning back. You gather intelligence on CIA operations. Use Yousef as witting source. Burn Chen's network. Free Yousef but destroy Chen's career and possibly expose people who thought they were protected." Lars glances over. "That's the calculation. Yousef's freedom versus everything else."

Just like Baqubah. The decision that costs more than you want to pay.

They drive back to the guest house. Park. Sit in the car.

"I need to talk to Yousef," Ethan says. "Tonight. Before I lose nerve."

"He's under surveillance."

"I know. But I need to tell him what Kamal wants. See if he'll do it."

"What if he says no?"

"Then I'm out of options."

Lars pulls out his phone. Types in Norwegian. Gets response. "Norwegian journalist I know. She has apartment in Erbil. Empty this week. She's covering Mosul from Baghdad. We can use it. Neutral location. I'll get Yousef there."

"How?"

"Leave that to me."

***

An hour later they're in a third-floor apartment. Modern building. Nice by Erbil standards. Two bedrooms, living room, small kitchen. Windows overlooking the street.

Lars made calls. Used his network. Got Yousef extracted from wherever Chen's people watch him. Brought him here through routes that avoid obvious surveillance.

But nothing in Erbil avoids all surveillance. Someone knows Yousef moved. Someone's tracking it. Question is whether they care enough to intervene or whether they're just observing.

Yousef arrives looking terrified. He enters the apartment like it might explode.

"What's happening? Lars said emergency. Said I needed to come. If Chen finds out I'm here—"

"Chen's going to find out eventually," Ethan says. "But we're out of time for being careful."

He explains. The meeting with Kamal. The offer. The price—intelligence on Chen's other operations. The promise—public refusal that forces Chen to release Yousef.

Yousef listens. Face going through emotions. Hope. Fear. Anger. Resignation.

"You want me to spy on Chen."

"I want you to gather information we need to free you."

"That's spying. If he finds out—" Yousef sits. Puts head in hands. "He'll destroy me. He'll expose my work. My family will know. Rochester community will know. I'll be known as American spy. My daughters will—" He stops. "I can't."

"Then you stay trapped."

"I know. But I can't spy on him. Can't betray him like that. He trusted me. He's—despite everything, he's been professional. He's not cruel. He's just committed to his mission. I can't—"

"He's keeping you prisoner," Ethan interrupts. "He's leveraging your family's safety. He's coercing your cooperation. That's not professional relationship. That's hostage situation with paperwork."

"I know. But if I betray him, I'm no better. I become the person he fears all sources become—the one who turns. The one who sells information. I can't be that person."

Lars speaks. "What if we frame it differently? You're not betraying Chen. You're protecting Kurdistan. Kamal needs information to protect Kurdish interests from American operations that might not serve Kurdistan. You're helping Kurdistan. Chen would say that's justified."

"That's manipulation. Using Chen's logic to justify betraying him."

"Yes. That's intelligence work. Everyone manipulates everyone. Chen manipulates you. Kamal manipulates everyone. You're just learning to manipulate back."

Yousef looks at Lars. Then at Ethan. "I came to Kurdistan thinking I could help people. Do good work. Go home. Instead I became spy. Then double agent. Now triple agent. Where does it end?"

"It ends when you're on a plane to Rochester," Ethan says. "It ends when your daughters ask when you're coming home and you can say 'next week.' It ends when you're free. That's where it ends."

Silence in the apartment. Traffic sounds from the street below. The hum of air conditioning. The pressure of impossible decisions.

"What information does Kamal want?" Yousef asks finally.

"Names of Chen's other sources. What networks he's mapping. What his priorities are. Who he's meeting with beyond you."

"I know some of that. Not all. Chen compartmentalizes. But I know some."

"Some is enough."

"When does he need it?"

"Three days."

Yousef laughs. Bitter. "Three days. From trapped asset to active spy in three days. The transformation is complete."

"Will you do it?"

Long pause. Yousef stares at the floor. Processing. Calculating. Making the decision that changes everything.

"Yes," he says finally. "I'll do it. Because I want to go home. Because I miss my daughters. Because I'm tired of lying." He looks at Ethan. "But if this goes wrong—if Chen catches me—you need to protect my family. Get them somewhere safe. Make sure they're okay."

"I will."

"Promise me."

"I promise."

Yousef nods. Stands. "How do I send the information?"

"Text it to the number that's been sending warnings. Kamal's monitoring it."

"And then?"

"Then we wait for Kamal to refuse Chen publicly. To make enough noise that Chen has to shut down the operation."

"What if Chen doesn't shut it down? What if he just gets more aggressive?"

"Then we have problem. But we'll deal with that when it happens."

Yousef moves toward the door. Pauses. "You've changed, Ethan. Since 2008. You're willing to do things I didn't think you'd do. Use people. Manipulate situations. Make calculations about acceptable costs."

"I learned from the best."

"From Chen?"

"From everyone. Chen. Petey. The war. You learn or you die or you get stuck in situations you can't escape." Ethan meets his eyes. "I'm sorry it came to this. Sorry I can't fix it with legal arguments and proper channels. Sorry the only way out is through betrayal and manipulation and burning someone's operation."

"Don't be sorry. Be effective. Get me home." Yousef opens the door. "I'll send the information tomorrow. Then we see if Kamal keeps his word."

He leaves.

Lars and Ethan sit in the empty apartment.

"Think he'll do it?" Lars asks.

"He'll do it. He's desperate enough and smart enough to see it's the only option."

"And if Chen catches him?"

"Then we improvise."

"Improvise how? If Chen arrests Yousef for spying, there's no improvising. That's game over."

Ethan doesn't answer. Because Lars is right. They're committed now. No turning back. The next seventy-two hours determine whether Yousef goes home or disappears into CIA detention somewhere.

His phone buzzes. The anonymous number.

*Good meeting. Information expected within 48 hours. After that, I move. Chen will know something's wrong. Be ready. —K*

At least they know it's Kamal now. No more anonymous warnings. Direct communication.

Another message arrives. Different number. US country code.

*Heard you met Kamal. Careful. He's playing his own game. So is Chen. So are you. Someone's game ends badly. Make sure it's not yours. —Petey*

"Petey's watching," Ethan says.

"Petey's always watching. That's what makes him valuable."

They leave the apartment. Drive back through night streets. The checkpoints are serious now. Past 11 PM. Curfew-adjacent. The Peshmerga check IDs more carefully. Ask more questions.

At the guest house, Lars parks. They sit in the car.

"Tomorrow Yousef gathers intelligence," Lars says. "Day after to-morrow he sends it to Kamal. Day after that, Kamal refuses Chen publicly. Then things get interesting."

"Interesting how?"

"Chen's not stupid. He'll know something happened. He'll investigate. He'll figure out someone fed you information. Someone compromised his operation. He'll narrow possibilities. Eventually he'll suspect Yousef or Kamal or both."

"What do we do then?"

"We get Yousef out before Chen moves on him. Fast extraction. No waiting for official channels. Just get him to the airport and on a plane."

"That's kidnapping from CIA's perspective."

"That's Tuesday in Kurdistan. Everyone's grabbing people. We'll just grab ours back."

The logic is sound. The legality is questionable. The morality is ambiguous. Just like everything else in this city.

They go inside. The guest house is quiet. Other residents sleeping or at the front or doing whatever foreign volunteers do in a war zone at night.

In his room, Ethan lies on the bed. Doesn't sleep. Thinks about the cemetery meeting. About Kamal's certainty that everyone's playing multiple games. About Yousef agreeing to spy on Chen. About the decision he made that committed everyone to a path that might end very badly.

Just like Baqubah. The decision in the moment that ripples forward. That costs things you can't predict until after it's done.

He touches the scar on his arm. The reminder. The permanent record of the night he learned that sometimes doing the right thing costs someone their life.

The man died because Ethan pulled the trigger. Because he saw the tactical situation and decided engaging was necessary. The math worked—they saved the village. But The man's wife—the wedding ring he wore—doesn't care about the math.

And tomorrow Ethan's asking Yousef to gather intelligence that could get him killed. For the same reason. Because the tactical situation requires it. Because the math works. Because one person's risk is acceptable cost for everyone's benefit.

The calculation Chen uses. The logic Ethan criticized. The framework he's now applying himself.

The cognitive dissonance is complete.

His phone buzzes. Petey again.

*DIA knows about the cemetery meeting. Kamal reported it to his handler. They're not happy you're operating independently. But they won't interfere yet. They want to see if you succeed where they couldn't. If you free Yousef, they claim credit. If you fail, they disavow knowledge. Classic intelligence play.*

Ethan types back: *Whose side is DIA on?*

Response comes immediately: *Their own. Same as everyone else. Loyalties are tactical in Kurdistan. Today's ally is tomorrow's problem. Just make sure when the music stops, you're not the one without a chair.*

Good advice. Hard to follow when the music keeps changing tempo and nobody knows when it stops.

Another message. The Kamal number.

*Chen suspects something. He's asking Yousef more questions. Being more careful. Time is shorter than I thought. Information needed within 24 hours. After that, too risky. —K*

Twenty-four hours. Not seventy-two. The timeline just compressed.

Ethan texts back: *Can Yousef gather it that fast?*

*He must. Or the opportunity closes. Chen becomes too cautious. Operation fails. Everyone loses. —K*

Everything accelerating. The window closing. The pressure building.

Ethan texts Yousef. Explains the new timeline. Twenty-four hours. Not forty-eight.

The response takes five minutes.

*I'll try. Chen meeting multiple sources tomorrow. I'll be there for some. I'll gather what I can. Send it tomorrow night. After that—if this works or not—I'm done. I can't keep doing this. —Y*

Translation: tomorrow night is end game. Yousef sends information. Kamal refuses Chen. Chen either releases Yousef or moves against him. No more waiting. No more calculating. Just results.

Ethan sets his phone down. Stares at the ceiling. The generator hums. The checkpoint sounds drift through the window. The city continues its complicated existence while secret wars play out in shadows.

# 6

## CHAPTER 6: THE INTELLIGENCE

*Erbil, Kurdistan Region — October 2015*

Morning comes too early. Ethan wakes at 6 AM to the sound of the call to prayer. Lies there listening. Five times a day, every day, the city stops for prayer. The rhythm of Muslim life continuing while intelligence services run operations in the spaces between.

His phone has three messages from Yousef. Sent at 4:17 AM.

*Chen scheduled meetings today. Four of them. I'll be at three. Will gather what I can.*

*Scared. If he suspects—*

*No. Can't think like that. I'll do this. For my daughters. —Y*

Ethan texts back: *Be careful. Don't push too hard. Better to get some intel than get caught getting all of it.*

No response. Yousef's phone is probably off. Standard protocol when you're gathering intelligence on your handler.

Lars is already up. Courtyard. Smoking. Looking like he didn't sleep.

"Coffee?" he asks.

"Always."

They walk to the bakery. Same routine. The owner recognizes them now. Brings chai without asking. Fresh bread. The morning ritual that makes foreign cities feel less foreign.

"Today's the day," Lars says.

"Yeah."

"Yousef gathers intel. Sends it to Kamal. Then Kamal moves."

"That's the plan."

"Plans are great until someone shoots at you." Lars drinks his chai. "We should be ready to move fast. If Chen figures out Yousef's compromised, he'll move to detain him. We'll have maybe an hour to get him to the airport."

"Can we get him through security that fast?"

"If we have to? Yes. But it won't be clean. Kurdish authorities will ask questions. Chen will make calls. It'll be messy."

"Better messy than Yousef in CIA detention."

"Agreed. But messy has costs. We burn bridges. Make enemies. Complicate future operations."

"I'm not running future operations. I'm getting Yousef home."

Lars looks at him. "You sure about that? Because once you start operating in places like Kurdistan, it has a way of pulling you back. You think you're done. Then someone calls. Then you're booking flights. Then you're in cemetery meetings with intelligence officers. The work finds you."

The conversation feels too familiar. Like something Chen would say. Or Petey. Or anyone who's been in the game long enough to recognize the pattern.

"Let's focus on today," Ethan says.

"Fair enough."

They finish breakfast. Walk back through morning streets. Erbil waking up. Shops opening. Traffic building. Peshmerga changing shifts at checkpoints. The city's daily rhythm overlaying the secret wars.

Back at the guest house, Ethan's phone rings. Unknown number. US country code.

"This is Ethan."

"It's Petey. You alone?"

"Lars is here."

"Good. Put me on speaker."

Ethan does. Lars leans in.

"DIA's nervous," Petey says. "They know about tonight. Know Kamal's planning to refuse Chen publicly. They're worried it'll blow their own operation."

"Kamal works for them," Ethan says. "They should be supporting this."

"DIA doesn't support anything that complicates their position. Kamal's valuable because he's access. If he burns his relationship with CIA, he's less valuable to DIA. They'd rather keep status quo—Kamal stringing Chen along, gathering intelligence, everyone maintaining plausible deniability."

"So they'll interfere?"

"They'll try. DIA handler's reaching out to Kamal today. Trying to convince him to slow down. Keep the recruitment alive longer. Maximize intelligence gathering."

"Fuck." Lars stubs out his cigarette. "If Kamal listens to DIA, Yousef stays trapped."

"Kamal won't listen," Petey says. "He's playing his own game. But he'll use DIA's concern as leverage. Ask for something in return for refusing Chen on their timeline."

"What does he want?" Ethan asks.

"Don't know yet. But be ready. Kamal doesn't do anything for free. If he's refusing Chen tonight, he's getting something from someone."

"As long as Yousef goes home, I don't care what Kamal gets."

"You should care. Because whatever he gets might cost you. Kurdistan's complicated. Every favor creates debt. Every debt has interest. You're accumulating obligations and you might not know what they are until someone calls them in."

The line goes quiet except for static.

"If Chen logs two more developmental touches on Kamal before Thanksgiving, Langley greenlights a burn notice on alternative access."

"Anything else?" Ethan asks.

"Yeah. Chen's meeting his network today. Four meetings. Yousef will be at three. The fourth is sensitive. Counter-terrorism source. Someone inside ISIS information networks. Chen won't bring Yousef to that one. Too compartmented."

"How do you know this?"

"Because DIA monitors CIA operations. They know Chen's schedule better than Chen does. They've been watching his Kurdistan network for two years. They know every source, every meeting, every safe house."

"And they're just now telling us this?"

"They're telling you this because I asked. And I asked because you're operating in the dark and that gets people killed." Petey's voice goes hard. "Don't mistake DIA's help for friendship. They're providing intelligence because it serves their interests. They want Yousef free because it embarrasses CIA. They want Chen's operation disrupted because it makes DIA look competent by comparison. You're useful. When you stop being useful, they'll stop helping."

"Noted."

"Good luck today. Call if you need extraction support. I've got people in theater who owe me favors."

"People in theater" means contractors. Private military. The kind who operate in gray areas and don't ask questions if the money's right.

"Thanks, Petey."

"Don't thank me. Just don't get killed. I don't want to explain to Margaret why her associate disappeared in Kurdistan." He hangs up.

Lars lights another cigarette. "DIA monitoring Chen's schedule means they're running surveillance on CIA operations. That's aggressive."

"That's inter-agency competition."

"Everyone watching everyone. Multiple operations running through same space. Sooner or later someone makes a mistake and it all collapses."

"We just need it to hold together for twenty-four hours."

"Twenty-four hours is a lifetime in intelligence work."

***

At 10 AM Ethan's phone buzzes. Text from Yousef.

*First meeting done. Chen introduced me to Kurdish business-man. Imports/exports. Front for tracking Iranian commercial networks. Chen's mapping Tehran's economic influence in Kurdistan. Business-man thinks he's helping Kurdistan resist Iran. Actually providing intelligence on Iranian business relationships. Classic recruitment.*

*Moving to second meeting. KDP official. Mid-level. Access to party communications. Chen's learning internal KDP dynamics. Who's ris-*

*ing. Who's falling. Post-ISIS positioning. Official thinks he's building relationship with Americans for Kurdistan's independence push.*

*Will send full details tonight. —Y*

Ethan types back: *Be careful. Don't get caught taking notes.*

*Not taking notes. Memorizing. Four years of doing this—I'm good at remembering. —Y*

Four years of practice. Four years of being asset. The skills you learn when you're trapped.

Lars reads the messages. "That's good intelligence. Businessman and KDP official. Two sources Chen's running. Kamal will want names."

"Yousef will have them."

"Question is whether Chen notices Yousef paying too much attention. Whether he's asking too many questions. Whether his behavior pattern changes enough that Chen gets suspicious."

"Yousef's been doing this for four years. He knows how to play the role."

"Yeah, but now he's playing it while actively betraying his handler. That's different. That changes your psychology. Makes you nervous. Makes you make mistakes."

Ethan doesn't argue because Lars is right. Yousef's in the most dangerous position—operational asset turned witting double agent. The stress must be immense.

His phone rings. Unknown number. Kurdish country code.

"This is Ethan."

"It's Kamal." The voice is calm. Professional. "We need to meet. Before tonight. Before I refuse Chen."

"Why?"

"Because DIA is pressuring me to delay. Because the timeline's compressing. Because there are things you need to know before this happens." Pause. "Can you come to Kurdistan Studies Center? Two PM. There's a lecture on water rights. Nobody attends lectures on water rights. We'll have privacy."

"I'll be there."

"Come alone. Bringing the Norwegian creates attention we don't need."

The line goes dead.

Ethan looks at Lars. "Kamal wants a meeting. Two PM. Kurdistan Studies Center. Alone."

"That's three hours from now. Could be legitimate meeting. Could be setup."

"It's legitimate. Kamal's not going to kidnap me from Kurdistan Studies Center in broad daylight."

"No, but he might manipulate you. Might change terms. Might ask for more than you agreed to." Lars crushes his cigarette. "That's how intelligence officers work. Get you committed. Get you invested. Then change the price."

"What choice do I have?"

"None. That's his leverage. He knows you're committed. Knows you'll pay the price whatever it is. So he can ask for anything."

"As long as Yousef goes home."

"Yeah. As long as that." Lars stands. "I'll drive you there. Wait outside. If you're not out in an hour, I'm coming in."

\*\*\*

The drive to Kurdistan Studies Center takes fifteen minutes. Traffic is heavy. Lunchtime in Erbil. The city functioning despite everything.

They pass through two checkpoints. The Peshmerga recognize Lars's vehicle. Wave them through. The familiarity is useful. Being known means not being questioned.

At the Studies Center, Lars parks across the street. "One hour. If you're not out, I'm coming in."

"Understood."

Ethan walks to the building. Security at the door checks his ID. Asks purpose. He says he's attending the water rights lecture. They look at him like he's crazy but let him through.

The lecture hall is on the second floor. Door open. Maybe fifteen people inside. Mostly Kurdish academics. One European man who might be from an NGO. The lecturer is already speaking. Something about aquifer depletion and cross-border water agreements.

Kamal is sitting in the back row. He nods toward the empty seat beside him.

Ethan sits. They don't speak for five minutes. Just watch the lecturer talk about declining water tables and irrigation challenges.

Finally Kamal leans over. Whispers. "This is actually interesting. Water is Kurdistan's next crisis. After ISIS. After independence questions. Water."

"Is that why you're here?"

"I'm here because nobody watches water rights lectures. Best place for private conversation in Erbil." He pulls out a notebook. Writes something. Shows it to Ethan.

*DIA pressuring me to delay refusal. Keep stringing Chen. They think current arrangement gives them more intelligence value.*

Ethan takes the notebook. Writes: *Will you delay?*

Kamal reads it. Writes back: *No. But I need something from you in exchange.*

*What?*

*After I refuse Chen, he'll investigate. He'll try to find who compromised his operation. He'll narrow suspects. Eventually he'll look at Yousef. I need you to protect Yousef from that investigation.*

*How?*

*Get him out of Kurdistan immediately. Tonight. Before Chen can move against him. And leave evidence suggesting someone else compromised the operation. Misdirection.*

*Who do we blame?*

*Iranian intelligence. Chen already suspects they're monitoring his operations. If evidence points to Iranian asset feeding you information, Chen investigates that direction. Buys Yousef time.*

*What evidence?*

*I'll provide it. Phone records. Meeting logs. Trail suggesting Iranian handler was your source. Chen will believe it because he wants to believe it. Fits his worldview—Iranians undermining American operations.*

Ethan writes: *That's manipulation. Lying to Chen.*

Kamal writes back: *Yes. That's intelligence work. Everyone lies. Question is whether lie serves good purpose. Does lie that saves Yousef from CIA detention serve good purpose?*

The moral calculation. The framework. The same logic Chen uses.

Ethan writes: *Yes. I'll do it.*

*Good. After I refuse Chen tonight, you have two hours maximum. Get Yousef to airport. Get him on plane. I'll provide the misdirection evidence. Chen will investigate Iranian angle. Won't pursue Yousef until he realizes Iranian trail is false. By then Yousef is in Rochester.*

*What if Chen realizes immediately?*

*He won't. Iranian intelligence does monitor American operations. Chen knows this. Evidence will be plausible. He'll investigate it because it's less embarrassing than admitting his own cultural advisor betrayed him.*

The psychology makes sense. People believe what they want to believe. Chen will want to believe external threat compromised his operation rather than internal betrayal.

Ethan writes: *When do you refuse him?*

*Eight PM. Kurdistan Regional Government building. Public event. International observers present. I'll refuse loudly enough that Chen must respond. Can't quietly shelve it. Must be public failure.*

*Why public?*

*Because private refusal lets Chen pretend it never happened. Continue operation with different approach. Public refusal forces him to accept failure. Move on. Let Yousef go.*

The lecturer is still talking. Something about transboundary water law. The few attendees are taking notes. The appearance of academic interest while intelligence business happens in the back row.

Kamal closes the notebook. Stands. Whispers one more thing. "Your friend Petey. Tell him DIA can stop watching me now. After tonight I'm done with Americans. All Americans. This operation costs too much. I'm going back to just serving Kurdistan."

"What does that mean?"

"It means I'm tired of playing multiple games. Tired of serving multiple masters. After I refuse Chen, I'll resign from American cooperation. Tell my DIA handler I'm out. Focus on Kurdistan's interests only." He pauses. "I've learned from watching Americans operate here. Learned that everyone uses everyone. Learned that loyalty to distant powers costs more than it's worth. Better to serve one master—my own people."

"DIA won't accept that."

"They'll have to. I'm not their asset. I'm their partner. Partnership ends when one partner decides it's done. They can't force me to continue. Can't threaten me. I'm Kurdish intelligence in Kurdistan. They need me more than I need them."

The calculation is clear. Kamal's been positioning for this. Building leverage. Making himself valuable enough to multiple sides that he can choose his exit. Smart.

"Good luck tonight," Ethan says.

"Luck is for people without preparation. I've been preparing for tonight for eight months. Since Chen first approached me through Yousef. I knew eventually I'd have to refuse. Just needed right moment. Right leverage. Right price." He moves toward the aisle. "You gave me right moment. Tonight I execute."

He leaves. Ethan sits through ten more minutes of the water rights lecture. Then leaves himself.

Outside, Lars is waiting. Smoking. Alert.

"How'd it go?"

"Complicated. Let's drive."

***

Back at the guest house, Ethan explains. Kamal's plan. The eight PM public refusal. The two-hour window to get Yousef to the airport. The misdirection evidence pointing at Iranian intelligence.

Lars listens. Then: "That's actually clever. Chen will investigate Iranian angle because it's plausible. Buys us time."

"But it's also manipulation. We're lying to Chen. Setting up false trail."

"We're doing intelligence work. Misdirection is standard tradecraft. Chen does it himself. We're just using his own methods against him."

"Still feels wrong."

"Lots of things in intelligence work feel wrong. That's the job. You make uncomfortable choices in service of objectives." Lars lights another cigarette. "Question is whether objective justifies uncomfortable choice. Does getting Yousef home justify lying to Chen?"

The same calculation. The same framework.

"Yeah," Ethan says. "It does."

"Then we prepare. Eight PM refusal. Two hours to airport. Need to have Yousef ready to move. Need transportation. Need tickets. Need exit strategy if Chen moves faster than expected."

They spend the afternoon planning. Lars makes calls. Arranges things. His network of contractors and volunteers and people who owe favors. The shadow infrastructure that operates parallel to official channels.

At 3 PM Yousef texts.

*Third meeting done. PUK intelligence officer. Provides Chen information on PUK internal politics. Rivalry with KDP. Officer thinks he's balancing power. Actually giving Americans leverage over both parties.*

*Chen's building comprehensive map. Every party. Every faction. Every player. He's not just gathering intelligence. He's positioning for post-ISIS Kurdistan. Trying to make sure Americans have influence over whoever comes out on top.*

*One more meeting. Then I'll compile everything. Send to Kamal tonight. —Y*

Ethan responds: *Good work. Be ready to move fast tonight. After Kamal refuses Chen, we extract you immediately. Airport. Plane. Home.*

*Home.* Yousef sends back. *I can barely remember what that means.*

Four years of being trapped. Four years of lying. Four years of serving Chen's operation. The psychological load must be crushing.

*Few more hours. Then it's over. —E*

*Or just beginning. If Chen figures out what I did—* Yousef doesn't finish the thought.

Ethan types: *He won't. We have misdirection. You'll be safe.*

But Ethan doesn't know that. Nobody knows that. They're operating in the confusion. Making bets with incomplete information. Hoping the calculation works.

At 5 PM Lars comes back with tickets. Turkish Airlines. Erbil to Istanbul. Istanbul to JFK. Arriving Rochester Sunday morning.

"Cost $2,800," Lars says. "Last-minute international. But it's booked. Yousef just needs to get to the airport."

"How do we get him through security?"

"His passport's at US Consulate, stamped 'Administrative Review' by KRG Interior—US request. We're not getting it without Chen's cooperation."

"So what's the plan?"

"Emergency travel document. US citizens can get emergency documentation from consular services if their passport is lost or stolen. We report Yousef's passport as stolen. Consulate issues emergency travel document. He uses that to board."

"Won't Chen block that?"

"Depends on timing. If we move fast enough—report passport stolen at 8:15, right after Kamal's refusal—consulate might issue document before Chen can intervene. It's gamble. But it's best option we have."

Everything's a gamble. Everything's betting on timing and misdirection and Chen being distracted long enough that Yousef slips through.

At 6 PM Yousef texts: *All meetings done. Compiling information now. Will send in two hours.*

Ethan: *Where are you?*

*Safe house Chen uses for operational meetings. North Erbil. He left thirty minutes ago. I'm alone. Writing everything down.*

*Be careful. If he comes back—*

*He won't. He has dinner meeting with Kurdish officials. Won't be back until ten PM. I have time.*

Time. The currency of intelligence work. You never have enough.

At 7 PM Yousef sends the intelligence. Long text. Names. Positions. Networks. Everything he gathered.

*Kurdish businessman: Hoshyar Mahmoud. Imports/exports. Tracks Iranian commercial networks. Believes he's helping Kurdistan resist Iranian economic influence. Actually providing CIA detailed intelligence on Iranian business relationships in KRG.*

*KDP official: Saman Aziz. Mid-level party administrator. Access to internal communications. Provides Chen information on KDP internal politics. Who's rising. Who's falling. Post-ISIS positioning. Thinks he's building US relationship for Kurdistan independence push. Actually giving Americans leverage over KDP decision-making.*

*PUK intelligence officer: Jamal Hassan. Counter-intelligence. Supposedly tracks foreign operatives in Kurdistan. Actually provides Chen information on PUK operations against Iranian intelligence. Creates back-channel for US-PUK intelligence cooperation outside official channels. Thinks he's protecting PUK interests. Actually compromising them.*

*Chen's objective: Map every faction. Every player. Every relationship. Position Americans to influence post-ISIS Kurdistan regardless of which party dominates. He's not picking winners. He's making sure Americans have leverage over everyone.*

*Additional: Chen mentioned fourth source. Counter-terrorism. Inside ISIS information networks. Wouldn't give details. Too sensitive. But this source provides tactical intelligence on ISIS operations.*

*Real-time. Chen very protective of this asset. Keeps completely compart-
mented.*

Ethan reads it twice. Saves it. Forwards to Kamal's number.

*Received. This is good intelligence. More than I expected. Yousef did
well. —K*

*Will you still refuse Chen tonight?*

*Yes. Eight PM. KRG building. Public event on regional security.
Perfect venue. Chen will be there. I'll refuse him with witnesses. Make it
impossible for him to continue operation quietly. —K*

*And the misdirection?*

*Already prepared. Phone records showing Iranian handler contact-
ing you. Meeting logs placing you near Iranian intelligence safe house.
Chen will investigate. Find evidence suggesting Iranian asset compromised his operation. Will pursue that angle while Yousef escapes. —K*

*Thank you.*

*Don't thank me. I'm not doing this for friendship. I'm doing it be-
cause it serves my interests. But result is same—Yousef goes home. That's
what matters. —K*

At 7:30 Lars and Ethan leave for the KRG building. The event is
public. Open to diplomats, academics, journalists. They'll blend in.

The drive takes twenty minutes. Evening traffic. The city transitioning to night mode. Generators starting. Checkpoints changing
shifts. The daily rhythm.

At the KRG building, security is heavy. Multiple checkpoints.
Asayish checking IDs. Looking for threats. ISIS is thirty kilometers
away. Security takes nothing for granted.

They clear security. Enter the building. Modern architecture. Kurdish flags. Photos of President Barzani. The infrastructure of regional
government.

The event is in the main conference hall. Maybe two hundred people. Kurdish officials. Peshmerga officers in dress uniforms. Foreign diplomats. NGO workers. Journalists. Everyone who matters in Kurdistan's security landscape.

And Chen. Standing near the front with other American diplomats. Talking with a Kurdish official. The easy rapport of someone who's been here long enough to be comfortable.

Ethan and Lars find seats in the back. Where they can see everything but aren't prominent.

At 8 PM the event starts. Kurdish Minister of Interior speaks. Talks about regional security cooperation. About Kurdish-American partnership. About shared interests against terrorism.

Chen's in the third row. Taking notes. The performance of engaged diplomat.

Then it's question period. Officials taking questions from the audience. Standard diplomatic event.

Kamal stands. He's in civilian clothes but everyone knows who he is. Asayish. Counter-intelligence. His presence means official Kurdistan security position.

"Question for the American delegation," Kamal says. His English is clear. Loud. Carrying through the hall. "Regarding intelligence cooperation and recruitment of Kurdish assets."

The room goes quiet. That's not standard diplomatic question. That's pointed. Aggressive.

Chen looks up. Recognizes Kamal. His face stays neutral but Ethan sees the calculation. Wondering where this is going.

"The United States values intelligence cooperation with Kurdish partners," an American official responds. Standard diplomatic answer. "We work together against shared threats."

"Yes," Kamal says. "But there's cooperation and there's recruitment. There's partnership and there's asset management. I want to clarify—for public record, with witnesses—that I am not American intelligence asset. I am Kurdish intelligence officer who cooperates with Americans when our interests align. But I am not recruited. I am not controlled. I serve Kurdistan first."

The room is silent. Everyone understands what just happened. Public refusal of CIA recruitment. With witnesses. Diplomatic incident.

Chen's face is stone. The official American position holds—we don't comment on intelligence matters. But everyone knows what Kamal just said. And everyone knows Chen runs CIA operations in Kurdistan.

"Furthermore," Kamal continues, "I am aware of approaches made to recruit me over the past eight months. Cultural introductions. Relationship building. Standard tradecraft. I am refusing these approaches publicly because I want clarity. I work with Americans. I do not work for Americans. That distinction matters."

He sits down. The Minister of Interior looks uncomfortable. The American delegation looks furious. Chen is already on his phone. Making calls.

Ethan and Lars slip out. They have two hours.

***

Outside, Ethan calls Yousef. "It's done. Kamal refused Chen publicly. We're moving now. Get to the airport. We'll meet you there."

"Oh God. Okay. Okay. I'm leaving now." Yousef sounds terrified. "What about my things? What about—"

"Leave everything. Just get to the airport. We have tickets. Emergency travel document being processed. Just move."

"Okay. Moving." The line goes dead.

Lars is already driving. Fast. Through evening traffic. Toward the safe house where Yousef is.

"Chen will move fast," Lars says. "He'll try to lock down Yousef before he can leave. We have maybe thirty minutes before Chen figures out what's happening and orders detention."

They reach the safe house. Yousef is outside. Waiting. One small bag. Looking like a man escaping prison.

He gets in the car. They drive.

"This is really happening," Yousef says. "I'm actually leaving."

"Not yet. Airport first. Security. Border control. Get on plane. Then you're leaving."

The drive to the airport takes twenty minutes. Yousef sits in back. Silent. Clutching his bag.

At the airport, security is tight. Evening flights. Multiple checkpoints. They park. Walk to terminal.

At the US Consulate counter—small presence inside the airport for citizen services—Ethan approaches.

"Need emergency travel document. US citizen. Passport stolen."

The consular officer looks skeptical. "Name?"

"Yousef al-Tamimi."

The officer types into computer. Face changes. "There's a hold on this passport. Security review. I can't issue emergency travel document without clearance."

"The passport was stolen," Ethan says. "He needs to travel. He's a US permanent resident. He has rights."

"I understand, but there's a security hold. I need to make a call." She reaches for the phone.

Lars leans in. Speaks quietly. "If you make that call, you're involving yourself in CIA internal operation. You're creating paperwork trail. Documentation of your involvement. Is that what you want?"

The officer pauses. Looks at Lars. At Ethan. At Yousef.

"If I issue this document and there's a problem—"

"There won't be a problem," Lars says. "He's permanent resident trying to go home. He has ticket. He has documentation. Issue the emergency travel document. Let him board. If someone has questions later, you followed standard procedure for stolen passport claim. You did your job."

The officer thinks. Then types. Prints. Signs.

"Emergency travel document valid for thirty days. Single use. Gets you to US. That's it."

Yousef takes it. Hands shaking. "Thank you."

They move to security. Yousef goes through. Bags checked. ID verified. Emergency travel document examined. Security looks at computer. Sees something. Looks at Yousef.

"Sir, can you wait here please?"

"What's wrong?" Yousef's voice cracks.

"Just need to verify something. Won't take long."

The security officer makes a call. Speaks in Kurdish. Low voice.

Ethan and Lars watch from the other side. Can't intervene. Can't help. Just watch.

The officer finishes the call. Looks at computer again. Then waves Yousef through.

"Safe travels."

Yousef moves through. Doesn't look back. Into the secure area. Toward the gate.

Lars and Ethan can't follow. Can't go past security without tickets.

"Think he'll make it?" Ethan asks.

"Depends how fast Chen moves. If Chen realizes what's happening in the next thirty minutes, he can order plane held. Have Yousef removed. But if he's distracted—investigating Kamal's refusal, dealing with diplomatic fallout—Yousef might board before Chen thinks to stop him."

They wait. Can't leave until they know.

Ethan's phone buzzes. Kamal.

*Chen investigating. Asking questions. Looking for who compromised operation. I've provided misdirection evidence. Iranian intelligence contact logs. He's pursuing that angle. Buys time. —K*

*How much time?*

*Few hours maybe. He'll realize Iranian trail is false eventually. But not tonight. Tonight he's chasing wrong lead. That's what you needed. —K*

*Thank you.*

*You're welcome. And we're done. I'm resigning American cooperation tomorrow. Tell your friend Petey—tell DIA—I'm out. Serving only Kurdistan now. No more games. —K*

At 9:47 PM Ethan's phone rings. Yousef.

"I'm on the plane. It's boarding. I'm actually on the plane."

"Stay calm. Don't attract attention. Just board. Sit down. Wait for takeoff."

"Ethan. Thank you. God, thank you. I don't know how to—"

"Get home. Hug your daughters. That's thanks enough."

"What about you? What about—Chen will know. He'll investigate. He'll figure out you helped."

"Let me worry about that. You just get home."

The line goes dead. Boarding announcement in background.

At 10:03 PM Lars checks the flight status on his phone. "Turkish Airlines 769. Departed on time. Istanbul. He's airborne."

Ethan lets out breath he didn't know he was holding. "He's out."

"He's out of Kurdistan. Still has to get through Istanbul. Through JFK. Through immigration in New York. Still has to make it all the way to Rochester before Chen can stop him."

"But he's out of Kurdistan. That's what matters. Chen doesn't have jurisdiction in Turkey or the US. Yousef's a permanent resident. He has rights. Chen can't just detain him in Rochester."

"Chen can make his life very difficult. Can investigate. Can question. Can create problems for his family. Can—"

"Let him try. Yousef's home. That's what we came here to do. He's home."

They walk back to the car. The airport behind them. The night cool. The city spread out. Lights and darkness.

In the car, Lars lights a cigarette. "What now?"

"Now we deal with Chen. He'll figure out eventually that I helped. That I fed information from Yousef to Kamal. That I facilitated the refusal. He'll come looking."

"And when he does?"

"I'll tell him the truth. That Yousef wanted out. That I helped him. That the operation was coercive and wrong. That I don't apologize."

"That's principled. Also stupid. Chen can make you disappear. This is Kurdistan. Things happen to people who interfere with CIA operations."

"I'm American citizen. He can't just disappear me."

"Maybe. Maybe not. Line between official detention and unfortunate accident is thinner than you think in places like this."

Ethan's phone rings. Unknown number. US country code.

He answers. "This is Ethan."

"It's Chen. We need to talk. Tomorrow morning. My office. Nine AM." The voice is cold. Professional. Angry underneath. "Don't make me come find you."

"I'll be there."

"Good. Because we have a lot to discuss. About Yousef. About Kamal. About your activities in my operational area." Pause. "You fucked up, Ethan. You interfered with intelligence operations. You compromised sources. You burned networks. Tomorrow we discuss consequences."

The line goes dead.

Lars looks at him. "That was Chen."

"Yeah."

"He knows."

"Yeah."

"What are you going to do?"

"Go to the meeting. Face the consequences." Ethan looks at the airport. At the departure boards visible through the windows. Turkish Airlines 769. Departed. Yousef in the air. Flying toward Istanbul. Toward New York. Toward home.

"It was worth it," Ethan says.

"Was it? You burned Chen's operation. Made an enemy of CIA. Put yourself in position where you might disappear. Yousef's free but you might pay for it with your career. Your safety. Your life maybe." Lars smokes. "Was it worth it?"

Ethan thinks about the grain field. About the math that never works.

"Yeah," he says. "It was worth it."

They drive back through night streets. The city quiet now. Past curfew. Only security moving. Checkpoints glowing. Peshmerga watching. The front line thirty kilometers away where men sit in trenches drinking chai and watching ISIS watch them back.

At the guest house, Ethan lies on the thin mattress. Stares at the ceiling. Processes what just happened.

Yousef's free. Flying home. That's success.

But Chen knows. Chen's angry. Tomorrow's meeting will be reckoning. The consequences of interfering with intelligence operations. The price of doing the right thing in the wrong way.

His phone buzzes. Petey.

*Heard Yousef's airborne. Well done. But Chen's furious. DIA monitoring his communications. He's talking about charges. About interference. About making you an example. Be careful tomorrow. He's dangerous when he's cornered. —P*

*I'll handle it.*

*That's what idealism looks like. Then Baqubah happened. Then someone was dead by his hand. Don't underestimate Chen. He's smarter than you. More connected. More ruthless. You pissed him off. That's dangerous. —P*

*Noted.*

*If you need extraction—if things go sideways—I have people. Can get you out of Kurdistan fast. Just say the word. —P*

*I'll keep that in mind.*

Ethan sets his phone down. Touches the scar on his arm. The reminder. The permanent record of the night he learned that doing the right thing costs something.

Tomorrow he finds out what this costs.

Tomorrow Chen explains the price.

Here we go again.

# 7

## CHAPTER 7: CONSEQUENCES

*Erbil, Kurdistan Region — October 2015*

Ethan doesn't sleep. Lies there listening to the city. Generator hum. Checkpoint sounds. Somewhere in the distance, a dog barking. The normal noises that mean the front line is holding. That ISIS is still thirty kilometers away. That life continues in the spaces between violence.

At 5 AM he gives up. Showers. The water pressure is weak but it's hot. Small mercy. He stands under it trying to prepare for what's coming.

Chen at nine AM. The reckoning.

Lars is already up. Courtyard. Coffee. He hands Ethan a cup without speaking.

They drink in silence for ten minutes.

"You're really going to the meeting," Lars says finally.

"Yeah."

"Could be trap. Could be Chen planning to detain you. Officially or otherwise."

"Maybe. But running means confirming I'm guilty. Going means I face it."

"Facing it might mean disappearing into CIA custody. Black site detention. The kind where you're held for investigation indefinitely while lawyers figure out jurisdiction."

"I'm American citizen. They can't just—"

"They can. Patriot Act. Material support for terrorism. Interference with intelligence operations in active theater. They can find legal justification if they want it badly enough."

Ethan drinks more coffee. It's thick and bitter. Turkish style. The kind that wakes you up whether you want to be awake or not.

"What would you do?" he asks.

Lars lights a cigarette. "I'd go to the meeting. Because running makes it worse. But I'd have extraction plan. Someone waiting. Someone ready to move if things go sideways."

"Petey offered that."

"Then use it. Tell Petey you're going to Chen's office. Tell him if you're not out in two hours, extract. Give him location. Give him authority. Then go to the meeting knowing you have backup."

The logic is sound. Ethan texts Petey.

*Meeting Chen at nine AM. US Consulate. If I'm not out by eleven, something's wrong. Can you extract?*

Response comes thirty seconds later.

*Already have team on standby. Two contractors. Good guys. They'll be nearby. If you're not out by 11:15, they move. Extraction to Turkish border. You'll be in Ankara by evening. —P*

*That seems extreme.*

*That's Kurdistan. Normal rules don't apply. Chen's furious. Furious people do stupid things. Better to have extraction ready and not need it than need it and not have it. —P*

*Understood. Thanks.*

*Don't thank me yet. Just get through the meeting. Answer Chen's questions. Take whatever punishment he dishes out. Then leave. Don't escalate. Don't argue. Just survive.* —P

At 7 AM Ethan walks. Needs to move. Needs to think. Lars goes with him. Armed. Carrying like he's expecting trouble.

They walk through morning Erbil. The city waking up. Shops opening. Chai sellers setting up. Traffic building. Peshmerga changing shifts at checkpoints. The daily rhythm that makes war zones feel normal until something reminds you they're not.

They pass through Ankawa. The Christian quarter. Churches visible. Morning mass at one of them. People going to pray. Life continuing despite everything.

"Chen's not wrong, you know," Lars says.

"About what?"

"About what you did. You interfered with intelligence operation. Compromised sources. Burned networks he spent years building. From his perspective, you're the problem. You're the one who damaged American interests for personal friendship."

"Yousef was being coerced."

"Maybe. But coercion is subjective. Chen would say Yousef volunteered. Accepted money. Did work. Made choices. That he used leverage doesn't make it coercion. Just makes it standard recruitment."

"You agree with Chen?"

"I'm saying I understand his perspective. Which doesn't mean I think you were wrong. Just means this isn't simple. Chen's not villain. You're not hero. It's complicated and nobody's hands are clean."

They walk past a park. Refugees living there. Tents and makeshift shelters. Families from Mosul. From Sinjar. From villages ISIS destroyed. Living in Erbil because it's safe. Because the Peshmerga held the line.

"That's why they're here," Lars says. "Those families. Because intelligence operations like Chen's provide warning. Because sources like the ones you compromised give tactical information that prevents attacks. That saves lives. So when you burn those sources—when you disrupt those operations—there are consequences beyond Yousef going home."

"You think I shouldn't have helped him."

"I think you made a choice. Choices have costs. Question is whether you're willing to pay them."

At 8:30 they're back at the guest house. Ethan changes into cleaner clothes. Trying to look presentable for whatever happens at the consulate.

Lars drives him. They don't talk. Just drive through morning traffic. Through checkpoints. Toward the US Consulate compound.

At the consulate gate, security is heavy. Multiple layers. Kurdish Asayish. American contractors. Marines in body armor. The infrastructure of protecting American interests in a war zone.

Ethan presents ID. Says he has meeting with David Chen. The guard checks a list. Makes a call. Waits.

Finally: "You're cleared. Through security. Building Three. Second floor. Someone will meet you."

Lars stays with the vehicle. Can't enter consulate grounds without clearance. Ethan goes through alone.

Security is thorough. Metal detector. Bag search. Pat down. Questions about purpose of visit. They take his phone. Standard procedure for entering classified spaces.

Through security, into the compound. It's like being transported to America. Manicured grass. American flags. Air conditioning. The cognitive dissonance of American suburb in the middle of Kurdistan.

Building Three is administrative. Offices for political officers, economic development, consular services. The civilian side of American presence.

A woman meets him at the entrance. Late twenties. Professional. State Department probably.

"Mr. Caldwell? Follow me please."

She leads him up stairs. Down hallway. To an office at the end. Door closed. She knocks.

"Come in."

Chen's voice. Ethan hasn't heard it in person since last night's event. Since Kamal's refusal. The voice is calm but there's something underneath. Anger. Disappointment. The controlled emotion of someone who's very good at not showing what they're feeling.

The woman opens the door. Gestures for Ethan to enter. Closes it behind him.

The office is small. Desk, chairs, bookshelf, window overlooking the compound. American flag in the corner. Photos on the wall—Chen with Kurdish officials, Peshmerga commanders, visiting dignitaries. The visual record of six years building relationships.

Chen is behind the desk. Same preppy look—khakis, Oxford shirt, wire-rimmed glasses. But he looks older than six days ago. Tired. Like he hasn't slept.

"Sit down, Ethan."

Ethan sits. Chen doesn't offer coffee or water. Doesn't do the courtesy rituals. Just gets to it.

"Yousef al-Tamimi is on a plane to New York. Via Istanbul. He used emergency travel document issued last night by consular services. Despite active hold on his passport. Despite ongoing security review. Despite explicit instructions that he was not to leave Kurdistan until operational requirements were met." Chen's voice is flat. Professional. "You facilitated this."

"Yes."

"You met with Kamal Barzani. Kurdish counter-intelligence officer. You provided him intelligence about my operations. Sources. Networks. Priorities. Information that came from Yousef. Information that Yousef gathered while pretending to continue working for me while actually working against me."

"Yes."

"And you coordinated with Kamal to refuse my recruitment publicly. At the KRG event. With witnesses. Creating diplomatic incident. Forcing me to terminate recruitment operation I'd spent eight months developing."

"Yes."

Chen leans back. Studies Ethan. The evaluation is clinical. Professional. Like he's analyzing a problem that needs solving.

"Why?"

"Because Yousef wanted to go home. Because you were keeping him trapped. Because the operation was coercive."

"Coercive." Chen says the word slowly. Testing it. "Yousef volunteered. Multiple times over four years. He took money. Accepted assignments. Provided intelligence. At what point does voluntary participation become coercion?"

"When you leverage his family's safety. When you threaten his visa status. When you make it clear that refusing has consequences he can't accept."

"That's called motivation. That's called ensuring asset reliability." Chen's voice softens slightly. Not much. Just enough to notice. "You think I enjoy this? Burning sources, leveraging families, keeping Yousef trapped? Six years here. Six years making calculations about acceptable costs. Eventually you stop feeling it. The fog becomes normal. That's what this work does."

He straightens. The crack closes. "But someone has to do it."

Chen opens a folder on his desk. "Let me read you something. This is from Yousef's agreement. Signed February 2011. 'I understand that my cooperation with U.S. government entities may be required for ongoing security matters. I understand that failure to cooperate may result in review of immigration status and visa privileges.' He signed this. Nobody forced him."

"The threat is implicit."

"The reality is explicit. We have leverage. We use it. Yousef understood this. He made informed choice to continue working. That's not coercion. That's consequence management."

"He wanted out. You wouldn't let him leave."

"Because the mission wasn't complete. Because I needed him for the Kamal recruitment. Because operational necessity required his continued participation." Chen closes the folder. "You think I kept him trapped out of cruelty? Out of ego? I kept him operational because the intelligence he provided saves lives. The networks he helped me map prevent attacks. The sources he introduced me to give us strategic advantage in region that matters."

"And Yousef's suffering was acceptable cost."

"Yes. One asset's discomfort versus intelligence that protects thousands of lives. That's not difficult calculation."

The logic is airtight. The morality is ambiguous. Chen's framework makes sense when you're the one making the calculations. Harder when you're the one being calculated.

"What about Kamal?" Ethan asks. "Your recruitment target. Did you know he was already recruited?"

Chen's face doesn't change but something flickers in his eyes. Surprise. Anger. Recognition.

"What did you say?"

"Kamal. He's been working with DIA for two years. Different agency. Different operation. You were trying to recruit someone who was already an asset. He was stringing you along. Gathering intelligence on CIA while you thought you were recruiting him."

The silence is heavy. Chen processes this. The implications. The operational failure. The embarrassment.

"How do you know this?"

"Sources. People who understand what's actually happening in Kurdistan. While you were building your network, other people were building theirs. You're not the only player. You're just one of many."

Chen stands. Walks to the window. Looks out at the compound. When he speaks, his voice is quieter. Different.

"I've been here six years. Six years building relationships. Learning the terrain. Understanding the players. I thought I knew what was happening. Thought I had comprehensive picture. But you're telling me I was running operation on someone who was already recruited. That I was being played. That I was the mark."

"Yes."

"And DIA didn't tell me. Different channels. Different operations. Competing instead of cooperating." He laughs. Bitter sound. "That's American intelligence. That's why we lose. Not because our enemies are smarter. Because we spend more time fighting each other than fighting them."

He turns back to Ethan. The anger is still there but it's mixed with something else now. Exhaustion. Disillusionment. The recognition that the system he serves is broken.

"You burned my operation to save your friend. That's understandable. Even admirable in its way. But it has consequences. Three sources—the businessman, the KDP official, the PUK officer—they're all compromised now. Kamal knows who they are. Which means Kurdish intelligence knows. Which means those sources are either arrested or turned. Years of work. Gone. Because you wanted to help Yousef."

"Those sources were being used without their knowledge."

"They were being cultivated with their cooperation. They thought they were helping Kurdistan. They were right—the intelligence they provided does help Kurdistan. Just also helps America. That's not betrayal. That's partnership."

"Partnership implies equal standing. They're assets. You control them."

"I coordinate with them. There's difference. They're not prisoners. They're participants. They benefit from relationship. We benefit from relationship. That's how intelligence work functions."

Ethan looks at the photos on the wall. Chen with Kurdish officials. Smiling. Professional. The appearance of friendship overlaying the reality of intelligence operations.

"What happens now?" Ethan asks.

"Now?" Chen sits back down. "Now I deal with consequences. I file report explaining how my operation was compromised by outside interference. I explain how Kamal refused recruitment. I explain how three sources are burned. I take the professional hit. My career absorbs the damage."

"Will you go after Yousef?"

"What would be the point? He's in America. He's permanent resident. I don't have jurisdiction. And pursuing him publicly means admitting I was running coercive operation on U.S. resident. That's bad optics. Bad policy. Bad intelligence practice. So no. Yousef's free. You succeeded."

"And me?"

Chen looks at him for a long moment. The evaluation. The calculation about what to do with person who interfered with CIA operations.

"You're American citizen. I can't detain you without cause. I can't make you disappear despite what your paranoid friends think. I can make you uncomfortable. I can flag you for enhanced screening. I can make sure every time you enter country where we operate, you get extra attention. But that's petty. That's not worth the energy."

"So I just leave?"

"So you just leave. Go back to Greenville. Back to estate planning. Back to comfortable life where the hardest decision is trust structure versus direct inheritance. You wanted to help your friend. You helped him. Mission accomplished. Now go home."

The dismissal stings more than threats would. Chen's not treating Ethan as threat. He's treating him as irrelevance. As amateur who stumbled into professional operation and got lucky.

"I'm sorry," Ethan says. "About your operation. About the sources. I didn't want to burn your network. I just wanted Yousef free."

"I know. That's what makes this tragic instead of malicious. You had good intentions. Good intentions executed poorly with bad consequences. That's most of human history in microcosm."

Chen opens a drawer. Pulls out a bottle of whiskey. Two glasses. Pours without asking.

"Last time we drank together, Baghdad, January 2009. You asked if any of it mattered. If we were making difference or just prolonging chaos. I said slightly more good than harm was the only honest metric."

"I remember."

"I still believe that. Everything I do here—recruiting Yousef, mapping networks, running operations—I believe it produces the right ends. Not for every individual. Not in every case. But aggregated across time and space, the intelligence I gather saves more lives than it costs."

"What about the lives it does cost?"

"They're real. They're tragic. They're acceptable cost for greater good." Chen drinks. "You disagree. You think individual suffering can't be justified by aggregate benefit. That's principled. Also naive. Because if you follow that logic to conclusion, you never act. You never intervene. You never make hard calls because someone always suffers."

"So you just accept the suffering."

"I acknowledge it. I account for it. I try to minimize it. But I don't let it paralyze me. Because paralysis also has cost. Inaction kills. Sometimes more than action does."

Ethan drinks the whiskey. It's good. Better than the beer in Baghdad six years ago. Chen's taste has improved with his access.

"Do you ever doubt?" Ethan asks. "Ever wonder if your calculations are wrong?"

"Every day. Every operation. Every recruitment. I doubt constantly. But I act anyway because doubt without action is cowardice. You make best decision with available information. You accept uncertainty. You live with consequences."

"And when consequences are wrong? When your calculations kill people?"

"Then I failed. Then I learn. Then I try to do better next time. That's all anyone can do. We're not gods. We're people making decisions with some of the information all of the time. Sometimes we get it right. Sometimes we don't."

The conversation feels familiar. Like the one in Baghdad. Like Chen's been having the same argument with himself for six years. Trying to justify the work. Trying to live with the costs.

"You've changed," Ethan says. "Since Baghdad. You're more certain now. Less willing to question."

"I've been here six years. I've run operations that prevented attacks. Saved lives. Shaped outcomes. The work validates itself. When you see results—when intelligence you gather stops truck bomb or prevents kidnapping—you get more certain. That's not arrogance. That's experience confirming framework."

"Or it's confirmation bias. You see what you want to see. You count successes. Discount failures. Convince yourself you're doing good when maybe you're just doing damage efficiently."

Chen pours more whiskey. Doesn't offer any to Ethan. Just drinks.

"Maybe. But I sleep at night. I look at myself in mirror. I believe the work matters. That's enough. Has to be."

They sit in silence. The office quiet except for generator hum from outside. The compound insulated from the city. From the war. From the reality thirty kilometers away where men sit in trenches waiting.

"What will you do?" Ethan asks. "After this. After the operation failed."

"Rebuild. Find new sources. Develop new networks. The work continues. Kurdistan matters too much to abandon because one operation went sideways. ISIS still exists. Iran still operates here. Turkey still interferes. Baghdad still threatens. Kurdistan needs America. America needs Kurdistan. So I keep working."

"Do they know? The Kurds. Do they know how much America uses them?"

"They know. They're not naive. They use us back. It's transactional relationship. We help them. They help us. Everyone benefits. That's partnership."

"Or it's exploitation with better PR."

"Cynical. Also partially true. But partial truth is still truth. We do help Kurdistan. We do provide intelligence that protects them. We do support their struggle. That it also serves American interests doesn't negate the help."

Ethan finishes his whiskey. Sets down the glass.

"Can I go?"

"You can go. Flight leaves when?"

"Don't have one yet."

"Get one. Today. Tomorrow latest. The longer you stay, the more complicated things get. My colleagues know you interfered. They're less forgiving than I am. You want to avoid those conversations."

"Understood."

Ethan stands. Chen doesn't. Just sits behind his desk. Looking tired. Looking older than thirty-four. Looking like someone who's carried weight for too long.

"One more thing," Chen says. "Baqubah. November 2008. You killed someone. Took a life. But the village survived. You made the right call. Hard call. But right call. Don't let the cost convince you otherwise."

"How do you know about that?"

"I read reports. I understand decision-making under pressure. I recognize when someone's carrying guilt that isn't earned." Chen meets his eyes. "You did what you had to do. You're responsible for the village that lived. That's the calculation. You made it work then. You made it work now with Yousef. Don't apologize for doing the right thing even when it costs something."

The validation from Chen feels wrong and right simultaneously. Permission from someone who understands the cost. Who makes the same calculations. Who lives with the same costs.

"Take care of yourself, Ethan. Go back to Greenville. Practice law. Help clients. Live quiet life. Leave this world to people who are built for it."

"You think I'm not built for it?"

"I think you have conscience. That's liability in intelligence work. Conscience makes you hesitate. Makes you question. Makes you do things like flying to Kurdistan to save one friend while risking larger operations. That's admirable. Also impractical. This work requires different temperament. Ability to calculate coldly. Accept costs dispassionately. I have that temperament. You don't. That's not criticism. That's observation."

Ethan walks to the door. Pauses.

"Do you ever regret it? The work. The costs. The people you've used."

Chen doesn't answer immediately. Just looks at the photos on his wall. Six years of relationships. Six years of operations. Six years of calculations about acceptable costs.

"Every day," he says finally. "I regret every day. But I do it anyway because someone has to. Someone has to make hard calls. Someone has to carry the load. I volunteered for that. I accept that. Whether I regret it doesn't change that it needs doing."

Ethan leaves. Door closes behind him. The woman from earlier escorts him back through the building. Through security. To the compound exit.

Outside, Lars is waiting. Smoking. Alert.

"How'd it go?"

"I'm not detained. I'm not disappeared. I'm just told to leave."

"That's good outcome. Better than expected."

"Yeah."

They drive back through the city. Late morning now. Heat building. Traffic heavy. Life continuing.

At the guest house, Ethan books a flight. Turkish Airlines. Tomorrow morning. Erbil to Istanbul. Istanbul to Charlotte. Home by Sunday evening.

His phone—returned at security exit—has messages. One from Yousef.

*In Istanbul. Layover. Everything okay so far. Nobody stopped me. Nobody questioned me. I'm actually going home. Thank you, Ethan. Thank you for everything. —Y*

*Good. Keep going. Don't stop until you're in Rochester. —E*

*What about you? Are you safe? Did Chen—*

*I'm fine. Meeting went okay. I'm leaving tomorrow. Going home too. —E*

*I don't know how to thank you. How to repay—*

*Be a good father. Hug your daughters. That's payment enough. —E*

Another message. Petey.

*Extraction team standing down. Glad the meeting went okay. Chen's filing reports. Making it official. But he's not pursuing you. You're clear. Come home. —P*

*Tomorrow. Flying out morning. —E*

*Good. Margaret's been asking about you. She's worried. Also annoyed you've been gone this long. Clients are piling up. —P*

*Tell her I'll be back Monday. Ready to work. —E*

*Will do. And Ethan? You did good. Yousef's free. That matters. Whatever Chen says, whatever doubts you have—you did good. —P*

The afternoon passes slowly. Ethan sits in the courtyard. Watches the gate. Processes what happened.

Chen's not wrong. The operation Ethan burned probably did provide valuable intelligence. The sources probably did help prevent attacks. The work probably did save lives.

But Yousef's free. That counts for something. One man trapped for four years. Now going home to his daughters. That's real. That's measurable. That's meaningful.

Maybe.

At evening, Lars comes back with food. Rice, kebab, flatbread. They eat in the courtyard. Don't talk much. Just eat.

"You leaving tomorrow?" Lars asks.

"Yeah. Morning flight."

"Good. Kurdistan's interesting but it's not home. Better to leave before you can't."

"What about you? When do you leave?"

"Don't know. Maybe never. I came here for the fight. Fight's not over. ISIS still exists. Still threatens. Until they're gone, I stay."

"That could be years."

"Yeah. But I don't have much pulling me back to Oslo. Software development. Cold weather. Social democracy that works too well. Here matters more. Here I can make difference."

"Or here you can get killed."

"That too. But if I'm going to die, rather it be for something that matters than something that doesn't." Lars drinks water. "That's what Chen understands. What you understand. What everyone who does this work understands. We're all choosing to be here. Choosing to make hard calls. Choosing to accept costs. Nobody forced us. We volunteered."

The philosophy sounds like Chen. Like Petey. Like everyone who's been in the game long enough to rationalize the choices.

"I'm going home," Ethan says. "Back to estate planning. Back to quiet life. Back to problems that can be solved with paperwork."

"Good. That's right choice. You're not built for this. You have too much conscience. Too much empathy. You care too much about individual suffering. That's good quality in lawyer. Liability in operator."

"Chen said the same thing."

"Because it's true. The people who last in this work—Chen, Petey, me—we've learned to calculate coldly. Accept costs. Move forward. You can't do that. You flew to Kurdistan for one friend. Burned CIA operation. Risked detention. That's loyalty. Also impractical. Can't operate like that long-term."

Ethan doesn't argue because Lars is right. And Chen was right. And Petey would say the same thing. He's not built for this world. He has conscience where he needs ruthlessness. Empathy where he needs calculation. Loyalty where he needs pragmatism.

But Yousef's free. That's what matters.

At midnight, Ethan's phone rings. Unknown number. US country code.

"This is Ethan."

"It's Kamal." The voice is tired. "Wanted to update you. Chen's investigating. Found my misdirection evidence. Iranian intelligence contacts. Meeting logs. He's pursuing that angle. Thinks Iranian asset compromised his operation. Buys Yousef time. Buys you time."

"Thank you."

"Don't thank me. I did what served my interests. But result is same—Yousef escapes. You escape. Chen investigates wrong direction." Pause. "I meant what I said. I'm done with Americans. All Americans. CIA, DIA, all of them. I'm resigning cooperation. Focusing only on Kurdistan. No more games."

"Will they let you?"

"They'll have to. I'm not their asset. I'm sovereign intelligence officer of autonomous region. They need me more than I need them. If
they push, I make things difficult. Reveal what I know about their operations. Create diplomatic problems. They'll accept my resignation
because fighting me costs more than losing me."

"Good luck with that."

"Don't need luck. Need leverage. I have leverage. That's what
six years working with Americans taught me—accumulate leverage.
Make yourself valuable. Then choose your exit." He pauses. "You
should learn that. You operate without leverage. That's dangerous.
Next time you interfere with intelligence operations, have better position. Have escape plan. Have leverage. Otherwise you get crushed."

"There won't be next time. I'm going home. Staying there."

"That's what they all say. Then someone calls. Then you're booking
flights. Then you're in another cemetery meeting another intelligence
officer. The work finds you. Especially people like you. People with
conscience. People who care. The work finds you because you can't
ignore it."

"I'll ignore it just fine."

"We'll see. Good luck, Mr. Caldwell. If you return to Kurdistan—which you won't—look me up. I owe you drink for helping free
me from Americans." He hangs up.

The conversation leaves Ethan unsettled. Everyone keeps saying the
same thing. The work finds you. You can't leave. Once you're in, you're
in forever.

But Ethan's going home. Back to Greenville. Back to Margaret's
firm. Back to clients and wills and trusts and problems that can be
solved without intelligence operations and calculations about acceptable costs.

He's leaving this world behind.

At 6 AM his alarm goes off. Lars drives him to the airport. Early morning traffic. The city waking up. Last time he'll see Erbil. Last time he'll be in Kurdistan.

At the airport, security is routine. They check his ID. Verify his ticket. Wave him through. No problems. No detention. Just normal traveler going home.

At the gate, Ethan texts Yousef.

*Where are you?*

*JFK. Immigration. They questioned me. Extra screening because of Kurdistan travel. But I'm through. Boarding to Rochester in two hours. Almost home. —Y*

*Good. Tell your daughters I said hello. —E*

*I will. And Ethan? Thank you. For everything. For caring enough to help. For risking everything. For—* The message cuts off. Then continues. *For reminding me that some people still choose loyalty over calculation. That matters. —Y*

At 9:30 AM the plane boards. Turkish Airlines. Istanbul. Then Charlotte. Then Greenville. Then home.

His phone shows final message. Petey.

*Welcome home. When you land, call me. We should talk about what's next. —P*

What's next. The assumption that there's always next. That the work continues. That once you're in, you're in forever.

But Ethan's done. He helped Yousef. Paid the price. Learned the lesson. Now he's going home to practice law and live quiet life and pretend Kurdistan never happened.

His phone rings. Chen.

Ethan debates not answering. Then answers.

"This is Ethan."

"It's Chen. I know you're at the gate. This will be quick." Pause.
"The extraction at Erbil airport. I reviewed the security footage.
Watched how you moved. How you adapted when plans changed.
How you executed under pressure with minimal resources and maxi-
mum constraints. That was good work."

"I wasn't trying to impress you."

"I know. That's what made it impressive. You weren't performing.
You were operating. There's difference." Chen's voice is different. Not
angry. Analytical. "You cost me an operation. Cost me a source. Cost
me eighteen months of network building. I should be furious. Part of
me is. But another part is impressed. You extracted an asset from active
operational zone using minimal support and significant opposition.
That's not legal work. That's operational work."

"What's your point?"

"My point is you're wasting yourself in Greenville. Doing estate
planning. Helping rich people minimize taxes. That's fine work. Safe
work. But it's not what you're built for. You're built for this. For operations. For hard decisions under pressure. For calculating acceptable
costs and living with consequences."

"I'm going home."

"I know. And you'll practice law. And you'll be fine at it. But you'll
be bored. You'll be underwhelmed. And when the phone rings at
2 AM with someone who needs help—someone like Yousef—you'll
answer. You'll book flights. You'll operate. Because that's who you are."
Pause. "I can be angry about what you cost me, or I can be strategic
about what you could do for me. I'm choosing strategic."

"I'm not interested."

"Not today. But circumstances change. Needs change. And when
you realize that estate planning doesn't matter compared to work
that saves lives—when you understand that slightly more good than

harm isn't philosophy, it's operational reality—call me. I have work for people like you. People who care too much. People who can't walk away. People who understand that someone has to carry this."

"I'm not calling."

"We'll see." Chen's voice softens slightly. "Yousef's free because you cared enough to help. That matters. Even though it cost me. Even though it complicated everything. You helped your friend. That's loyalty. Also impractical. But rare. And useful if channeled correctly."

"I have to board."

"Go. Fly home. Practice law. Live quiet life. But Ethan? Keep your phone on. Keep your passport current. Keep your skills sharp. Because the work finds people like you. And when it does—when someone needs help and official channels can't provide it—you'll need to decide whether to ignore it or answer it. I think you'll answer. I think you can't help yourself. And when you do, I'll be here. With resources. With support. With framework that makes answering sustainable instead of suicidal."

"I don't need your framework."

"Not yet. But you will. Because operating alone is exhausting. Operating without support is dangerous. Operating without cover is impossible. When you realize that, call me. I'll help you do this work professionally instead of desperately."

Chen hangs up.

Ethan stares at the phone. The manipulation is obvious. The recruitment pitch is transparent. Chen planting seeds. Making offers. Positioning himself as solution to problems Ethan doesn't have yet.

But under the manipulation, there's truth. The extraction was operational work. And Ethan was good at it. And some part of him—small part he doesn't want to acknowledge—felt alive doing it. Felt useful. Felt like it mattered more than anything he does in Greenville.

The boarding announcement starts. First call for Turkish Airlines to Istanbul. Then Charlotte. Then Greenville. Then home.

Ethan settles into his seat. Economy. Middle seat. The indignity of last-minute booking. But it's a seat on a plane leaving Kurdistan. That's what matters.

The plane pushes back. Taxis. Takes off. Erbil falls away below. The city spreading out. Checkpoints visible. Refugee camps. The front lines in the distance. The berm where Peshmerga and ISIS watch each other across four hundred meters.

As they climb, Ethan thinks about Chen. About the six years he's spent here. About the operations and sources and calculations. About the certainty that the work matters even when it costs things.

Chen will rebuild. Find new sources. Continue operations. The work continues because someone has to do it. Someone has to make the hard calls. Someone has to carry it.

But it doesn't have to be Ethan.

He's going home.

Kurdistan disappearing behind him.

The plane levels off. Flight attendants begin service. Ethan accepts water. Refuses food. Just wants to sleep.

The plane flies west. Over the Zagros mountains. Over Turkey. Over the Mediterranean. Away from the war zone. Away from the calculations about acceptable costs.

The scar on his arm doesn't itch anymore.

Maybe that means something.

Maybe it means he's finally done.

# 8

— · —

# CHAPTER 8: ROCHESTER

*R*ochester, New York — *Three weeks later*

The flight from Erbil lands in New York at 6:23 PM on a Tuesday in mid-November. Twelve hours in the air plus layover in Istanbul. Ethan's body doesn't know what timezone it's in. Doesn't matter. Yousef needs help now, not after jet lag recovery.

He rents a car at JFK. Drives upstate. Four hours through darkness. Empty highways. The landscape transitioning from city to suburbs to rural. November in upstate New York. Cold. Gray. The kind of weather that makes you understand why people leave.

At 11:47 PM he reaches Rochester. Drives to Yousef's neighborhood. Eastside. Working class. The kind of place where Iraqi refugees can afford rent and find halal groceries.

The surveillance is obvious.

Two cars parked on Yousef's street. Both occupied. One person reading newspaper nobody reads anymore. Another on phone. Both vehicles too clean for the neighborhood. Both positioned with sight lines to Yousef's apartment building.

Not hiding. That's the point. Visible surveillance sends message: We're watching. We know. Behave.

Ethan drives past without stopping. Doesn't look too hard. Just notes positions, vehicles, patterns. He parks three blocks away. Texts Yousef from the burner phone he bought at JFK.

*I'm here. Don't come outside. Don't acknowledge. I'll call in thirty minutes. —E*

He walks to a 7-Eleven. Buys prepaid phone. Cash. The tradecraft feels excessive but probably isn't. If someone's running surveillance, they're monitoring communications.

At a Dunkin' Donuts—still open at midnight, upstate staple—he activates the burner. Calls Yousef.

"Who is this?"

"Ethan. Burner phone. Your regular line is compromised. This one too probably, but less obviously."

"I saw the cars. I thought—" Yousef's voice is strained. Scared. "I thought maybe police. Immigration. But police don't do this."

"It's not police. Could be FBI. Could be contractors working for someone who wants you nervous. Either way, it's pressure. They want you scared. Isolated. Reaching out for deal."

"What kind of deal?"

"That's what I'm here to figure out. Where can we meet? Somewhere not near your apartment. Somewhere public but not obvious."

Yousef thinks. "Wegmans. Grocery store. East Avenue. Open twenty-four hours. Big. Crowded enough at night with third-shift workers. We can talk in parking lot."

"Twenty minutes."

Ethan drives to the Wegmans. The parking lot is half-full despite midnight. Night shift workers buying groceries before going home. The fluorescent glow of American consumerism at all hours.

Yousef arrives in his old Honda. Parks three spaces away. Gets out. They walk toward the entrance but don't go in. Just stand near the shopping cart return. Cold air. Visible breath. Two men having conversation that looks like nothing.

"How bad is it?" Ethan asks.

"Two cars since Friday. Different vehicles, same pattern. They follow me everywhere. Work, mosque, store. They photograph me. Document who I talk to. My wife is terrified. Thinks ICE is deporting us. I can't explain without telling her about Chen. About Kurdistan. About everything I've been hiding for four years."

"Have they approached you? Made contact?"

"No. Just watching. Just documenting. Like building case but not ready to act."

"That's because it's not official investigation. If this was FBI, they'd have interviewed you by now. This is something else. Pressure operation. Making you nervous so you'll reach out. So you'll cooperate."

"Cooperate with what? I'm done. I'm free. Chen said I could go home."

"Chen says a lot of things. Doesn't mean they're true."

Yousef leans against the cart return. The exhaustion is complete. "What do I do?"

"You do nothing. You live normally. You don't react to surveillance. Don't change patterns. Don't give them ammunition. I'll figure out who's running this and why. Then we deal with it."

"And if they arrest me?"

"Then you call the lawyer Margaret recommended. You say nothing until he arrives. You don't explain, don't justify, don't try to help. You just shut up and wait for counsel. Understand?"

"Yeah."

They separate. Yousef back to his Honda. Ethan to the rental. Both being watched probably. Both documented. Both part of some operation neither fully understands.

Ethan drives to an airport hotel. Marriott near the terminal. Anonymous. Corporate. He checks in using cash and real ID. No point hiding—whoever's watching already knows he's here.

In the room he sits on the bed. Thinks about the surveillance. About who's running it and why. About Chen and whether this is his play or someone else's.

His phone rings. The burner. Unknown number.

"This is Ethan."

"It's Petey. You're in Rochester. I know because I'm watching too. Different surveillance than what you saw on Yousef's street. Mine is professional. Theirs is theater."

"Whose theater?"

"That's complicated question with complicated answer. Too complicated for phone. Can you come to Charlotte? Tomorrow. There's thing you need to see. People you need to meet. Information that explains what's actually happening."

"Why Charlotte?"

"Because that's where I am. Because warehouse I use for meetings is there. Because I have people who can explain this better than I can." Pause. "Also because what I'm showing you is sensitive enough that it can't be digital. Has to be in person. Has to be face to face."

"When?"

"Tomorrow afternoon. Two PM. I'll text address. Come alone. Tell no one. And Ethan? Leave your phones. All of them. Nothing electronic. Nothing that can be tracked or recorded."

"That careful?"

"That careful."

\*\*\*

The drive to Charlotte is six hours. Ethan leaves at 6 AM. Stops for coffee in Virginia. Crosses into North Carolina around 10:30. The landscape shifting from upstate winter to mid-Atlantic November. Still cold but less gray.

The address Petey texted is industrial area near the airport. Warehouses. Shipping containers. The infrastructure of logistics and commerce. The kind of place contractors use for meetings that don't appear on calendars.

Petey's truck is parked outside a warehouse. He's leaning against it. Smoking. Same as always. Mid-fifties. Compact. The bearing of someone who's spent career downrange and survived by being smarter than his enemies.

"You came."

"You asked."

"Asking isn't always enough. Some people don't listen. You listen. That's good trait. Means you might survive this."

They walk inside. The warehouse is mostly empty. High ceilings. Concrete floor. A few shipping containers along walls. Office area at back.

In the office, Petey is waiting. Not contractors. Petey himself. The first time Ethan's seen him in person since Kurdistan. The first time they've had face-to-face conversation since this started.

Petey looks older than his voice suggests. Gray hair. Weathered face. The accumulated wear of decades doing work that costs pieces you can't get back. But his eyes are sharp. Alert. The eyes of someone who still operates even though his body should be retired.

"Sit," Petey says. "This is going to take a while. You'll want coffee."

There's a pot already made. Ethan pours cup. Sits. Waits.

Petey opens laptop. Turns it toward Ethan. Screen shows map. Northern Iraq. Syria. ISIS-controlled territory marked in red. Kurdish-controlled territory in yellow.

"This is current situation. November 2015. ISIS controls Mosul, Raqqa, significant territory across Iraq and Syria. Caliphate at peak strength. Coalition airstrikes degrading capability but slowly. Ground forces—Peshmerga, Iraqi army, Syrian rebels—holding lines but not advancing. It's stalemate."

"I know this. I was just in Kurdistan."

"You saw the front. You didn't see the intelligence operations underneath. The recruitment networks. The defector programs. The proxy wars playing out through human assets." Petey clicks to different screen. "Chen's operation—the one you burned by extracting Yousef—it wasn't just mapping Kurdish political networks. That was cover. Surface layer. Real objective was something else."

"What?"

Petey shows organizational chart. Names. Photos. Connections.

"Chen was running operation to identify and recruit ISIS defectors. Foreign fighters who joined the Caliphate and became disillusioned. Western passport holders specifically. Americans. Europeans. Canadians. People who could return home. Who could provide intelligence on ISIS operations in the West. Who could help prevent attacks."

Ethan looks at the chart. Studies the faces. Young men. Mostly. The faces of people who made terrible choices and now live with consequences.

"This is ISIS intelligence network?"

"This is Chen's recruitment target list. People he was cultivating. People who might defect if approached correctly." Petey points to one photo. "Ahmed Khalil. Born Michigan. Joined ISIS in 2014. Got disillusioned. Chen identified him as potential defector. Started cultivation through Yousef."

"Yousef was access."

"Exactly. Yousef speaks Arabic. Understands Iraqi culture. Has family connections. Chen used him to make indirect contact with ISIS fighters' families. To pass messages. To facilitate communication that couldn't happen through official channels. Yousef thought he was helping with refugee work. Actually he was facilitating ISIS recruitment operation."

The pieces connect. Yousef's assignments. The meetings Chen sent him to. Not just mapping Kurdish networks. Facilitating contact with potential ISIS defectors.

"So when I extracted Yousef—"

"You disrupted active ISIS recruitment operation. Cost Chen access to network that took two years to build. Compromised ongoing cultivations. Potentially cost lives because defectors who might have warned about attacks are no longer accessible."

Ethan sets down the coffee. The consequences settling. He thought he was helping friend escape coercion. Actually he was disrupting operation that might prevent terrorist attacks.

"But there's more," Petey continues. "The ISIS recruitment—that's not even the real operation. That's layer two. Underneath is layer three. The actual objective."

He clicks to another screen. Different organizational chart. Iranian names. Persian script. English translations below.

"These are Iranian intelligence officers. MOIS. Ministry of Intelligence and Security. Operating in United States. New York specifically. They run networks. Monitor dissidents. Facilitate operations. Maintain pressure on regime critics who fled Iran and built lives in America."

"What does this have to do with ISIS recruitment?"

"Everything. Chen's ISIS defectors—he's not just using them for terrorism intelligence. He's using them to infiltrate Iranian networks. To identify MOIS officers. To map Iranian operations on American soil. That's the real objective. ISIS recruitment is cover for domestic counterintelligence operation against Iran."

Petey shows intercepts. Communications. Arabic and Farsi text with English translations.

"ISIS and Iran are enemies. Sunni extremists versus Shia regime. They hate each other. But they have overlapping networks. Overlapping recruitment pools. Overlapping operational spaces. Chen realized—if you recruit ISIS fighter, you don't just get terrorism intelligence. You get access to communities where Iranian intelligence also operates. You get introductions to people who might know MOIS officers. You get mapping capability CIA can't get any other way."

"That's illegal. CIA doesn't have domestic authority."

"Technically it's FBI operation. FBI has domestic authority. CIA is 'liaison.' Providing expertise. Offering access through ISIS defectors. It's joint task force. Structured carefully to stay barely legal. But the access—the operational intelligence—that's all Chen. That's all CIA capabilities deployed on American soil through FBI cover."

Ethan processes this. The operation is elegant. Terrible but elegant. Use ISIS recruitment as justification for domestic counterintelligence. Use defectors as access to Iranian networks. Wrap it in counterterrorism so it's barely legal.

"And the surveillance on Yousef?"

"That's FBI. They're watching him because he was Chen's primary access point. Because he facilitated the ISIS recruitment that provides Iranian access. They're documenting his activities. Building case file.

Not for prosecution—for leverage. They want him operational again. Want him to restart the access Chen lost when you extracted him."

"So the surveillance isn't punishment. It's recruitment pressure."

"Exactly. Make him nervous. Make him isolated. Make him desperate for solution. Then offer deal: cooperate or face consequences. Standard coercion playbook."

"And what about me? Am I under surveillance?"

"Not yet. But you will be. FBI knows you extracted Yousef. Knows you disrupted operation. They're deciding whether you're threat or asset. Whether to prosecute you or recruit you."

"Recruit me for what?"

Petey closes the laptop. Looks at Ethan directly. "For what Chen's always wanted. Replacement for Yousef. Someone with legal background, operational capabilities, cultural understanding. Someone who can navigate gray areas. Someone who thinks like operator but has lawyer credentials. That's you. That's what this whole thing has been building toward. The surveillance on Yousef isn't about him. It's about pressuring you. Making you choose: help rebuild the operation or watch your friend get prosecuted."

The trap is complete. Yousef is leverage. The surveillance is pressure. The FBI investigation is theater. All of it designed to force Ethan into cooperation.

"There's one more thing," Petey says. "The ISIS recruitment operation. The one Chen's running. The defectors he's cultivating. One of them—the main one—is already compromised."

"How?"

"Because he's not Chen's asset. He's DIA's asset. Defense Intelligence Agency. Different chain of command. Different objectives. They recruited him first. Two years ago. He's been providing intelligence to DIA while Chen thinks he's recruiting him for CIA."

"Who?"

"Kamal Barzani. The Kurdish intelligence officer you met in Erbil. The one Chen tried to recruit through Yousef. He's been working with DIA for two years. Chen doesn't know. DIA doesn't tell CIA. Agencies don't share sources. So Chen's been trying to recruit someone who's already recruited. And Kamal's been playing along. Gathering intelligence on Chen. Understanding CIA priorities. Using the recruitment attempt to map American intelligence operations in Kurdistan."

The chessboard is complete. Multiple agencies. Multiple operations. Multiple layers of recruitment and counter-recruitment. Everyone using everyone.

"So what do I do?"

"That's your call. But understand—if you go to New York, if you try to help Yousef, you're walking into active counterintelligence operation. Multiple agencies. Multiple agendas. Multiple ways to get caught in crossfire. Chen wants to recruit you. FBI wants to leverage you. DIA wants to use you without telling CIA. Iranian intelligence probably knows about all of it and has their own play. That's the situation. That's what you're walking into."

"What would you do?"

"I'd go. Because Yousef needs help. Because walking away means he stays trapped. Because sometimes you operate in the gray not because you see clearly but because staying still means getting run over." Petey stands. "But I'd go with eyes open. I'd know I'm being played. I'd accept that every move has consequences I can't predict. I'd make best decisions with imperfect information and live with whatever ripples forward. That's operational reality. That's the work."

Ethan sits in the warehouse office. Processing. The layers. The complexity. The trap closing from multiple directions.

"There's more," Petey says. "Something you need to know about Chen's Iranian operation. The target. The reason he's running domestic counterintelligence."

He shows photo. Iranian man. Mid-forties. Professional clothes. The look of someone comfortable in both Persian and American cultures.

"Reza Hosseini. MOIS officer. Operates in New York under diplomatic cover. He runs Iranian intelligence networks in tristate area. Monitors dissidents. Tracks regime critics. Facilitates operations."

"What kind of operations?"

"Assassinations. Seven Iranian dissidents. American residents. All regime critics. All vocal. All vulnerable. Reza's planning to kill them. Not himself—he'll use assets. Proxies. Make it look like accidents. But it's coordinated assassination campaign. Targeting people who think they're safe in America. Seven people. Seven lives. That's what Chen's operation is trying to prevent. That's why he needs the ISIS defectors. That's why he needs Iranian access. To stop the assassinations before they happen."

Petey shows list. Seven names:

**Sohrab Madani** - Journalist. Writes about human rights abuses in Iran. Queens. Wife and two teenage sons.

**Mina Karimi** - Activist. Organizes protests against regime. Brooklyn. Single mother, one daughter.

**Farhad Rezaei** - Former government official who defected. Testifies to Congress. Manhattan. Married, no children.

**Nasrin Tavakoli** - Academic. Professor at Columbia. Writes about women's rights. Widowed.

**Arash Mohammadi** - Businessman. Funds opposition groups. New Jersey. Family in Tehran.

**Leyla Ahmadi** - Poet. Her work circulates in Iran underground. Brooklyn. Young, twenties.

**Kamran Sabeti** - Former military officer. Provides intelligence on IRGC to Western agencies. Queens. Divorced, three children.

Seven people. Seven families. Seven lives at stake.

"These are real?" Ethan asks.

"According to Chen's intelligence, yes. According to FBI counter-intelligence assessment, yes. According to DIA independent analysis, probably yes. The targeting is specific. The timeline is established. Early January. Two-month window. Reza's moving forward with operation unless something stops him."

"And Chen thinks disrupting his network stops the assassinations."

"Chen thinks mapping Reza's network, identifying his assets, understanding his capabilities—that prevents the operation. Whether he's right—" Petey shrugs. "That's the calculation. That's what intelligence work is. Making bets about future based on incomplete information. Chen's betting his operation saves seven lives. Maybe he's right. Maybe he's wrong. Can't know until January when we see if people die or don't."

Ethan looks at the photos. The seven faces. Real people. Real families. Real lives depending on operations they don't know exist.

"Why are you showing me this?"

"Because you need to understand what you're deciding between. Chen's going to offer you recruitment. He's going to pitch you on helping rebuild operation. On using your skills to facilitate Iranian access. And you need to know—the pitch isn't abstract. It's not about strategic objectives or intelligence priorities. It's about seven people who might die if Chen's operation fails. That's the calculation. Your cooperation versus seven lives. You understand that framework. Chen taught it to you. Now he's applying it to recruit you."

"That's manipulation."

"That's operational reality. Seven dissidents are real. Assassination plot is real. Chen's operation is real attempt to stop it. Whether recruiting you is moral or immoral—that's separate question from whether operation serves legitimate purpose. Both can be true. Chen can be coercing you while also preventing murders. That's the gray area. That's why this work is hard."

Petey walks to window. Looks out at parking lot. At the normal world continuing beyond the warehouse.

"One more thing. Kamal. The Kurdish intelligence officer. The one DIA recruited. The one Chen's trying to recruit. He's Reza's cousin."

"What?"

"Reza Hosseini. MOIS officer planning assassinations. Kamal Barzani. Kurdish counter-intelligence. They're cousins. Grew up together. Family connection. That's why Kamal's so valuable to DIA. That's why he has access to Iranian networks. That's also why he might be compromised. Family loyalty versus operational objectives. Can't know which wins until moment of crisis."

The layers multiply. Kamal protecting cousin. Chen targeting cousin. DIA using Kamal while CIA doesn't know he's theirs. Everyone playing everyone. Everyone carrying multiple loyalties. Everyone calculating from their own perspective.

"So what do I do?" Ethan asks again.

"You go to New York. You see what Chen offers. You understand the stakes. Then you make calculation about whether helping him is collaboration with coercion or prevention of murder. Maybe both. Probably both. That's what makes it impossible. That's what makes it operational."

Petey hands Ethan business card. Name and number. "This is Richard Holbrook. Lawyer. Former DOJ. Specializes in national security cases. You'll need him. Whether you cooperate with Chen or fight him, you'll need legal representation. Call him today. Get him read in. Start building defense or negotiation position. Don't try to navigate this alone."

"Will he understand?"

"He's represented contractors, intelligence officers, whistleblowers, everyone who operates in gray areas. He understands those shades better than most lawyers. He'll help you figure out what's legal, what's illegal, what's barely legal, and what's worth doing regardless. That's his specialty. Gray area navigation."

Ethan takes the card. Puts it in wallet.

"Thank you. For showing me this. For explaining. For—"

"Don't thank me. I'm not doing this out of friendship. I'm doing it because you're walking into situation where ignorance gets you destroyed. I'd rather you understand the game before playing it. Gives you better chance of surviving. Improves odds you make good decisions instead of reactive ones. That's all. Professional courtesy between people who operate."

They walk back to parking lot. The afternoon sun is bright. Cold but clear. The November light that makes everything sharp.

"Where will you be?" Ethan asks.

"Watching. I always watch. That's my role. I don't intervene directly. Don't take sides explicitly. But I watch. I provide intelligence to people who might use it well. That's you. That's why I showed you this. Use it well."

Petey gets in his truck. Drives away. Leaving Ethan alone in the parking lot with warehouse full of classified information and decision that keeps getting harder.

His phone rings. Regular phone. Chen.

"Ethan. We need to talk. I know you're with Petey. I know what he showed you. I know you understand the situation now. So let's talk. Face to face. No games. No manipulation. Just honest conversation about what's happening and what I need from you."

"When?"

"New York. Tomorrow. I'll text address. Come ready to listen. Come ready to understand that this isn't about coercion. It's about prevention. It's about seven people who deserve to live. It's about stopping operation that shouldn't happen. Come ready to hear the pitch. Then decide."

"I'll be there."

"Good. Because time is short. Because Reza's moving forward. Because every day we wait is day closer to January when people die. See you tomorrow."

Chen hangs up.

Ethan sits in the rental car. Thinking about seven names. Seven faces. Seven families. About Yousef under surveillance. About Chen's operation. About Kamal's family loyalty.

He books flight to New York. LaGuardia. Evening departure. Lands at 9:47 PM.

Tomorrow he meets Chen. Tomorrow he hears the pitch. Tomorrow he decides whether preventing assassinations justifies cooperating with operation that compromised his friend. Whether slightly more good than harm applies when both good and harm are measured in lives he'll never meet.

Tomorrow the calculation gets real. Tomorrow the fog either lifts or gets impossibly thicker.

Here we go again.

# 9

## CHAPTER 9: THE GAME

*Greenville, South Carolina — November 2015*

The flight back is three hours of thinking.

About FBI investigations and federal charges and prison time. About the ultimatum—cooperate or face maximum prosecution. About Yousef trapped in Rochester with surveillance outside his apartment. About choices made in Kurdistan and consequences that won't stop rippling.

But mostly about what Chen actually wants.

Because something doesn't add up. The surveillance is too obvious. The FBI involvement is too quick. The ultimatum is too clean. Like pieces arranged deliberately. Like someone running operation rather than investigation.

Chen's smart. Six years in Kurdistan. Successful operations. No blown covers. Good tradecraft. He doesn't make mistakes. Doesn't operate sloppily. Doesn't run obvious surveillance if he wants actual intelligence.

So why is the surveillance obvious? Why is FBI involved so quickly? Why the ultimatum demanding cooperation within forty-eight hours?

Because Chen wants something. Something beyond revenge. Something beyond punishing Ethan for burning his operation. Something operational.

Question is what.

The plane lands in Charlotte at 8:47 PM. Ethan drives to Greenville. Sunday night. Empty roads. The comfortable South Carolina darkness that feels nothing like Kurdistan darkness.

At his apartment he unpacks. Checks messages. Margaret sent contact information for the attorney. DC-based. Former DOJ. Specializes in national security cases. Name is Richard Holbrook.

Ethan emails him. Brief explanation. Kurdistan. CIA operation. FBI investigation. Need representation. Urgency high.

Response comes twenty minutes later despite being Sunday night.

*Received. We should talk tomorrow. 9 AM call? I'll need full brief but initial read suggests complicated case with operational dimensions beyond legal charges. —RH*

Operational dimensions. That's telling. Not just legal defense. Something more.

Ethan confirms the call. Then sits in his apartment trying to piece together what's actually happening.

FBI doesn't move this fast on counterintelligence cases. Typical investigation takes months before contacting suspects. Surveillance. Intercepts. Building evidence. Then approach. Interview. Maybe arrest if evidence warrants.

But this moved in days. Kurdistan operation collapsed three weeks ago. Ethan returned to US two weeks ago. FBI contacted Margaret less than a week later. Timeline is compressed. Too compressed for normal investigation.

Which means either:

1. FBI had been investigating before Kurdistan. Ethan walking

into existing case.

2. Chen pushed FBI to move fast. Using bureau resources for personal objective.

3. This isn't actually investigation. It's operation. Something else disguised as investigation.

Option three feels right. Feels like Chen. Feels like intelligence officer using available tools for operational objective rather than legal one.

His phone rings. Petey.

"You back in Greenville?"

"Yeah. Just got in."

"Good. We need to talk. Not on phone. Can you come to Charlotte tomorrow? There's thing you need to see."

"What thing?"

"Thing that explains what Chen's actually doing. Why FBI is involved. What the real objective is." Pause. "This isn't about punishing you. This isn't about prosecuting Yousef. This is something else. Something operational. You need to see it to understand."

"Can't you just tell me?"

"No. Has to be in person. Has to be face to face. Too sensitive for phone." Pause. "Trust me. Come to Charlotte. Two PM tomorrow. I'll text address. Bring nothing electronic. No phone. No laptop. Nothing that can be tracked or recorded."

"Petey—"

"Two PM. Come alone. Tell no one." He hangs up.

Ethan sits holding dead phone. The cloak and dagger routine feels excessive but Petey doesn't do excessive. If he's being this careful, there's reason.

***

Monday morning. 9 AM call with Holbrook.

The voice is calm. Professional. The sound of someone who's navigated national security cases before.

"Tell me what happened. All of it. Kurdistan, the CIA operation, what you did, what they're investigating. Don't leave anything out. I can't help if I don't have complete picture."

Ethan tells it. Baghdad 2008. Yousef as interpreter. Chen as CIA officer. The relationship six years later. The call from Kurdistan. The trip to Erbil. The operation to extract Yousef. Kamal. The burned sources. The return home. Rochester. FBI.

Holbrook listens without interrupting. When Ethan finishes, silence on the line for thirty seconds.

"Okay. First thing—you're right to not talk to FBI without representation. Second thing—this case is more complicated than standard counterintelligence investigation. There are operational elements. Political elements. Things beyond legal charges."

"What do you mean?"

"I mean FBI counterintelligence doesn't typically move this fast unless there's pressure from above. Someone pushed them to investigate you quickly. Someone with access. Someone at Agency probably. That's unusual. That suggests operational objective beyond prosecution."

"Chen."

"Probably. But Chen doesn't have unilateral authority to direct FBI investigations. He'd need cover. Legitimate national security concern. Plausible threat. Something that justifies fast-tracking investigation." Pause. "Which means either you're actually threat—which I doubt—or you're tool for something else. Means for some other end."

"What end?"

"Don't know yet. But I'll find out. I have contacts at bureau. At DOJ. At Agency. I'll make calls. Figure out what's actually happening beneath the surface. In the meantime—don't talk to FBI. Don't answer questions. Don't try to explain. Just refer them to me. I'll handle communication."

"What about Yousef? He's getting his own attorney but he's scared. Surveillance outside his house. Doesn't know what's coming."

"Yousef should get good attorney and follow same advice. Don't talk. Don't engage. Let lawyers handle it. These investigations take time. Use that time to understand what's really happening. What the actual objective is. Then we build appropriate response."

"What if the objective is just prosecution? What if they really do want to charge us?"

"Then we defend. But I don't think that's what this is. Prosecution would be messy. Complicated. Would expose CIA operational details. Would create congressional attention. Agency hates that. They avoid prosecution when possible. Prefer administrative solutions. Quiet resolutions. This feels like something else."

After the call Ethan sits processing. Holbrook's right. Prosecution makes no sense. Too much exposure. Too much attention. Too much risk for Agency.

So what does Chen want? What's the operational objective?

At noon Ethan drives to Charlotte. Leaves his phone at home. Brings nothing electronic. Just wallet and keys and burner phone still in package.

The address Petey texted is industrial area. Warehouses. Shipping containers. The kind of location where contractors store equipment and hold meetings that don't appear on calendars.

Petey's truck is parked outside a warehouse. He's leaning against it. Smoking. Waiting.

"You came alone?"

"Yeah. No phone. Nothing electronic. Like you said."

"Good. Come inside."

The warehouse is mostly empty. High ceilings. Concrete floor. A few shipping containers along one wall. Office area at the back.

In the office, three other men. Contractors probably. Mid-forties. Fit. The bearing of people who've spent careers downrange. They nod at Ethan but don't introduce themselves.

Petey closes the door. "What I'm about to show you doesn't leave this room. Understand?"

"Yeah."

"I'm serious. You can't tell your attorney. Can't tell Margaret. Can't tell Yousef. No one. This is compartmented information that could get people killed if it gets out."

"I understand."

Petey opens a laptop. Turns it toward Ethan. Screen shows map. Northern Iraq. Syria. ISIS-controlled territory marked in red. Kurdish-controlled territory in yellow. Turkish border. Iranian positions.

"This is current situation. November 2015. ISIS controls Mosul, Raqqa, significant territory in Iraq and Syria. Caliphate at peak strength. Coalition airstrikes degrading capability but slowly. On the ground, Peshmerga hold the line in Kurdistan. Syrian Kurds—YPG—fighting ISIS in Syria. But it's stalemate. ISIS can't advance but isn't collapsing either."

"I know this. I was just in Kurdistan."

"Right. But what you don't know is what's happening beneath the surface. The intelligence operations. The recruitment networks. The proxy wars." He zooms in on Kurdistan. "Chen's operation—the one you burned—wasn't just about Kamal. Wasn't just about mapping Kurdish political networks. That was cover. The real objective was something else."

"What?"

"Chen's been cultivating this network for eighteen months. You disrupted it in October. He's spent the last month trying to rebuild."

Petey clicks to different screen. Shows organizational chart. Names. Photos. Lines connecting them.

"Chen was running operation to identify and recruit ISIS defectors. Foreign fighters who joined the Caliphate and became disillusioned. Western passport holders specifically. Americans, Europeans, Canadians. People who could return home. Who could provide intelligence on ISIS operations in the West. Who could help prevent attacks."

Ethan looks at the chart. Recognizes nothing. Just names and photos.

"This is ISIS intelligence network?"

"This is Chen's recruitment network. Targets. Potentials. People he was cultivating. People who might defect if approached correctly." Petey points to one photo. Young man. Western features. "This is Ahmed Khalil. Born in Michigan. Parents Iraqi. Joined ISIS in 2014. Fought in Syria. Got disillusioned. Started questioning. Chen identified him as potential defector. Started cultivation process."

"How does this relate to Yousef?"

"Yousef was access. Yousef speaks Arabic. Understands Iraqi culture. Has family connections in Iraq. Chen used him to make indirect contact with ISIS fighter families. To pass messages. To facilitate communication that couldn't happen through official channels. Yousef didn't know he was doing it. Thought he was helping with refugee work. But Chen was using him for ISIS recruitment operation."

The pieces start connecting. Yousef's assignments. The meetings Chen sent him to. The people he talked to. Not just mapping Kurdish networks. Facilitating contact with ISIS-adjacent networks.

"And when I extracted Yousef—"

"You disrupted active ISIS recruitment operation. You cost Chen access to network that took two years to build. You compromised ongoing cultivations. You potentially cost lives because defectors who might have provided warning about attacks in the West are no longer accessible."

Ethan sits back. Processing. The consequences he didn't know he was causing.

"So Chen's not pursuing me for revenge. He's pursuing me because I disrupted operational priority. Because ISIS recruitment matters more than one interpreter's freedom."

"Exactly. And the FBI investigation—that's not really investigation. That's leverage operation. Chen's trying to force you back into play. Trying to make you cooperate. Not to punish you. To recruit you."

"Recruit me for what?"

Petey clicks to another screen. Shows list of names. Western names.

"These are ISIS foreign fighters. Western passport holders. People who joined Caliphate. Chen's been trying to recruit them. Get them to defect. Come back to West as intelligence assets. Provide warning about attacks. Help disrupt ISIS operations in Europe and America." He looks at Ethan. "But recruitment requires access. Requires cultural understanding. Requires people who can navigate both worlds. Chen had Yousef for that. You took Yousef away. Now Chen needs replacement."

"He wants me to replace Yousef."

"He wants you to help him rebuild the operation. To use your legal background, your Iraq experience, your connections to navigate the network. To help identify potential defectors. To facilitate recruitment. To be new access point for ISIS cultivation operation."

"That's insane. I'm not intelligence officer. I'm lawyer. I don't have training or clearance or—"

"You have something better. You have credibility. You helped interpreter escape CIA coercion. That story—if properly framed—makes you hero to people who distrust American government. Makes you sympathetic to ISIS fighters who feel trapped by their choices. Makes you potential access point Chen can't get any other way."

The operational logic is elegant. Terrible but elegant. Use Ethan's interference as recruitment credential. Frame him as someone who opposes CIA coercion. Use that reputation to access ISIS defectors who fear American prosecution.

"Chen thinks I'll do this?"

"Chen thinks he can force you to do this. FBI investigation is pressure. Threat of prosecution is leverage. Cooperate or face federal charges. Work for us or go to prison. That's the play."

"And if I refuse?"

"Then prosecution moves forward. You and Yousef both face charges. Material support for terrorism. Providing intelligence to foreign nationals. Obstruction of intelligence operations. Stack enough charges, threaten enough prison time, eventually you cooperate to reduce sentence. That's standard recruitment playbook when voluntary cooperation fails."

One of the other contractors speaks up. First time. Deep voice. Southern accent. "It's coercion. Same thing Chen did to Yousef. Just different target. Different leverage. Same methodology."

Petey nods. "Chen's good at coercion. Six years in Kurdistan taught him how. He learned from best—from Mossad officers, from Iranian intelligence, from all the players operating in that space. Learned that leverage works better than ideology. That fear motivates better than money. He's applying those lessons to you."

Ethan stands. Walks to the window. Looks out at empty parking lot. Gray November day. Cold. Everything cold.

"So what do I do? Cooperate or fight?"

"Neither. You do third option. You expose the operation. You make it public. You create so much attention that Chen can't run coercion play anymore. Congressional inquiry. IG investigation. Media attention. All the things CIA hates. That's how you stop this."

"Exposure means burning the ISIS recruitment operation. Means potential defectors go underground. Means losing intelligence that might prevent attacks. Means more people die."

"Maybe. Or maybe Chen's operation was always questionable. Maybe recruiting ISIS fighters as assets is too risky. Maybe some operations shouldn't happen even if they might produce intelligence. That's the calculation you have to make."

The calculation. That's weighing the balance. Chen's framework. The math that never works cleanly.

Expose the operation—stop Chen's coercion but cost potential intelligence that might save lives. Stay silent—protect the operation but accept being coerced into becoming asset yourself. Cooperate—become part of operation and live with consequences.

Three options. All bad. All costs. No clean answers.

"I need to think," Ethan says.

"You have time. FBI investigation will take weeks to develop. Chen's patient. He'll apply pressure gradually. Wait for you to crack. But you don't have unlimited time. Eventually pressure becomes prosecution. Eventually you have to choose."

"What would you do?"

Petey lights a cigarette. "I'd expose it. I'd take the hit. I'd burn the operation and accept the consequences. Because being coerced into intelligence work—into recruiting ISIS defectors—that's line I won't cross. That's selling too much of yourself for operational objective. But I'm not you. I don't have your obligations. Your relationships. Your conscience. You have to make your own calculation."

The other contractors nod. Agreement without words. These are men who've made similar calculations. Who understand the gravity. Who respect whatever choice Ethan makes.

"Can I tell my attorney? Holbrook?"

"Tell him general outline. ISIS recruitment operation. Chen's leverage play. Don't give him specifics. Don't show him the chart. Don't name names. Keep it abstract enough that he can build defense without compromising sources. Holbrook's good. He'll understand."

Ethan nods. "What about Yousef? Does he know? About the ISIS recruitment operation?"

"No. He thinks he was doing refugee work. Cultural liaison. He doesn't know Chen was using him for ISIS access. Better he doesn't know. Keeps him clean. Keeps him sympathetic. Makes defense easier."

"Should I tell him?"

"That's your call. But think carefully. Telling him means he carries that burden too. Means he knows his four years of work wasn't refugee assistance—it was ISIS recruitment facilitation. That's heavy knowledge. Might break him. Might be kinder to let him keep his version of events."

The question of mercy. Of burden sharing. Of whether truth helps or hurts. No clean answer.

They talk for another thirty minutes. Details about the operation. About Chen's methods. About the targets on the recruitment list. About the successes—two defectors so far, both providing valuable intelligence. About the costs—families threatened, leverage applied, coercion normalized.

Then Ethan leaves. Drives back to Greenville. Thinking. Processing. Calculating.

Chen's not pursuing revenge. He's running operation. Trying to recruit Ethan as replacement for Yousef. Using FBI investigation as leverage. Building pressure until cooperation seems like only option.

It's elegant. It's terrible. It's classic intelligence work.

And Ethan has to decide whether to expose it or submit to it or find third option nobody's mentioned yet.

***

That evening Ethan calls Holbrook. Explains. ISIS recruitment operation. Chen using FBI investigation as leverage. Operational objective rather than legal prosecution.

Holbrook listens. When Ethan finishes: "That makes sense. Explains the timeline. Explains the pressure. Explains why prosecution threats feel performative rather than serious."

"What do we do?"

"We build defense around it. We document the coercion. We prepare to expose the operation if necessary. We create leverage of our own. Make Chen choose between pursuing you and protecting his operation. That's how we win."

"Winning means burning ISIS recruitment operation. Means losing potential intelligence."

"Maybe. But that's not your problem. Your problem is protecting yourself and Yousef. Agency's problem is running ethical operations that don't rely on coercion. They've created this situation. They can live with consequences."

The lawyer's logic is clean. But Ethan knows the real world doesn't work that way. Consequences ripple. Burned operations cost lives. Stopped attacks that don't happen because intelligence was lost. Invisible costs of exposure.

"I need to think about this," Ethan says.

"Think fast. FBI will move soon. Once they formalize investigation, options narrow. Better to act before that happens. Before pressure becomes prosecution."

After the call Ethan sits in his apartment. The calculation is impossible. The calculus doesn't work when good and harm are measured in different currencies across different timescales.

His phone rings. Regular phone. Unknown number.

"This is Ethan."

"It's Chen. We should talk. Face to face. Without lawyers. Without recording. Just you and me. Like Baghdad 2009. Before everything got complicated."

"I don't think that's good idea."

"It's excellent idea. Because you need to understand what's actually happening. What I'm actually trying to accomplish. What's at stake beyond your friend's freedom." Pause. "Come to DC. Wednesday. I'll meet you. No surveillance. No recording. Just conversation. Then you can make informed decision about what to do."

"My attorney says—"

"Your attorney doesn't understand operational realities. Doesn't understand ISIS threat. Doesn't understand what I'm trying to accomplish. You do. You've been downrange. You've made hard calls. That's why I want to talk to you directly. Not to coerce. Not to threaten. Just to explain."

"And if I don't come?"

"Then FBI investigation proceeds. Prosecution develops. You and Yousef face federal charges. That's not threat. That's just what happens when people won't talk. When they won't listen. When they choose lawyers over conversation."

"That sounds like threat."

"It's consequence. There's difference." Pause. "Come to DC. Wednesday. Two PM. I'll text address. Come alone. Hear what I have to say. Then make your choice. That's all I'm asking."

He hangs up.

Ethan sits holding the phone. The invitation is dangerous. Meeting Chen without lawyer present. Without protection. Without recording. Everything Holbrook would tell him not to do.

But Chen's right about one thing. Ethan does understand operational realities. Does understand the cost. Does understand the calculations that don't work cleanly but have to be made anyway.

And maybe—maybe—there's third option. Maybe there's compromise between exposure and submission. Maybe there's way to protect Yousef without burning operation. To resist coercion without costing lives.

Maybe.

He texts Holbrook: *Chen wants to meet. Wednesday. DC. No lawyers. Should I go?*

Response comes five minutes later: *Absolutely not. Terrible idea. Meeting without representation creates problems. Anything you say can be used against you. Plus physical risk. Chen has operational capabilities. Could detain you. Could coerce you. Could—*

Another text before Holbrook finishes: *But if you're going anyway—and I suspect you are—then document it. Record the conversation if possible. Tell someone where you're going. Have extraction plan. Be smart.*

Smart. That's the hard part. Being smart while walking into lion's den. Being smart while making impossible calculations. Being smart while carrying a load that keeps getting heavier.

Ethan books flight to DC. Wednesday morning. Returns evening. One day. One meeting. One chance to understand what Chen actually wants before choosing whether to expose him or submit to him or find third option.

One day to figure out if the logic really applies when both good and harm are measured in lives.

One day to make calculation that might determine whether people live or die based on choice he makes in conversation with man who tried to coerce his friend.

One day.

Then the weight crushes him or he carries it.

Then he makes the choice and lives with consequences.

The scar on his arm itches.

He doesn't touch it this time.

Just sits in the dark apartment thinking about all the calculations that ripple forward forever.

Wednesday in DC.

Then he decides.

# 10

## CHAPTER 10: THE PITCH

*Washington, DC — Early December 2015*

The flight to Reagan National lands at 11:42 AM on a Wednesday. Ethan takes the Metro into the city. No rental car. No paper trail. Following tradecraft he learned from people who do this for living.

The address Chen texted is in Georgetown. Residential street. Expensive brownstones. The kind of neighborhood where intelligence officers live on government salary supplemented by family money or book deals or speaking fees.

Number 2847. Red brick. Black door. Brass fixtures. The appearance of wealth without ostentation.

Ethan arrives at 1:55 PM. Five minutes early. Stands on the sidewalk looking at the building. Thinking about walking into a trap. About meeting without lawyer. About all the ways this could go wrong.

But he's here. Committed. Time to see what Chen actually wants.

He climbs the steps. Rings the bell.

Chen answers. Same preppy look. Khakis, button-down, wire-rimmed glasses. But he looks tired. Older than Kurdistan. Like the world has gotten heavier.

"Ethan. Come in."

The interior is nice. Hardwood floors. Oriental rugs. Art on walls. Books everywhere. The home of someone who reads. Who thinks. Who's spent years accumulating knowledge.

"Drink?" Chen asks.

"Water's fine."

They sit in a study. Leather chairs. Fireplace. Window overlooking small garden. The civilized space for uncivilized conversation.

Chen pours water for both of them. Sits. Looks at Ethan.

"Thank you for coming. I know your lawyer advised against it."

"He did. I came anyway."

"Because you want to understand. Because you know there's more to this than FBI investigation. Because you're smart enough to recognize operational play when you see it." Chen drinks water. "That's why I wanted you here. Because you understand. Because we can talk frankly without legal theater."

"So talk. Tell me what you want."

"I want to rebuild what you destroyed. The ISIS recruitment operation. The network that took three years to develop. The access that might prevent attacks in New York or Paris or London. I want to rebuild it and I want your help."

"Why me? You have resources. Personnel. Professional recruiters who know what they're doing."

"Because you have something they don't. Credibility. You helped interpreter escape CIA coercion. That story—properly framed—makes you sympathetic to people who distrust American government. Makes you accessible to ISIS fighters who feel trapped by their choices. They'll talk to you. They won't talk to Agency officers."

"So I'm recruitment tool. Asset to facilitate access to targets."

"You're potential partner. Someone who understands stakes. Who's been downrange. Who knows costs of war and costs of peace. Someone who can help me prevent attacks before they happen." Chen leans forward. "Do you know how many ISIS fighters are American citizens? How many hold Western passports?"

"I've heard estimates."

"Three hundred Americans. Five thousand Europeans. Canadians, Australians, all over. They joined Caliphate thinking they'd build paradise. Found hell instead. Brutality. Slavery. Public executions. Rape as policy. Many are disillusioned. Want to leave. But they're terrified of coming home. Terrified of prosecution. Life in prison. Guantanamo. Death penalty potentially."

"They joined terrorist organization. Consequences are appropriate."

"Are they? Some joined at eighteen. Nineteen. Kids who were radicalized online. Who made terrible decision and now want out. Should we punish them forever? Or should we offer path back? Amnesty for cooperation. Protection for intelligence. Help them defect and prevent next attack."

"That's not how justice works."

"Justice is luxury during war. During war, you use available tools. You recruit defectors. You flip enemies. You make deals with bad people to stop worse people. That's reality. That's what I'm trying to do."

The argument is seductive. The logic sound. Save potential terrorists by offering them amnesty. Prevent attacks by recruiting from inside. Use bad people against worse people.

"And when defectors you recruit commit attacks anyway?" Ethan asks. "When the ISIS fighter you promised amnesty blows himself up in shopping mall? Who takes responsibility?"

"I do. That's burden. That's cost of this work. Some will betray us. Some will lie. Some will take amnesty and attack anyway. But most won't. Most will provide intelligence. Most will help prevent attacks. Net calculation works."

"Net calculation. You sound like actuary."

"I sound like someone who's been doing this long enough to know you can't save everyone. Can't prevent every attack. Can't make moral choices in immoral world. You just make best calculation with available information and live with consequences."

Chen stands. Walks to bookshelf. Pulls down a file folder. Opens it.

"Ahmed Khalil. Twenty-three. Born in Dearborn. Joined ISIS in 2014. Fought in Syria. Participated in executions. War crimes. By any standard, he's criminal. Terrorist. Should be prosecuted." He shows photo. Young man. Hard face. Dead eyes. "I recruited him in March. Offered amnesty for cooperation. He provided intelligence on ISIS command structure. Safe houses. Communication methods. That intelligence prevented attack in Brussels. Six months before the actual Brussels attacks happened. Prevented it because Ahmed told us about the cell. Told us about plans. We disrupted it."

"You can't verify that. Can't prove the attack would have happened."

"No. But Belgian intelligence confirms the cell was real. The plans were real. The targets were real. We stopped it because Ahmed cooperated. Because I offered him deal his conscience could accept." Chen closes folder. "That's what I do. That's what the operation you burned was accomplishing. Preventing attacks by recruiting terrorists who want out."

Ethan looks at the photo. At the dead eyes. At the face of someone who's seen things and done things and can't unsee or undo them.

"How many have you recruited?"

"Four. Two Americans, one British, one German. All providing intelligence. All preventing attacks. Small number but significant impact. Could have been more but you disrupted the operation. Took away Yousef. Took away my access to the network."

"So you want me to replace him."

"I want you to help me rebuild. Use your credibility. Your Iraq experience. Your legal background. Help me identify candidates. Help me approach them. Help me offer deals that save lives." Chen sits back down. "I'm not asking you to join ISIS. Not asking you to commit crimes. Just asking you to facilitate conversations. Help me reach people who might defect. That's all."

"And if I refuse?"

"Then FBI investigation proceeds. You and Yousef face charges. Federal prosecution. Years in prison potentially. That's not threat. That's what happens when people interfere with national security operations and refuse to make it right."

"Make it right. By becoming your asset."

"By becoming partner in work that matters. By helping prevent attacks. By using your talents for something beyond estate planning." Chen drinks water. "You're wasting yourself in Greenville. Doing work that doesn't matter. Helping rich people avoid taxes. You could be doing work that saves lives. Work that prevents next Paris. Next San Bernardino. Next whatever comes next because we failed to recruit the person who could have warned us."

The pitch is complete. The logic elegant. The appeal to purpose and meaning and significance. Everything designed to make cooperation feel like moral choice rather than coercion.

But it's still coercion. Still leverage. Still threat of prosecution backing every word.

"I need to think," Ethan says.

"Of course. Take time. Consider options. Talk to your lawyer if you want—though he'll tell you not to cooperate. Lawyers always do.

They don't understand operational necessities. Don't understand that sometimes you work with people who coerce you because the work matters more than your feelings about how you were recruited."

Chen stands. Walks Ethan to the door.

"One more thing. Baqubah. You've been carrying that. Thinking you made wrong call. Thinking his death is your fault."

"How do you—"

"I read reports. I understand decision-making under pressure. And I want you to know—you made right call. Village survived. Intel package was recovered. Mission succeeded. That you killed someone doesn't negate that success. It just means success had cost. That's war. That's life."

"Don't use my dead to recruit me."

"I'm not using him. I'm helping you understand that you're already someone who makes hard calls. Who accepts costs. Who does what needs doing even when it hurts. That's why I want you. That's why you're right for this work." Chen opens the door. "Think about it. You have one week. After that, FBI moves forward. After that, choices narrow. After that, only option is prosecution or cooperation. Choose wisely."

Ethan steps outside. The door closes behind him. The cold November air feels good after the warm study. The street is quiet. Expensive cars parked. Expensive people living expensive lives.

He walks toward the Metro station. Thinking. Processing. Calculating.

The pitch was good. The logic sound. The appeal to purpose real. Chen's right that estate planning doesn't matter. Right that Ethan's wasting talents. Right that preventing attacks is meaningful work.

But it's still coercion. Still wrong. Still shouldn't work this way.

His phone buzzes. The burner he bought in Rochester. Text from unknown number.

*Don't trust Chen. Meeting was recorded. You're being played. Get to Union Station. Track 12. Train leaving in 30 minutes. Someone needs to talk to you. —K*

K. Kamal. But Kamal's in Kurdistan. Can't be in DC. Unless—

Another text: *I'm in DC. Emergency. Can't explain on phone. Get to Union Station. You'll understand when you see what I brought. —K*

Ethan looks at his phone. At the messages. At the choice between going home or going to Union Station to meet intelligence officer who shouldn't be in DC.

Every instinct says go home. Go to airport. Fly to Greenville. Talk to lawyer. Build defense. Do sensible thing.

But every instinct also says Kamal wouldn't risk coming to DC without reason. Wouldn't contact him without cause. Something happened. Something that changes the calculation.

He changes direction. Walks toward Union Station instead of Metro. Fifteen minutes. Moving fast. Checking for surveillance. Seeing nothing obvious but assuming it's there.

Union Station is crowded. Tourists. Commuters. The anonymity of public spaces. Ethan goes to Track 12. Amtrak to New York. Boarding in twenty minutes.

Kamal is standing near the track entrance. Civilian clothes. Baseball cap. Sunglasses despite being indoors. The tradecraft of someone trying not to be recognized.

"Ethan. Thank you for coming."

"What are you doing in DC? You're Kurdish intelligence. You resigned American cooperation. You should be in Erbil."

"I should be. But something happened. Something that changes everything. Something you need to know before you decide whether to cooperate with Chen." Kamal looks around. Checking for surveillance. "We can't talk here. Get on the train. I have tickets. We'll talk en route. Away from surveillance. Away from recording devices."

"I'm not getting on train to New York with you. I don't know what game you're playing but—"

"Not playing game. Saving your life. Chen's not just recruiting you for ISIS operation. He's setting you up. The FBI investigation is real but the objective isn't prosecution. It's elimination. You're loose end. You know too much. You burned his operation. Now he's cleaning up. The recruitment pitch was test. If you cooperate, he has asset. If you refuse, he has excuse to recommend prosecution. Either way, you're controlled or eliminated."

"That's paranoid. Chen's intelligence officer, not assassin."

"Chen's both. Six years in Kurdistan taught him wet work. Taught him how to eliminate threats that can't be prosecuted. You think his operations were all recruitment? All intelligence gathering? Some targets disappeared. Some sources stopped communicating. Some problems got solved quietly." Kamal pulls out envelope. "I brought evidence. Photos. Operational reports. Things Chen did in Kurdistan that you don't know about. Things that explain what he's really doing now."

Ethan takes the envelope. Doesn't open it. Just holds it.

"Why should I trust you? You played Chen. You played DIA. You play everyone. Why should I believe anything you say?"

"Because I'm here. In DC. Risking arrest. Risking extradition. Risking everything to warn you. I wouldn't do that if this wasn't real. If you weren't in actual danger." Kamal checks his watch. "Train leaves in fifteen minutes. Get on it. Come to New York. Let me show you what's really happening. Then decide whether to trust Chen's pitch or trust my warning."

The calculation is impossible. Trust Chen—intelligence officer who coerced Yousef for four years. Trust Kamal—intelligence officer who manipulates everyone. Trust nobody—stay in DC, face FBI investigation alone.

Three bad options. No clean choice.

"Why New York?" Ethan asks.

"Because that's where the real story is. That's where Chen's actual operation is running. Not ISIS recruitment. Something else. Something using ISIS recruitment as cover. Something you need to see to believe." Kamal starts walking toward the train. "Coming or not? Train leaves whether you're on it."

Ethan looks at the envelope. At Kamal walking away. At the choice between safe and curious. Between going home and following the thread.

The same calculation he made in October when Yousef called. The same decision that got him here. The same pattern of choosing involvement over safety.

He follows Kamal onto the train.

Track 12. Amtrak Northeast Regional. DC to New York. Three hours. Enough time for Kamal to explain. Enough time for Ethan to decide whether he's being helped or played or both.

They find seats in quiet car. Coach section. Anonymous. Kamal waits until train starts moving before speaking.

"Open the envelope."

Ethan opens it. Photos inside. Surveillance photos. Kurdish men. Some alive. Some dead. Dates and locations marked.

"These are Chen's targets. People he eliminated in Kurdistan. Not recruited. Eliminated. Killed to protect operations. Killed to prevent exposure. Killed because they knew too much or threatened too much or complicated things."

"Chen's not assassin. He's case officer."

"Case officers in Kurdistan do wet work. When necessary. When targets can't be prosecuted or recruited or contained. Chen learned from Israelis. From Iranians. From all the players who operate in that space. Learned that sometimes elimination is cleanest solution." Kamal points to one photo. "This man. Hamid Talabani. PUK intelligence. He discovered Chen was running operation without PUK knowledge. Threatened to expose it. Died in car accident three weeks later. Brakes failed. Very convenient."

"That's not proof. That's coincidence."

"This woman. Shilan Aziz. Journalist. Writing story about American intelligence operations in Kurdistan. Interviewed Chen's sources. Getting too close to operational details. Died of apparent heart attack. Thirty-two years old. No history of heart problems. Very convenient."

Kamal shows more photos. More deaths. More convenient accidents. Building pattern.

"You're saying Chen kills people who threaten his operations."

"I'm saying Chen protects operations by any means necessary. Usually that's recruitment. Sometimes that's blackmail. Occasionally that's elimination. He's been operating in gray area for six years. He's good at it. He's comfortable with it. And now you're threat. You burned his operation. You know his methods. You're loose end that needs either controlling or cutting."

The train moves through Maryland. Past suburbs. Past empty fields. The landscape flowing past while Ethan processes what Kamal's saying.

"Why tell me this? What do you gain?"

"Revenge. Chen tried to recruit me for two years. Used Yousef against me. Tried to coerce me into betraying Kurdistan. I refused. But I can't move against him directly. I'm foreign intelligence officer. No jurisdiction. No authority. But you can. You're American citizen. You can expose him. You can create investigation that brings him down. That's what I want. That's what I'm here to facilitate."

"So you're using me for your revenge."

"I'm giving you information that saves your life. What you do with it is your choice. But if you cooperate with Chen—if you accept his recruitment pitch—you become his asset. You become controlled. And eventually, when you're no longer useful, you become eliminated. That's pattern. That's his methodology. That's what these photos prove."

Ethan looks at the photos again. The dead faces. The dates. The pattern Kamal's describing.

Could be real. Could be fabrication. Could be Kamal manufacturing evidence for his own objectives. No way to verify without investigation.

But if it's real—if Chen really has killed to protect operations—then cooperation is death sentence. Delayed but inevitable.

"I need to verify this," Ethan says.

"Of course. That's why we're going to New York. That's where evidence is. That's where Chen's actual operation is running. Not ISIS recruitment. Something else." Kamal looks out window. "Chen told you he recruited four ISIS defectors. Told you they're providing intelligence. Told you they're preventing attacks."

"Yeah."

"He lied. There are no defectors. There's no ISIS recruitment operation. That's cover. Smoke screen. The real operation is something else. Something in New York. Something using ISIS threat as justification for actions that have nothing to do with terrorism."

The train continues north. Past Baltimore. Toward Philadelphia. Toward New York. Toward whatever Kamal's leading him to.

Ethan texts Holbrook: *Change of plans. Going to New York. Will explain later. Don't worry. —E*

Response comes immediately: *Worry is my job. What's in New York? —RH*

*Not sure yet. But might be evidence that changes everything. Will update tonight. —E*

The burner phone buzzes. Chen.

*Where are you? You missed your flight to Greenville. —DC*

Ethan doesn't respond. Turns off the phone. Sits in silence as train rolls north.

Either Kamal's telling truth and Chen's more dangerous than anyone realized. Or Kamal's lying and Ethan's walking into trap. Or both are playing games and Ethan's piece being moved across board he doesn't understand.

The calculation impossible.

But he's committed now. On train to New York. Following thread. Trying to find truth in world where everyone lies and truth is just another operational tool.

Except this time the math involves assassinations and cover operations and whether Chen's been running something much darker than anyone suspected.

This time the calculation might determine whether Ethan lives or dies based on whose story he believes.

Kamal or Chen. Kurdistan intelligence or CIA. Revenge or recruitment. Truth or manipulation.

No way to know until New York. Until whatever evidence Kamal wants to show him.

The train rolls on.

The calculation that never ends.

Here we go again.

# CHAPTER 11: NEW YORK

*New York City — December 2015*

Ethan arrives at LaGuardia at 4:17 PM. The city is already dark. December. The sun sets before offices close. He has three hours before meeting Kamal.

He takes the subway into Manhattan. Gets off at 72nd Street. Walks. No destination. Just movement. The cold air feels good after the recycled airplane atmosphere. The city hums around him. Eight million people living compressed lives.

On Broadway he passes a Persian restaurant. Saffron House. The window shows warm light, copper pots on walls, Persian calligraphy. The kind of place that serves as cultural anchor for diaspora communities. He's hungry. He goes in.

The interior is comfortable. Not fancy. Family-run clearly. Older woman at the register. Younger man cooking. Smell of rice and saffron and grilled lamb. Three tables occupied. Late afternoon crowd. Early dinner.

He sits at a corner table. Orders lamb kabob and doogh. The waiter—mid-forties, graying—brings tea while he waits.

"First time here?" the waiter asks. Accented English. Friendly.

"Yeah. Just visiting."

"Welcome. You'll like the kabob. My brother makes it. Family recipe." He pauses. "You have Persian friends? Most Americans don't know about this place."

"I work internationally. Pick up food preferences."

The waiter nods. Approving. He goes back to the kitchen.

The tea is strong. Good. Ethan sits drinking it. Watching the other diners. Mostly Persian. Families. Couples. The comfortable scene of people maintaining culture in adopted country.

The door opens. Man enters. Fifties. Well-dressed. Wool coat. Wire-rimmed glasses. Professional. He orders takeout. While waiting, he sits at the bar. Pulls out phone. Scrolls absently.

The waiter brings Ethan's food. Sets it down with pride. "Enjoy. My brother, Farhad, he cooks like our mother did in Tehran. Before revolution. Before everything changed."

"You're from Tehran?"

"All of us. Thirty years here now. But some things you don't lose. Food. Music. Language. The things that make you who you are."

He returns to the kitchen. Ethan eats. The food is excellent. The rice is perfectly prepared. The lamb is tender. This is someone's grandmother's recipe preserved across continents and decades.

The man at the bar receives his takeout. Pays. Before leaving, he speaks to the waiter in Farsi. Quick exchange. Familiar. The ease of compatriots.

The waiter laughs. Responds. Then says in English, probably for Ethan's benefit: "Tell Nasrin I'll bring proper fesenjan this weekend. None of this grocery store walnut paste."

"She'll appreciate it. She misses your cooking." The man smiles. Then to Ethan, in English: "Have you tried the fesenjan here? Pomegranate walnut stew. It's what I dream about when I'm traveling."

"Not yet. Should I?"

"Absolutely. Farhad makes it traditional style. The way our mothers made it." He extends hand. "I'm Sohrab Madani. I write about food sometimes. Among other things."

Ethan shakes his hand. "Ethan Caldwell."

"American? Your accent is pure."

"South Carolina originally. You?"

"Tehran originally. Queens now. Thirty-two years. Long enough that I dream in English but think in Farsi." He smiles. Sad smile. "That's immigrant life. You're always between languages. Between homes."

"What kind of writing do you do?"

"Journalism. Human rights mostly. Iran. Middle East. The things that make governments uncomfortable." He shrugs. "Someone has to write them. Someone has to remember what happened. What's still happening."

"That's important work."

"It's necessary work. Whether it's important—that's for others to judge. I just write what needs writing. What someone would want to read if they could. The people still living under the regime who can't speak freely." He picks up his takeout bag. "I have two sons. Teenagers. They think I'm paranoid. They don't understand why I write about Iran when we're safe here. But that's the thing—we're only safe because people keep writing. Keep remembering. Keep speaking. The moment we stop, we become invisible. And invisible people are easy to forget."

Something in his tone. Something about the way he said "safe here" with quotes implied.

"Do you feel safe?" Ethan asks.

Sohrab pauses. Studies Ethan. Evaluating whether to answer honestly.

"Honestly? No. Not entirely. Iranian intelligence watches diaspora. Monitors critics. Some of us are careful. We watch who we talk to. Where we go. We don't talk on phones about certain things. We assume we're being monitored. It's—" He stops. "It's the cost of speaking freely. You accept surveillance as price of not being silent."

"That's a hell of a price."

"It is. But the alternative is worse. The alternative is silence while people suffer. I have daughter back in Iran. Nasrin. My niece. She's twenty-six. Studying medicine. She can't say what she thinks. Can't protest. Can't even post online without risk. Someone has to speak for her. Someone has to say the things she can't say. That's why I write. Even with the cost. Even with the risk."

The waiter calls from the kitchen. Something in Farsi. Sohrab responds. Laughs.

"He's telling me my food is getting cold. I should go. My wife worries when I'm late." He nods to Ethan. "Enjoy your meal. If you're in New York long, come back. Try the fesenjan. Farhad only makes it Saturdays, but it's worth planning around."

He leaves. The door closes. The restaurant returns to its quiet rhythm.

Ethan finishes his meal. Pays. The waiter thanks him. Hopes he'll return.

Outside, the December cold has intensified. Ethan walks toward Penn Station. Thinking about Sohrab. About writing what needs writing. About the cost of speaking freely. About diaspora journalists who accept surveillance as price of not being silent.

About daughters in Tehran who can't speak. About uncles in Queens who speak for them. About the people who think they're safe in America while Iranian intelligence watches and monitors and plans.

Seven names. Seven people. Seven lives.

Sohrab Madani is one of them.

Ethan didn't know that when they talked. Didn't know he was meeting someone on Chen's list. Someone marked for assassination. Someone whose work made regimes uncomfortable enough to kill him.

But in two hours, Kamal will show him the organizational charts. The surveillance locations. The targeting lists. And Ethan will see Sohrab's name. Journalist. Human rights. Queens. Two teenage sons.

And he'll remember the man talking about fesenjan. About writing what needs writing. About his niece Nasrin in Tehran who can't speak freely.

Seven people. Seven lives. Not abstract. Real.

The calculation just got harder.

***

Penn Station at 6:47 PM. Rush hour chaos. Commuters flooding platforms. The anonymity of crowds. Good place to disappear if you need to. Bad place to notice surveillance if it's there.

Kamal moves fast through the station. Up stairs. Through tunnels. Out onto Eighth Avenue. Cold. Dark. November in Manhattan. The city humming with energy and indifference.

They walk west. Away from the tourist areas. Into Hell's Kitchen. Old neighborhood trying to stay authentic while gentrification creeps in. Kamal stops at a building. Pre-war. Six stories. Brick. Fire escapes.

"Safe house?" Ethan asks.

"Apartment. Friend lets me use it. Kurdish community here. We help each other." Kamal unlocks the street door. They climb to the fourth floor. Another lock. Inside.

The apartment is small. Studio. Kitchen in one corner. Futon. Desk. Window overlooking the street. Functional but not comfortable. The space of someone passing through.

Kamal goes to the desk. Opens laptop. Types. Pulls up files.

"What I'm about to show you—this is classified material. Operational intelligence. Intercepts. If anyone knows I have this, I'm arrested. If anyone knows you've seen it, you're arrested. Understand?"

"Yeah."

"Good. Because what Chen's doing—it's not just ISIS recruitment. That's cover. Layer one. Public story. What he tells his superiors. What he tells FBI. What he tells anyone who asks. But underneath—underneath it's something else."

Kamal turns the laptop. Screen shows organizational chart. Names. Photos. Lines connecting them.

"These are Iranian intelligence officers. MOIS. Ministry of Intelligence and Security. Operating in United States. New York specifically. They run networks. Facilitate operations. Maintain contacts with Iranian diaspora. Monitor dissidents. Run influence operations."

"Why would Iranian intelligence be in New York?"

"Because New York has largest Iranian population in America. Because UN is here. Because financial systems are here. Because it's intelligence target like any major city. MOIS has been operating here for twenty years. Everyone knows. FBI monitors them. But they're hard to disrupt because they hide behind diplomatic cover. Behind cultural organizations. Behind legitimate business."

Ethan looks at the chart. Recognizes nothing. Just names and photos.

"What does this have to do with Chen?"

"Everything. Chen's ISIS recruitment operation—the defectors he's cultivating—he's not just using them for terrorism intelligence. He's using them to infiltrate Iranian networks. Using them to identify MOIS officers. Using them to map Iranian operations in United States. That's the real objective. That's what he's actually doing."

"How?"

"ISIS and Iran are enemies. Sunni extremists versus Shia regime. They hate each other. But they have overlapping networks. Overlapping recruitment pools. Overlapping operational spaces. Chen realized—if you recruit ISIS fighter, you don't just get terrorism intelligence. You get access to communities where Iranian intelligence also operates. You get introductions to people who might know people who work for MOIS. You get mapping capability CIA can't get any other way."

Kamal clicks to different screen. Shows intercepts. Communications. Arabic and Farsi.

"These are conversations Chen's ISIS defectors are having. Not about terrorism. About Iranian cultural centers. About community leaders. About who's connected to who. About suspicious activities. About money flows. Chen's using ISIS recruitment as cover for domestic counterintelligence operation against Iran. Operation CIA can't legally run because CIA doesn't have domestic authority. But if it's framed as ISIS intelligence—if it's sold as preventing terrorism—then FBI allows it. Then it's joint operation. Then it's legal. Barely."

The pieces start connecting. The domestic surveillance. The FBI involvement. The pressure on Ethan. Not about ISIS recruitment. About Iranian counterintelligence. About operation that exploits terrorism threat to run domestic intelligence gathering.

"How do you know this?"

"Because I'm counter-intelligence. Because I monitor everyone operating in Kurdistan. Including MOIS. Including CIA. Including the places where they overlap. I've been tracking Chen's operation for two years. Watching how he uses ISIS recruitment. Seeing where intelligence goes. Realizing it's not about terrorism. It's about Iran."

"So Chen's running illegal domestic operation using ISIS recruitment as cover."

"Exactly. And it's working. He's identified MOIS officers FBI didn't know about. He's mapped networks no one else has access to. He's providing counterintelligence that helps U.S. But he's doing it by violating CIA charter. By operating domestically. By using ISIS defectors as intelligence assets against target that has nothing to do with terrorism."

Ethan sits on the futon. Processing. The operation is elegant. Terrible but elegant. Use ISIS recruitment as justification for domestic operations. Use defectors as access to Iranian networks. Wrap it in counterterrorism so FBI cooperates. Build counterintelligence capability CIA isn't supposed to have.

Illegal but effective. Wrong but productive.

"What does this have to do with me? Why am I threat?"

"Because you know about the ISIS recruitment. Because if you expose it, you expose the Iranian operation. Because Chen can't risk that. The Iranian counterintelligence work is producing real intelligence. Valuable intelligence. Intelligence agencies want. If you burn it—if you create investigation—it collapses. All of it. The ISIS recruitment, the Iranian mapping, the entire operation. That's why he's pressuring you. Not to punish you. To control you. To ensure you don't expose what's really happening."

Kamal clicks to another screen. Shows locations. Addresses in New York. Queens. Brooklyn. Manhattan.

"These are surveillance sites. Places Chen's operation monitors. Iranian cultural centers. Community organizations. Businesses. Places where MOIS operates. Chen has eyes on all of them. Uses ISIS defectors to access them. Uses their community connections to map networks. It's comprehensive surveillance of Iranian diaspora in New York. Surveillance that's technically illegal. But productive."

"And you brought me here to see this because—"

"Because you need to understand what you're deciding. Chen offered you recruitment. Cooperation. Chance to help prevent attacks. That sounds noble. But the attacks you'd be preventing—they're not ISIS attacks. They're Iranian intelligence operations. Chen's using ISIS threat as cover for Iran focus. If you cooperate, you're not fighting terrorism. You're fighting Iran. That's different calculation."

Ethan looks at the screens. The organizational charts. The surveillance locations. The intercepts. The evidence of operation that's both wrong and effective. Illegal and valuable.

The gray darkens.

"How did you get this intelligence? This is classified material. Operational details. How does Kurdish counter-intelligence officer access CIA operational files?"

Kamal smiles. Tired smile. "Because I'm not just Kurdish counter-intelligence. I've been doing this for twenty years. I have sources. I have relationships. I have access. Some of what you're seeing came from CIA leaks. Some came from Iranian intercepts I ran. Some came from third parties who monitor both sides. I've built comprehensive picture. That's my job. That's what I do."

"And you're showing me this because you want revenge on Chen."

"I'm showing you this because you deserve to know what you're walking into. Chen's pitch was seductive. Help prevent attacks. Save lives. Do meaningful work. But the reality is messier. You'd be helping run illegal domestic surveillance. You'd be facilitating operation CIA isn't supposed to run. You'd be asset in gray area that might collapse any moment. Is that worth it? Is that the calculation you want to make?"

Ethan stands. Walks to window. Looks at Manhattan. The lights. The density. Eight million people living compressed lives. Some of them Iranian. Some of them MOIS officers. Some of them targets of operation they don't know exists.

"What do you want me to do?"

"Expose it. Document it. Create investigation that brings it down. Congressional inquiry. Inspector General. Media attention. All the things CIA hates. Make Chen choose between protecting operation and protecting himself. Force him to shut it down. That's how you survive. That's how Yousef survives. That's how this ends."

"And Iranian intelligence operations continue unmonitored. MOIS officers operate freely. Networks remain unmapped. Whatever attacks they're planning go undetected."

"That's not your problem. That's FBI's problem. That's legitimate law enforcement's problem. You're not responsible for stopping Iranian intelligence operations. You're responsible for stopping illegal CIA operations. There's difference."

The lawyer's logic. Clean distinctions. Clear lines. Legal versus illegal. Right versus wrong.

But operational logic is different. Messier. Chen's operation is illegal but effective. Wrong but productive. Violates charter but produces intelligence.

The calculation that never works cleanly.

Ethan's phone vibrates. Regular phone. He turned it back on getting to New York. Text from number he doesn't recognize.

*Know you're in New York. Know you're with Kamal. Know what
he's showing you. It's real. The Iranian operation exists. But Kamal's not
telling you everything. He has his own agenda. Be careful. —P*

Petey. Watching. Always watching.

Another text: *Kamal worked with MOIS. Before he worked with
Americans. Before he worked with anyone. He was Iranian asset in
Kurdistan in the 90s. He flipped. But he still has relationships. Still has
contacts. He's playing his own game. Don't trust him completely. —P*

Ethan shows the texts to Kamal. "Want to explain?"

Kamal reads them. Nods slowly. "It's true. I worked with MOIS.
In the 90s. During Kurdish civil war. I was young. Desperate. Needed
protection. MOIS offered it. I gathered intelligence for them. For two
years. Then I realized what they were. What they wanted. I flipped.
Started working against them. But yes, I have history with Iranian
intelligence. Your friend Petey is right to mention it."

"Why didn't you tell me?"

"Because it's complicated. Because intelligence work is dirty. Because everyone has history with someone. You think Chen's clean? You
think he hasn't worked with questionable people? Everyone in this
business has compromised themselves. The question isn't who you
worked for. It's who you work for now. What your loyalties are now.
What you're trying to accomplish now."

"And what are you trying to accomplish?"

"Revenge on Chen. I'm honest about that. But also—stopping
operation that shouldn't exist. Chen's domestic surveillance of Iranian
diaspora is wrong. Violates charter. Violates rights. Turns every Iran-
ian-American into potential surveillance target. That's not countert-

errorism. That's ethnic profiling wrapped in national security. That's wrong regardless of whether it produces intelligence."

The ideological argument. The principled position. The moral clarity Kamal's been missing until now.

But Petey's right. Kamal has agenda. Has history. Has reasons beyond principle.

"What aren't you telling me?" Ethan asks.

"What do you mean?"

"Petey says you're playing your own game. That you have agenda beyond revenge. What is it? What do you really want?"

Kamal looks at the laptop. At the organizational charts. At the evidence he's compiled.

"The Iranian intelligence officer Chen's targeting—the one at center of his operation—his name is Reza Hosseini. He runs MOIS operations in New York. Cultural centers. Community organizations. All of it. Chen's been building case against him for three years. Mapping his networks. Documenting his activities. Preparing to expose him. To have FBI arrest him. To disrupt Iranian operations completely."

"So?"

"So Reza is my cousin. My mother's sister's son. We grew up together in Kurdistan. Before the civil war. Before I worked for MOIS. Before everything got complicated." Kamal looks at Ethan. "Chen's operation succeeds, Reza goes to prison. Life sentence probably. Espionage. MOIS officer on American soil. That's serious charges. My cousin spends rest of his life in American prison. That's what Chen's building toward. That's what I'm trying to stop."

The truth. The actual motivation. Not revenge. Not principle. Family.

"So this is about protecting your cousin."

"This is about stopping illegal operation that happens to target my family. Both can be true. Operation is wrong. Also costs me personally. Those things coexist."

"Does Reza know you're doing this?"

"No. He doesn't know I'm in New York. Doesn't know I'm working against Chen. Doesn't even know I know about the operation. If he knew—if MOIS knew—they'd either recruit me or kill me. Probably kill me. Too dangerous to trust former asset who flipped once. Might flip again."

The complexity is complete. Kamal protecting family. Running operation against Chen. Using Ethan as tool. Risking his own life. All simultaneously. All true.

Multiple games. Multiple loyalties. Multiple calculations.

"So what's real?" Ethan asks. "The evidence against Chen? The illegal domestic operation? Or is that fabricated to protect Reza?"

"It's real. All real. Chen's domestic operation exists. Iranian surveillance exists. Reza is target. All true. What's also true is I want to stop it. For personal reasons and principled reasons. Both motivate me. Both matter."

Ethan sits back down. Every piece of information adds complexity. Every revelation makes calculation harder. Every truth comes with lies attached.

Chen's running illegal operation that produces valuable intelligence. Kamal's exposing it to protect family while claiming principle. FBI's investigating Ethan to pressure cooperation. Petey's watching everyone. Yousef's trapped in Rochester. And Ethan has to decide whose story to believe. Whose side to take. Whose calculation to accept.

Slightly more good than harm. The framework that never works when everyone's good and harm point different directions.

His phone rings. Unknown number.

"This is Ethan."

"It's Chen. I know you're in New York. I know you're with Kamal. I know what he's showing you." The voice is calm. Tired. "He's telling you about Iranian operation. About domestic surveillance. About how I'm violating charter. He's right. About all of it. But he's not telling you why."

"I'm listening."

"Reza Hosseini. MOIS officer in New York. Kamal's cousin. He's planning attack. Not terrorism. Intelligence operation. Against Iranian dissidents. Against people advocating regime change. People who've fled Iran and built lives here. People who think they're safe. Reza's planning to kill them. Not himself. He'll use assets. Proxies. Make it look like accidents. But it's assassination operation. Targeting seven people. Seven Iranian-Americans who've criticized regime. Who've organized protests. Who've testified to Congress about human rights abuses."

"How do you know this?"

"Because my ISIS defectors provided access. Because the Iranian community overlaps with terrorist community in ways most people don't understand. Because I've been mapping Reza's network for three years and I've seen the planning. Seen the targeting. Seen the operational preparation. He's moving forward. Two months. Maybe three. Seven assassinations on American soil. That's what I'm trying to stop. That's why the operation exists."

"So you're running illegal domestic surveillance to prevent assassinations."

"I'm running gray area operation to stop Iranian intelligence from killing American residents. Yes. It's illegal. Yes, it violates charter. Yes, I should have gone through official channels. But official channels are slow. Official channels require evidence. Official channels take years while people die. I'm preventing deaths. Now. With tools available. That's the balancing. That's the calculation."

"Why should I believe you? Why should I believe Reza's planning assassinations?"

"Because I'll show you. Tomorrow. If you're still in New York. I'll show you the intelligence. The intercepts. The planning. Everything Kamal's not showing you. Everything he's hiding to protect his cousin. Then you can decide. Then you can make informed choice." Pause. "Meet me tomorrow. 10 AM. Address I'll text. Come alone. See the evidence. Then choose. Expose the operation or help me stop assassinations. That's the real choice. That's the actual calculation."

Chen hangs up.

Ethan looks at Kamal. "Chen says Reza's planning assassinations. Seven Iranian dissidents. Two months out. Says that's why the operation exists."

Kamal's face doesn't change. "Of course he says that. That's justification. That's how he sells illegal operation. Create threat. Manufacture urgency. Make it seem like only option. Classic intelligence manipulation."

"Is it true? Is Reza planning assassinations?"

"I don't know. Maybe. MOIS does that. Targets dissidents. Kills regime critics. Happens in Europe. Happens in Middle East. Could happen here. But Chen could also be inventing it. Could be creating justification after the fact. Could be using real MOIS capability to justify operation that exists for other reasons."

"So you don't know if your cousin's planning to kill people."

"I know Reza's MOIS officer. I know he follows orders. If Tehran ordered him to kill dissidents, he would. But I don't know if those orders exist. Don't know if Chen's telling truth. Don't know if threat is real or manufactured."

The fog is impossibly thick now. Chen says Reza's planning assassinations. Kamal says Chen might be lying. Both have motivations to lie. Both have reasons to tell truth. No way to verify without evidence.

"I need to see Chen's evidence," Ethan says.

"Don't. It's trap. He'll show you what he wants you to see. Manipulated intercepts. Translated documents. Context-free intelligence that supports his narrative. You won't get truth. You'll get recruitment pitch version 2.0."

"Maybe. But I need to see it. Need to understand what he's actually stopping. Whether the illegal operation is justified by prevention of worse thing." Ethan stands. "I'll meet Chen tomorrow. See his evidence. Then decide."

"And if his evidence is convincing? If it looks real?"

"Then I have harder decision. Expose illegal operation or help stop assassinations. But I need to see evidence first. Need to understand what's actually at stake."

Kamal nods. Tired. Defeated. "You'll meet him tomorrow. He'll show you convincing intelligence. He's good at that. Good at making case. Good at justifying operational necessities. That's how he recruited Yousef. That's how he'll recruit you."

"Maybe. But at least I'll have complete picture. At least I'll understand what I'm deciding between." Ethan moves toward the door. "Where should I stay tonight?"

"Hotel. Pay cash. Use different name if possible. Chen knows you're in New York but doesn't know where. Keep it that way. Stay mobile. Stay anonymous. Meet him tomorrow but on your terms. Public place. Witnesses. Recording device if possible. Document everything. That's how you protect yourself."

"Where will you be?"

"Gone. I've shown you what I can show you. Warned you what I can warn you. Now you decide. I'm going back to Kurdistan. Back to where I belong. This is your fight now. Your calculation. Your choice." Kamal looks at Ethan. "Good luck. Whatever you decide, I hope it's right one. For your sake. For Yousef's sake. For everyone caught in this."

He leaves. Out the door. Down the stairs. Disappearing into New York night.

Ethan sits alone in the apartment. Looking at the laptop. At the organizational charts. At the evidence of operation that's both wrong and necessary. Illegal and protective.

Tomorrow he sees Chen's evidence. Tomorrow he learns if assassinations are real or manufactured. Tomorrow he decides.

Expose the operation—stop illegal surveillance but allow potential assassinations. Cooperate with operation—help prevent deaths but become asset in illegal program. Walk away—let everyone else handle it and accept whatever consequences come.

Three options. All costs. No clean answers.

Except this time the math involves assassinations and domestic surveillance and whether stopping illegal operation costs seven lives.

This time the calculation determines whether people live or die based on choice Ethan makes in meeting with man who might be lying about everything.

Tomorrow in Manhattan.

Then the weight crushes him or he finds way to carry it.

Then he makes choice and lives with consequences.

The scar itches.

He touches it in the empty apartment.

The reminder. The permanent record. The calculation that never ends.

Tomorrow decides everything.

Tonight he just sits here carrying the impossible.

# 12

---

# CHAPTER 12: THE EVIDENCE

*New York City — December 2015*

Ethan finds a hotel in Midtown. Small place. Not a chain. The kind of establishment that takes cash and doesn't ask questions if you don't volunteer them. Two hundred a night for a room the size of a closet with a window overlooking an air shaft.

Perfect.

He sleeps poorly. The city noise is constant. Sirens. Traffic. Voices from the street. The sound of eight million people living compressed lives. Different from Kurdistan quiet. Different from Greenville silence. Different from anywhere.

At 3 AM he gives up on sleep. Sits by the window. Watches the empty air shaft. Thinks about Chen and Kamal and whose story to believe.

Both told compelling narratives. Both showed evidence. Both had motivations to lie and reasons to tell truth. No clear sight lines. No obvious answer.

Chen says Reza's planning assassinations. Seven Iranian dissidents. Two months out. Stopping that justifies illegal domestic surveillance.

Kamal says Chen's manufacturing threats. Creating justification for operation that exists for other reasons. Protecting his cousin while claiming principle. Also the correct bad call, just a different calculation.

Who's lying? Who's telling truth? Or are both lying and both telling truth simultaneously?

Multiple games. Multiple truths. Multiple calculations all coexisting.

The intelligence world in microcosm.

At 7 AM Ethan showers. Dresses. Goes downstairs. Finds a diner. Sits at counter drinking coffee while morning shift workers eat breakfast. Construction guys. Cab drivers. Night shift nurses. The people who keep cities running while everyone else sleeps.

His phone buzzes. Text from Chen.

*10 AM. 225 Varick Street. Suite 1840. Come to lobby. I'll meet you. —DC*

Varick Street. Downtown Manhattan. Commercial building. Office space. More discrete than Georgetown townhouse. More professional than clandestine safe house.

Chen's learning. Or Chen's always known and Georgetown meeting was first act of performance.

Ethan texts back: *I'll be there. —E*

He sits drinking coffee. Watching the diner. The morning rhythm. People coming and going. Each carrying their own weight. Their own calculations. Their own impossible choices that look easy from outside but crush from inside.

At 9:15 he takes the subway. Crowded morning train. Bodies pressed together. The democratic intimacy of public transportation. Billionaire and homeless person sharing same space. Same air. Same indignity.

At Varick Street he emerges into cold November morning. The building is modern. Glass and steel. Anonymous corporate architecture. The kind of place where intelligence agencies rent office space under shell company names.

He enters the lobby. Security desk. Sign-in required. He gives name. They check list. Make call. Wait.

Chen appears from elevator. Same preppy look. But he looks harder today. More focused. Like Georgetown exhaustion has been replaced with operational intensity.

"Ethan. Thank you for coming."

They ride elevator in silence. Eighteenth floor. Hallway. Unmarked door. Chen uses keycard. Inside.

The office is small. Conference room. Table. Chairs. Screens on walls. Computer equipment. The infrastructure of modern intelligence work. No windows. No connection to outside world. Just the controlled environment where secrets are processed.

Two other people in room. Man and woman. Mid-thirties. Professional. The bearing of intelligence officers. They don't introduce themselves. Don't shake hands. Just nod acknowledgment.

"These are colleagues," Chen says. "FBI counterintelligence. They're working the Reza Hosseini case. They're here because what I'm showing you is their investigation. Their evidence. Not mine alone."

The FBI presence changes dynamics. This isn't just Chen's operation. It's joint task force. Official. Sanctioned. Still questionable but less rogue than Kamal suggested.

"I thought CIA doesn't have domestic authority," Ethan says.

"We don't," Chen responds. "This is FBI investigation. FBI authority. FBI warrants. FBI oversight. I'm liaison. Providing context. Offering expertise. Facilitating access to ISIS defectors who provide intelligence relevant to investigation. But it's FBI case. FBI lead."

The woman speaks. Quiet voice. Professional tone. "I'm Special Agent Morrison. Counterintelligence Division. I've been investigating Iranian intelligence operations in New York for three years. The Reza Hosseini network specifically. What we're about to show you is classified. Sensitive Compartmented Information. You're not cleared for it. But circumstances require your knowledge. Require your cooperation. What you see doesn't leave this room. Understood?"

"Understood."

Morrison opens laptop. Connects to screen on wall. Display shows organizational chart. Similar to what Kamal showed but more detailed. More complete.

"Reza Hosseini. Iranian intelligence officer. MOIS. Operating in New York under diplomatic cover. Cultural attaché at Iranian Interests Section. He runs networks. Assets. Operations. Everything from influence campaigns to industrial espionage to targeted surveillance of dissidents."

She clicks. Shows photos. Surveillance photos. Reza meeting with various people. Cafes. Parks. Cultural centers. The tradecraft of modern intelligence work.

"We've been watching him for three years. Building case. Documenting activities. Preparing prosecution. But he's careful. Uses diplomatic immunity. Maintains plausible deniability. Operates through cutouts and proxies. Hard to build criminal case against him personally."

"What changed?" Ethan asks.

"Your friend," Chen says. "The ISIS defector. Ahmed Khalil. The one I told you about in Georgetown. He provided access. Ahmed's cousin works at Iranian cultural center. Has contact with Reza's network. Ahmed introduced me. Facilitated relationship. Gave us access to Iranian community we didn't have before."

Morrison clicks again. Shows intercepts. Conversations. Farsi text with English translations below.

"These are communications we intercepted through that access. Reza discussing operation. Targeting Iranian dissidents. Seven people. All American residents. All regime critics. All vulnerable."

She highlights names. Seven people. Photos. Brief bios.

Sohrab Madani. Journalist. Writes about human rights abuses in Iran. Lives in Queens.

Mina Karimi. Activist. Organizes protests against regime. Lives in Brooklyn.

Farhad Rezaei. Former government official who defected. Testifies to Congress about regime corruption. Lives in Manhattan.

Four others. Seven total. Seven lives.

"Reza's planning to kill them," Morrison says. "Not personally. He'll use assets. Iranian agents already in place. Make it look like accidents. Car crashes. Home invasions. Medical emergencies. But it's assassination operation. Coordinated. Systematic. Targeting regime critics on American soil."

"How certain are you?" Ethan asks.

"Ninety percent. The intercepts are clear. The targeting is specific. The timeline is established. Two months. Early January. They're planning to execute all seven within two-week period. Make it look random. Make it seem like coincidence. But it's systematic elimination of regime critics."

Morrison shows more evidence. Operational planning. Surveillance photos of targets. Logs of their movements. The infrastructure of assassination.

The evidence is compelling. Detailed. Professional. The kind of intelligence that takes months to develop. Years probably.

"This is why the operation exists," Chen says. "Why I recruited ISIS defectors. Why I've been running access to Iranian community. To develop intelligence like this. To stop operations like this. To prevent assassinations on American soil."

"So Kamal's wrong. Reza really is planning murders."

"Kamal's not wrong about operation being legally questionable," Morrison says. "He's right that CIA providing access stretches author-ities. Right that joint task force operates in gray area. But he's wrong about motivation. Wrong about objectives. This isn't ethnic profiling. This isn't surveillance for surveillance sake. This is counterintelligence investigation of genuine threat. Assassination plot against American residents."

The man speaks. First time. Deep voice. Boston accent. "I'm Spe-cial Agent Romano. Morrison's partner. I want to be clear about something. The people Reza's targeting—they're not just dissidents. They're not just critics. They're people who've built lives here. Who've raised families here. Who think they escaped Iran and found safety. Killing them sends message. No one's safe. No escape. Regime reaches everywhere. That's terrorism. On American soil. Against American residents. Stopping that justifies uncomfortable tactics."

The moral framework. The justification. The gray area calculus from law enforcement perspective.

Seven lives. Seven assassinations prevented. Seven families saved. That's real. That's measurable. That's good.

But achieved through operation that's legally questionable. That profiles community. That uses ISIS defectors as access to Iranian net-works. That operates in gray area between terrorism investigation and counterintelligence operation.

The gray shades; the balancing. The calculation Chen's been mak-ing all along.

"What do you need from me?" Ethan asks.

Chen leans forward. "Cooperation. Help rebuilding ISIS recruitment network. Help maintaining access to Iranian community. Help developing intelligence that stops Reza. You have credibility. You have story. You helped interpreter escape CIA coercion. That makes you sympathetic to communities that distrust government. That makes you valuable access point."

"You want me to be informant."

"I want you to be partner. Someone who understands stakes. Who helps prevent assassinations. Who uses your unique position to facilitate intelligence gathering that saves lives."

"And if I refuse?"

Morrison speaks. "Then investigation proceeds differently. Without access you could provide. Without intelligence you could develop. We'll still try to stop Reza. But harder. Slower. Maybe not in time. Maybe those seven people die because we didn't have access we needed."

The leverage is implicit but total. Cooperate or people die. Help us or live with consequences. That's the pitch. That's the recruitment.

"I need to think," Ethan says.

"Of course," Chen responds. "But think fast. Reza's operational timeline is fixed. Early January. That's eight weeks. We need access now. Need intelligence now. Need cooperation now. Delays cost lives."

Ethan stands. Walks to the window. Realizes there is no window. Just walls. Just the controlled environment where decisions get made that ripple outward into real world where real people live or die based on calculations made in rooms like this.

"Can I see Ahmed? The ISIS defector. The one who provided access. I want to talk to him."

Chen and Morrison exchange looks. Morrison nods.

"He's in protective custody," Chen says. "Safe house in New Jersey. We can arrange meeting. But why? What will that accomplish?"

"I want to understand his choice. Why he cooperated. How he lives with it. Whether he thinks it's worth it."

"He thinks it's worth it because he's not in Guantanamo. Because he got amnesty for cooperation. Because he's building new life instead of rotting in prison. That's simple calculation."

"Maybe. But I want to hear it from him. Want to understand how someone makes that choice. How they live with becoming informant. How they reconcile cooperation with conscience."

Chen checks his watch. "We can arrange it. This afternoon. Three PM. I'll text address. You meet him. You talk. You hear his story. Then you decide. But decide today. Tomorrow we need answer. Cooperate or walk away. No more delays."

Morrison adds: "One more thing. Kamal. The Kurdish intelligence officer. He's in New York illegally. No visa. No diplomatic status. FBI's looking for him. If you're in contact, you should know—helping him means obstruction. Means harboring foreign intelligence officer. That's felony. Separate from everything else we've discussed. Just FYI."

The warning is clear. Kamal's burned. Radioactive. Associating with him creates problems Ethan doesn't need.

"I'll keep that in mind," Ethan says.

***

Outside the building Ethan breathes cold air. The relief of being out of controlled environment. Of seeing sky even if it's gray. Of being in space not designed to manipulate every variable.

He walks. No destination. Just movement. Thinking.

The evidence looked real. The threat seemed genuine. Seven people targeted for assassination. Seven lives at stake. That's not abstract. That's real.

But Kamal's warning echoes. Chen's good at making case. Good at showing convincing evidence. Good at manufacturing urgency. Maybe the intercepts are real. Maybe they're selectively edited. Maybe the threat is genuine. Maybe it's exaggerated.

No way to verify without independent source. Without someone who isn't Chen or Morrison or Kamal. Someone who has access to truth without agenda.

His phone rings. Petey.

"You saw Chen's evidence."

"How do you know?"

"Because I'm watching. Because the building on Varick Street has cameras. Because I track everyone. You were inside ninety minutes. Long enough for comprehensive brief. Long enough to see evidence. Long enough to hear pitch." Pause. "What did they show you?"

"Assassination plot. Reza Hosseini targeting seven Iranian dissidents. Two months out. Evidence looked convincing."

"It would. FBI's good at building cases. Good at presenting evidence. Question is whether evidence supports conclusion. Whether assassination plot is real or whether Reza's doing something else that's being framed as assassination plot."

"You think they're lying?"

"I think they're shading truth. Highlighting evidence that supports their narrative. Downplaying evidence that complicates it. That's what intelligence officers do. They don't lie explicitly. They just manage perception until you believe their version."

"So is the plot real or not?"

"Plot's real. Reza's planning something. Something that involves surveillance of dissidents. Something that involves operational planning. But whether that's assassination or something else—I don't know. Can't verify without access to raw intelligence. And Chen's not giving you raw intelligence. He's giving you processed intelligence. Interpreted intelligence. Intelligence that supports recruitment pitch."

Ethan stops walking. Leans against building.

"What should I do?"

"That's your call. But understand—once you cooperate, you're asset. You're controlled. Chen owns you. Can't walk away. Can't change mind. Can't expose operation without exposing yourself. That's how recruitment works. That's the trap."

"But if plot's real—if seven people die because I didn't cooperate—"

"Then you live with that. Same way Chen lives with people who died because his operations failed. Same way everyone in this business lives with ghosts. You make calculation. You accept consequences. That's the work." Pause. "The grain field. You've been carrying that. Thinking you should have made different call. But you made right call. Village survived. Intel was recovered. Mission succeeded. That you killed someone doesn't negate success. Just means success had cost. This is same calculation. Cooperate—maybe save seven lives but become Chen's asset. Refuse—maybe seven people die but you stay free. Both choices have cost. You decide which cost you can carry."

"That's not helpful."

"It's honest. That's better than helpful. I can't tell you what to do. Can't make calculation for you. Can only tell you—whatever you decide, commit to it. Don't half-ass it. Don't cooperate with reservations. Don't refuse with regrets. Make choice. Live with it. Move forward. That's only way to survive this work."

After Petey hangs up, Ethan continues walking. Downtown Manhattan. Toward Financial District. Past Office workers on lunch breaks. Tourists taking photos. Normal people living normal lives while secret wars play out in rooms they'll never see.

At 2 PM his phone buzzes. Text from Chen.

*Address for Ahmed meeting: 447 Boulevard East, Weehawken, NJ. Apartment 3B. Three PM. Come alone. —DC*

Weehawken. New Jersey. Across the river. Thirty minutes by subway and bus.

Ethan heads that direction.

***

Weehawken is quiet. Residential. Working class neighborhood with million-dollar views of Manhattan. The contradiction of geography and economics.

Boulevard East runs along the cliff. Apartment building at 447 is six stories. Brick. Pre-war. The kind of building that's survived eighty years and will survive eighty more.

Ethan rings apartment 3B. Buzzer sounds. He climbs stairs. Third floor. Door opens before he knocks.

Ahmed Khalil is younger than his photo suggested. Twenty-three but looks nineteen. Thin. Nervous energy. The face of someone who's seen things and can't unsee them.

"You're Ethan. Chen said you'd come."

"Yeah. Can I come in?"

"Sure. Sorry. Yes."

The apartment is small. Studio. Generic furniture. The space of someone who's starting over with nothing. Through the window, Manhattan skyline. The view is spectacular. The irony complete. ISIS fighter in New Jersey apartment overlooking city he once wanted to destroy.

"Chen says you want to talk. About my choice. About cooperation."

"If you're willing."

Ahmed sits on the couch. Gestures for Ethan to take the chair. The hospitality of someone trying to build normal life out of abnormal circumstances.

"What do you want to know?"

"Why you joined ISIS. Why you left. Why you cooperated with Chen."

"That's three different questions. Three different answers. Or maybe same answer three times. I don't know." Ahmed looks out window. At Manhattan. "I joined because I was angry. Because America invaded Iraq. Because Muslims were dying. Because I believed propaganda about Caliphate. About building Islamic state. About restoring glory. I was eighteen. Stupid. Angry. I joined."

"What was it like?"

"Hell. Absolute hell. Not paradise. Not Islamic state. Just brutality wearing religious mask. Executions. Slavery. Rape. Torture. Everything I thought I was fighting against, ISIS was doing. Everything I believed about Islam, they perverted. I realized—maybe six months in—that I'd made terrible mistake. But by then I was trapped. Couldn't leave. They kill deserters. Couldn't come home. America would arrest me. I was stuck."

"How did Chen find you?"

"I didn't. He found me. Or his people found me. Iraqi contacts. People who monitor ISIS. People who look for defectors. They reached out. Said there might be path back. Amnesty for cooperation. Protection for intelligence. I didn't believe them at first. Thought it was trap. But I was desperate. So desperate. I took the chance."

"What did Chen want?"

"Intelligence. About ISIS. About networks. About people I knew. About operations. But also—" Ahmed pauses. "Also access to Iraqi community in America. To Iranian community. To places where I had connections. Family connections. Cultural connections. He wanted me to maintain relationships. Talk to people. Report conversations. Facilitate his access to communities he couldn't reach directly."

"And you did it."

"What choice did I have? Go to prison for life? Get sent to Guantanamo? Disappear into black site somewhere? Chen offered alternative. Cooperation for amnesty. Freedom for intelligence. I took the deal. I'm not proud of it. Not comfortable with it. But I took it because it's better than alternatives."

"Do you trust Chen?"

Ahmed laughs. Bitter sound. "No. I don't trust anyone. Not Chen. Not FBI. Not Iraqi community. Not Iranian community. Everyone wants something. Everyone has agenda. I cooperate because it's survival. Because it's only way to build life that isn't prison or death. But trust? No. Trust is luxury I can't afford."

"The Iranian operation. The assassination plot. Is it real?"

"The intelligence I provided is real. The conversations I reported are real. Whether that adds up to assassination plot—I don't know. I'm not analyst. I'm just source. I report what I see. What I hear. How Chen interprets it—that's not my problem. That's not my responsibility."

The honesty is refreshing. The clarity about his role. Ahmed's not trying to justify Chen's operation. Not defending the methodology. Just explaining his part in it.

"Do you think you're doing good? Preventing attacks? Saving lives?"

"I think I'm surviving. I think I made terrible choice joining ISIS and now I'm trying to make less terrible choices recovering from that. Whether that's good—" He shakes his head. "I don't know. Some days I think Chen's using me. Using my guilt. Using my desperation. Other days I think maybe I am helping. Maybe the intelligence I provide does stop attacks. Does save lives. I can't know for certain. I just survive day by day and try not to think too hard about larger implications."

"That's honest."

"That's realistic. You want to know if cooperation is worth it? If becoming informant is justified? I can't answer that. Can only tell you—it's better than alternatives I faced. It's survival. Whether it's moral, whether it's good, whether it's worth carrying—those are questions I can't answer. Those are questions you answer for yourself."

They sit in silence. The Manhattan skyline fills the window. The absurdity of the view from this particular apartment. ISIS fighter looking at city he once wanted to destroy while working as informant for same government he once fought against.

The complexity. The calculations that never work cleanly.

"Thank you," Ethan says. "For being honest. For not sugarcoating it."

"Chen tells stories about preventing attacks. About saving lives. About meaningful work. Maybe that's true. Maybe it's bullshit. I can't tell the difference anymore. I just cooperate because it's survival. You decide if that's enough. You decide if the work justifies the costs. But don't let Chen tell you it's noble. Don't let him tell you it's clean. It's not. It's just survival with better narrative."

Ethan leaves. Down the stairs. Out onto Boulevard East. The cold air. The view of Manhattan across the river.

Ahmed's honesty was gift. The clarity about what cooperation actually means. Not noble work. Not meaningful service. Just survival with complications. Just trading one trap for different trap. Just choosing which to carry.

His phone buzzes. Chen.

*Have you decided? —DC*

Ethan looks at Manhattan. At the city of eight million people. Seven of them targeted. Seven lives hanging on his decision.

He types: *Not yet. Need more time. —E*

*You have until tomorrow morning. Nine AM. After that, investigation proceeds without you. After that, Reza moves forward with operation. After that, whatever happens is on you. Choose wisely. —DC*

The ultimatum. The pressure. The forced calculation.

Ethan takes the bus back to Manhattan. To his hotel. To the small room overlooking the air shaft. To the space where he has to decide.

Cooperate with Chen. Become informant. Help stop assassination plot. Accept becoming asset.

Or refuse. Walk away. Let FBI handle it differently. Accept that seven people might die.

Two choices. Both crushing. Both impossible. Both real.

But this time the stakes are measured in lives he'll never meet. People targeted for assassination because they criticized regime. People who think they're safe in America. People whose lives depend on whether Ethan cooperates with operation he doesn't trust to stop plot he can't verify.

That's the calculation.

That's the balance when both good and harm are measured in ghosts you'll carry forever.

He sits in the small room. Staring at nothing. Thinking about everything.

Tomorrow morning. Nine AM. The choice.

Tonight he just carries the weight.

Tomorrow he decides.

# 13

— • —

## CHAPTER 13: 4 AM

*N*ew York City — *December 2015*
　　　　The decision comes at 4 AM.

Not from thinking. Not from calculation. Not from weighing options until one seems less terrible than the other.

It comes from his phone ringing. From a number he doesn't recognize. From a voice he hasn't heard in weeks.

"Ethan. It's Yousef."

The voice is wrong. Scared. Urgent.

"What's wrong?"

"They took her. They took my daughter. Layla. She didn't come home from school. My wife called. Called police. Called everyone. They can't find her. She's gone. Ethan—someone took my daughter."

The world stops. The calculation ends. The consequences multiply.

"When?"

"Three hours ago. School ended at three PM. She walks home with friends. Two blocks. She never arrived. We've looked everywhere. Police are involved but they think she ran away. They don't understand. She's eleven. She doesn't run away. Someone took her."

"Have you gotten any contact? Any demands?"

"No. Nothing. Just gone." Yousef's voice breaks. "Chen did this. I know it. This is pressure. This is leverage. This is him making me cooperate. Making you cooperate. He took my daughter to force the decision."

"You don't know that."

"I know. I know how this works. You taught me. You showed me. Intelligence agencies use family. Use leverage. Use whatever pressure works. Chen needs cooperation. Needs you. Needs me. So he took Layla. So he's holding her until we comply."

The logic is sound. The methodology is classic. Take what matters most. Create immediate urgency. Force decision. That's recruitment 101. That's how intelligence services operate when subtle approaches fail.

But would Chen do this? Would FBI allow it? Would American intelligence service kidnap eleven-year-old girl to pressure cooperation?

Maybe. In gray area where authorities blur. Where operational necessity justifies methods. Where 'the ends justify the means' becomes excuse for anything.

"I'm calling Chen," Ethan says. "I'm finding out if this is him. If it is, I'm getting her back. I promise you—I'm getting her back."

"Hurry. Please. My wife—she's—" Yousef can't finish. Just breaks. The sound of parent whose child is missing. The sound of everything collapsing.

Ethan hangs up. Calls Chen immediately. The phone rings. Once. Twice. Chen answers.

"It's four AM, Ethan."

"Did you take Yousef's daughter?"

Silence on the line. Long silence. Then: "What?"

"Layla. Yousef's daughter. Eleven years old. Didn't come home from school. Missing for three hours. Rochester police think she ran away. Yousef thinks you took her. Did you?"

"No. Jesus Christ, no. I don't kidnap children. I don't—" Chen stops. Silence. "She's really missing?"

"Since three PM. No contact. No demands. Just gone."

More silence. Then Chen's voice, different now. Harder. "This isn't me. This isn't FBI. This isn't any American operation. We don't take children. We don't—" He stops again. "Reza. This is Reza."

"What?"

"The Iranian operation. The assassination plot. It's accelerated. Moved up timeline. They're not waiting until January. They're moving now. And Layla isn't random target. She's pressure. Leverage against Yousef. Against you. Against the investigation."

"How would Reza know about Yousef? About the investigation?"

"Because we have leak. Because someone inside the operation told him. Because—" Chen goes quiet. Processing. "Kamal. Kamal's in New York. Kamal warned Reza. Told him about the investigation. About FBI surveillance. About everything. And Reza responded by taking Layla. By creating leverage of his own."

The pieces connect. Kamal protecting his cousin. Warning him about FBI investigation. Giving him operational intelligence. And Reza responding by going offensive. By taking hostage. By creating pressure that forces shutdown of investigation.

"You're sure?" Ethan asks.

"I'm not sure of anything at four AM with missing child. But the timing is suspicious. The target is specific. This isn't random. This is operational response to our investigation. This is Iranian intelligence pushing back."

"What do we do?"

"You make decision. Right now. No more delays. No more thinking. Cooperate or walk away. Because if you cooperate, I use every resource to find Layla. FBI, CIA, every asset we have. We find her. We get her back. That's what cooperation means. That's what partnership provides. But if you walk away—if you refuse—then you're on your own. Yousef's on his own. Layla's fate is whatever it is. Choose now."

The ultimatum. The leverage. The forced decision at four AM with child's life hanging.

But it's also clarity. No more moral ambiguity. No more weighing abstract goods against abstract harms. Just concrete reality. Girl is missing. Help find her or don't. That's the choice.

"I'm in," Ethan says. "I cooperate. I help. Whatever you need. Just find her. Get her back."

"Get to the Varick Street office. One hour. We're activating everything. FBI, NYPD, every resource. You're part of team now. You're in. No walking away. No changing mind. You understand?"

"I understand. One hour."

Ethan dresses fast. Leaves hotel. The city is different at 4:30 AM. Emptier. Quieter. The space between late night and early morning where the city breathes.

He takes taxi to Varick Street. Expensive at this hour but fast. The driver doesn't talk. Doesn't ask questions. Just drives.

At the building, security is ready. They're expecting him. Buzz him through. Elevator to eighteen. The office is lit. Active. Multiple people. Screens glowing. The energy of operation launching.

Chen is there. Morrison. Romano. Three other agents. Everyone moving with purpose. Making calls. Checking databases. Building operational picture.

"Ethan. Good. You're here." Chen hands him coffee. "Layla al-Tikriti. Eleven years old. Disappeared from Rochester at approximately 3 PM yesterday. Last seen leaving school. Should have arrived home by 3:15. Never arrived. Mother called police at 4:30. Rochester PD treating as runaway. We know better."

Morrison pulls up photo on screen. Layla. School picture. Smiling. Dark hair. Dark eyes. The face of child who should be worried about homework and friends, not intelligence operations and leverage.

"What do we know?" Ethan asks.

"Not much. No witnesses to abduction. No security footage. No contact from abductors. No demands. Just missing child and timing that's too coincidental." Morrison types. Shows map. Rochester. Yousef's neighborhood marked. "We're reviewing traffic cameras. Looking for vehicles. Checking known Iranian intelligence assets in upstate New York. It's long shot but it's what we have."

"How did Reza know about Yousef? About his connection to the investigation?"

"Kamal," Chen says. "Has to be. Kamal warned his cousin. Told him FBI was closing in. Told him about our sources. About our access. Reza responded by going after our source's family. Creating leverage. Forcing shutdown of investigation."

"Where's Kamal now?"

"We don't know. He left the apartment in Hell's Kitchen. Disappeared. Could be anywhere in the city. Could be gone. But he set this in motion. He warned Reza. He created situation where taking Layla seemed like good operational response."

Romano speaks up. "FBI's issuing BOLO. Be On Lookout. Every law enforcement agency in tristate area. Looking for girl, looking for vehicles, looking for known Iranian intelligence assets. We're also pressuring Iranian Interests Section. Making it clear—if Reza took this girl, if Iran is involved, there will be consequences. Diplomatic consequences. Political consequences. We're applying every available pressure point."

"Will that work?" Ethan asks.

"Depends on whether Iran wants escalation. Whether they're willing to trade diplomatic incident for operational advantage. Whether they care about American political pressure." Morrison shakes her head. "Honestly? Probably not. If Reza took the girl, he did it with approval from Tehran. Or he went rogue and Tehran will disavow him. Either way, diplomatic pressure is slow. We need operational response. We need to find her."

"How?"

Chen walks to different screen. Shows organizational chart. Reza's network. Dozens of names. Dozens of connections.

"We hit every asset. Every contact. Every person in Reza's network. We question them. We pressure them. We make it clear—help us find the girl or face consequences. We activate every source. Use every relationship. Apply maximum pressure until someone breaks. Until someone talks. Until we find her."

"That could take days. She could be anywhere. Could be hurt. Could be—"

"Could be dead already," Chen finishes. "Yes. That's possible. But it's also possible she's alive and being held. Possibly as leverage. Possibly as insurance. We find out which by acting fast. By using every resource. By doing what needs doing."

The methodology is brutal. The logic sound. Maximum pressure applied quickly. Force someone to break. Force someone to give up location. It's how intelligence operations work when time matters more than finesse.

"What do you need from me?" Ethan asks.

"Access to Iraqi community. To Iranian community. To networks where we don't have trust. You helped interpreter escape CIA. That story makes you sympathetic. Makes you trusted. Use that. Talk to people. Ask questions. Find out if anyone's heard anything. Seen anything. Knows anything. You're not federal agent. You're not threatening. You're just guy trying to help friend find missing daughter. That's access we don't have."

"Where do I start?"

Morrison writes address. Hands it to Ethan. "Iranian cultural center. Queens. Opens at 8 AM. Director is Mahmoud Sadeghi. Iranian American. Community leader. Not MOIS as far as we know. But he knows everyone. Sees everything. Hears everything. Talk to him. Feel him out. See if he knows anything."

"What do I say?"

"The truth. Friend's daughter is missing. You're trying to help. You're asking if he's heard anything. Seen anything. Keep it simple. Keep it honest. Don't mention FBI. Don't mention investigation. Just concerned friend looking for missing child. That's all."

Ethan takes the address. Looks at the photo of Layla on the screen. The smiling face. The child whose life depends on decisions made in rooms like this. On calculations about pressure and leverage and operational responses.

"I'll find her," Ethan says. "Whatever it takes. I'll find her."

Chen nods. "I believe you. That's why you're here. That's why you're in. Because you don't calculate coldly. Because you care too much. Because you'll do whatever it takes when it's personal. That's what makes you valuable. That's what makes you operational asset."

The classification. The formal acknowledgment. Ethan's not consultant anymore. Not helping friend anymore. He's asset. He's in. He's part of the operation.

The weight settles. Different weight. Heavier weight. The weight of being inside the machine instead of watching from outside.

At 6 AM Ethan leaves the office. The city is waking up. Early risers. Morning shift workers. The world continuing while eleven-year-old girl is missing and intelligence services scramble to find her.

He takes subway to Queens. Forty minutes. Crowded train. He stands holding rail. Surrounded by strangers going to normal jobs. Living normal lives. Not knowing about secret wars playing out in their city.

At 7:45 he arrives at the cultural center. Small building. Community space. Signs in Farsi and English. The infrastructure of diaspora life. The place where Iranians gather. Where they maintain culture. Where they help each other navigate American life while staying connected to homeland.

The director arrives at 7:55. Older man. Sixties. Gray hair. Kind face. The look of community leader who's spent decades building bridges.

"Can I help you?" he asks in accented English.

"My name is Ethan Caldwell. I'm looking for information about missing child. Girl named Layla al-Tikriti. Eleven years old. Disappeared yesterday in Rochester. Her father is Iraqi. Her mother is Iraqi. But they have connections to Iranian community. I'm hoping someone might have heard something. Seen something. Anything that could help."

Mahmoud studies Ethan's face. Evaluating. Deciding whether to trust.

"Come inside. We'll talk."

The interior is simple. Community room. Library. Kitchen. The functional space where community maintains itself. Mahmoud makes chai. They sit.

"This girl. Layla. Why are you looking for her? Are you family?"

"I'm friend of her father. He helped me in Iraq. Now his daughter is missing. I'm trying to help him find her."

"And you think Iranian community is involved?"

"I don't know. I'm asking everyone who might know something. Iranian community. Iraqi community. Anyone who might have heard anything."

Mahmoud drinks chai. Thinking.

"There are rumors. In community. About American government pressure on Iran. About investigations. About people being questioned. People are nervous. Scared. Some think FBI is targeting community. Others think Iranian government is watching. Monitoring. Everyone's careful about what they say. Who they talk to."

"Have you heard about missing children? About anyone taking children?"

"No. Nothing like that. But—" He pauses. "There are people in community who are more than community members. Who work for Tehran. Who monitor dissidents. Who report on activities. Everyone knows this. No one talks about it. But it's real. If child was taken—if this is political—then those people might know. Might be involved."

"Can you give me names?"

"No. Too dangerous. I have family. I have community to protect. If Tehran thinks I'm cooperating with Americans, there are consequences. Not just for me. For everyone I know."

The fear is real. The caution justified. Iranian intelligence has long reach. Targets dissidents. Punishes cooperation. Mahmoud's right to be careful.

"I understand," Ethan says. "But this is eleven-year-old girl. Child who has nothing to do with politics. Nothing to do with intelligence operations. Just child whose father helped Americans and now she's missing. If you know anything—if you can help—please."

Mahmoud sits in silence. Wrestling with decision. Community loyalty versus helping child. Self-preservation versus doing right thing.

Finally: "There is man. Kasra Ahmadi. He works at import/export business. But everyone knows he's more than businessman. He has connections. Access. Information. If anyone in community knows about missing children, it's him. But approaching him is dangerous. He reports everything to Tehran. Talking to him means your conversation gets monitored. Gets analyzed. Gets used."

"Where do I find him?"

"His office is in Brooklyn. Sunset Park. I'll write address. But be careful. Very careful. He's not community member. He's operator. He's dangerous."

Mahmoud writes address. Hands it to Ethan. They finish chai in silence.

Outside, Ethan texts Chen: *Got lead. Kasra Ahmadi. Import/export. Brooklyn. Possible MOIS asset. Worth investigating? —E*

Response comes immediately: *We know Ahmadi. He's on watch list. Suspected MOIS. Never had evidence to act. If he's involved with Layla, that changes things. Do NOT approach him alone. Wait for backup. Sending Romano to meet you. —DC*

Outside the cultural center, Ethan's phone rings. Yousef.

"Ethan. I have something. Maybe nothing. But something."

"Tell me."

"I've been calling people. Iraqi community. People I know from Baghdad. From refugee resettlement. People Chen had me contact when I was working for him." Yousef's voice is steadier now. Focused. "One of them—Tariq—he works at import/export business in Brooklyn. Sunset Park. He said there's been unusual activity. Iranian men coming and going. Meetings in back office. He didn't think much of it until I asked about Layla. Then he remembered—yesterday afternoon, a van. Dark green. Pennsylvania plates. Parked behind the building for two hours. When it left, there were blankets in the back. The kind you'd use to cover something. Or someone."

Ethan's pulse quickens. "Did he get the plate number?"

"Partial. He texted me a photo. The van. The building. Everything he could see from his shop across the street." Pause. "Ethan, the building—it's owned by man named Kasra Ahmadi. Tariq says everyone knows he's more than businessman. That he has connections. That Iranian intelligence uses his building for meetings."

"Send me everything. Address. Photos. All of it."

"Sending now. But Ethan—Tariq is scared. He doesn't want to be involved. Doesn't want Iranian intelligence knowing he talked. He has family in Iran. They'll use them as leverage if they find out."

"He won't be involved. This is anonymous tip. Nobody knows where it came from."

"Thank you. For protecting him. For—" Yousef's voice cracks. "For finding my daughter. I know you're risking everything. I know—"

"I'm not losing her. We're getting her back. I promise."

Yousef sends the information. Address. Photos. The van. The building. Everything Tariq documented.

Ethan forwards it to Chen. Then texts: *Lead from Iraqi community source. Building in Brooklyn. Possible MOIS connection. Checking it out. —E*

Chen responds immediately: *Do NOT approach alone. Wait for backup. That's direct order. Ahmadi's dangerous. —DC*

Ethan checks time. 9:17 AM. Layla's been missing eighteen hours. She doesn't have time for careful approaches and tactical planning. She needs someone acting now. Every hour decreases chances. Every delay risks worse outcome. Waiting for backup means more time. More time means more danger.

He gets on subway to Brooklyn. Moving toward the address. Toward Kasra Ahmadi. Toward whatever answers the man has.

His phone rings. Romano.

"Chen says you got lead. Ahmadi. I'm en route to Brooklyn. Don't approach without me. That's order. Ahmadi's dangerous. Trained intelligence officer. You approach alone, you're at risk."

"How long until you arrive?"

"Forty minutes. Traffic's heavy. Just wait. We'll go in together."

"Layla doesn't have forty minutes. She doesn't have time for careful approach. She needs action now."

"And you'll help her better by getting yourself killed? By alerting Ahmadi that we're onto him? By spooking potential source? Wait. For. Backup."

Romano hangs up.

Ethan sits on subway watching stations pass. Brooklyn approaching. The address getting closer. The choice getting clearer.

Wait for backup. Follow protocol. Approach carefully. That's professional. That's smart. That's how operations run.

Or go now. Risk contact. Push for immediate answers. That's dangerous. That's stupid. That's how operations fail.

But it's also how sometimes you get results. When time matters more than method. When eleven-year-old girl's life matters more than operational protocols.

The subway reaches Sunset Park. Ethan gets off. Checks address Mahmoud gave him. Three blocks.

His phone rings again. Chen.

"Romano says you're not waiting. Says you're going to approach Ahmadi alone. Don't. That's direct order. Wait for backup. Wait for professional approach."

"How long has Layla been missing?"

"Eighteen hours."

"How long before we assume worst case? Before we assume she's dead?"

"Twenty-four hours is statistical cliff. After that, outcomes get significantly worse."

"So we have six hours. Six hours before odds shift dramatically. You want me to wait forty minutes for backup? To spend another hour on careful approach? To use protocols that waste time we don't have?"

"I want you to stay alive. I want you to not compromise investigation by alerting Ahmadi. I want you to—"

Ethan hangs up. Turns off the phone. Continues walking.

Three blocks. Import/export business. Ahmadi's office.

This is the calculation, the balancing.

This is that moment.

This is where Ethan decides whether operational protocols matter more than eleven-year-old girl.

He reaches the address. Industrial building. Loading docks. The legitimate business front for intelligence operations.

He goes inside.

The reception is empty. Nobody at desk. He walks further. Down hallway. Toward voices. Toward office at end.

The door is open. Inside, two men. One is older. Fifties. Hard face. The look of someone who's done bad things and made peace with it. That's Ahmadi probably. The other is younger. Thirties. Nervous. Talking fast in Farsi.

Ethan knocks. They stop talking. Turn. Look at him.

"Can I help you?" Ahmadi asks. Accented English. Careful pronunciation.

"My name is Ethan Caldwell. I'm looking for missing girl. Layla al-Tikriti. I think you might know where she is."

The reaction is immediate. The younger man goes pale. Ahmadi's face hardens.

"I don't know what you're talking about. You should leave."

"She's eleven years old. She didn't come home from school yesterday. Her father is my friend. I'm trying to find her. If you know anything—if you can help—please."

"You're American intelligence. FBI probably. This is harassment. This is targeting Iranian community. I have rights. I have lawyer. Leave now or I call police."

"I'm not FBI. I'm just man trying to help friend. Trying to find missing child. That's all."

Ahmadi stands. Walks toward Ethan. The posture is threatening. Professional threatening. The movement of someone trained.

"You need to leave. Now. This conversation is over."

Then the younger man speaks. Rapid Farsi. Urgent. Panicked. Ahmadi turns. Snaps response. The younger man argues back.

Ethan doesn't speak Farsi but the tone is clear. Disagreement. Fear. The younger man is nervous about something. About Layla probably. About being involved.

Ahmadi makes decision. Turns back to Ethan.

"You want to find the girl? You want answers? Then you need to make trade. Information for information. You tell me what FBI knows about our operations. What surveillance they're running. What investigation they're building. Then maybe—maybe—I tell you something useful."

"I don't have that information."

"You're working with them. Chen. Morrison. Romano. You're their asset. You have access. You know things. So make choice. Information trade or leave empty-handed. That's offer."

The leverage play. The counter-operation. Ahmadi's doing what intelligence officers do. Using situation to gather intelligence of his own. Using Layla as leverage to extract information about FBI investigation.

This is the moment. The decision. The calculation.

Trade information about investigation to potentially save Layla. Compromise operation to save life. That's the call.

But it's also betrayal. It's compromising active investigation. It's giving Iranian intelligence operational details they can use. That's cost. Real cost. Cost measured in future operations compromised. Future sources endangered.

Except this time the stakes are immediate. This time the calculation is simple. Trade information or walk away from child who might be savable.

Ethan makes the choice.

"What do you want to know?"

# 14

## CHAPTER 14: THE TRADE

*Brooklyn, New York — December 2015*

*B*rooklyn, New York — December 2015
Ahmadi closes the office door. Locks it. The click is loud in the small space. The younger man looks at Ethan with fear and something else. Guilt maybe. Knowledge of something he shouldn't know.

"Sit," Ahmadi says. Not request. Command.

Ethan sits. The chair is plastic. Uncomfortable. The office is sparse. Desk, filing cabinets, computer that looks ten years old. The minimal infrastructure of front operation.

Ahmadi remains standing. Controlling the space. The dynamics. "You want information about the girl. I want information about FBI investigation. Fair trade. Both sides get something. Both sides give something. That's how intelligence work functions."

"I'm not intelligence officer. I'm just trying to help friend."

"You're working with Chen. With Morrison. With FBI counterintelligence. That makes you asset. That gives you access to information I need. So stop pretending you're innocent civilian. You're operational. We both know it."

The younger man speaks. English this time. "Please. This is wrong. The girl is just child. She has nothing to do with—"

"Quiet," Ahmadi snaps. "You've said enough already." He looks at Ethan. "My associate here has conscience. Has doubts. That's weakness in our business. But it's useful weakness right now because it means you'll get what you want. If you give me what I need."

"What do you want to know?"

"Everything. What FBI knows about Reza Hosseini. What evidence they have. What surveillance they're running. What sources they're using. What their timeline is for moving against him. Everything."

The request is comprehensive. Operational intelligence that would compromise entire investigation. That would expose sources. That would give Reza—and through him Tehran—complete picture of FBI activities.

Giving that information means betraying Chen. Betraying Morrison. Betraying everyone working to stop Iranian intelligence operations in New York. It means compromising years of work. It means endangering sources. It means potentially allowing assassination plot to succeed.

But it might mean finding Layla. Might mean saving eleven-year-old girl. Might mean preventing worst outcome.

Intelligence operation versus child's life. National security versus individual existence.

"If I tell you what you want to know, you'll tell me where Layla is?"

"If I know where she is, yes. But understand—I don't control everything. I'm not holding her. I'm not involved directly. But I might know who is. Might know where. Might be able to facilitate exchange. Information for location. That's the trade."

"How do I know you're telling truth? How do I know you'll honor the deal?"

Ahmadi smiles. Cold smile. "You don't. You trust or you don't. You trade or you walk away. But understand—walking away means girl stays missing. Means you tried nothing. Means you protected FBI investigation at expense of child's life. Can you live with that?"

The manipulation is obvious. The pressure is effective. Ahmadi's good at this. Years of experience. Decades probably. He knows how to find pressure points. How to exploit them. How to force decisions people don't want to make.

Ethan thinks about the grain field. About the calculation he made that got someone killed but saved the village. About when the math doesn't work cleanly.

This is that calculation again. Trade intelligence to save life. Compromise operation to prevent worst outcome. Accept that both choices have costs. Both choices create consequences. Neither choice is clean.

"FBI knows about Reza's assassination plot," Ethan starts. "Seven Iranian dissidents. American residents. Targeted for elimination. Timeline moved up from January to now. Maybe because of investigation. Maybe because something changed."

Ahmadi listens. Absorbing. Processing. The younger man looks horrified but stays quiet.

"FBI has intercepts. Communications. Planning documents. They know targets. Know methods. Know timeline. Approximately two months was original schedule. Now it's accelerated. They're preparing to arrest Reza. To disrupt the operation. To prevent assassinations."

"What evidence do they have?"

"Surveillance. Phone intercepts. Financial tracking. Source reporting from inside Iranian community. Someone with access to Reza's network. Someone providing real-time intelligence."

"Who?"

That's the line. The question that crosses from general information to specific betrayal. Naming sources means exposing them. Means potential death sentences. Means consequences Ethan can't take back.

"I don't know names. Compartmented. Chen doesn't share that level of detail."

Ahmadi studies Ethan's face. Evaluating truth. "You're lying. You know more than you're saying. But we'll come back to that. Tell me about surveillance. What methods? What locations?"

Ethan continues. Describing the surveillance operation. The technical methods. The locations being monitored. The cultural centers. The businesses. The networks being mapped. Everything he learned in the Varick Street briefings.

With every word, he feels the pressure increasing. The betrayal deepening. Chen trusted him. Morrison trusted him. They brought him in. Showed him classified information. Made him part of the team. And he's repaying that by trading operational details to Iranian intelligence officer.

But Layla is missing. Eleven years old. Somewhere in this city. Scared probably. Maybe hurt. Maybe worse. And this trade might be only way to find her.

Slightly more good than harm. The calculation that justifies anything if you're desperate enough.

After twenty minutes, Ahmadi holds up hand. "Enough. You've given me useful information. Some I knew. Some I didn't. Now I'll give you something. The girl—Layla—she's not in New York."

The statement hits like punch. "What?"

"She was taken in Rochester. She's still in Rochester. Or near it. Somewhere upstate. The operation isn't mine. Isn't Reza's directly. It's separate cell. Different handlers. Different objectives. But I know who runs it. I can make contact. I can facilitate communication."

"Do it. Now."

"Not yet. First, more information. You said FBI has source inside Reza's network. Someone providing intelligence. I need to know who. That's not optional. That's requirement for me making the call that gets you to the girl."

The ultimatum. The deepest betrayal. Naming sources means their death probably. Means families destroyed. Means everything intelligence work tries to protect.

But saving Layla means everything to Yousef. Means everything to mother whose daughter is missing. Means something real and immediate versus abstract future consequences.

"Ahmed Khalil," Ethan says. "ISIS defector. He provided access to Iraqi community. To Iranian community. Through family connections. Through cultural relationships. He's the source."

The younger man gasps. Ahmadi nods slowly. "The ISIS defector. Of course. Chen's been running him for months. Using him for terrorism intelligence. But also using him for Iranian access. Clever. Using extremist to infiltrate exile community. Very American solution."

"I gave you what you want. Now make the call."

Ahmadi pulls out phone. Not smartphone. Old flip phone. Burner probably. He dials. Speaks in Farsi. Brief conversation. Tense. The younger man watches nervously.

Ahmadi hangs up. "The girl is alive. She's being held at location in Finger Lakes region. About ninety minutes from Rochester. Cabin on lake. I'll give you address. But understand—going there means confrontation. Means people with guns. Means dangerous situation. You want FBI involved? Or you want to handle this differently?"

"I want location. I'll decide what to do with it."

"Smart. FBI involvement means complications. Means questions about how you got information. Means exposure of my role. Means problems for everyone. Better you handle quietly. Extract girl. Return her to family. Everyone walks away. Nobody asks questions."

Ahmadi writes address on paper. Hands it to Ethan. "Cabin 47. Otisco Lake. South shore. Three men holding her. Armed. Professional. They're not going to just give her back. You'll need leverage. You'll need force. You'll need plan."

Ethan takes the paper. Looks at address. "Why are they holding her? What do they want?"

"Leverage against FBI investigation. Pressure to stop. Message that Iranian intelligence can reach anyone anywhere. Take that message to your handlers. Tell them—stop investigating Reza or next time it's not just Kurdish girl. Next time it's FBI agent's child. Next time it's something worse."

The threat is clear. The escalation is explicit. Iranian intelligence pushing back against FBI pressure. Using kidnapping as counter-operation. This is intelligence war playing out through civilian casualties.

Ethan stands. Moves toward door.

The younger man speaks. "Wait. I'm sorry. About the girl. About all of this. I didn't want—they made me—I'm not—" He stops. Breaks down. The gravity of participating in something he knows is wrong.

"What's your name?" Ethan asks.

"Dariush. My name is Dariush. I work for Kasra. I do what he tells me. But I have daughter too. Same age as Layla. I can't—I couldn't—" He looks at Ahmadi. "Tell him the rest. Tell him what they're planning."

Ahmadi's face goes hard. "Shut up."

"No. He traded information. He deserves truth. They're going to kill the girl anyway. After FBI backs off. After message is sent. They're going to kill her and make it look like accident. She's dead girl no matter what. They're just using her for leverage first."

The revelation hangs in the air. Layla is dead already. Not yet physically but operationally. Her death is planned. Expected. Inevitable. The kidnapping isn't for ransom. It's temporary use of asset before disposal.

"Is that true?" Ethan asks Ahmadi.

"Get out. Now. Before I change my mind about giving you address."

Ethan leaves. Down hallway. Out of building. Into Brooklyn morning. Cold air. Clear sky. The normal world continuing while he carries knowledge of child marked for death.

He turns phone back on. Immediately it buzzes. Multiple texts from Chen. Multiple calls from Romano. Everyone angry that he went in without backup. Everyone demanding contact.

He calls Chen.

"Where the hell have you been? Do you understand how dangerous—"

"I have location. Layla is alive. Being held upstate. Finger Lakes. Otisco Lake. Cabin 47. Three armed men. Professional operation."

Silence on line. Then: "How did you get this information?"

"I made trade."

"What kind of trade?"

"The kind I can't take back. The kind that compromises investigation. The kind that probably got sources killed." Ethan keeps walking. Away from Ahmadi's office. Away from the scene of betrayal. "But I have location. I know where she is. We can get her back."

"What did you trade? Exactly?"

"Everything. Surveillance methods. Investigation timeline. Sources. I gave Ahmadi everything he wanted. In exchange for location and contact that led to the girl."

More silence. Longer this time. Then Chen's voice, different now. Harder. "You just compromised eighteen months of work. You exposed sources. You gave Iranian intelligence complete operational picture. You—" He stops. Breathes. "But you got location. You found the girl. That's—I don't know if that's acceptable trade or catastrophic error. Probably both."

"She's going to die anyway. The kidnapping isn't for leverage. It's temporary use before disposal. They're planning to kill her even if FBI backs off. So we need to move now. Need to extract before that happens."

"How do you know this?"

"Inside source. Guy in Ahmadi's office. Dariush. He broke protocol. Told me the truth. He's risk now. Ahmadi will probably kill him for talking."

"Jesus." Chen exhales. "Okay. We're activating tactical team. FBI HRT. Best extraction team we have. They'll be at Otisco Lake in three hours. You're not going. You're staying here. You've done enough. You've compromised enough. Leave this to professionals."

"I'm going. I found her. I'm part of extraction. That's not negotiable."

"You're not trained. You're not equipped. You're liability in tactical situation."

"I'm going anyway. You can bring me or I'll go alone. But I'm going."

Silence. Chen calculating. Then: "Fine. You come. But you follow orders. You stay behind tactical team. You don't engage. You don't make decisions. You're observer. Understand?"

"Understood."

"Get back to Varick Street. We're launching in forty-five minutes. Helicopter to Otisco Lake. Full tactical package. We're getting her back. And then—then we deal with consequences of what you traded to make this happen."

***

The helicopter ride is ninety minutes. FBI HRT team. Six operators in full tactical gear. Chen. Romano. Morrison. Ethan. Flying low over upstate New York. The landscape below transitioning from city to suburbs to rural. The Finger Lakes region spreading out. Gray water. Bare trees. November emptiness.

Morrison briefs the team. Cabin 47. South shore of Otisco Lake. Three hostiles. Armed. Professional. One hostage. Eleven-year-old girl. Extraction objective. Minimize casualties. No heroics.

The plan is simple. Fast insertion. Overwhelming force. Secure perimeter. Breach structure. Extract hostage. Neutralize threats if necessary. Standard tactical operation executed by people who've done this hundreds of times.

The helicopter lands in Rochester. Not at the airport. At a secure facility on the outskirts. FBI field office. Private landing pad. The kind of place where operations conclude away from public eyes.

As the helicopter settles, Ethan sees figures waiting on the tarmac. Chen. Morrison. Local FBI personnel.

And Yousef.

He's standing apart from the agents. Wrapped in borrowed jacket. Looking small and desperate and hopeful. When he sees the helicopter, sees Layla through the window, his knees nearly buckle.

The helicopter door opens. Medical personnel move first. Checking Layla. Vitals. Assessment. Making sure she's stable. She's dehydrated. Scared. But alive. Whole.

"Daddy?" Her voice is small.

Yousef breaks. Runs forward. "Layla. Habibi. I'm here. You're safe."

The agents step aside. Let him through. This isn't their moment. This is father and daughter. This is the reason for everything.

Yousef reaches her. Grabs her. Holds her like he'll never let go. Crying. Saying her name over and over. Saying words in Arabic—prayers, thanks, promises.

Layla holds him back. Crying too. The relief. The terror releasing. The nightmare ending.

Ethan watches from the helicopter. The reunion makes everything feel worth it. Makes the information trade feel justified. Makes the compromised operation feel like acceptable cost.

One girl saved. One father reunited with daughter. One family not destroyed.

That's the good. The harm comes later. Always does. But right now, this moment, it's just good.

Yousef looks up. Finds Ethan through the crowd. Mouths *thank you* silently. The gratitude too big for words. The debt impossible to repay.

Ethan nods. Turns away. Gets back in helicopter. Leaving them to their reunion. Leaving them to rebuild. Leaving them to the work of recovering from trauma.

Chen appears at the helicopter door. "Good work. Extraction was clean. Hostage is safe. Mission accomplished."

"What happens now? To Yousef? To Layla? Are they safe? Is Reza—"

"Reza's network is compromised now. We'll increase protection on Yousef's family. Surveillance. Security protocols. He's no longer an asset—he's a protected witness in ongoing counterintelligence investigation. That comes with resources. Support. Safety measures." Chen pauses. "They'll be okay. Not immediately. Trauma takes time. But they'll recover. They'll rebuild. That's what people do. That's why the work matters."

They drive to staging area. Half mile from cabin. The team moves on foot from there. Through woods. Cold. Quiet. The forest empty except for them.

Ethan stays with Chen and Romano. Behind the tactical team. Watching through trees as operators position themselves. Surrounding the cabin. Establishing fields of fire. Getting ready.

The cabin is small. One story. Wood construction. Dock behind it extending into lake. Two vehicles parked outside. Lights on inside. Smoke from chimney. People home. Unaware of what's coming.

Team leader signals. Three fingers. Countdown.

Three. Two. One.

Flashbang through window. Explosive sound. Blinding light. Door breach. Operators flowing inside. Shouting. Commands. "FBI! Down! Down! Down!"

Gunfire. Three shots. Quick succession. Then silence.

More shouting. "Clear! Clear! Target secure! Hostage located!"

Thirty seconds. Start to finish. Professional extraction. Clean operation.

Chen moves forward. Romano and Ethan follow. Into the cabin. Interior is chaos. Flashbang debris. Broken glass. Three men on floor. Zip-tied. Faces down. One has blood on leg. Wounded but alive.

And in the back room. Layla. Tied to chair. Blindfolded. Crying. Alive.

Operator removes blindfold. Removes restraints. Gentle hands. Professional comfort. "You're safe. You're okay. We're FBI. We're getting you out."

Layla looks confused. Terrified. Then sees Ethan. Doesn't know him but recognizes him as not-captor. Something safe. She reaches toward him.

Ethan moves forward. Kneels. "Your dad sent me. Yousef. Your dad. He sent me to find you. You're safe now. You're going home."

She breaks. Crying. Grabbing him. The release of terror held for twenty-four hours. The relief of being found. Of being saved. Of nightmare ending.

Morrison makes call. "Package secure. Hostage alive. Three suspects in custody. Extraction successful. ETA to Rochester ninety minutes."

The operation is over. Layla is safe. The hostage situation resolved. By standard metrics, this is success. This is victory. This is the outcome everyone wanted.

But Ethan knows the cost. Knows what he traded. Knows Ahmed Khalil is probably dead already. Knows Iranian intelligence now has complete picture of FBI investigation. Knows Reza will adjust. Will go deeper underground. Will be harder to catch. Will potentially succeed with assassination plot because FBI's advantage is compromised.

One life saved. Seven lives potentially lost. That's the trade. That's the calculation. That's best choice you can make, regardless, when you have to choose between concrete suffering and abstract future consequences.

The helicopter ride back is quieter. Layla wrapped in blanket. Medic checking her. No serious injuries. Dehydrated. Scared. But alive. Whole. Savable.

She looks at Ethan.

"You came," she says in English. Careful, practiced words.

From her jacket she pulls folded paper. Crayon drawing. Stick figure with weapon. "THANK YOU MR ETHAN" in careful letters. A child's version of a soldier. Knight protecting her.

She hands it to him. "Keep safe."

Ethan folds it. Puts it in his jacket pocket. The weight of it—paper, nothing more—feels heavier than it should.

They land in Rochester. Ambulance waiting. But also Yousef. Running across tarmac. Not caring about security protocols. Just running toward daughter.

Layla sees him. Breaks free from medic. Runs. Father and daughter colliding. Grabbing each other. Crying. The reunion that makes everything else seem worth it. That justifies every cost. Every compromise. Every betrayal.

Yousef looks at Ethan over Layla's shoulder. Tears streaming. Mouths "thank you" silently. The gratitude that can't be expressed in words. The debt that can't be repaid.

Ethan nods. Turns away. Gets back in helicopter. Leaving Yousef and Layla to their reunion. To their recovery. To rebuilding life that was nearly destroyed.

Chen sits next to him as helicopter lifts off.

"What you did—the information trade—it was unauthorized. Reckless. Possibly criminal. You gave classified information to foreign intelligence officer. That's espionage. That's felony. That's prison time if we prosecute."

"I know."

"But you also found the girl. You saved her life. You did what needed doing when operational protocols would have taken too long. That's—" Chen pauses. "That's what operators do. Make impossible choices. Live with consequences. Accept that success has costs."

"So what happens now?"

"Now we deal with fallout. Ahmed Khalil is missing. Probably dead. Iranian intelligence is probably interrogating him right now. Getting everything he knows. Or he's already dead and they're cleaning up. Either way, we lost him. Lost our primary source into Iranian community."

"I'm sorry."

"Don't be sorry. Be responsible. You made the call. You live with consequences. That's how this works." Chen looks out window. At Rochester falling away below. "The Iranian operation—the assassination plot—it's compromised now. Reza knows we're onto him. Knows our methods. Knows our sources. He'll go deeper. Change tactics. Maybe succeed in killing those dissidents because we lost our advantage. That's on you. That cost is yours to carry."

"I know."

"But Layla's alive. Yousef has his daughter back. That's real. That's measurable. That's good. Whether it's more good than harm—we won't know for months. Maybe years. Maybe never. But you made the calculation. You accepted the cost. That makes you operational. That makes you one of us."

The classification. The acknowledgment. Ethan's not civilian anymore. Not lawyer playing at intelligence work. He's operator. He's made the call.

They fly back to New York. Landing at FBI facility in Queens. Debriefing. Questions. Reports. The administrative aftermath of tactical operation.

Morrison pulls Ethan aside. "Ahmadi. The man you met with. He's gone. Cleared out his office. Disappeared. Probably left country already. Diplomatic flight to Tehran via Canada maybe. Gone."

"What about Dariush? The younger guy. The one with conscience."

"Also gone. Ahmadi probably killed him. Probably disposed of body. Probably cleaning up loose ends. That's how intelligence services operate. You broke protocol. Talked too much. You get eliminated. That's the cost of conscience in this business."

Another cost. Another ghost. Another person dead because of choices made in desperate moment.

"How many?" Ethan asks.

"How many what?"

"How many people died because of the information I traded? Ahmed probably. Dariush probably. Who else? How many consequences haven't rippled out yet?"

Morrison looks at him. "I don't know. Can't know. Maybe just those two. Maybe more. Maybe operations we don't know about get compromised. Maybe sources we don't know about get exposed. Maybe families get destroyed. Maybe nobody else. Can't predict consequences. Can only make calls and live with whatever ripples forward."

Chen walks over. Sits across from Ethan in the debriefing room.

"One more thing. The FBI investigation. The surveillance on Yousef. The potential charges against both of you for interfering with federal operations. That's done. Closed. I made calls this morning. Explained operational circumstances. Your cooperation in Brooklyn—the information trade, the extraction assistance—that demonstrated good faith. Showed you're not hostile actor. You're asset who made hard call under pressure."

"So we're clear?"

"You're clear. Yousef's clear. Surveillance stops tomorrow. No prosecution. No charges. No administrative consequences. Clean slate." Chen leans back. "That's the trade. You helped me in Brooklyn. I clean up the legal mess. We're even on the extraction. Now we move forward on new terms. Professional terms. That's how this works."

Ethan processes this. The legal threat that's been hanging since Kurdistan—gone. Just like that. Because he became useful. Because he proved operational value. Because the machine rewards cooperation and punishes resistance.

"And if I hadn't cooperated? If I'd refused in Brooklyn?"

"Then FBI investigation proceeds. Holbrook builds your defense. Maybe you win. Maybe you don't. Either way, it's expensive, time-consuming, career-damaging. This is better. This is clean. This is how smart people resolve these situations."

The manipulation is explicit. The leverage is clear. But the result is real. Yousef is free. Ethan is clear. The FBI problem is solved.

"Thank you," Ethan says. Hating that he means it.

"Don't thank me. This is transaction. You provided value. I resolved problem. That's professional relationship. That's what contractors do. They solve each other's problems. That's what you are now. Contractor. Asset. Operator. Welcome to the life."

"That's supposed to be comforting?"

"That's supposed to be honest. Intelligence work creates ghosts. Creates debts. Creates consequences you can't see or control or undo. You accept that or you leave. Those are options."

Ethan sits in the debriefing room. Alone. Processing. Thinking about Ahmed. About Dariush. About choices made in Ahmadi's office. About the trade that saved one life and cost others.

The grain field. The first kill. Layla. The calculations that never work cleanly. The costs that ripple forever.

His phone rings. Unknown number.

"This is Ethan."

"It's Kamal. I heard about Layla. About the extraction. About what you traded. I wanted to say—you made right call. Child's life matters more than investigation. More than operational security. More than any of it. You chose correctly."

"Your cousin warned them about the investigation. Your cousin ordered the kidnapping. This is your fault."

"Partially. Yes. I warned Reza. Tried to protect family. Created situation where kidnapping seemed like good response. That's on me. That's weight I carry. But you—you didn't create situation. You just responded to it. You saved child. That's good. Whatever else comes, that's good."

"Where are you?"

"Leaving. Going back to Kurdistan. This city—this operation—it's not mine anymore. I did what I came to do. Warned my cousin. Protected my family. Now I'm going home. Back to where I belong."

"What about Reza? About the assassination plot?"

"That's FBI problem. American problem. Not mine. I'm done playing games with American intelligence. Done serving multiple masters. Done carrying loads that aren't mine to carry." Pause. "Advice—go home too. Go back to Greenville. Go back to estate planning. Go back to life that doesn't involve kidnappings and information trades and ghosts you'll carry forever. Get out while you still can."

"Can't. I'm in now. I'm asset. I'm committed."

"Then God help you. Because this work—it doesn't end. It doesn't get better. It just creates more ghosts. More impossible choices. Until you're carrying so much you can't function. Can't feel. Can't be human anymore. Get out before that happens."

Kamal hangs up.

Ethan sits in silence. The debriefing room empty except for him. The walls closing in. The weight settling.

Chen enters. "We need to talk. About next steps. About Kurdistan."

"What about Kurdistan?"

"Ahmed Khalil's family. They're in Kurdistan. Erbil. If he's dead—if Iranian intelligence killed him—someone needs to notify family. Someone needs to explain. Someone needs to—" Chen pauses. "I want you to go. To Kurdistan. To deliver the news. To explain what happened. To make it right."

"Why me?"

"Because you traded his life for Layla's. Because you made the call that got him killed. Because you owe him. Because—" Chen stops. "Because I need you to understand what this work costs. Need you to see consequences firsthand. Need you to carry them properly. You're operational now. You're one of us. Time to learn what that means. Time to meet the families. Time to look into their eyes and explain why their son is dead. That's the job. That's the real work. Not the tactical operations. Not the intelligence gathering. The aftermath. The ghosts. The families left behind."

"When do I leave?"

"Tomorrow. Flight to Istanbul. Connect to Erbil. Ahmed's family will be waiting. You tell them everything. You answer their questions. You accept their anger. You carry their grief. That's how you become operator. That's how you earn the classification."

Ethan nods. Can't speak. Can't process. Just accepts the consequence. The cost of choices made in desperate moment.

Tomorrow Kurdistan. Tomorrow the families. Tomorrow the reckoning.

Tonight he just sits here. Thinking about the grain field. About Ahmed. About Dariush. About all the people whose lives ended because of calculations made in rooms like this.

The weight is crushing. The costs keep accumulating.

And Ethan's just beginning to understand what Chen meant. What Kamal warned. What everyone tried to tell him.

This work doesn't end. It doesn't get better. It just creates more ghosts you carry forever.

Welcome to operations. Welcome to the real work.

Welcome to the load you can't put down.

# 15

## CHAPTER 15: ERBIL (REPRISE)

*Kurdistan Region, Iraq — January 2016*

The flight to Istanbul is twelve hours. Ethan doesn't sleep. Just sits watching the Atlantic pass below. Thinking about Ahmed. About the information trade. About the family waiting in Erbil who don't know yet that their son is dead.

Or maybe they do. Maybe Iranian intelligence already told them. Maybe the body already arrived. Maybe Ethan's trip is just formality. Administrative cleanup. The American government going through motions of notification and apology.

At Istanbul he has six-hour layover. Sits in airport watching travelers. Families. Business people. The normal movement of normal lives. None of them carrying weight like his. None of them flying to war zone to tell parents their son died because of intelligence trade gone wrong.

The connection to Erbil is smaller plane. Regional jet. Half empty. The other passengers are Kurdish businessmen, aid workers, a few journalists. People who operate in complicated spaces. Who understand that Kurdistan is safe-ish but not safe. Stable-ish but not stable.

Landing at Erbil at 11:47 PM. The airport is quiet. Night operations limited. He clears customs. Kurdish Asayish check his passport.

See the stamps. Multiple entries. They ask questions. He answers. Lawyer. International case. They let him through with suspicion but no problems.

Outside, the November night is cold. Colder than October was. Winter approaching. The city lights spread out below the airport. Familiar now. The place he thought he'd left. The place that keeps pulling him back.

The compound café is the same. Same bad coffee. Same Kurdish news on the television. Same contractors passing through on their way to somewhere worse.

Lars is at a corner table. Older somehow. More weathered. He's grown a beard.

"Ethan." Lars stands. They shake hands. "Heard you were back. Thought you went home."

"I did. Briefly."

"Briefly." Lars smiles. Tired smile. "That's how it works. You think you're done. Then something pulls you back."

They sit. Order coffee neither of them wants. The television shows footage from Mosul. ISIS retreating. Slowly.

"How long you been back?" Ethan asks.

"Never left. Three years now. Mosul, Sinjar, Tal Afar. Wherever they need bodies who know what they're doing." He looks at the television. "We're winning. Slowly. People forget that takes time. Years. Bodies."

"You ever think about going home?"

"To Norway? What for? To explain why I spent three years fighting someone else's war?" Lars drinks his coffee. "My family stopped asking. Friends stopped calling. There's no home anymore. Just this."

The weight in his voice. The acceptance. The same thing Ethan hears in Petey's voice. Chen's voice. Everyone who stays too long.

"You hear about Ukraine?" Lars asks.

"Some."

"Wagner. Russian contractors. Mercenaries. Fighting in Donbas. Same shit, different country. Some of the guys here are talking about going. After ISIS collapses. After this ends." He pauses. "You always need somewhere to fight. Someone to fight. Otherwise what's the point of knowing how?"

"That why you stay? Because you need it?"

"No. I stay because they need help. Because ISIS is evil. Because someone has to." Lars looks at Ethan directly. "You stay because you need it. I stay because they need me. Different reasons. Same result."

"What happens when ISIS is gone? When there's no one left who needs you?"

Lars shrugs. "Ukraine. Syria. Wherever Wagner shows up next. Wherever evil needs fighting. There's always somewhere." He finishes his coffee. "You're not like me. You don't need the fight. You're here for other reasons. Chen's reasons. Intelligence reasons. That's different. That's sustainable. What I do—fighting because it's right—that ends when you're too old or too dead."

"You ever regret it?"

"Every day. And never." He stands. "Good seeing you, Ethan. Don't stay too long. You've got option to leave. Use it before you don't."

He walks out. Back to the war. Back to wherever Peshmerga need Norwegian volunteers who believe.

Ethan sits alone. Thinking about Lars's question. Why he came back. Chen's reasons. Not ideology. Not belief. Just calculation. Just slightly more good than harm.

Different reasons. Same result.

The television shows more Mosul footage. The war continuing. Slowly.

Chen arranged driver. Kurdish man. Forties. Professional. Doesn't talk much. Just drives through empty streets toward the address Chen provided.

The safe house is different from before. Not the guest house where Lars stayed. Different part of city. Nicer area. Two-story house. Walled compound. The infrastructure of American presence in Kurdistan. Places where officials stay. Where operations get planned. Where Americans hide from the reality outside the walls.

The gate opens. Driver drops him. Leaves without speaking.

Inside, Chen is waiting.

"You made it. Good flight?"

"Long."

"Always is." Chen gestures toward the house. "You're staying here tonight. Tomorrow morning we meet Ahmed's family. I'll be with you. Translator will be with you. We'll explain what happened. Answer their questions. Make available whatever resources they need. It's—" He pauses. "It's not easy. Meeting families. But it's necessary. It's part of the work."

"Have you done this before?"

"Three times. Twice in Iraq. Once in Syria. Each time—" Chen stops. Shakes his head. "Each time I think it gets easier. It doesn't. You just get better at hiding how hard it is."

They go inside. The house is comfortable. American furniture. American amenities. The bubble of Western life dropped into Kurdistan. Ethan gets a room. Small but adequate. He lies on the bed. Stares at ceiling. Doesn't sleep.

At 6 AM there's knock on door. Chen.

"We leave in an hour. Breakfast is ready if you want it. Otherwise just get ready. Dress respectfully. This is grieving family. This is serious."

Ethan showers. Dresses. Dark pants. White shirt. Simple. Respectful. The clothes of someone delivering bad news.

At 7 AM they leave. Different driver. Same silence. Through morning Erbil. Traffic building. The city waking up. Generators humming. Checkpoints operational. The daily rhythm.

They drive to residential area. Middle class. The neighborhood where Kurdish professionals live. Doctors. Engineers. Teachers. People building normal lives in not-normal place.

The house is modest. Two story. White walls. Garden in front. The home of family that worked hard. That saved money. That believed in education and opportunity and future.

Chen knocks. The door opens. Woman answers. Forties. Wearing black. Her face is wrong. The face of mother who already knows. Who already received the news somehow. Who's been crying for days.

She looks at Chen. Recognition. Then anger. "You killed him. You killed my son."

Chen speaks in Arabic. Soft voice. Respectful. The translator—young Kurdish woman—translates even though the mother clearly understands English.

"Mrs. Khalil. I'm deeply sorry for your loss. Ahmed was brave man. He helped save lives. He—"

"He was twenty-three. He was child. You recruited child. You used him. You got him killed." She's crying now. The anger mixing with grief. "He called me three days ago. Said he was scared. Said something was wrong. Said people were watching him. I told him to stop working for you. To come home. To be safe. He said he couldn't. Said you wouldn't let him. Said he was trapped."

The accusation hangs in the air. Chen trapped him. Same as Chen trapped Yousef. Same methodology. Different asset. Same coercion.

"Can we come in?" Chen asks. "Please. Let us explain. Let us talk about what happened. What we're doing to make this right."

She stands aside. Lets them enter. The interior is modest. Clean. Photos on walls. Ahmed as child. Ahmed graduating school. Ahmed before ISIS. Before everything went wrong.

They sit in living room. Ahmed's father appears. Older man. Sixties. Wearing suit. Traditional Iraqi formality. His face is stone. Controlled. The grief buried under dignity.

"You are CIA," he says. Not question. Statement.

"Yes sir."

"You recruited my son. Promised him amnesty. Promised him safety. Promised him future. Then you got him killed."

"We tried to protect him. We provided security. We—"

"You used him. Same as ISIS used him. Different flag. Different ideology. Same result. My son is dead because powerful people needed him for their operations. That's truth. That's reality."

The accusation is comprehensive. The parallel complete. ISIS recruited Ahmed for their purposes. CIA recruited him for theirs. Both got him killed. The only difference is which organization claims moral high ground.

Chen doesn't argue. Just sits taking the measure. The anger. The grief. That's his job. That's what notification means. Accept the family's rage. Carry their grief. Be target for their need to blame someone.

Ethan watches. Learning. Understanding. This is what operational consequences look like up close. This is the cost that gets calculated in abstract terms—"acceptable losses," "necessary sacrifices"—but lived in concrete reality by families left behind.

"How did he die?" Ahmed's father asks.

Chen looks at Ethan. Meaningful look. Your turn. Your trade. Your consequence. You explain.

Ethan clears his throat. "Ahmed was providing intelligence on Iranian operations in New York. He had access through family connections. Through community relationships. He was helping FBI investigate assassination plot. Seven Iranian dissidents targeted for murder. Ahmed's intelligence was crucial. Was preventing attacks. Was saving lives."

"But?" the mother asks. "There's always but. My son was helping. Doing good. But—"

"But information got compromised. Iranian intelligence learned about the investigation. About Ahmed's cooperation. They—" Ethan stops. Forces himself to continue. "They abducted him. Interrogated him. We believe they killed him. His body hasn't been found yet but given the circumstances—"

"How did information get compromised?" the father asks. "How did Iranian intelligence learn about my son?"

This is the moment. The confession. The acceptance of responsibility. Ethan looks at Chen. Chen nods slightly. Go ahead. Tell them. Own it.

"I compromised the operation. There was emergency. Friend's daughter was kidnapped. I needed information to find her. I traded operational details to Iranian intelligence officer. Told him about FBI investigation. About sources. About Ahmed. I—" Voice breaks. "I traded your son's life for the girl's. That was the calculation. That was my decision. That's why he's dead."

The silence is complete. The mother stares. The father's face remains stone. Processing. Understanding.

Finally the mother speaks. "You killed my son to save someone else's child."

"Yes."

"Did you save her? The girl you traded for?"

"Yes. She's alive. She's home. She's safe."

"Then my son died for something. Someone lived because he died. That's—" She breaks down completely. The grief overwhelming. "That's what he wanted. When he called. When he was scared. He said—he said if he was going to die, let it be for something that matters. Let it be to save someone. You gave him that. You gave him meaning in his death."

The forgiveness is unexpected. The grace is impossible. Ahmed's mother is offering absolution Ethan doesn't deserve. Can't accept. Won't ever feel entitled to.

"I'm sorry," Ethan says. "I'm so sorry. He was brave. He was trying to build new life. He deserved better than being caught between operations. Between intelligence services using him. He deserved—"

"He deserved to never join ISIS," the father interrupts. "Deserved to never make terrible choices that put him in position to be used. But he made those choices. We accept that. We grieve that. But we don't blame you for consequences of his choices. We blame ISIS. We blame extremism. We blame everyone who recruited him—you, them, all of you. But we don't blame you for trying to save child. That's human. That's what anyone would do."

The conversation continues for two hours. Questions about how Ahmed died. About whether he suffered. About what happened to his body. About whether they'll ever get closure. Chen answers what he can. Avoids what he can't. Maintains professional sympathy without crossing into false emotion.

Before leaving, Chen hands envelope to father. "This is compensation. For Ahmed's service. For your loss. It's not adequate. Nothing is adequate. But it's what we can offer. Use it however you need. For funeral. For family. For whatever helps."

The father opens envelope. Sees check. His face hardens. "Blood money."

"Compensation for services rendered. For sacrifice made. For—"

"Blood money." He hands it back. "Keep it. We don't want American money. Don't want anything from people who got our son killed. We just want to grieve in peace. We just want to be left alone."

Chen takes the envelope back. Doesn't argue. "If you change your mind. If you need anything. Contact information is in here. You call. We help. That's promise. Regardless of how you feel about us. Regardless of blame. If you need help, we're here."

They leave. Walking back to car. The morning sun is bright. The neighborhood is busy. Normal life continuing while families grieve. While consequences ripple. While the machine grinds on producing casualties and calling them operational necessities.

In the car, Chen is quiet. They drive in silence for ten minutes.

Finally: "That went better than expected."

"How?"

"They didn't throw us out. Didn't curse us. Didn't attack physically. Mother offered forgiveness. Father maintained dignity. That's good outcome given circumstances. That's better than most notifications."

"They lost their son."

"They did. And we're responsible. You're responsible. I'm responsible. Everyone involved is responsible. That's how this works. But they granted grace. Offered forgiveness we don't deserve. That's gift. That's something to hold onto."

They drive toward the safe house. But Chen diverts. Different direction. Out of city. Toward the front lines. Toward Gwer. Toward the berm where Ethan watched Peshmerga and ISIS stare at each other across four hundred meters.

"Where are we going?"

"There's someone who needs to talk to you. Someone who's been waiting."

Twenty minutes later they reach checkpoint. Peshmerga recognize Chen's vehicle. Wave them through. They continue to the berm. Park. Walk up.

At the top, Lars is waiting.

"Ethan. Didn't expect to see you back here."

"Didn't expect to be back."

They stand looking at the other berm. ISIS positions visible. Smoke from their fires. Movement of fighters. The static war continuing. The line holding.

"I heard what happened in New York," Lars says. "Heard about the trade. About Ahmed. About saving the girl. Word travels fast in contractor community. Petey told everyone. You're famous now. Or infamous. Depends on perspective."

"What's your perspective?"

"That you made hard call under pressure. That you saved child. That you accepted consequences. That's what operators do. That's the work." Lars lights cigarette. Offers one to Ethan. Ethan takes it. "But also that you're fucked. That you're in now. That you can't leave. That this work owns you whether you want it to or not."

"Chen said the same thing."

"Because it's true. You made the trade. You became operational. You compromised investigation. You got sources killed. You're part of the machine now. You walk, it follows. Always. Can't go back to Greenville and pretend this didn't happen. The work found you. The work owns you. Welcome to the life."

They smoke in silence. Watching the line. The war. The waiting.

"Why did Chen bring me here?" Ethan asks.

"Because I asked him to. Because I wanted to tell you something. Something important." Lars drops cigarette. Grinds it out. "Ahmed Khalil. He's not dead."

The words don't process. Ethan stares.

"What?"

"He's not dead. Iranian intelligence didn't kill him. They grabbed him. Interrogated him. Got some information. But then—" Lars smiles. "Then he escaped. Or someone helped him escape. Or something. Details are unclear. But he's alive. He's in Turkey. He's safe."

"How do you know this?"

"Because Petey told me. Because contractor network sees things official channels don't. Because Ahmed reached out to people he knew. Made contact. Asked for help getting to safety. People responded. Got him out. Got him to Turkey. He's safe."

"Does Chen know?"

"Chen knows. Just found out this morning. That's why he brought you here. So I could tell you. So you could understand—the trade you made, the cost you thought you paid—it's not what you thought. Ahmed's alive. Dariush is probably alive too. Iranian intelligence isn't as efficient as Chen suggested. They're messy. They make mistakes. They let assets slip through."

The relief is overwhelming. Ahmed alive. Not dead. Not ghost. Not consequence to carry forever.

But then the other shoe.

"Why didn't Chen tell me? Why send you?"

"Because Chen wanted you to sit with it first. Wanted you to meet Ahmed's family believing he was dead. Wanted you to feel the full consequence of the trade. That's how he teaches. That's how he makes operators understand what the work costs. You let you carry that. Then he lifts it. Shows you it's not as bad as you thought. But the lesson stays. The understanding stays. You still made the trade. Still betrayed investigation. Still compromised sources. Those costs are real even if Ahmed survived."

"That's manipulation."

"That's training. That's Chen making you into operator. Making you understand that you can't know consequences when you make decisions. Can't predict outcomes. Can only make best call with available information and live with whatever happens. Ahmed being alive doesn't make your trade right. Doesn't erase the betrayal. Doesn't change that you compromised investigation. It just means this particular cost was less than you thought. Next time you might not be lucky. Next time the trade might cost exactly what you fear."

Ethan looks at the berm. At ISIS positions. At the war that continues whether he's here or not. Whether he's part of it or not.

"So what now?"

"Now you decide. Chen's going to offer you choice. Come work for him full-time. Become contractor. Become operator. Do this work professionally. Or go home. Go back to Greenville. Go back to estate planning. Try to pretend this never happened. But understand—going home doesn't mean you're out. Doesn't mean the work stops finding you. It just means you're not getting paid for it. You're still asset. Still operational. Still trapped in the machine. Just trapped differently."

"And if I take Chen's offer?"

"Then you become what I am. What Petey is. What everyone in this game is. Professional operator. Contractor. Someone who works in gray areas. Who makes hard calls. It's not bad life. It's honest about what it is. But it's also not clean. Not noble. Not heroic. It's just work. Hard work. Complicated work. Work that costs pieces of yourself every time you do it."

Chen appears at the berm. Walking toward them. Timing perfect. Probably listening. Probably waiting for right moment to make offer.

"Ethan. Can we talk?"

Lars nods. Leaves. Down the berm. Back to Peshmerga positions. Back to the war.

Chen and Ethan stand on the berm. Two Americans in Kurdistan. Looking at ISIS across kill zone. The absurdity complete.

"Ahmed's alive," Ethan says.

"Yes. Just confirmed this morning. He's in Turkey. Safe. We're arranging proper protection. Proper relocation. He'll be fine."

"You knew before I met his family. Before you made me think he was dead."

"I suspected. Wasn't confirmed until after. But yes, I let you carry the burden of believing he was dead. That was intentional. That was teaching moment. You needed to understand what this work costs. What trading information means. What compromising operations means. You needed to feel the full consequence before learning it was less severe than feared."

"That's fucked up."

"That's training. That's making sure you understand the stakes before I offer you what I'm about to offer." Chen turns to face him. "Come work for me. Full-time. Contractor. Advisory role. You help with cultural access. With legal frameworks. With navigating gray areas between law and operations. You use your skills. Your background. Your understanding. You get paid well. You do work that matters. You become professional operator instead of amateur stumbling through."

"Why?"

"Because you're good at this. Because you make hard calls. Because you accept consequences. Because you understand. Because you're already in—might as well get paid for it. Might as well do it professionally instead of getting dragged back every few months for another emergency."

The offer is seductive. The logic sound. Accept reality. Get paid for what he's already doing. Make it career instead of series of crises.

"What about Greenville? Margaret's firm? The life I built?"

"Keep it if you want. This is contractor work. You do it remotely. You travel when needed. You maintain cover as lawyer. Makes you more useful actually. Gives you access. Gives you legitimate reason to be places. Margaret probably won't mind. Probably knows already that you're doing more than estate planning. She's smart woman. She sees what you are."

"And if I say no?"

"Then you go home. You try to live normal life. And in three months, six months, year—someone calls. Someone needs help. Someone pulls you back in. That's how this works. The work finds you. Might as well accept it. Might as well get paid."

Ethan looks at the berm. At ISIS. At Kurdistan. At the place he thought he'd left. The place that keeps pulling him back.

"I need to think."

"Of course. Take time. But decide soon. Because Ahmed being alive doesn't change that your trade compromised operation. Doesn't change that Reza Hosseini is still planning assassinations. Doesn't change that FBI investigation is damaged. We need to rebuild. Need new sources. Need new access. You can help with that. Or you can walk away and let someone else handle it. But either way, consequences continue. Either way, the work continues. Question is whether you're part of it or not."

Chen walks away. Down the berm. Toward the vehicles. Leaving Ethan alone on the line.

Ethan sits. Watching the front. Thinking about Ahmed alive. Layla safe. Yousef reunited with daughter. Thinking about costs and consequences and calculations that never work cleanly.

His phone buzzes. Text from Margaret.

*Heard you're in Kurdistan again. Heard you're having crisis of career conscience. Here's my advice: Stop pretending you're lawyer who does intelligence work. Accept you're operator who has law degree. Stop fighting what you are. Either commit or quit. Half-assing helps nobody. —M*

Direct. Honest. Margaret's specialty.

Another text. Petey.

*Chen's making you offer. I know because I trained him. He learned from me. Here's what I'll tell you: contracting is good life if you accept what it is. It's work in gray areas for gray money doing gray things. But it's honest about being gray. That's something. Question is whether you can accept the gray. If yes, take the offer. If no, go home and stop answering phones. Choose. —P*

Another text. Yousef.

*Layla is doing better. Therapy helps. She asks about you. Wants to thank you. We all do. Whatever happens next—whatever you decide—know that you saved my daughter. You saved my family. That matters more than anything else. That's real. That's good. That's debt I can never repay. Thank you. —Y*

The messages stack up. Everyone weighing in. Everyone offering perspective. Everyone trying to help him decide.

But the decision is his. The calculation is his.

Stay or go. Commit or quit. Accept the gray or fight for clarity that doesn't exist.

He sits on the berm for two hours. Watching the line. Thinking.

Finally he stands. Walks down. Gets in vehicle. Chen's waiting.

"Have you decided?"

"Not yet. But I'm going home first. To Greenville. To Margaret's firm. To the life I built. I need to see if it still fits. If I still fit in it. Then I'll decide. Then I'll tell you yes or no."

"Fair enough. When will you know?"

"Give me a week. One week to go home. To sit with the consequences. To understand what I'm choosing between. Then I'll call you. Then I'll tell you."

Chen nods. "One week. Then I need answer. Because the work continues whether you're part of it or not. Because Reza's still operational. Because seven dissidents are still targeted. Because the fog doesn't clear just because one operator quits. Someone has to carry it. Question is whether that's you."

They drive back to the safe house. Ethan packs. Books flight to Istanbul. Istanbul to Charlotte. Charlotte to Greenville. Home by Saturday.

One week to decide whether home is Greenville or Kurdistan. Whether the work is estate planning or operations. Whether he's lawyer or operator. Whether he accepts the gray shades or keeps fighting for clarity.

One week to choose.

Then the consequences ripple forward forever based on the calculation he makes.

The grain field. The first kill. Ahmed. Layla. All the people whose lives intersected with his. All the costs that rippled.

Now he decides whether to accept more. More costs. More ripples.

Or whether to walk away and try to believe that's possible.

The flight leaves in six hours.

One week to decide everything.

# 16

— • —

# CHAPTER 16: OF COUNSEL

*G*reenville, *South Carolina – January 2016*

The flight lands at Charlotte Douglas at 9:32 AM on a Saturday in late January. Twenty-seven hours in transit. Three months since the phone call that started everything. Istanbul to JFK. JFK to Charlotte. The exhaustion is complete. Physical and otherwise.

The rental car waiting. The drive to Greenville. The landscape transitioning from airport sprawl to suburbs to downtown. Everything familiar. Everything alien. Like returning to childhood home and finding furniture smaller than memory suggested.

His apartment is exactly as he left it. Mail piled up. Refrigerator empty except for condiments that expired weeks ago. The evidence of life suspended mid-stride. Of person who left thinking he'd be gone days and stayed gone weeks.

He showers. The American water pressure. The reliable temperature. The small luxuries that feel obscene after Kurdistan. After seeing Ahmed's family. After sitting on the berm watching men wait for war.

He sleeps for sixteen hours. The body reclaiming what it's owed. The mind shutting down. Processing nothing. Just empty unconsciousness.

Sunday morning he wakes at 10 AM. Makes coffee. Sits at his small kitchen table. Looks at nothing.

His phone has accumulated messages. Texts from clients. Emails from Margaret's firm. The administrative debris of normal life. The work that continues whether he's in Greenville or Kurdistan. Whether he's lawyer or operator. Whether he's present or not.

He doesn't answer them. Not yet. Just sits drinking coffee. Thinking.

The drawing is on the table. He'd emptied his jacket pockets when he got home. Keys. Wallet. Passport. And Layla's crayon drawing.

Stick figure holding weapon. "THANK YOU MR ETHAN" in careful letters. A child's version of a soldier. Knight protecting her.

He picks it up. Studies it. The simple lines. The careful coloring. The misspelled gratitude.

This is what the calculation looks like. Not abstract philosophy. Not utilitarian math. Not "slightly more good than harm" written in Chen's briefing documents.

It's a child's drawing. Alive because of information trade. Because Ahmed Khalil died. Because Dariush Ahmadi got exposed. Because Ethan accepted costs he can't quantify or justify, only carry.

The good and the harm, never balancing. Never clean. Just this: girl making crayon drawing because she's alive to make it.

He sets it down. Drinks coffee. Watches winter light through kitchen window.

The week starts Monday. The decision is due Friday. Chen waiting for answer. The choice between staying or going. Between accepting what he is or fighting for what he was.

Seven days to figure out if Greenville still fits. If the life he built still makes sense. If estate planning still matters when he knows what's

happening behind the curtain. In the spaces between wills and channels where decisions get made about acceptable costs.

He looks at the drawing again. Folds it carefully. Puts it in his
wallet behind his driver's license. The weight of it—paper, nothing
more—feels heavier than it should.

***

Monday morning. Margaret's office. 8 AM.

She's already there. Always is. First one in. Last one out. The discipline of someone who built firm from nothing and maintains it
through relentless presence.

Margaret's office hasn't changed. Same law books. Same files
stacked carefully. Same photograph on her desk—new detail Ethan
notices now. Man in contractor gear. Desert background. Mosul,
maybe. Baghdad.

"That's Richard," Margaret says, following his eyes. "2005. Three
months before he quit the firm permanently. Stopped pretending
he was coming back to practice law." She touches the frame briefly.
"He sent that photo with a letter. Said he'd found his real work. Said
estate planning felt like pretending to matter when real things were
happening somewhere else."

She turns the frame toward Ethan. The man in the photo looks
tired. Competent. Alive in a way office photos never capture.

"He lasted five more years. Died in Kandahar. IED. Never got to
practice law again. Never wanted to." She looks at Ethan. "That's the
cost. Not just dying. Living halfway. Being somewhere else even when
you're here."

She turns the frame back toward herself. Leaves it there. Facing her, not him.

"I knew what Richard was doing before he told me. Recognized the signs. The late calls. The careful language. The weights he carried." She pauses. "I'd seen it before. Different context. When I was younger, before law school, I worked at Langley. Administrative. Clearances. Personnel files. You see a lot from that desk. Who breaks, who adapts, who disappears into the fog and never comes home."

"You never mentioned—"

"It's not relevant to estate law. But it's relevant to this conversation. I've watched men like you and Richard make these choices for thirty years. I know where it leads. Not from books. From files. From funerals. From wives who call asking where their husbands really are." She sits back. "That's why I'm telling you this isn't sustainable. I'm not guessing. I'm not theorizing. I'm reading a file I've read before. Different name. Same ending."

Silence. The kind that carries weight. The kind where truth settles.

"You think I should walk away," Ethan says.

"I think you should be honest about what you're choosing. Don't tell yourself you're doing both. Don't pretend you're maintaining balance. Richard did that. Lasted five years lying to himself. Then the lie collapsed and he had to choose. By then he'd already lost everything worth choosing for."

"And you're telling me this because—"

"Because I've seen this file before." She opens drawer. Pulls out contract. Revised. "And because you've already decided. You just won't admit it yet."

She slides the contract across desk. Of counsel agreement. The classification that means something and nothing. Lawyer but not quite. Part of firm but separate. In but with distance.

"This is what compromise looks like. Legal cover for operational life. Lets you keep license. Keep clients. Keep appearance of normal practice. But we both know what it really is. It's permission structure. Framework for living in the gray. Contract that acknowledges you're both things and neither thing and mostly the thing you won't say out loud."

Ethan reads it. The terms are generous. Flexible schedule. No billable hour requirements. Of counsel classification. The legal framework for being halfway.

"Richard had the same contract," Margaret says. "Used it for three years. Told himself he was maintaining both lives. Practicing law part-time. Operational work part-time. Perfect balance." She laughs. Bitter sound. "Then he just stopped showing up to the office. Forgot to return client calls. Missed court dates. The operational life consumed the legal life until the legal life was just paperwork he filed between deployments."

"You think that'll happen to me."

"I think you're already halfway there. I think the phone call from Kurdistan pulled you out of life you were building and dropped you into life you've been avoiding. I think Chen's offer isn't offer. It's acknowledgment of reality you won't admit."

She stands. Walks to window. Looks out at Greenville. The small city. The normal life. The world that operates without knowing about rifles and intelligence trades and calculations about acceptable costs.

"But you're not Richard. You're younger. More self-aware. More honest about costs. Maybe you can maintain the balance he couldn't. Maybe the of counsel structure works for you. Maybe you find way to be both things without destroying everything." She turns back. "Or maybe you're just better at lying to yourself. Time will tell."

"You're not very encouraging."

"I'm not trying to encourage you. I'm trying to warn you. Because I've seen this file before and I know how it ends and I'm not interested in watching another good man disappear into work that never ends." She sits back at desk. "So sign the contract or don't. Take Chen's offer or don't. But don't lie to yourself about what you're choosing. That's the only advice worth giving."

Ethan looks at the contract again. The legal language that creates space for living in between. The framework that acknowledges reality without requiring commitment.

"Thank you. For understanding. For not making this harder."

"You're making it hard enough on yourself. Don't need my help with that." She hands him pen. "Sign this. Make it official."

Ethan signs. The ink making it real. Of counsel. The classification that means he's part of firm but separate. Lawyer but not quite. In but with distance.

Same as being contractor. In but not quite. Operator but not official. Part of machine but separate.

Everything becomes gray area. Everything becomes both/and instead of either/or. Everything becomes living in fog and accepting that's normal.

Margaret watches him sign. Says nothing. Just witnesses the choice being made.

"My husband Richard—I told you he lasted five years trying to do both. Lawyer and contractor. Normal life and operational life. You know what he told me when he finally chose? When he quit the firm and went full-time with Agency work?"

"What?"

"He said 'I've been lying to myself. Pretending I was choosing both. But I chose operations years ago. The law was just cover I maintained because I was afraid to admit what I'd become.' He called it the fog.

Said it was permanent once you accepted it. Said there was no coming home after that."

She looks at Ethan directly. No sympathy. No judgment. Just truth.

"You think you're choosing both. You're choosing operations with a law license as cover. Eventually you'll admit it. I just hope you do it before you destroy everything else in service of the work. Richard didn't figure it out until after the divorce. After his kids stopped talking to him. After he'd burned every bridge to normal life."

"You think I'll do the same?"

"I think the work finds people who can't say no. Who care too much. Who make impossible choices because someone has to. That's you. That's Richard. That's everyone who lasts in that world." She stands. "Just don't lie to yourself about the cost. Don't pretend you can have both forever. And when you have to choose—and you will have to choose—make the choice honestly. Not because you ran out of other options."

She walks to the door. Stops.

"Mrs. Patterson needs estate documents by Monday. Her son's getting married. She wants trusts finalized before wedding. Do that work. Do it well. That's how you maintain the cover. But don't confuse maintaining cover with having two lives. You've got one life. You're just hiding parts of it from different people."

***

At noon Ethan sits in his office. Looking at the contract he signed. Looking at his phone. Looking at Layla's drawing in his wallet.

The three objects. The three versions of reality. The legal framework. The operational connection. The emotional weight.

He picks up his phone. Calls Chen.

"I'm in. I take the offer. Contractor. Advisory role. Whatever you need. I'm in."

"Good. I knew you would be. Knew you'd come around. Knew you'd accept what you are." Pause. "There's paperwork. Clearances. Process. Takes a few weeks. But you're in. You're operational. Welcome to the team."

"What's first assignment?"

"Reza Hosseini. The Iranian operation. It's compromised but not dead. We're rebuilding. Finding new sources. Developing new access. You'll help with that. Cultural understanding. Legal frameworks. Community access. You start January. After holidays. After paperwork clears. Until then—rest. Decompress. Enjoy Christmas. Live normal life while you can. Because once you start, it's harder to stop. Harder to remember what normal feels like."

"Understood."

Chen hangs up. The call ending. The decision made. The future locked.

Ethan sits in his office. Looking at estate documents on screen. Looking at phone showing call with Chen. Looking at two futures existing simultaneously.

This is his life now. This is what he chose. This is what accepting reality looks like.

He returns to the documents. Finishes the trusts. Emails Mrs. Patterson. Schedules meeting to review and sign. Does the work. Does it well.

Because that's what operators do. They maintain cover. They function in normal world while operating in gray world. They live multiple lives. They accept complications without resolution.

The drawing is in his wallet. The contract is signed. The call is made.

The fog doesn't clear. The weights don't lift. The costs keep accumulating.

But slightly more good than harm. That's the metric. That's the calculation. That's what makes it sustainable.

Maybe.

Probably not forever. Probably until something breaks. Until choice becomes necessary. Until carrying all of it becomes impossible.

But that's future problem. That's Book 3 of the story. That's next crisis. Next calculation. Next impossible choice.

Today he's lawyer in Greenville. Tomorrow he might be contractor in Istanbul. Next week he's both. Next month he's something else.

The work finds you. The work owns you. The work continues whether you accept it or fight it.

He chose acceptance. He chose commitment. He chose honoring what he is instead of fighting for what he was.

Time will tell if that was right choice. If this all works when applied to your own life. If the costs are sustainable or crushing.

But today—sitting in office in Greenville on Monday afternoon reviewing estate documents—it feels manageable. Feels possible. Feels like he made decision he can live with.

At least for now. At least until the next call. The next crisis. The next moment when someone needs him and he has to calculate whether saving them costs more than walking away.

That moment will come. It always does. That's the work. That's the life. That's what he accepted.

The scar itches. He doesn't touch it. Just lets it remind him. The permanent record. The calculation that never ends.

Slightly more good than harm. That's enough. Has to be. Because it's all anyone can manage when they're honest about costs.

The work continues. The fog persists. The weights accumulate.

And Ethan Caldwell—lawyer, contractor, operator, whatever he is now—carries them forward into whatever comes next.

# 17

## EPILOGUE

*B*aqubah, Iraq — *November 2008*

The culvert stinks of stagnant water and fear.

Ethan presses himself against the concrete, rounds snapping overhead. The firefight has been going for ten minutes. Feels like hours. The insurgents knew exactly where they were. Ambush. Coordinated. Professional.

"Counselor!" Ramos grabs his shoulder. "You got your rifle?"

"Yeah—"

"Then use it! Anything that moves out there is trying to kill us!"

Through the chaos—AK fire, RPGs, Kozlowski's M240 hammering—Ethan sees him.

A man appears in the grain field. Fifty meters out. Raising an AK.

Ethan's body moves before his brain catches up. Muscle memory from training. Adrenaline. Pure survival instinct.

M4 to shoulder. EOTech red dot on center mass. Squeeze.

The rifle bucks. Once. Twice. Three times.

The figure drops.

Ethan stares, frozen. The rifle still at his shoulder. He'd done it. Put rounds into a human being and watched him fall.

"Good shot, counselor!" McKnight yells. "Keep firing!"

But Ethan can't move. Can't process. The red dot sight. The man dropping. The first time he'd ever—

An RPG hits the culvert edge. The explosion is deafening. Something hot slashes across his left arm. Blood wells up. Shrapnel. He keeps firing. Has to. The man is dead but there are more of them. So many more.

The QRF arrives. Five minutes to spare. The insurgents flee. The firefight ends.

They sweep the field afterward.

The man Ethan killed lies in the grain. Young. Maybe twenty-five. Wedding ring on his finger. Three holes in his chest. An AK beside him. A phone in his pocket.

Someone's son. Maybe someone's father.

Dead because Ethan had put three rounds in him.

"Clean shoot," Ramos says. "He was about to light us up. You saved lives tonight."

Both things are true.

The man deserved to die and didn't deserve to die. Ethan had to shoot and will never forget shooting. The team survived because someone else died.

Slightly more good than harm.

The math: one insurgent dead, five Americans alive, intelligence recovered, mission accomplished.

The cost: everything. Always everything. The first time you cross that line, you can't uncross it.

That night Ethan looked at his arm. At the wound from the shrapnel. The medic stitched it—seven stitches, neat and professional. Said it would scar.

He touched it then. Knew it would itch forever. Knew he'd carry the man in the grain field forever. Knew the calculation would never feel right even when it was right.

The first kill never leaves you. Even when justified. Even when necessary. Even when it saved everyone else.

You killed someone. You're alive because of it. Both things are true. Both things will always be true.

***

*Greenville, South Carolina — January 2026*

The scar itches.

Ethan touches it now. Sitting in his office. Looking at estate documents and phone showing Chen's number and the two futures existing simultaneously.

Baquba taught him the calculation. Kurdistan reinforced it. Brooklyn proved it. Now he lives it.

Every day. Every choice. Every moment when someone needs him and he has to decide what costs more—acting or walking away.

The man in the grain field died because Ethan made a split-second call. Because survival required someone dying. Because self-defense doesn't erase the fact that a young man with a wedding ring never went home.

Ahmed nearly died for Layla's life. Sohrab Madani will live or die based on operations playing out in shadows he doesn't see.

The math never works cleanly. The weights never balance. The costs always exceed the benefits if you count honestly.

But slightly more good than harm. That's the metric. That's all anyone can manage.

The man in the grain field fell so Ethan's team could live. Died knowing nothing. No last words. Just the red dot sight, center mass, three rounds.

Seven years later, Ethan finally understands what Ramos meant: "You did good, counselor. Right call."

Right call. Hard call. Good call.

***

Operator. Lawyer. Both. Neither. Something in between. Something honest about being complicated.

The calculations never stop. The work continues. The weights accumulate.

And Ethan Caldwell—lawyer, contractor, operator, whatever he is now—carries them forward into whatever comes next.

Carrying the man in the grain field. Carrying Ahmed. Carrying Sohrab and the six others whose names he knows. Carrying Layla and Yousef and everyone whose lives intersected with his choices.

The scar itches. It always will.

That's the permanent record. That's the cost. That's what slightly more good than harm looks like when you're honest about both parts of the equation.

Welcome to operations. Welcome to the real work. Welcome to the rest of his life.

Whatever that means. However long it lasts. However it ends.

# 18

## HISTORICAL NOTE

*Between 2007 and 2015, over 70,000 Iraqis applied for Special Immigrant Visas based on their service to and with U.S. forces.*

*Fewer than 15,000 were approved.*

*The interpreters are real.*

*The bureaucracy is real.*

*The lists are real.*

*The rest is fiction.*

BAD
ACTOR

# CHAPTER 1

THE STREETS OF CANOGA PARK looked defeated in a way
Ellis Dunaway didn't remember from when he was a kid riding
his black Schwinn Tornado through them—to school, and the
ballfields at Knapp Ranch Park, to Fallbrook Square Mall, and the
7-Eleven on Saticoy Street to spend his allowance on candy and
comics, and sneak peeks at the porn magazines. On nights when
his mom worked late, he biked to the Baronet Theatre on
Topanga Canyon Boulevard and saw whatever was playing. She
was never the wiser. Pedaling home, alone, after dark, never
scared him until he saw *The Swarm* in the summer of 1978.

As a third grader, killer bees, birds, bugs, fish, and dogs were
scarier than roving psycho killers, with whom he believed he
might reason. His anxiety over nature run amok was confirmed
and compounded by doomsayers on the nightly news who
prophesied wildfires, acid rain, holes in the ozone layer, global

warming, and, of course, The Big One, which was due any minute. Until marijuana came along in the seventh grade, it was tough to relax. But then, his bike rides took on a psychedelic, therapeutic quality. Where before there had been danger, there was now order. Rewatching *The Swarm* as an adult, his fears of animals and psycho killers long since transposed, he hoped for a kiss of transcendent nostalgia. Instead, despite the stellar ensemble cast, the film bored him so bad he returned the tape to Blockbuster unfinished but kindly rewound.

Cruising the neighborhood streets today in his battered, classic Porsche 911, only every third or fourth three-bedroom, single bath house was decorated, mostly with inflatable Snoopys, Grinches, Sponge Bobs, and Baby Yodas. And most of those were toppled or deflated and lying on dead lawns like heaps of laundry. A house on Welby Way had a fifteen-foot-tall Jack Skellington in front of it that had been there since Halloween. It now sported a Santa hat and a scarf. Very clever. When Ellis was a kid, all these houses had been decorated, none cleverly and none with pop culture icons, unless you counted Rudolph and Santa Claus. The streets were an unbroken strand of electric candles in living room windows and multi-colored bulbs framing rooflines and doorways. The only reference was to Christmas.

"Can we puh-*leeease* change the station?" asked Prashanth, shaking Ellis out of his reverie. Carly Rae Jepsen's cover of Wham!'s "Last Christmas" was playing on Sunny96.

"Yeah, go 'head," said Ellis. "I don't know why anybody would cover that song anyway. I mean, it's perfect. You're just setting yourself up for failure."

"I guess."

Seventeen-year-old Prashanth's long black hair hung in his eyes as he flipped through ads on the Porsche's original Blaupunkt AM/FM stereo and cassette deck. *...for a limited time! ...spending the holidays alone? ...a thinner, younger-looking you ...no interest until next year!* He stopped on KT102 just as "Enter Sandman" by Metallica was starting.

"I can play this riff on guitar." Prashanth started headbanging.

"It's a cool song," said Ellis, "but why are they playing it on this station? This is a classic rock station."

"Dude, this is classic rock."

"The hell it is."

"It's like, thirty years old."

"Yeah, but still..." The kid had a fair point, which made it that much more annoying. Ellis struck back. "I have to be honest with you. I think your band name needs work."

Prashanth stopped whipping his hair. "What's the matter with it?" he asked, trying to sound indifferent.

"I think Unholy Sodomy is a little... let's say, gauche."

"No duh. It's supposed to be gross."

"Not *gross,* though it is certainly that—*gauche.* It's going to repel more people than it attracts."

"It'll attract black metal fans and that's all that matters."

"I thought you were a thrash band."

"We were, but then we got a new drummer and he kind of sucks. He can't play fast enough for thrash. So, now, we're a black metal band."

"He's black, the drummer?"

"No, man. Black metal means it's Satanic."

"Uh-huh. Well, in that case, I guess Unholy Sodomy makes sense."

Score two for Prashanth. The boy pointed to one of the shabbier, undecorated houses on the block and said, "That's it right there."

Ellis pulled to the curb and helped Prashanth pry his guitar case from the tiny back seat.

"Thanks for the ride, E."

"Anytime, Master P."

All Ellis had had to eat that day was a microwavable breakfast burrito and a 25-mg. Dr. Zonker's weed cookie that was still going strong. Waiting in the In-N-Out drive-thru at Topanga

Canyon and Vanowen, the top-of-the-hour news report came on the radio:

*In a letter to Los Angeles police and local media outlets, the Southland Sniper claimed responsibility for another murder in a string of shootings that have occurred over the last five weeks, the latest happening early this morning in Reseda. So far, the police have found no link between the victims. The killings appear to be unprovoked and totally random. Authorities are asking anyone with any information to contact them. A wrong-way crash on the northbound Four-Oh-Five in Brentwood has traffic at a standstill. Traffic on the Five is moving again after an earlier three-car collision near Whittier Boulevard has been cleared. Thanks to the Santa Ana winds, temperatures are higher than normal all over Los Angeles County. Right now, it's seventy-six Downtown, eighty in the Valley, and a little cooler at the beaches. You're listening to KT102 FM, where classic rock lives forever. Coming up in the next hour, we've got Soundgarden, Stone Temple Pilots, and lots more. Stick around.*

Ellis gagged on a hunk of his animal-style Double-Double. Soundgarden? Stone Temple Pilots? He cleared his throat with a swig of Diet Coke and changed the station back to Sunny96, where what sounded like a teenage girl with all the range and charisma of an empty paper sack was butchering "Jingle Bell Rock." Ellis sighed. Some people just couldn't leave well enough alone.

As he merged onto the 101, the comforting smell of fast food was replaced by exhaust. Watching the rearview for an opening to move left, a lane-splitting motorcycle cut in front of him from the right. The driver was wearing a yellow leather jacket. Ellis had to slam on the brakes to keep from hitting him.

"Shit!"

He took a deep breath and clocked in to work.

PER USUAL, Jay Arliss exited the Prestige Import Auto Sales showroom in Studio City at one o'clock sharp and headed to the employee parking lot. He had the beefy build of a high school athlete gone to mid-life flab. He was wearing the same sharkskin suit and Oxfords with sneaker treads he'd worn yesterday. Ellis imagined that if Jay were selling an Aston Martin and someone tossed him a football, he would catch it and the deal would be off, so irresistible and preferable was grab-assing with the fellas.

Ellis tailed Jay's blue Maserati from Ventura Boulevard to Tujunga Avenue to the 170 to an apartment house in Valley Glen. Now that Ellis thought about it, he could have just gone there and waited for Jay to show up. But then again, the day Ellis did that would be the day Arliss changed his pattern (*Get 'Em*, Chapter 3: Due Diligence Before It Does You).

A minute later, Jay's wife's cousin Kirra, (pronounced *Kye-ruh*), a petite bottle-blonde with collagen lips and fake tits, hopped in the Maserati. She was half Arliss's age, and he wasn't the only middle-aged middle manager she was seeing. They started making out. Ellis zoomed in on the action with his newish secondhand Canon video camera. After a minute, the lovers pulled apart, and

Arliss started the car. Ellis followed it to an inexpensive Asian fusion restaurant in a strip mall on Woodman Avenue. He parked on the street with a view of the front door, which had a Hello Kitty wreath on it. Four-point-seven out of five stars on Yelp! but not the kind of place Arliss's wife, Kaitlynn, or any of their friends were likely to pop into.

Ellis shot video of Jay and Kirra entering, then sat back, waiting for them to come out again. A man wearing gym shorts and nothing else pushed a grocery cart heaped with junk down the sidewalk. The layer of grime on his skin made it impossible to tell his age and ethnicity. He paused in front of the Veda Holistic Wellness Boutique and Spa to shout obscenities and swat flies only he could see. A woman in pink athleisure wear and designer sunglasses, carrying a pink Birkin bag and matching yoga mat, walked by the flailing, shouting man, completely unbothered, like he wasn't even there. Apparently, the Zen techniques one learned at Veda Holistic Wellness Boutique and Spa really worked.

*Get 'Em*, Chapter 21: Staking Out and Cashing In instructed PIs to maintain situational awareness while also staying focused on the subject under surveillance. Common sense, really, but Ellis's attention span, wrecked as it was by decades of TV and weed, wouldn't allow strict adherence to this rule or many of the others. So, he opened the L.A. Times app on his cracked iPhone and scrolled through the headlines.

*City panics as Southland Sniper*
*promises more killings*

*Extreme fire danger in parts of L.A.*
*County, red flag warnings begin*
*tomorrow*

*Reckless driver pursuit ends in fiery*
*crash in Pomona*

*Roaming dog packs in South Central*
*leave a trail of blood and terror*

(Ellis's childhood fear made manifest!)

*Peaceful protest at the Farmers Market*
*leaves two dead, sixteen critically injured*

*Urs Schreiber's legacy of toxic privilege*

Ellis stopped there and opened the article.

Urs Schreiber—early twenties, handsome, thin, with sharp cheekbones and thick, unruly blonde hair—was the breakout star of the mega-hit show *Graveyardland*. This summer, his portrayal of a narcoleptic junkie trumpet player, in the arthouse sleeper *Brass Hearts*, won over critics who had previously written him off as just another pretty face. Ellis had no intention of seeing the movie and only occasionally hate-watched *Graveyardland*, but the kid's charisma was undeniable. At least it used to be. In interviews on late-night talk shows, he exuded a playful egotism and insouciance that, like *Brass Hearts* itself, beat the odds and clicked with the ticket buyers. But then, leaving a Halloween party in the Palisades, Urs crashed his bright-blue Lotus Evora into the parked Mercedes-Benz G Wagon of a "Hollywood housewife". He was arrested, charged with drunk driving, leaving the scene of an accident, possession of cocaine and Ketamine, and resisting arrest. He only spent six-and-a-half hours in jail before he was bailed out, sentenced to time served, and paroled.

The op-ed Ellis read was the same as all the others. Where before, Urs had been exalted as "Ashton Kutcher with an attitude" and "Robert Pattinson for the TikTok generation", now, he was nothing more than a rich, white, male, nepo baby leveraging his privilege to avoid the consequences of his antisocial behavior. Like Prashanth's point about classic rock, the media backlash wasn't unfounded, but that didn't make it less dispiriting. Ellis rubbed his chin and sighed. Getting Urs back on top might prove more difficult than he thought, never mind reclaiming his own position in The Industry.

Looking at the ubiquitous paparazzi picture of Urs being handcuffed against his crumpled sportscar, costumed as a member of the Iapetusian Brotherhood of Eternal Tranquility, the L.A.-based doomsday cult that committed mass suicide in 1988—three-piece suit, single black leather glove, and gold chain necklace with a medallion shaped like the planet Saturn—Ellis flashed back to the night he wrecked his Porsche on Cahuenga

Boulevard. All over again, he saw Nazario's demonic face glowing red in the taillights—

*WHAM!*

Ellis jumped at the sight of Jay Arliss slamming his fat mitt on the hood of the Porsche.

"Why you following me, asshole?"

Ellis reached for the handle, but it was too late. Arliss reached in the car window and grabbed his shirt collar.

"Let go of me! I'm not following you. This is a public street. I have every right—"

"Don't gimme that shit. You been following me for a week now. I wanna know why." He tightened his grip, ripping fabric and drawing his knuckles tight against Ellis's windpipe. "Whadda you want?"

"Nuh… thing…" Ellis was short of breath. He wondered what a heart attack felt like. Probably worse than this. But not much worse than what came next.

Arliss's punch caught him high on the cheek. A cloud of stars accompanied the ringing in his ears, but the warning cut through.

"I better never see your stupid face or this piece of shit car in my rearview mirror ever again or I'm really, *really* gonna fuck you up! Got me?"

*NO LIFEGUARD ON DUTY – SWIM AT YOUR OWN RISK – NO DIVING.*

Allegro48 was the new name of an apartment building in North Hollywood that had been recently and perfunctorily renovated. The cursive ghost of the building's original name—Palm Breeze Apts.—was still visible on the façade. Ellis let himself in the security gate with the code he'd been texted and climbed the concrete steps. Gaps in the sloppy gray paint job revealed that the crumbling stucco used to be pink. A trio of palm trees in the courtyard leaned toward the sun and dropped withered fronds into the shaded, kidney-shaped swimming pool.

On the terrace, Reshma was leaning against the railing, like the palm trees, for the best light to take a selfie. Ellis crept up behind her and photo bombed just as she snapped a sunny portrait.

She spun around and gasped.

"What happened to you?"

"Ugh. The One-Oh-One was jammed," said Ellis, knowing full well she was talking about his cheek.

"I'm talking about your cheek." She stepped in close and inspected the swollen bruise. "What happened?"

"Nothing. It's nothing. I walked into a door." He relished her concern, but showing up late and looking terrible was an old pattern he, and especially Reshma, had moved on from, and Ellis hated to repeat it.

Reshma was a whole new woman from the one who, a couple of years ago, used to be his secretary. Back then, sitting behind the desk in his office, waiting hours, days, *weeks* for the phone to ring, her black hair was streaked with silver and hung in a ponytail to the middle of her back; she wore no make-up to mask her tired eyes, and cinched her huge breasts into tops that were too small or else draped them in material that made her look heavier than she was. To offset the boredom of Dunaway Private Investigation foundering under Ellis's neglect to its current state—just him and an iPhone—she had a divorce, a troubled teenage son, a second job, and studying for her realtor's license to worry about.

Now, Reshma was in bloom with success. Her hair was styled into bouncy layers, the silver dyed away. Her wardrobe flattered her curvy figure. She displayed her bosom proudly to the delight of twenty-five thousand Instagram followers. Though her account was ostensibly dedicated to L.A. real estate, almost all the comments were about her looks, plus emojis of hearts, flames, cakes, peaches, eggplants, and water drips.

Good for her.

"What really happened?" she asked, looking like she expected the drunken worst.

"Nothing. Really. Just a clumsy accident." Before she could push the matter further, Ellis gestured toward the door of apartment 2-C. "Shall we?"

Reshma unlocked the door and held it open for Ellis to enter. She turned on realtor mode and gave him the pitch. But she needn't have bothered; Ellis could see the entire studio apartment from where he stood.

"This is the epitome of comfort and style," she said unironically. "Four hundred square feet of elegance and practicality. It's recently remodeled with fresh paint and floors inspired by the natural beauty of real wood. The kitchenette is a culinary haven with stainless steel appliances and a granite-like countertop."

A mouse scuttled along the baseboard. Reshma missed it because she had turned to flip on the light in the bathroom, which was right next to the refrigerator, and Ellis was glad she was spared the embarrassment.

"With a cute shower curtain and some candles, this can be your tranquil retreat for relaxation and rejuvenation."

Squeezing past Reshma to take a look, Ellis smelled the peppery perfume he liked so well. It was just a tiny bathroom—a pedestal sink and a toilet, a foot and a half away from the bathtub—but Ellis played along.

"Very nice," he said, happy to bolster Reshma's joy in her new life and job. "Very tranquil."

Back in the main room, she said, "The laundry facility is right downstairs." Ellis could hear the thump of the dryer and smell the cloying fabric softener. "There's assigned on-site parking.

And," she opened the vertical blinds of the apartment's only window, "of course, you saw the swimming pool."

Two kids were playing in it: a boy doing a handstand on the pool's edge, and a girl floating face down with the tree litter, pretending, Ellis hoped, to be dead.

"It gets sun in the mornings, so you can work on your tan," said Reshma.

"What are you trying to say?"

"It's your pastoral oasis."

Ellis took his phone out of his pocket to call 911 when the girl in the pool finally raised her head, panting.

"So, what do you think?" asked Reshma.

"How much is the rent?"

"It's a one-year lease. Fourteen-ninety-five a month, with a fourteen-ninety-five deposit."

"Fourteen-ninety-fi— Are any of the utilities covered?"

"No, but in a place this cozy, they aren't much."

They're enough, thought Ellis. Fourteen-ninety-five was more than he was paying now for two bedrooms and a bathroom that made up for in size what it lacked in pastoral tranquility.

"I'm not trying to rush your decision," said Reshma, "but I'm showing a house in Silver Lake in half an hour, so…"

Houses in Silver Lake weren't cheap; Reshma had bigger fish to fry. Ellis understood she was doing him a favor by showing him (relatively) low-rent apartments. A dog was barking in another unit. The dryer downstairs hummed and thumped. The kids in the pool were playing Marco Polo now. Ellis could already imagine going stir crazy living and working in an oasis this cramped and noisy. But maybe it would provide extra motivation to reignite his writing career so that he could leave behind the hand-to-mouth, paycheck-to-paycheck drudgery of private investigation. Especially now that he was *so close*…

"I'll take it."

"Yay! I'm so glad. You're going to love being just a short walk from the Arts District," said Reshma, preparing the paperwork. "NoHo isn't just a convenient place to live, it's a whole lifestyle."

Ellis smiled, happy she was happy.

"If there's no problem with the credit check…" The way she looked at him was another reminder of a messier time.

"There won't be."

"Of course not," she said. "The deposit is due within forty-eight hours, so if you want to go ahead and pay that now…?" She had a card reader on her iPhone.

"Uh, yeah. Sure." Things were moving too fast. "I'll cut you a check."

Ellis still wrote the occasional check because, along with goods and services, it bought time. And every little bit counted. He post-dated the check for extra insurance and folded it before handing it to Reshma so she wouldn't notice.

Walking to their cars—Reshma was the proud lessee of a new Cadillac SUV—Ellis craved a shot of whisky. Or two. Instead, Reshma's approval would provide the desired hit of well-being.

He couldn't think of a lead-in, so he just said outright, "I have a meeting in Hollywood tonight with Kent Moran. He's producing a new show for Urs Schreiber, and he asked me to write it."

"Really? That's so great!"

A hug would have gone great there, but Reshma was rooting through her purse for her keys.

"Yeah, Urs is looking for a project to try and turn his image around, y'know, so, Kent gave me a call."

"That's amazing! He is *such* a genius. Is it a zombie show? This season of *Graveyardland* is my favorite one so far."

Ellis hated disappointing Reshma, but in this case, he was happy to say, "No. No, it's not a zombie show. It's something totally new. I'm not really supposed to talk about it, since we're still in development, trying to find it a home and everything, but yeah, it's pretty exciting."

"I'm so glad you're writing again. I'm really proud of you."

There it was. Validation. "Thanks. It feels good." To bask in the moment's warmth a little longer, he said, "And hey, talk about being proud. I gave Prashanth a ride to band practice today, and he's a really cool kid. You can be proud of—"

Reshma's smile and professional posture collapsed. "You gave him a ride to band practice?"

"Yeah. He called me and said he needed a ride. He's really a cool kid. We talked about classic rock. He's got some learning to do, but—"

"He's being grounded. He's not supposed to leave the house."

"Oh… Shit. I'm sorry. I— He didn't say anything about that."

"Of course, he didn't." Reshma unlocked her car.

"I'm sorry, really."

"It's okay. It's not your fault. How's he getting home?"

"I don't know. That didn't come up."

Reshma put on her sunglasses and sighed.

"Well, thanks for all your help finding me an apartment. I'm super-excited about it. Really."

"Okay."

"Good luck in Silver Lake."

"Thanks. I'm going to be late."

This time of day, rush hour, she was correct.

WHEN IT WAS ELLIS'S TURN, he washed the lingering crumbs of a flavorless, gluten-free vegan donut from between his teeth with a swallow of weak, organic, free-trade coffee, and addressed the circle.

"Hey, everyone. I think most of you know me at this point, but my name is Ellis. I'm an alcoholic and a drug addict."

"Hi, Ellis!" said the group in the Fellowship Room of Pathways Church in Burbank.

"It's been a year and three months since my last drink."

He paused for the pro forma approbation from the others.

Across from him was Antonio, who had been arrested fourteen times on drunk charges in the last ten years. Currently in his late thirties, but still wearing Vans, tube socks, Dickies shorts, and XXXL T-shirts, he was six months sober and ready to take another crack at his GED.

To his left sat Ricky, in his early twenties. He got clean after his grandmother kicked him out of the house for stealing her pills and selling her EBT cards to buy drugs. He was now working nights at 7-Eleven to raise the money to have the *LUSH LIFE* tattoo lasered off his neck.

Sanya, a former homeless sex worker who used to break open batteries for the lithium inside, today had a new set of teeth and a vegan diet to go with it. She was the one who provided the coffee and donuts.

Next to her, Lucinda, a fifty-something former nurse practitioner—probably cute before opiate addiction took hold—chewed gum and bounced her knee. She hit rock bottom when, on a bender, she gave the wrong medication to a patient and put him in a coma. It lasted a month, but in the screenplay she was writing about herself, he died.

Overweight and balding, Darren, an investment banker with empty folding chairs on either side of him, knew he had to make a change when he crashed his "Beemer" (his word) through the picture window of a ranch house in Pasadena, putting a "retarded kid" in the hospital. "Luckily," Darren was blacked out when it happened and he "didn't remember shit about it." At least twice per meeting, his phone would ring—a "business call" he "had to take" in flagrant violation of the posted no-cell-phone rule.

Shereé, (pronounced *Sher-ay*), late thirties/early forties, no prize but still the best looking of the bunch, passed out behind the wheel on her way to pick up her kids from school, causing a six-car pile-up on the 405. Getting sober and selling handmade, small-batch beeswax candles on Etsy—"featured in *Martha Stewart Living*"—gave her the strength to forgive herself.

Ellis shot nineteen-year-old narco initiate Nazario Sanchez in the neck at point-blank range. That Sanchez had just killed the King of Cable Television and was trying to do likewise to Ellis didn't make living with the memory any easier. Especially not stone-cold sober. But the group didn't know any of that. Nobody did. As far as they knew, Ellis was just another no-name television writer who, stumbling between alcohol-and-cocaine-induced blackouts and hallucinations, had flushed his career down the toilet and wrecked the 1987 Caramel Beige Porsche 911 Carrera he had inherited from his father in like-new condition with all the original components. That the inheritance also included a trust fund and a profitable private investigation agency, which Ellis also squandered, he kept secret from the group, too. "Private" was a full half of his job title, and he only trusted the "anonymous" aspect of the sobriety program as far as he could pick up the Porsche and throw it.

"As I guess you can see," he pointed to his swollen purple cheek, "I've had a pretty crazy day. Lotta triggers."

Darren's phone rang. "Whaddya want?" He said into it. "Talk fast. I'm in a meeting."

"Yep," said Ellis. "A lotta triggers."

# CHAPTER 2

THE VOLUME OF THE MUSIC inside the Century Club rendered conversation practically useless. Still, Ellis, Urs Schreiber, his CAA uber agent Larry Price, and Kent Moran, the writer, producer, director, and showrunner of *Graveyardland*, were tucked into a back booth, trying. They were discussing, kind of, the development of a limited streaming series for Urs to star in to salvage his reputation. "To show how much he's grown," in Larry's words.

Although it was occasionally graced by a curious/slumming A-lister, *Time Out Los Angeles* counted the Century Club among the 18 Best Bars for Spotting B-List Celebrities. Taking up space between the occasional Kit Harrington, Ashley Tisdale, Spencer Pratt, and Evan Rachel Wood were wannabe models, actors, influencers, and content creators from all obscure corners of the Industry and the internet. Besides the whiff of danger that came with an after-dark visit to the seedy east end of Hollywood—Zac Efron had been mugged at a gas station down the street—the Century Club offered, per *Time Out*, "a cloak of deafening music and near-total darkness under which Hollywood's hip and hopeful can really let their hair down." The only light came from the exit sign and a red neon *100* above the bar with just enough glow underneath it for the pierced and tattooed bartender to mix the overpriced cocktails and crack open the beers. All in all, an odd place for a development meeting, Ellis thought. But Urs had insisted.

He was also insisting on playing Rico Tubbs, the African American detective, in the *Miami Vice* reboot Ellis had written at Kent's behest.

"I like the script," said Urs; Ellis nodded, *thank you*, "but it needs to be like, a thousand percent more woke."

"A thousand more jokes?" asked Ellis.

"Exactly! And here's another twist—Crockett and Tubbs are gay."

Larry shut his eyes and pinched the bridge of his nose.

"Gay stuff is really hot right now," said Kent, "no doubt, but cultural appropriation is going to be an issue if you try to play a gay black guy."

"Then get a black guy to play Crockett," said Urs, beaming. "Race swap. Boom."

"That's just going to be confusing."

"Who's a foodie?"

"Wait… what?"

Ellis was having a hard time following. Not only could he not hear much of what was being said over the off-kilter electronic racket squeezing his skull and thudding behind his bruised cheek, he was distracted by the sweating, jewel-like cocktails in everybody's hands. Urs knocked back the last of his fourth Paloma and went to the bar for another.

Kent and Larry exchanged shrugs and eye rolls.

Like Reshma with her appointment in Silver Lake, Kent didn't need *Miami Vice* to happen the way Ellis did. If the show fell through, so what? Kent would just go back to running one of the most popular shows on television, but Ellis might have to downgrade further, from a studio apartment to a tent.

Larry's belief in the project and in Urs was also hard to ascertain. Only occasionally did he look up from his phone to offer non-sequiturs about "Sundance," "marketing synergy," and "digital rights management" without taking the swizzle stick out of his mouth.

Ellis sipped his soda and bitters and scanned the club. He could just make out Urs at the bar talking to a girl in a bikini top and stack heels. Her ass looked like a pair of volleyballs wrapped in spandex. Porn, Ellis assumed. The red neon *100* revealed enough body language—her crossed arms and haughty contrapasso; Urs's head thrown back in exasperation, then hanging in weariness—to tell they were arguing. Ellis's stare was broken when the crowd shifted, and people blocked his eyeline.

He turned back to the conversation, such as it was, between Kent and Larry.

"…four-quadrant…"

"…franchise potential…"

"…new normal…"

"…refuses to read for the part…"

"…circle back…"

They laughed. At what? Ellis joined in without knowing.

He marveled. Despite, or maybe somehow because of, people talking past one another in clichés, thousands upon thousands of new shows were being churned out all the time. And here he was, after thirty years of exiled dreaming, once again a cog in the cultural wheel. Almost.

Fate announced itself four weeks ago when Kent called out of the blue and asked if Ellis was interested in writing a *Miami Vice* reboot for Urs to star in, as the white detective Sonny Crockett, they both assumed. Ellis took the gig, of course, but had to ask, "Why me?"

"Because, dude, you're a genius," said Kent. As much as Ellis loved hearing it, he suspected the reason was budgetary: Ellis was a nobody and thus cheap. "And because you gave Urs his start. It's only right that you be a part of his *rebirth*. That's Larry's word, by the way."

Ellis was also being reborn.

Back when "Enter Sandman" was a new song, Ellis and Kent were staff writers on the underrated and short-lived military drama *SEAL Team Trident*. The show was executive produced by Aaron Grant, then regarded as the King of Cable Television. He earned the crown as the creator, writer, and producer of *Southland HEAT*, one of the most successful police procedurals of all time. *SEAL Team Trident*, however, was cancelled after just thirteen episodes.

Kent moved on to other increasingly successful shows, and Ellis washed out. Depressed over his father's sudden, mysterious death in 1994, he quit writing, earned his private investigator's license, and took over his father's agency.

Twenty-five years later, with the business gathering exponential downhill velocity, Aaron Grant's wife, Bettina, hired Ellis to tail Aaron and gather evidence she could use against him in divorce court. She also had Ellis deliver her nephew, Urs Schreiber's, headshot to Kent, the reigning King of Streaming. Ellis did, Urs was cast on *Graveyardland*, and the rest was history.

Urs dropped back into his seat, sloshing his drink on his shirt.

Larry said, "Put a pin in it, circle back."

"The dog groomer is attached to produce?" asked Kent.

"Nope," said Urs, spinning the gold Saturn-shaped medallion on his necklace, the one he'd been wearing as part of a Halloween costume the night of his arrest. "Gemini, just like John Wayne."

"…good friend of mine!" said Kent.

Ellis wondered if he was having a stroke or they were.

"…three-dimensional," said Larry, "and ethnically ambiguous…"

"…why I'm perfect to play Rico Tubbs!" said Urs.

Larry threw his hands up. "Oh, for fuck's sake."

"Again," said Kent, "cultural appropriation—"

"I'm not talking about black face," said Urs.

"Forget it!" said Larry. "Let it go already."

"I'm about to let *you* go! This whole show is my idea. If you're not gonna listen to me, I'm gonna go do coke with Evan Rachel Wood and her friends."

"Like hell you are."

"Watch me."

"You dumb sonofabitch, you're on probation—legally, and more important, publicly. You're supposed to have *grown*. You're supposed to be *reborn*."

"I'm the fuckin' boss here, Larry, not you. You get paid to back me up. But you never take my ideas seriously. Why is that, huh?"

"Rico Tubbs? That's a serious idea? You think you're going to bring something to that role that Philip Michael Thomas *and* Jamie Foxx didn't?"

"Yeah, being white and gay. How many times do I have to fuckin' say it? …Don't fuckin' roll your eyes at me, motherfucker! You know what? Fuck this." Urs stood, spilling more Paloma on himself. "And fuck you. I don't need this shit. I got Netflix offering me everything."

With that, he turned and disappeared into the dark crush of bodies.

Larry shook his head and said something to Kent, who made a *no-need-to-apologize* gesture. Then, without so much as a glance at Ellis, Larry stood and shouldered his way toward the exit.


IN THE PARKING LOT, a balmy wind washed over Ellis. Breathing in the fresh air and quiet night, he spotted Larry, fifteen yards away, walking up Hollywood Boulevard.

"Larry! Hey, wait up."

Larry stopped and looked back. When he saw Ellis trotting over, he continued on his way.

"Larry, hang on. Hang on, man." Ellis caught up, ashamedly winded. "Let's—*whew*… Let's reschedule. Somewhere not so noisy. There's obviously been a misunderstanding—"

"Urs thinks he's perfect to play Rico Tubbs for fuck's sake. He won't let it go. Nope, I'm done."

Ellis dogged Larry past a computer repair shop, Thai restaurant, French café, and weed dispensary. "I agree, it's a strange choice, but I mean, you're his agent. You could—"

"Not anymore. I'm done. I'm dropping him."

"Wait, stop. Let's—"

"You heard that little bastard. He's about to let *me* go? Uh-uh. I am letting *him* go!"

"Let's reschedule the meeting, okay? Let's everybody cool off, and we'll reschedule. My calendar is completely open."

"Listen, Alan, the best thing—"

"It's Ellis."

"—for Urs to do is disappear for a while, let this blow over, let this whole *woke*," he put air quotes around it, "bullshit cultural moment pass and use the time to grow up."

"But—"

"Kent tells me you're desperate for work."

Ellis cocked his head. "I wouldn't say *desperate*."

"You seem like a nice enough guy, so I'll be straight with you. Give up. If there's anything else you know how to do besides write, do it. The landscape is different now. Nobody's hiring old white guys."

*Old?!* "Okay, white guy, I'll give you, but I'm not that old."

"Ha! I hate to break it to you—"

"But Netflix—"

"There's no Netflix without me. I'm the one," Larry thumped his chest, "with the Netflix connections. Not that it matters anyway. Nobody, and I mean nobody, wants to work with Urs at this point. I'm not convinced Kent really does." Larry stopped at his BMW 7-Series and beeped the key fob. "Well, thanks for walking with me."

It struck Ellis as an odd thing to say. "Uh, sure. No problem."

"It's not safe out here." Larry cocked his head to the passenger side, still chewing the swizzle stick. "Get in. Lemme show you my dick."

"What the—?" Had Ellis heard right?

He would never know because in that second, a gunshot cracked.

Blood spattered his face. Something sharp hit his lip, and Larry dropped to the pavement, his skull broken open, oozing brains.

# CHAPTER 3

*I'M PLAYING THE BEST GOLF OF MY LIFE, thanks to Zyxeltra!*

Ellis blinked. Usually, the pharmaceutical commercial struck him funny. Especially when he was stoned. That line reading was so big, almost manic, it cracked him up. But today, stoned though he was, seated in a warm patch of yellow sunlight on the floor of his not-even-half-packed apartment, the comedy wasn't coming through.

Last night, when Ellis finally got home from Hollywood, after having told and re-told the story of Larry Price's murder to the police, he was exhausted but too wired to sleep. The adrenaline still surging through him made him want a drink to dampen the voltage, but there hadn't been a drop in the place for more than a year. And he was way past drinking mouthwash, though it did cross his mind. He was more or less used to the hundreds of random addiction triggers he encountered every day—song lyrics, billboards, certain streets, certain kinds of weather, good days, and bad—but nothing made him want to get wasted like seeing a dead body, let alone witnessing the killing. And he'd witnessed more than his share. Four, including Nazario.

Back then, he'd had the narcotizing bosoms of cocaine and alcohol to nurse. Last night, it took a hot shower, a gram-and-a-half of Pineapple Kush, a fistful of 5-mg. melatonin gummies, and three mugs of Natur-Ganic Valerian/Passionflower Sleep Tea he got at Whole Foods on West Olive Avenue to finally knock him out sometime around three a.m. during a rerun of *Southland HEAT*.

*Thanks to Zyxeltra, I shot an eighty-six, and no soreness!*

Usually, it was funny.

Ellis yawned, and his bruised cheek smarted. He sparked the joint he had been working on back to life.

*Do not use Zyxeltra if you are pregnant or plan on becoming pregnant.*

He toked and reached beside him for his .38 Smith & Wesson revolver. He placed it, sheathed in its holster, in a Jack Daniels box packed with random bric-a-brac he intended never to unpack: die-cast metal cars he'd had since he was a kid, paperbacks he was never going to finish—*Crime and Punishment, Helter Skelter, The DaVinci Code*—a red frisbee he hadn't tossed since 1993, a framed Polaroid of the woman he had tossed it with and hadn't seen since, and VHS tapes he had no way to view—

*Apocalypse Now, Navy SEALs, Total Recall, Lethal Weapon 2*. He taped the box shut and wrote *STRANGE ERA – DO NOT REVISIT* on the top with a pungent broad-tip Sharpie. He looked around at the other boxes full of CDs he abandoned after downloading Spotify—*Appetite for Destruction, Hotel California, Candy-O, Diver Down*—kitchen utensils he never used, and unfashionable clothes that no longer fit. And there was still so much more to pack. Now would have been the perfect time to get rid of such junk, but sentiment snuck up behind him every time he tried and paralyzed him with guilt. So, true to his nature, he gave up and determined to pack everything.

*Hollywood residents are on edge today after talent agent Larry Price was shot and killed last night after leaving the Century Club, a popular night spot. The shooter is on the run*, said Tayleigh Tompkins on MaxxNEWS.

Instantly, in a jolt of nausea and blood pressure, Ellis was right back on Hollywood Boulevard: red and blue flashing lights, police cordoning off the area and taking statements, the ambulance idling… No rush.

*The deadly gunfire has rocked the community and the entertainment industry to its very core. Police will not confirm or deny whether they believe this to be another killing by the Southland Sniper, the serial shooter who has claimed responsibility for three random murders in Los Angeles in the last five weeks.*

CUT TO: FULL SHOT of a shirtless man in pink bedroom slippers pushing a grocery cart of garbage up the street. Tayleigh in VOICE OVER: *Witnesses report hearing a loud gunshot ring out at approximately eleven-fifteen last night on Hollywood Boulevard west of Winona Boulevard, about a block from the Century Club.*

CUT TO: LONG SHOT of police cars in the parking lot. *A witness who preferred not to appear on camera*—Ellis, as a PI or a TV writer, preferred the faceless side of the camera—*told us that CAA agent Larry Price left the Century Club last night at approximately eleven-fifteen and was walking to his car parked on Hollywood Boulevard when a gunshot struck him in the head and killed him instantly. Other witnesses heard the shot and saw Price fall, but none saw the shooter.*

CUT TO: CLOSE UP of a young Asian American woman with a nose ring: *I heard the gunshot, y'know—bam!—and I go like, whoa! and then start runnin', goin' like, whaaat? Am I about to get shot right now? Aaah! And that's when, all of a sudden, I see the guy just layin' there, y'know, and I'm like, wow, this guy has a BMW and nice clothes and everything, but like, he's dead and I'm not. So…* She shrugged.

CUT TO: Tayleigh in the studio: *Police are still on the scene. They have been working through the night collecting evidence and conducting interviews, but all they will say at this point is that the motive remains under investigation. Anyone with any information is asked to call the Los Angeles police. Larry Price's clients included Urs Schreiber, Walton Goggins, and Mary Elizabeth Winstead. He will be missed.*

Ellis toked, but the joint had gone out again.

His phone rang: a local number he didn't recognize.

"Dunaway Priv—" Ever since Kent hired Ellis to write *Miami Vice*, Ellis started immediately trying to break the habit of answering the phone, "Dunaway Private Investigation," in anticipation of when it would no longer apply. He cleared his throat. "Hello?"

It was Urs.

"I just left the police station." His voice was anxious and exhausted. "They think I did it."

"Did what?"

"Killed Larry. What else?"

"Why do they think that?"

"They said a witness saw me running up Hollywood Boulevard with a rifle." There was a rushing sound and pop music in the background, like Urs was driving with the top down and the radio on.

"The news just said nobody saw the shooter."

"Yeah, well, for the last six fuckin' hours the cops said somebody *did* see the shooter and it was *me!*"

"They're just trying to sweat you," said Ellis. Or maybe they were withholding from the press that Urs was a suspect for some reason. "They obviously don't have enough to hold you."

"They said they'd see me again."

"And they probably will, but not necessarily to arrest you."

Urs said the cops didn't believe his alibi. "After I left the Century Club, I stopped to get gas at the Mobil on Sunset and North Bronson, and the card reader was fucked up, so while I was fucking with it, these two guys jumped me. They threatened to shoot me and then took my chain."

"The necklace with the Saturn medallion?"

"Yeah, they took that and like, seven hundred bucks."

"You report it to the police?"

"Fuck no, I didn't report it. I'm on probation, and I was high as hell, and I had an eight ball on me."

The way Urs sounded—stretched thin, scraped out—Ellis doubted much of the eight ball was left. Just thinking about it made Ellis's nose twitch.

He relit the roach, inhaled—"Y'know, Zac Efron was mugged at that same gas station a couple years ago"—and exhaled.

"Yeah, one of the cops that interrogated me worked the case. He said Zac smelled like cinnamon and sandalwood."

"Oh yeah?"

"You gotta help me out, man, please. You gotta clear my name. Everybody fuckin' hates me now. They wanna make an example out of me. They wanna put me in jail, dude. For fucking murder!"

"Relax. I'm sure there are security cameras at the gas station that will back up your story. You might even get your necklace back."

Urs wasn't listening. "I know you used to be a cop—"

"My father was a cop. I was never—"

"—or a private eye or some shit."

"Some shit, yeah."

"So, I wanna hire you to find out who killed Larry—"

"I mostly do divorce work, man. I'm not—"

"—or at least prove I'm innocent. The cops have already made up their minds I did it. You gotta help me out."

Urs sounded like the paranoid, over-tired, dehydrated cokehead he was. Probably tomorrow, after he crashed, he would realize he didn't have anything to worry about; he had an expensive attorney. The last thing Ellis wanted to do was get mixed up in Larry's murder investigation—in any investigation. He was eager to tape that box shut.

"I want to help you, man—"

"Great!"

"—but taking your case would be a conflict of interest, y'know, since we're going to be working together and everything." Ellis paused for Urs to confirm that they were... But he didn't.

"Just like the cops thinking you're guilty, I can't take the case already thinking you're innocent."

"But I am!"

"I don't doubt it. And that's the problem. It's called confirmation bias." (*Get 'Em*, Chapter 3: Ethics is More than Just a Six-Letter Word). In the not-too-distant past, Ellis had taken any work he could get, ethics be damned, like tailing Aaron Grant, but now, on the threshold of a new life, he didn't want to take any backward steps. "Try to relax. The security cameras at the Mobil station—"

"I'll pay you double your usual fee. Triple!"

Larry's murder was a horrible omen for Ellis's show business rebirth, but only if he let it be. Urs wouldn't be able to focus on developing a show or himself—he wouldn't be able to grow—if he were in and out of police stations, lawyers' offices, and courts all the time. Contrary to the adage, there was, now, such a thing as bad publicity. Urs was proving it. If Ellis could help exonerate him and there was any credibility to the myth of karma, surely Ellis would be rewarded with a contract and a salaried writing job. And besides that, he needed money in the meantime to cover the deposit on his new apartment. The nominal payment he'd gotten for writing *Miami Vice* had been spent on debts and living expenses in almost as little time as it had taken him to earn it.

Ellis sighed and rubbed his forehead. "Okay, man. I'll see what I can find out."

"Awesome! …text it to you…can't forget…"

"What? Urs…? You're breaking up."

"…in the canyon…breaking up… Remember…"

"Remember what? Hello?" The call dropped.

Ellis tossed his phone aside and took a deep toke. Looking around the apartment, he was bummed. He was almost out of boxes, and now the *Miami Vice* deal had devolved into… this.

There was a knock at the door. Ellis knew without looking through the peephole who it was. He roached the joint and got to his feet with a groan.

"Hi, Lucky," he said as he opened the door, stirring the smoke in the air.

"What happened to your face?" asked his Chinese American landlord, Lily Luk. She was a four-feet-and-eleven-inch spitfire in heavy eyeshadow and doused in perfume that over the years, Ellis had come to, if not like, no longer hate.

"It's nothing." He gingerly touched his cheek and winced for sympathy. "Just an acci—"

There was no sympathy. "You know the rules. No smoking allowed. It's against apartment policy and California state law to smoke in a multi-dwelling building."

"Yeah, I know, but what difference does it make anymore? They're tearing the building down. Almost everybody else has already moved out."

Regent Villa, the Mid-Century, rent-controlled apartment complex in Burbank—it looked like a Swiss chalet—where Ellis had lived for the past 30 years, had been sold to a Chinese development company planning to demolish and replace it with a concrete and steel five-over-two building called Pacific Synergy Plaza. Ellis had to be in a new apartment by the start of the new year.

Lucky was adamant. "California state law says—"

"I don't know if you've been outside lately, but California state law says a lot of things and none of it means shit."

"It means no smoking in a multi-dwelling unit. Get a vape pen. That's what I have." She pulled it out of her pocket and clicked it to LED-blinking life.

"I don't like vape pens. Those stupid cartridges get all clogged up, and the battery's always dead. There's no finesse, no human touch. The cannabis ritual is robbed of some essential…" he couldn't think of a better word, "thing."

Lucky drew on the pen and exhaled an odorless cloud. "See? No smell."

"Exactly. No smell, no soul."

"California state law and apartment policy is very clear."

They went around and around like that for another couple of minutes.

Ellis was glad for the distraction.

# CHAPTER 4

THE DOOR OF HI-HAT DISCOUNT LIQUOR on North
Glenoaks Boulevard was hung with red and gold tinsel. Ellis
walked in with his phone to his ear. He was surprised to hear Judy
Garland singing "Have Yourself a Merry Little Christmas"
through the ringing. These days, he only ever heard the hip-hop
version. The replacement of iconic intellectual properties, like
*Miami Vice*, with inferior remakes and reboots had started
gradually. Now, the practice was common, and the resultant
cultural swamp had trapped even Ellis. But, he thought, it was
probably delusional to pretend he was important enough even to
be part of the problem. Besides, he was lucky to have another
shot at a writing career, no matter how crass.

Sunil, who ran the store, was wearing a Santa Claus hat. A
lush snow-white beard—his own—completed the look. Ellis

waved, but Sunil didn't see because he was finishing up with a customer.

After six rings, Kent answered. "What's up, dude? I got you on speakerphone. Jillian is in the car with me."

The name meant nothing to Ellis. "Hi, Jillian."

Last night, Kent was in the crowd watching Larry Price get loaded into the ambulance. He was envious that Ellis had witnessed the shooting and was still talking about it. "It must have been *sooooo* insane! A piece of his skull actually hit you?"

"Uh-huh. In the lip."

To keep from picturing Larry's exploding head, Ellis admired the autumnal rainbow of labels on the bottles lining the shelves: brown antlers and eagle feathers, orange oak leaves, red family crests, silver filigree, sepia-toned antebellum Romanticism.

"Awesome! It's like *Faces of Death* or something," said Kent. "Fuck me, I wish I'd been there."

"Well, it wasn't like *Faces of Death* because it was actually real, and I wish you'd been there too, and I'd been the one drinking in the bar. Anyway, that's why I called. When I went after Larry, did you catch up with Urs? …Hello…? Kent? You there?"

"…Evan Rachel Wood and her friends… generate buzz at Sundance…"

The wind howling around his convertible Jaguar F-Type and the spotty cell reception garbled most of what Kent was saying.

Still, the upshot seemed to be that he didn't see Urs again after he stormed off because he, Kent, was gossiping about the Sundance Film Festival with Evan Rachel Wood and her friends.

"So, with Larry Price out of the picture, where else are we thinking about taking the show?" asked Ellis. "Hulu, HBO, Maxx Plus maybe?" Kent was the last person to whom Ellis was worried about coming across as insensitive. "Hello…? Kent?"

"…in the canyon… not the best timing…"

"Not the best timing for the show or this call? …Hello?"

"…put a pin in it, circle back after the holidays…"

Kent kept talking, but it was just more fractured jargon. Ellis picked up a fifth of Old Grand-Dad, which had become his brand, replacing Jim Beam, after he bought a bottle one night when he was blacked out.

"…private jet to Aspen…" said Kent. "…committed to a deal with Sony… hope you…"

"Dude, you're breaking up pretty bad. Anyway, uh, I'm really excited about the show. We're gonna get Urs his heat back." And mine too, thought Ellis. "I can feel it."

"…in the canyon …no signal…"

"Hello…? Hello…?"

The call failed. Ellis pocketed his phone and walked to the front of the store. He was almost at the register before he realized he was still carrying the bottle of Old Grand-Dad. He waffled a moment but then put it back.

"No boxes today," said Sunil Claus. "Somebody came before you and took everything."

# CHAPTER 5

*I'M PLAYING THE BEST GOLF OF MY LIFE.*

Century Club owner Terry Montero was looking over Ellis's shoulder at the 42-inch HDTV on the back wall of his office. His eyes sparkled as he mouthed the words along with himself. *Thanks to Zyxeltra!*

"This is the seventeenth time I've seen my commercial today," he said, rapt in his own image.

"That's awesome, man. I love this commercial," Ellis said, looking behind him.

*I shot an eighty-six,* Terry rubbed his shoulder and flashed his capped teeth the way he did on screen, *with* no *soreness!*

Ellis chuckled. The comedy was back.

*Do not use Zyxeltra if you are pregnant or plan on becoming pregnant,* he lip-synched, cocking an authoritative eyebrow, but Terry missed it. With his part over, he had turned his attention back to chopping out lines of cocaine with a credit card.

"I saw it twenty-two times yesterday," he said. "And to think, I owe it all to you."

"Maybe you'll remember me in your acceptance speech when you win an Oscar," said Ellis, wiping his sweaty palms on his knees. He pulled his eyes off the coke and focused on the framed *Night Street* promo poster on the wall.

When Ellis gave Urs Schreiber's headshot to Kent, he also gave him Terry's, who, at sixty-six years old, also landed a part on *Graveyardland* as a featured extra, which led to the Zyxeltra commercial. Ellis doubted it aired twenty-two, or even sixteen, times a day, but it was indeed a lot. Enough to encourage Terry to invest in a battery of plastic surgery procedures to expedite his super-stardom. The scars from his chin tuck and eye lift were still healing. His Latin complexion precluded the need for a tanning booth, but he was an early and enthusiastic ambassador of the technology. His skin looked like religiously moisturized saddle leather, but sure enough, the camera liked it.

Since the late 1970s, back when Ellis was another Schwinn-riding kid and his father, Hank, was still a detective for the LAPD, Terry had owned discos, bars, and pizza places. According to him, he would trade information to Hank in exchange for him looking the other way on Terry's procuring and drug dealing for a clientele that included not only the adult film stars of the day—"your John Holmeses, your Sekas, your Vanessa del Rios"—but also mainstream celebs like John Belushi, Harrison Ford, and "sweet kid" Dana Plato from *Diff'rent Strokes*.

In 1989, Terry appeared in three episodes of a by-the-numbers LAPD procedural called *Night Street* and hadn't worked as an actor since. Until *Graveyardland*. In the years between, Terry reverted to type, dealing drugs and laundering the money through the nightclubs he operated. And Hank resigned from the LAPD, founded Dunaway Private Investigation agency, and wrote the book that would become the PI industry bible, *Get 'Em: The Private Investigator's Ultimate Guide to Tracking Missing Persons and Fugitives for Profit and Vengeance*. When he died in a helicopter crash in 1994, Ellis, still in a tailspin from the cancellation of *SEAL Team Trident*, abandoned hope of succeeding in television and assumed liability of his father's agency. Terry came along with it. Occasionally, he would give Ellis a tip on an investigation, usually it was nothing, but it provided a pretext for buying Terry's high-grade and wholesale cocaine.

"So, what's up, babe? Where the hell have you been? I was startin' to get my feelings hurt. I mean, you never even called me to congratulate me on my commercial, and I know you saw it. It's on TV twenty-five times a day."

Ellis cleared his throat and uncrossed, then re-crossed, his legs. Since getting sober, or what passes for it in L.A., there was little reason for him to come to the Century Club and endure Terry talking about himself over the blaring television in his cramped office. Watching him toy with the glittering mound of blow, his typical little demonstration of relative wealth and power, Ellis was eager to move things along and slip back out of temptation's grip.

"Yeah, yeah. I'm sorry about that, man. I've been pretty busy lately." He traced a finger over his tender, swollen cheek, which Terry hadn't mentioned, if he even noticed. "I'm writing again, and last night—"

"Rachel Evan Woods was in here last night," said Terry, rolling up a hundred-dollar bill.

"It's Evan Rachel Wood, and I know. I was here."

"You were here? What the fuck, babe? Why the hell didn't you say hi? I thought we were better friends than that. I'm about to get my feelings hurt."

"We are friends, man, but I was having a meeting with Kent Moran and Urs and—"

"I let Rachel and her friends get high in my office."

"Oh yeah? Was Urs with them?"

"Nah, it was like four or five chicks. They were hot as fuck, too, except for one who was kinda fat and had half of her head shaved. I think she was Rachel's assistant."

"*Evan's* assistant. And can you turn down the TV a little?" Terry changed channels, but the volume stayed up. "Okay. Well, anyway, I was having a meeting with Kent and Urs and his agent, Larry Price—"

"How 'bout that shit? The Southland Sniper fuckin' kills him, and now my club *and* my commercial are all over TV and the internet. Haha! MaxxNEWS is coming here to interview me in a little while. I gotta get into character." He snorted a line of coke with the rolled C-note.

"I don't think the Southland Sniper has taken responsibility for the killing yet, but that's awesome how it worked out for you."

Terry winked, missing the sarcasm.

"The cops questioned Urs last night and told him a witness saw him fleeing the scene with a rifle."

"Pfft! Urs isn't a killer," said Terry, massaging his nose. "The cops're just sweating him because he beat the rap on all that other DUI shit."

"That's what I told him, but he's freaking out. So, did you see him at all last night, like around the time of the murder? About eleven?"

"Hell no, babe, I was in here getting high with Rachel and her friends."

"*Evan* Rachel. Her name is Evan Rach—" Ellis shook his head. "Forget it. Anyway, Urs wasn't with them?"

"No. Are you deaf?"

"I will be if you don't turn the TV down…" He didn't. "Did Larry Price come in here a lot?"

"Huh?"

"I said, *did Larry Price come in here a lot?!*"

"My office?"

"No, the club."

"Nah. I never even heard of him until he got his head blown off."

Ellis agreed that the Southland Sniper most likely killed Larry. The shooting fit the serial killer's MO, except that he still hadn't contacted the police claiming responsibility. Thinking how easily it could have been Ellis who was gunned down, that only by random chance was he alive and Larry Price dead, made him want to bury his face in the mound of cocaine on Terry's desk. Then again, maybe Larry had an enemy who, acting as a copycat, used chance as camouflage...

"Last night, Urs was arguing with a girl with a big ass in a mini skirt. She had a tattoo on her left thigh," said Ellis.

"White girl?" asked Terry. "That's probably Brandii Bunnz. Sweet kid."

"Brandy what?"

"Brandii—with two Is—Bunnz—two Ns and a Z."

"Porn?"

"She's an influencer."

"What's her beef with Urs?"

"No tellin'." Terry snorted another line. Ellis used to hate waiting for Terry to offer him a toot, but now he hoped Terry didn't. Ellis wasn't sure he'd pass the test. "A lotta people have beef with him."

"How come?"

"You know him. He's an arrogant little shit. He talks down to people. Not to me, of course. Me and Urs, we're like this," Terry crossed his fingers, "But, y'know," he hoovered another line, "he can be rude to the security guys and the bartenders. Especially when he's been over-served. I had to hold Jamichael back from kicking his ass more than a couple times."

"Aren't you interested in why I was meeting with him and Kent and Larry last night?"

Whether Terry didn't hear or didn't care, he didn't respond. However, he did push the coke mirror across the desk to Ellis.

Ellis sat back and crossed his arms. His armpits were damp. "No thanks. I, uh— I'm good. I'm trying to kinda clean up my act a little bit."

"Is that why you don't come see me anymore?"

"No, man. In fact, I was just gonna say, I've been—"

"That really hurts my feelings, babe. I thought I was your friend, not just your drug dealer."

"You are my friend. Like I said, I—"

"Your dad and I, we were like *this*." Terry crossed his fingers again.

"For sure, yeah. I know all about you and my dad. It's just— I've been really busy writing this show for Urs. I can't say too much about it because we're still in development, and now with Larry getting killed and everything—" Ellis sat forward and licked his lips. "Maybe I will do a line, just a little one, to freshen up."

Again, Terry didn't seem to hear. The coke mirror stayed where it was while he aimed the remote over Ellis's shoulder, changing channels, undoubtedly searching for his commercial.

"Since I gave you some information, I got a favor to ask you. A little tit for tat."

Ellis hung his head and sighed. The last favor he did for Terry started the chain of events that led Ellis to kill Nazario Sanchez. But it also allowed him to finish an investigation his father had begun twenty years prior and expose a high-profile crime family. "What is it?"

Terry tossed Ellis an oversized manila envelope.

"What's this?" he asked, even though the moment it hit his hands, he knew.

"Sixty thousand dollars." Bingo. "Do me a solid and deliver it, huh?"

The envelope was addressed to Ramsey Skillern in North Hollywood. "I haven't done a solid in six weeks. My doctor says I need more fiber in my diet. Or is it less…?"

"Anytime tomorrow is fine."

"I dunno, man. This isn't exactly tit for tat. I asked you for a name, and you're asking me to deliver drug money to some gangster."

"It's not drug money, and Ramsey runs a prop rental business. I'm just the middleman between him and a colleague who utilized his services."

Ellis squinted. "Uh-huh. A colleague…" Hinky. He wanted to tell Terry where he could stick his sixty thousand dollars, but something, like a premonition or maybe simply hedging his bets against an inevitable relapse and drug purchase, prevented Ellis from burning another bridge his father had built.

He tucked the envelope under his arm and opened the office door.

"This has something to do with porn, doesn't it?"

*I'm playing the best golf of my life.*

Terry pumped his fist at the TV. "I'm back, baby, thanks to Zyxeltra!"

STROLLING DOWN HOLLYWOOD BOULEVARD, retracing the steps he took alongside Larry Price last night, Ellis remembered Urs fidgeting, spinning his gold Saturn medallion and twisting cocktail napkins into ropes, his manicured hands never still. They didn't look like hands that spent much time at the rifle range. And whoever killed Larry had been a dead shot.

Other reasons Ellis doubted Urs was the gunman: A) he seemed like a complete wuss—not that you had to be brave to commit gun murder, quite the opposite, but still… B) while clearly Urs had been high on something last night, he was agitated, not insane, and killing his agent would be insane; C) Urs was paying Ellis three times his usual fee to investigate, and D) he sounded more sincere on the phone, even with the call dropping in and out, than he had in his big monologue in *Brass Hearts*, no matter what the critics said.

When Ellis got to the blood stain on the pavement where Larry had fallen dead, he admitted to himself that he was acting in bad faith. He wasn't thinking of how to help Urs, and he had no expectations whatsoever of discovering anything on the street that would positively exonerate him. Ellis just wanted—*needed*—to rack up billable hours while the racking was good. Probably tomorrow or the next day, the Southland Sniper would send a letter to the *Times* owning up to Larry's murder, and following the pattern, taunt that there were killings yet to come and he would never be caught. Then, with Urs's name clear, he, Ellis, and Kent could get back to *Miami Vice*.

Confirmation bias was a bitch.

Backtracking to the Century Club, an emaciated yellow bobtail cat abandoned the roadkill it was eating and started walking with Ellis, a couple of steps ahead, like it was leading the way.

Right when Ellis unlocked and opened the Porsche, a motorcycle engine revved and startled him. A streak of yellow flashed under a streetlight. Ellis took a deep breath to recover his pulse and pivoted to drop into the car, but stopped.

"What the—?"

The yellow bobtail cat was sitting in the driver's seat, licking its chops and flashing a broken fang.

"Get the fuck outta there… I mean it. C'mon, let's go."

As he waved and shooed, the cat curled up, hooked a paw over its nose, and started to purr.

"You should know better than to get into a stranger's car." He reached in and scooped the female cat onto the pavement with one hand, surprised at how little she weighed. "Now, stay out of trouble," he said as she trotted away, flicking her stubby tail.

# CHAPTER 6

AMONG OTHER ACTION STARS, autographed headshots of Sylvester Stallone, Jason Statham, and Charlie's Angels—Drew Barrymore, Cameron Diaz, and Lucy Liu—gridded the morning-sun-soaked wall behind the counter of Bullseye Props in North Hollywood.

"So, how do you know Terry?" asked Ramsey Skillern, locking the manila envelope full of cash in the reception desk, casual but wary. His skin was Crayola-crayon brown. He had close-cropped hair and a goatee so small Ellis wondered what the point was. Ramsey wore his official Bullseye Props polo shirt, with a bullseye embroidered on the breast, tucked into black jeans that fit like slacks.

"Terry's an old friend of the family," said Ellis.

Ramsey nodded like he knew there was more to the story but wasn't going to press.

"I work in the industry too," said Ellis. "I'm a writer," he was curious enough about the sixty grand to linger and see what kind of vibe he got, "but I've never been in a prop house before."

"That right? Lemme show you around."

Ellis waited while Ramsey punched in the code that unlocked the metal door to the warehouse, then followed him in. Like a well-organized pawn-shop-cum-army-surplus-store, rack after rack, shelf after shelf was stocked with badges, machetes, riot helmets, web belts, and artillery shells. Every kind of bicycle, rowboat, and wheelchair from the last two centuries hung from the ceiling.

"We specialize in action and stunt props mostly," said Ramsey. "Anything military and police, fire and rescue, tactical, medical, sci-fi, western…" Ellis eyed the racks of gas masks, syringes, Kevlar vests, AK-47s, and M-16s. "Replica weapons—from six shooters to rocket launchers—functional electronics, fake currency, jewelry, diamonds, drugs…" Ziplock bags full of white powder made Ellis's nose itch. "We've even got a 3D printer, CNC machines, and laser cutters, so we can custom-make just about anything you can think of. There's lots of places to go for Mid-Century lamps and toasters and TV sets, but you gotta come here for something like that there." Ramsey pointed to a Gatling gun that looked like it had just rolled off a Civil War battlefield.

Ellis began to doubt his assumption that the "colleague" of Terry's who had utilized Ramsey's services worked in porn. Not that there weren't action-genre-themed porn movies, but not many of the producers were likely to spend sixty grand on props this sophisticated. Ellis could, however, imagine lots of ways that Terry and his underworld cohorts could make use of fake guns, drugs, police uniforms, jewels, and money. It crossed Ellis's mind that maybe the money he delivered to Ramsey wasn't even real.

"We supply all the props for *Graveyardland*," said Ramsey, straightening a row of hand grenades. "You know the big wooden cross wrapped in barbed wire the bishop used in season two?"

Ellis had no idea but nodded. "Uh-huh."

"We made that."

"No kidding? That's awesome. I'm co-writing a new series with Kent Moran."

"For real? What's it about?" Ramsey's tone was more polite than genuinely interested.

"It, uh— Actually, we're still in development, so I can't say too much about it, but it's gonna be..." Ellis stopped short of saying, "woke as fuck," and went with, "action packed. Kent and I used to write *SEAL Team Trident* together." Ramsey's face was blank. "Maybe you remember it... on Maxx...? Back in the nineties?"

Ramsey shook his head. Of course, he didn't remember it. Nobody did. "When your new show goes into production, you know where to come get your props."

"For sure, for sure." Ellis instigated a handshake. "Thanks for showing me around. I gotta run. I have a meeting at Warners."

Ramsey smiled like he heard that all the time.

BETWEEN WARNER BROS. STUDIOS to the north and the Hollywood sign to the south, Forest Lawn Drive was lined with RVs, camper vans, and trailers, most of them wrecked and missing parts essential to automobility. Every fifth or sixth one had fire damage—meth lab mishaps.

Electrified by the midday sun and Santa Ana wind, the people who lived in the makeshift camp bickered, smoked crack, shot dope, disassembled appliances, defecated, and pitched fits in plain view of the traffic rushing by. It seemed to be an odd place for Brandii Bunnz to be creating content, shaking her big ass in a hot-pink thong, until Ellis noticed her videographer was positioned in the trash-strewn but otherwise empty bike lane trying to get the gigantic *Bachelorette* billboard in the background. "Marketing synergy," Larry Price might have called it.

"Make sure you get *Bachelorette* in there—" Brandii said as she twerked, "—the whole word. It's literally the whole point of being here."

"I am, I am," said the spindly, white-haired man with the camera. "Looks really hot, baby. Move to the left a little... No, no, *your* left. That's it. That's really hot."

"I can tell the angle's not low enough," said Brandii. "Get the fuck down there!" With a grunt, the old man got to his knees. "And watch the shadows. I don't have all day to fuck with this."

When they stopped to watch the playback, Ellis approached and introduced himself.

"Like I said when I messaged you, I'm writing Urs Schreiber's next project and—"

"You said Kent Moran was writing it." Brandii's heart-shaped face with its ski-slope nose was probably cute, but it was hard to tell under all the makeup and attitude.

"He's producing it," said Ellis, "and we're hoping you can help us out."

Brandii lit up and stepped closer. "You want me to be in it?"

"Sure, I guess. That's not my decision to make. We were hoping—"

"Dad!" Brandii yelled at the old man futzing with the camera. "Go get me a headshot and my bio outta the car!"

"That's not necessary," Ellis said to both of them, but the old guy was already on the move. "It's not my decision to make."

"Is it Kent's decision?"

"Yes and no. It's complicated. Anyway, I— Kent and I were hoping you could give us some perspective on Urs Schreiber. I know you're a friend of his and—"

"Okay, to be honest, I wouldn't say we were friends. I've known him for a long time and I love him as a person, y'know, but we don't like, hang out or anything like that. Trust me though, on the set, in front of the cameras, I am one hundred percent professional."

"Yeah, I saw that. So, you've known Urs a while?"

"We went to high school together in Orange County. That's where I'm from, Costa Mesa. Me and my ex-boyfriend and Urs and his ex-girlfriend double-dated a couple of times. It was nothing major, but we had fun. But then, when Urs moved up here and got famous though, he just like, ghosted everybody. Christian, that's my ex, he hates Urs to this day, not just because he's a snob, but Christian says Urs stole his part in *Brass Hearts*."

"What's Christian's last name?"

"Cooper. You won't have heard of him. He's never really been in anything. That's why he was so mad when he lost that part to Urs. But I'm a professional, y'know? I believe in letting the past stay in the past. Like, I one hundred percent don't blame Urs for focusing on his career. I'm really focused like that, too. When I'm working, it's like, I'm all about the work, y'know? I did a play in middle school, so I can memorize lines and all that stuff. And I'm like, honestly *obsessed* with being on time. You'll never have to worry about me being late to the set—"

"That's awesome. I love your enthusiasm, but I'm not the casting director."

"Here's your headshot, baby," said Brandii's father, winded and sweaty.

"What about the bio?" asked Brandii.

"We're out of them. I didn't make it to Kinko's yet."

"Goddamnit, dad! I swear to God—"

"Don't worry about it, please," Ellis said, looking from one to the other. "I don't make casting decisions."

"Well, could you like, give this to Kent for me anyway?" Brandii asked, fluttering her false lashes.

"Sure." Ellis took her headshot.

"I have like, almost a million followers on Instagram and I've partnered with a bunch of hot brands like—"

"Synergy, yeah, awesome. So, was Christian Cooper also mad at Urs's agent, Larry Price, over losing the part in *Brass Hearts*?"

Brandii wrinkled her little nose. "Not that I know of. Why?"

"Like I said, I'm just trying to get some perspective on Urs and gauge how ready he is to work. He's obviously got a lot going on. You don't think Urs could have had anything to do with Larry's murder, do you?"

Per *Get 'Em*, Chapter 3, it wasn't the proper way to frame the question, suggesting the answer you wanted from the interviewee. Again, confirmation bias… The only answer you were supposed to want was the unfettered truth.

"No fucking way!" she said, sputtering a laugh. "Urs—I don't mean this to sound like, mean or anything—but Urs is like, way too soft to kill anybody. He just talks shit behind people's backs."

"When you and he were talking in the Century Club the other night, it looked like things were kind of tense."

"That was nothing. That was just some stupid drama from a long time ago that he can't let go of. But honestly, it wouldn't affect our working relationship. On set, I would be one hundred percent professional."

"I'm sure." The sun was directly overhead, and the Santa Anas were stirring the foul odors of the mile-long homeless camp. Time to wrap it up. "So, after your argument, did you see Urs again that night, like around eleven o'clock or so?"

"No, and we weren't arguing. I told you. It was just some stupid drama—" Brandii's demeanor calcified. She took a step back and squinted at Ellis from under the visor of her hand. "Are you a cop?"

"What? No. I'm a writer."

"I dunno… I'm getting cop vibes all of a sudden."

Just when Ellis opened his mouth to assure her—

*BAH-WOOOM!!*

—an explosion shook the street.

He ducked, covering his head. When he looked up, one of the RVs was on fire. Brandii and her father were jogging toward the blaze.

"Make sure you get the flames," she said, bouncing her ass before the fiery backdrop.

"I am, I am," said her father, crouching for the best camera angle. "You're lookin' good, baby. Really hot."

# CHAPTER 7

ELLIS'S FIRST VISIT to the set of a porn movie ended with a couple of security guards kicking the shit out of him in a warehouse parking lot in Sylmar. Today, in a Woodland Hills ranch house, he was hoping for a better outcome.

It was clear from the pictures lining the hallways and shelves that the house belonged to a proud and photogenic family of five. They appeared to be of Greek or Armenian descent and take lots of expensive vacations: mom and dad in a gondola, the twin girls on the slopes, little brother holding up the Tower of Pisa, all together in Giza, Machu Picchu, Epcot Center. In addition to the living room furniture, there were C-stands and LED lights. Cables and extension cords snaked across the carpet. Ellis added it up that the family defrayed the cost of their lavish vacations by renting their house to porn shoots. He wondered if the kids knew what happened in their bedrooms when they were gone.

A young woman wearing only bikini bottoms and rollers in her hair sat on an overstuffed floral-print armchair, vaping and flipping through a magazine. Two grips in backward ball caps and work boots were asleep and snoring on the matching sofa. Huddled around the grand piano, a man in chinos and a button-down shirt was in conference with a woman in a tracksuit and a muscular naked guy.

On the patio on the other side of the sliding glass door, two men were fucking a woman in a stand of lights and reflectors while the crew watched, and the camera operator circled the action.

In the kitchen, a woman wearing a bathrobe, high heels, and sunglasses was snorting coke with a guy in a black leather jacket and a shirtless guy with a beach towel wrapped around his waist.

Standing across the room at the sink, with his back to the others, Christian Cooper, also shirtless, was raking the cream filling out of Double Stuf Oreos with his teeth and washing it down with swigs of Red Bull. Ellis introduced himself.

Christian was far less impressed by the dropping of Kent Moran's name than Brandii, which gave Ellis a modicum of respect for the lanky young man in tight jeans running his fingers through his wavy hair and avoiding eye contact.

"First of all, Brandii is a fucking idiot," he said, twisting open another Oreo. "It's true, Urs and I aren't tight like we used to be, but that's bullshit about me being mad at him because he stole *Brass Hearts* out from under me. That's how the business is— friendship doesn't mean shit. I know that. And he didn't ghost me, okay? He mighta ghosted Brandii because she's a fucking idiot, but there's nothing but love between me and Urs. I could call him right now if I wanted to." He licked the filling out of the cookie, dropped the empty halves in the sink, switched on the garbage disposal, and stared into it.

Ellis noticed a shadow on Christian's neck and assumed it was a hickey. "What about his agent, Larry Price?" he asked over the grinding noise. "How did you feel about him?"

"I didn't feel any way about him," Christian said loud enough to raise the heads of the three people snorting coke off one of the Armenian, or Greek, family's dinner plates. He switched off the disposal and said, quieter, "I mean, it's too bad he's dead I guess, but it sounds like he was kind of a douchebag. I met his assistant at Bella Thorne's birthday after-party at One Oak, and she said he was talking about dropping Urs."

"Bella Thorne said that?"

"No, Larry's assistant Kendra. I don't know her last name."

"She say why?"

"Why what?"

"Why Larry wanted to drop Urs."

Christian ran his hand through his hair some more, pushing it this way and that. "I dunno, she said Larry thought Urs wasn't talented enough to put up with what a two-faced asshole he can be. Those are Larry's words, not mine. Me and Urs, we got nothing but love."

"So, like, you don't think Urs had anything to do with Larry's murder, do you?" It was the same leading question Ellis had put to Brandii. However, Christian's response was slightly, but significantly, different.

"Hmm…" He gulped some Red Bull and then looked Ellis in the face for the first time. "They say everybody is capable of murder under the right circumstances."

"Yeah. Yeah, that's what they say, alright."

He cut his eyes over at the motley crew doing coke, half hoping, half fearing they were going to offer him some. He saw the lights go out through the sliding glass door and the boom mic come down. The crew began to stir, getting ready for the next setup.

"But, no, yeah. I mean, Urs probably definitely had more reasons than most people for wanting to kill Larry, but I seriously doubt he would actually do it. He's more the kind of guy who would get somebody to do it for him. I'm not saying he *did*, I'm just saying."

Ellis was mulling over Christian's equivocations when the actor added, "I was at my parents' house."

"Pardon me?"

"The night Larry got killed. I was at my parents' house. It was my stepdad's birthday."

"Oh. Okay."

A middle-aged man hustled into the kitchen, wearing the kind of vest fly-fishermen wear—khaki with lots of pockets—and the harried expression of an assistant director. "Five minutes, Christian. Wha—...? What the hell did you do to your hair?"

Christian ran his hand through it and let it fall back in his face. "Nothing."

"Whaddya mean, nothing? It's all messed up. Go have Jules fix it. And tell him to touch up that bruise on your neck, too." Christian clapped his hand over it. "You look like Dracula bit you. Chop chop! Five minutes."

Christian huffed and stalked out of the kitchen, bare feet slapping the linoleum, still holding his neck.

The AD looked at Ellis. "Who the hell are you?"

"You remember the show *SEAL Team Trident?* From the nineties?"

He didn't.


AT THE BOTTOM of the driveway, a pair of pre-teen boys on bikes, wearing helmets and knee and elbow pads, stopped Ellis.

"What's going on in there?" one of them asked, pointing at the house. "A party or something?"

Ellis looked up at the house and back at the snickering boys.

"No, they're shooting a movie called *Stop! Or My Mom Will Squirt.*"


VENICE BEACH was one of the places Ellis liked the least in the city he loved the most. Since he wasn't a surfer, skater, weightlifter, busker, hula hooper, goggle-eyed tourist, or mentally ill vagrant, and since he wasn't in the market for a tattoo, glass bong, corporate logo parody T-shirt, shitty tacos, or meth, the boardwalk offered little more than people watching, albeit of a world-class caliber.

On weekends, the freakishness was amplified by the Venice Beach Drum Circle, an impromptu institution—two hundred or so free spirits pounding away on bongos, djembes, tablas, tambourines, buckets, boxes, and trash cans. The hands that weren't busy doing that were passing joints or waving ecstatically in the air. Ellis wouldn't have been there (especially on a weekend!) except that that's where Larry Price's ex-assistant Kendra texted she'd be indulging a visiting cousin from Minnesota.

Ellis found them taking magic-hour selfies. Kendra was petite with long, layered, and streaked blonde hair. She wore a gray T-shirt, high-waisted jeans in a light wash, and pointed mules. Her fourteen-year-old cousin Boyd, in floral board shorts and a tie-dyed *I ♥ L.A.* tank top, had bad skin and green hair. Under his arm was a spanking-new skateboard.

Kendra barely remembered Bella Thorne's birthday after-party and didn't remember Christian Cooper at all.

"I was doing ketamine that night," she said, but just the same, she was "happy to meet a friend of Kent Moran's and spill the tea on Larry and Urs. I'm out of job, so, what the fuck?" She took a vape pen out of her purse and clicked it on.

"I wanna meet Bella Thorne," said Boyd. "What's ketamine? That guy over there is smoking weed. Look."

Ellis looked. "Oh, no. That guy is smoking crack."

"What about him?"

Ellis looked the other way. "Yeah, he's smoking weed, but judging by the way he's twitching, it's probably laced with something."

"Whoooa! Cool."

"Not cool."

"Go get a henna tattoo or something," Kendra said to Boyd. "Give us a minute."

Boyd stuck out his bottom lip playfully and hopped on his skateboard. Immediately, he hit a rock and fell off.

Kendra shook her head. "So, anyway, Urs is as toxic as everybody says he is, but I definitely don't think he killed Larry. This isn't a very feminist thing to say, okay, but honestly… he's way too much of a pussy. If he were in jail like he should be though, it wouldn't even be a question, right?"

"Are people asking that question—did Urs kill Larry?"

"Isn't that what you're asking?"

"I'm just trying to gain some perspective, y'know, since I'm writing his next project."

Kendra was wearing sunglasses, but Ellis could tell she rolled her eyes. "Uh-huh. Well, here's my perspective—quit now. Take any other job. And tell Kent the same thing. I can't believe he didn't fire Urs from *Graveyardland*. I mean, I feel like I can't even watch it anymore, and it's my favorite show. Like, how is Kent this total genius and can't read the room better than that?"

Ellis gave a rueful shrug. "He's never been able to read a room. And listen, I don't mean to talk shit. Kent and I have been friends a long time. I love him like a brother, y'know? We're like this," he crossed his fingers. "Nothing but love. And I'm super-happy for him that people think he's a genius, but honestly," he lowered his voice to a conspiratorial level, just above the incessant drumming, "he's *not* a genius."

"I'm starting to wonder," said Kendra. "Urs is cancelled, and anybody who works with him will be cancelled too. If Urs weren't a celebrity—a white male nepo baby—if he were a person of color, he'd be in jail, that is, if the cops didn't murder him first, in broad daylight, like they did to, uh… what was that guy's name? You know who I'm talking about…" Ellis shrugged. "Anyway, Urs Schreiber wouldn't even be a celebrity in the first place if his uncle wasn't Aaron Grant—another notorious scumbag."

"Mm-hmm. Yep." Kendra hadn't been born yet when *SEAL Team Trident* was on the air, but Ellis made a mental note not to mention it or his one-time employment under notorious scumbag Aaron Grant.

"Plus, Urs is a racist. He was practically in black face when he got arrested."

"No way."

"He was dressed as a pimp—in a suit and that ridiculous necklace. How have you not seen the pictures?"

Ellis thought it was racist to assume that because somebody wore a suit and a gaudy medallion, he was imitating a black person—a pimp at that—but kept it to himself.

"He was dressed as a member of the Iapetusian Brotherhood of Eternal Tranquility. They were a cult that committed mass suicide in the eighties. The costume was in bad taste, for sure, but not because it was racist."

"Well, the whatever-you-said Brotherhood—that's the patriarchy, so…"

"The leader was a woman."

"Urs is a racist."

"He's immature. I'll give you that."

"He wants to play the African American guy on some stupid *Miami Vice* reboot. That's not the show you're writing, is it?"

Ellis nodded, embarrassed that he was embarrassed.

Again, Kendra rolled her eyes. "Sorry, not sorry. A couple days ago, Urs and Larry got into this big fight over it in Larry's office. You could hear them all the way down the hall. The only reason Larry hadn't already dropped him was because he hadn't figured out how to fuck him yet."

"You mean literally or…?"

"I mean in any way a person can fuck another person. Larry loved fucking people and fucking them over. But he would settle for just being a sadistic creep. He used to make me go into the bathroom with him and take dictation while he pissed."

*Lemme show you my dick*—BANG! "Yeah, he liked to show it off, didn't he?"

"And this one time he sent me to Erewhon to get him a chicken salad sandwich for lunch and told me to bring it to him while he was in a meeting with Kat Dennings and some ODL people. So, I did, and he threw the sandwich in the trash and bitched me out for interrupting the meeting and forgetting that he was a vegan. But he's not a vegan. He just did the whole little routine to impress Kat. After the meeting, he made me go get him another chicken salad sandwich, which he ate on the toilet."

"That's disgusting," said Ellis. "What's ODL?"

"The Order of the Divine Light."

"Those Satanists from the sixties?"

"They're not specifically Satanists anymore. Now, they call themselves a," Kendra made air quotes, "*non-profit research library.* But it's really just a bunch of rich people playing dress up and throwing parties for themselves. Larry got kicked off the board for calling one of the volunteer docents a cunt. He was trying to get back on by having Kat Dennings photographed entering the mansion—a publicity stunt. Kat Dennings is a vegan, that's why the whole routine with the sandwich."

"The mansion?"

"The ODL headquarters are in this old mansion in Los Feliz."

"So, it kind of sounds like, if the Southland Sniper didn't kill Larry, there are other people who—"

"There ain't no Southland Sniper," said a bearded homeless man, swilling from a half-gallon jug of something that smelled like diesel fuel. "Newspapers made the whole thing up. Video killed the radio star. The CIA trains ninja assassins up in the Valley and brings 'em down here to kill people on TV. You can hear it on the radio, see it on the video."

"Ninja assassins?" said Boyd, who appeared, eating a piece of pizza and wearing a crisp new Venice Beach University trucker's cap and mirrored shades with neon frames. "For real?"

Kendra tugged his arm and said through gritted teeth, "I told you, don't engage with the beach crazies."

"The CIA trains ninjas up in the Valley," said Diesel Breath. "The Karate Kid built the city on rock' n' roll cereal bowls."

"The Karate Kid? You mean Jaden Smith?" asked Boyd.

Kendra pulled him along as she and Ellis walked away.

"Sounds like a lot of people might have had it in for Larry."

"One hundred percent," said Kendra. "But most people in the industry—even though they're total narcissistic psychopaths, like Urs—are way too chickenshit to actually kill anybody, especially not just for being a chauvinist pig. Which, I guess, is good in a way, right? I mean, murder, that's like… another level."

"You can say that again," said Ellis, looking out at the drummers on the beach.

"Will you introduce me to Bella Thorne?" Boyd asked Kendra.

"No."

"What about Jaden Smith?"

"I don't know Jaden Smith."

"So anyway, what's next for you?" asked Ellis. "Another position at CAA?"

Kendra sighed. "I moved out here to be a singer. But, yeah," she took a hit of the vape pen, "yeah, probably another position at CAA."

Ellis wished her luck.

As they parted ways, Diesel Breath, who had been following them, yelled, "The Beverly Hills ninja strikes again! Down periscope!"

It struck Ellis so funny that he laughed out loud. Was it possible he had a contact high?

The drumming on the beach was locked into a coherent rhythm, and the sunset was uncommonly vivid.

# CHAPTER 8

THE MAYAN-REVIVAL MANSION, which housed the Order of the Divine Light Research Center, was located on top of a hill between Los Feliz Boulevard and the Griffith Observatory. The walk from the car and then up the stone steps to the glossy black front door left Ellis short of breath. He fanned cool air down his shirtfront before entering.

Seated at a card table in the vaulted entry hall, a woman dressed as the Wicked Witch of the West, complete with warty rubber nose and green face paint, was selling admission to the Krampus Night festivities, which included a costume party and a screening of obscure gore films from the '60s directed by somebody Ellis had never heard of, and culminating with the arrival of Krampus, per the ODLRC website, "a goat-horned, cloven-hooved demon who accompanies St. Nicholas to punish naughty children." Ellis tried not to blanche as he coughed up twenty-five bucks. Conveniently, the website didn't mention the price.

"There are spirits in the courtyard," said the Wicked Witch, handing him a drink ticket.

Down a long hallway glowing red with the flickering light of gothic sconces, Ellis followed the echoey tittering of a cocktail party. The mansion made Ellis think of a private liberal arts college decorated with props from *The Munsters*. He paused to admire the fangs on a taxidermy grizzly bear.

"That's Bernard," came a bell-like voice beside him.

It belonged to a young woman in an empire waist gown. Her yellow wig had a braid so long it looped around her arm twice and still dragged the ground. She introduced herself as Rapunzel.

"Is this your first time here?" Ellis confirmed that it was. "I'll show you around, if you want." He did. "The house was built in 1933 and once belonged to Jean Harlow before it was acquired by Maximillian Vance in 1952."

Rapunzel stopped before a life-size portrait of a man in a Bela Lugosi-style Dracula costume, cape, amulet, and all. He had a waxed moustache, a pointed Van Dyke beard, and a predatory scowl.

"Vance personally collected the more-than-thirty thousand volumes of western esoterica in the library."

The two-story room smelled of lavender and dust. Green-shaded desk lamps gave just enough light to make out the titles of the moldering leather-bound editions—*A Pre-History of Demonology*; *Rekindling Canaanite Magik*; *Queen of Heaven: UFOs and Marilyn Monroe*—and view the cracked oil paintings depicting violent myths: Shiva, in a skirt of severed arms, decapitating someone; Saturn cannibalizing his son; Tengu lashing a priest to a tree while a temple burns in the background. Glass display cases contained animal skulls and skeletons. A pair of mounted taxidermy rams' heads stared down from facing walls.

"That's Anton and Aleister," said Rapunzel.

She and Ellis exited the library through a different door than they entered, then immediately took a right, climbed a few steps, and passed through a set of double doors guarded by a pair of stuffed black goats.

"What are their names?" asked Ellis.

"I dunno," said Rapunzel, frowning like it had been a weird question. "So, anyway, in 1989, Vance opened his home and archive to the public as a non-profit multi-cultural research center to aid seekers of wisdom in art, philosophy, mysticism, mythology, and metaphysics. And so, the One Divine Light Research Center was born. We host lectures and panel discussions on alchemy, astrology, cryptozoology, sex magik, folkloric tradition, somatic healing, all kinds of cool things. Our arts program includes live music, film screenings, poetry readings, celestial sound meditations, and ecstatic movement recitals. And the Death Café on Wednesday nights is a lot of fun."

"Death Café? It sounds like fun."

"Oh, it is. I never miss it."

In the courtyard, fifty or sixty nymphs, ghosts, imps, devils, Wicked Queens, Nosferatus, and grim reapers milled about sipping highballs and red wine from plastic cups. Ellis wasn't the only person not in costume, but he was in the minority.

"You want something to drink?" Rapunzel asked, motioning to the bar.

Ellis did. Very much. For some reason, he was nervous, and there was no better, faster cure for anxiety than a shot or two. He stuck his hand in his pocket and touched the drink ticket...

"No. Thanks. I'm okay. I'd rather keep looking around." It almost sounded convincing.

Rapunzel led Ellis through the masquerade—"I got a callback for the part of Richard Ramirez." "My guru is teaching me Tantric pranayama." "We broke up. He didn't know the difference between rhodonite and pyrite. Now we just sleep together." "Is that Kat Dennings over there?"—and through a door to the mansion's east wing.

"Down this way is the lecture hall." Rapunzel led Ellis left, then right, right, and left again. Walking past a row of open doors: "These are all offices, classrooms, reading rooms, conference rooms..." Right, right, left, up a stairwell, right, down a stairwell. Rapunzel presented the dining hall—"Seating for two hundred."—chapel—"Interfaith."—and solarium—"Nudie Tuesdays are a big draw as you can imagine."

Each room had the same whiff of decay. There were cobwebs in all the corners and melted candle wax and cigarette burns on the antique furniture and fraying carpets. All the taxidermy owls, foxes, and rabbits needed dusting. Down a spiral staircase and up a sloped, curving hallway carpeted in a dizzying geometric pattern were dance and sound studios. Certain halls and doors were roped off, others impenetrably dark, and Ellis was happy to skip them. He attributed his mounting anxiety to his inability to fathom how the interior of the mansion fit the exterior, and to the Dr. Zonker's 25-mg. weed cookie he ate on the way over, which was kicking in sooner, and much harder, than he expected.

By the time they arrived at the bookstore/gift shop, he was unsure of which floor of which wing they were on.

"Do you have any questions?" asked Rapunzel, smiling.

Ellis wanted to say, "Yeah. How the hell do you get out of here?" Instead, he swam against the cannabinoid riptide and got down to cases. "Did you know Larry Price?"

Rapunzel's smile flatlined. "Yeah. He called me a cunt in front of group of fifth graders."

"That was you? I heard about that."

"I didn't ask for him to get kicked off the board. I was content for karma to take its course," her smile bounced back, "and sure enough…"

Ellis didn't think getting shot in the head seemed like equitable karmic balance for calling someone a cunt, but then he'd always found the idea of karma, and in fact, most all spiritualism and metaphysics to be total bullshit. Déjà vu, synchronicities, and coincidences were amusing but meaningless in themselves, just like everything else—empty happenstance. He didn't begrudge anyone their belief in gods, devils, monsters, and ghosts, but he couldn't take the ODLRC seriously. Except for the nagging air of danger. But surely, that was down to nothing uncannier than Dr. Zonker.

Focus.

"I, uh… I was surprised when I heard Larry was on the board of directors here. I didn't take him for a mystical seeker."

"Mysticism is a big tent. There are lots of selfish reasons a person might explore the occult. It doesn't mean you're enlightened. Far from it. Larry was a regular at the Death Café. He had a lot of fears and a very murky aura."

"What is the Death Café?"

"A group of us get together and have coffee and tea, and whatever herbal sacrament anybody happens to prefer, and talk about death. Larry talked a lot about a premonition he had that he would be killed by a male Gemini, someone who had an early advantage in life because of an inheritance, someone disgraced and striving for redemption but was held back by resentment and pain."

Ellis swallowed. His ears were ringing. Was Rapunzel describing Urs, or him?

She checked her Apple Watch. "The screening is about to start. The theatre is just down those stairs, right at the end of the hall, then the first left. The second door on the right opens onto a stairwell. At the top, go left, then right, and it's the third room on the right. You'll see it... You okay? You got it? You look a little bewildered."

"No, yeah. I got it." Hearing the directions again wouldn't help.

"I would take you," Rapunzel said, backing through a dark doorway, "but I have to go help set up for Krampus. It was fun showing you around. Bye."

Fuck the screening. Ellis hopped down the stairs and took the turns he thought he needed to to exit the mansion. He opened a door onto the now-empty courtyard. The bar was already packed up. He entered the wing of the house where the tour began. But the two nameless black goats weren't there. He had never been in this room before. Mason jars containing frogs, snakes, and mutated animal fetuses in formaldehyde lined the built-in shelves.

Through the door at the end of a long hallway was a downward set of stairs. At the bottom, another door, another hallway, this one concrete, lit by bare low-watt lightbulbs. Ellis turned back, but the door to the stairs was locked. He doubled back down the corridor at a trot, panic tightening his chest, making him lightheaded.

"You're just stoned," he said to himself. "You've been stoned millions of times... It'll pass... It'll pass. Oh *shit!* Don't freak out. It'll pass, it'll pass..."

He turned left and found himself at a dead end. On his right was a closed door. It opened onto a windowless room with new parquet floors that reflected buzzing overhead fluorescents. On the freshly painted walls were photographs of the Eiffel Tower and Marilyn Monroe that looked like they had come with the frames. There was a mattress on the floor in one corner, with a pillow and tangled sheets. Beside it was a digital alarm clock blinking *12:00*. Heartened by signs of life, Ellis entered.

A pair of crutches and a pile of mismatched, overstuffed luggage were in one corner. In the opposite corner, a heart-shaped mylar balloon was tied to the back of a plastic patio chair, leaking helium and hanging in mid-air. Before he could add it all up, he was startled by the sound of hard-soled shoes in the corridor behind him. He spun around.

They weren't shoes, but hooves. Krampus. Fixed in the panting monster's red-eyed stare, Ellis looked for the seams in the costume, the dead giveaway—a wristwatch, a shoelace, anything. The beast ducked its horns to enter the room, bringing with it the smell of rot. Its nostrils flared and lips curled back to reveal long yellow fangs and a flicking forked tongue.

"But I've been good," Ellis said as Krampus threw a bag over his head.

# CHAPTER 9

*I'M PLAYING THE BEST GOLF OF MY LIFE, thanks to—*

Ellis muted the Zyxeltra commercial. After waking up under a bush across the street from the Order of Divine Light Research Center at four a.m. and finding the Porsche missing, he wasn't in the mood for Terry Montero's hamminess.

Sipping coffee in the early afternoon sunlight, Ellis's memory of last night had the blurry contours of an evaporating nightmare. Getting to his feet and brushing himself off, he had taken stock: no injuries and still in possession of his phone, wallet, and keys. The ODLRC mansion was quiet and locked. Ellis reported the theft of his car to the police but left out the part about being attacked by a mythical creature from Alpine folklore. Had it even really happened? Indeed, Dr. Zonker made a potent weed cookie, and drug-induced panic attacks, hallucinations, and blackouts were nothing new to Ellis, but last night was... different.

Riding home in an Uber, if liquor stores had still been open, Ellis would have told the driver to stop at one. There was virtually no hope of the police recovering the Porsche, and he was heartsick over never seeing it again. He cracked his knuckles. Another piece of his father's legacy, lost at his only son's hands.

Ellis unmuted the television when MaxxNEWS anchor Tayleigh Tompkins appeared, and drew on his new vape pen. Or, tried to. It was clogged.

*In a letter received by Los Angeles police early this morning, the Southland Sniper, the serial gunman who, over the last month, has been terrorizing Los Angeles by killing random individuals, has claimed responsibility for three more murders. The shooting started last night at seven-twenty p.m. when a middle-aged Caucasian male was shot in the head as he loaded groceries into the trunk of his car at the Ralph's supermarket on West Olympic Boulevard.*

CUT TO: LONG SHOT of the parking lot cordoned off by police tape. *An hour later, a Hispanic woman was killed as she gassed up her car at the ARCO station on Highland Avenue.*

CUT TO: MEDIUM SHOT of a blood-spattered gas pump. *At nine-seventeen p.m., an African American man sitting on a bench outside a taqueria on Washington Boulevard. Law enforcement sources say the weapon in all three shootings was a high-powered rifle fired from a distance.*

CUT TO: CLOSE UP of a young man in a chef's coat: *We had just closed,* he said, *and I saw the guy lying there with all this blood coming out of his head. It was a lot of blood, and I was like, whoa, that's not good.*

Tayleigh in VOICE OVER: *All together, three bullets, three apparently random victims in two hours. Police are stunned.*

CUT TO: CLOSE UP of Los Angeles Police Chief Malcom Davies: *We're obviously dealing with a highly skilled shooter. The random nature of the killings presents a particularly difficult and serious problem for us.*

CUT TO: Tayleigh in the studio: *Police have little to go on—just one witness's description of a white male fleeing the scene of talent agent Larry Price's killing three days ago. However, in the letter received this morning by police, the Sniper denies responsibility for that murder but claims six others. And promises to commit more. A massive manhunt is ongoing, but police admit they don't know who they're dealing with or what his motive might be, other than, in the killer's own words,* a demonic compulsion. *And that is making the people of Los Angeles nervous.*

Ellis tried the pen again. Nothing. Maybe it was just as well. Maybe weed was another soured relationship.

There was a knock at the door.

"Hey, Lucky. I know the rent is late. I'm gonna get paid in a day or two, and I'll cut you a check then, okay?"

"You said that last time." She craned her neck to see around him. "It costs extra to keep a pet."

"What are you talking about? I don't have a pet."

"Oh yeah?" Lucky pointed inside. "What's that, huh? Your girlfriend?"

Ellis turned around, and his breath caught. Sitting in his father's orange bamboo chair, the chair he'd been sitting in seconds before, was the yellow bobtail cat that had tried to stowaway with him outside the Century Club.

"What the fuck?"

"One hundred and fifty dollars extra to keep a pet," said Lucky.

The cat was licking her scrawny shoulder in the sun. Ellis shook his head.

"Hold on. This— That's not my cat. I have no idea how it got in here."

"And you still owe this month's rent."

The cat rolled over on her back, exposing her pale, concave belly to the sun, and murmured.

"Lucky, gimme a break. I had a terrible night last night. My car got stolen, and somebody mugged me or something. I'm still trying to put it together and now there's this cat—"

"I give you a break all the time."

"The bulldozers are coming in like, three weeks, aren't they? Can't we just... be cool?"

"I am cool. It's not my policy. It's building policy."

"Uh-huh, well, speaking of building policy, I'm going back to smoking in here. This thing," he held up the vape pen, "sucks. Actually, it doesn't suck. That's the problem. It's always clogged. Or else the battery's dead."

"Maybe you just don't try hard enough."

Ellis sighed. "Probably not."

THE PERGOLA was strung with multi-colored Christmas lights, the big incandescent kind. Boyz II Men's "Let It Snow" piped from hidden speakers. The volume was well within the city ordinance, and the harmonies blended with the good cheer coming from inside the 1,500-square-foot ranch house in Northridge. It was the kind of place a rookie LAPD officer like Courtland Hollender and his new bride could buy for about $30,000 in 1972, but that now went for more than a million.

Even in the heyday of the afro, Hollender kept his hair short and the moustache he'd had since high school trimmed. Now, his hair was almost all white; the moustache, he'd been dyeing black since 1989. Every year, his naturally stocky build softened and expanded. Cradling a can of Michelob Ultra to his belly, he flipped and prodded burgers, bratwursts, and assorted chicken parts on the grill.

The aroma triggered an urge in Ellis, but the weak beer selection made it easy to defend his sobriety. He took a swig of

Diet Coke and said, "Retired. Wow. I never thought I'd see it. I always figured you'd go out with your boots on."

"Well, you were wrong about that," said Hollender. "When I do go out, I sure as hell don't wanna be wearing boots. I'ma be wearing flip-flops or golf shoes."

"Since when do you play golf?"

"I'm thinking about taking it up."

Ellis squinted. "Really?"

"Yeah. Why're you looking at me that way?"

They turned at the sound of the back door popping open. An LAPD patrolwoman in uniform came through it.

"There's my baby girl!" said Hollender, throwing his arms wide to envelope the rushing cop into a twisting, growling bear hug. On release, she patted Hollender's tummy.

"Where you been hiding?" he asked.

"Hiding? I've been *working*. A *lot*."

He kissed the crown of her head with a theatrical, "Mmmm-*waaa!*" and turned her around. "Meet a friend of mine. This is Ellis Dunaway. Ellis, this is my niece, Officer Tameka Settles."

Despite the dimness of the patio and the darkness of her skin, Ellis detected a blush. Though stepping out from under her uncle's arm to give Ellis a dry, brief handshake, she mustered a police officer's authoritative poise.

Her wide-set eyes and pug nose gave her an impish quality belied by the huskiness of her voice. "Nice to meet you. My uncle misspoke though. I'm his *favorite* niece."

"Ha! You wish." Hollender crushed his beer can and tossed it toward the recycling bin, but missed.

"Pfft! How many of those have you had?" Officer Settles asked.

Ellis wondered that himself. In all the years he'd known him, he had never seen Hollender in party mode, or even really in relaxation mode. That's what made it so difficult to picture him on a golf course or in any other capacity than official police business. Even when he and Ellis met for lunch, no matter where it was—#1 Sushi & Pet Grooming, Fiesta Pizza, East Side Tandoori Boys, Luigi's Korean BBQ—Hollender was dressed as if he was about to testify before the grand jury, in a necktie, sport coat, khakis, and loafers. He would bolt his food and wash it down with black coffee before rushing back to work.

Ellis also wondered why Hollender had never mentioned his favorite niece, a police officer no less.

"When I was a rookie detective," Hollender said to Tameka, cracking another beer, "Ellis's dad and I were partners. But then—I'm being for real, now—Hank got inspired by *Magnum P.I.* and retired from the cops, started a private investigation agency, and went on to write the definitive manual of tricks of the trade. Ellis here followed in his footsteps."

"Oh yeah? As a private investigator or a writer?" Tameka asked Ellis, a hand resting on her duty belt.

"Both, actually. But in reverse order. I started out as a writer on the show *SEAL Team Trident*—"

"With David Boreanaz?"

"No. No, this was the original." Tameka blinked. "In the nineties?" Total deadpan. "Kent Moran worked on it, too."

Tameka grinned. It worked every time. Her teeth were flawless. "Okay, now, I never miss *Graveyardland*," she said. "I love my zombies."

"Same, same," said Ellis. "Such a great show, right? So, anyway, not long after *SEAL Team Trident* came to the end of its run," (it was cancelled after half a season), "my dad died—"

"In a helicopter crash in Hawaii," said Hollender, "in the same kind of helicopter TC flew on *Magnum P.I.* Ain't that some shit? Hank even used to call me TC, and I called him TM."

"All true," said Ellis, nodding.

He added two to the number of beers he thought Hollender had had, bringing the total to six. Blurting out the details of the single most tragic thing that had ever happened to Ellis, the flush handle of his downward spiral, was uncharacteristic of the typically reserved Hollender. But whatever. He deserved to enjoy his party. Besides, on the scale of drunken offenses, insensitive garrulity hardly rated.

"So, um, yeah, my dad died, and I earned my PI license and took over his agency." And bankrupted it. But of course, he didn't mention that, and hoped Hollender wouldn't either.

Tameka said, "Hmm. Interesting," like she meant the opposite.

Ellis knew how to win her back: "Uh-huh, so, now, I'm writing a new show that Kent and I are co-producing."

"Oh yeah?" Every, single, time. She was back on the hook. "Is it about zombies?"

"I don't know how y'all can watch that mess," said Hollender. "Zombies and the living dead and all that voodoo bullshit." Shaking his head, he headed for the house, carrying a platter stacked high with barbecued meat. "Real life is ugly enough." Tameka opened the door for her uncle. "Y'all, come on. Time to eat."

"Be there in a minute. I'ma have a cigarette real quick," said Tameka, tapping an American Spirit out of the box.

Hollender stopped in the doorway, gas heat and merry voices rolling out around him. "I thought you quit."

"I did." Tameka lit the cigarette. "And I will again. I've just been really stressed. Working a lot, like I said."

"That's an excuse."

"I know it is. But it's true."

"Well, go over there, away from the door. And don't you let your aunt Cheryl catch you. She's not sweet and compassionate like I am."

"Pfft," came out with a puff of smoke.

On the far side of the patio, Tameka asked Ellis to elaborate on his and Kent's new zombie show.

"Sure. Well, I can't say too much, because we're still in development, but I *can* tell you it's *not* about zombies. It's something totally new—well, not like, totally, *totally* new. It's a reboot of an iconic IP. I can't say which one," Tameka took a drag on her cigarette and raised a polite eyebrow, "but people are going to be blown away when they see what we do with it."

Ellis sipped his Diet Coke, waiting for Tameka to ask a follow-up question. When she didn't, he went on. "Speaking of being blown away, Kent and I were in a meeting with Urs Schreiber and his agent, Larry Price, the night he was killed. I was standing right beside him when it happened."

"No shit," said Tameka, reinterested. "That was you?"

"Unfortunately. You know what's happening with the case?"

"Not much. All we have to go on is the anonymous witness who says he saw Schreiber running down the street with a rifle. It's a long way from being able to arrest him, but it's enough to make him the main—which is to say, the only—suspect at this point."

"What about the security camera footage from the gas station where he was mugged and got his necklace stolen?"

"Can't be retrieved."

"How convenient."

"None of that about his necklace being stolen was in the news. How do you know about it?"

Ellis rubbed the back of his neck. "TV writing and private investigation are two sides of the same coin lately."

"Uh-huh. So, you're out to prove Urs is innocent so he can star in your new show."

"The dignity of the private investigator's cause lies in the impartial pursuit of the truth," said Ellis. "That's a line from my father's book. But also, Urs didn't shoot his agent. He talks a lot of shit but he's not dangerous like that."

"You haven't seen the videos of him resisting arrest after crashing his car driving drunk? Looks pretty dangerous to me and a lotta other cops, too."

"I see where you're coming from, I do. But apparently, Larry Price pissed off everybody he ever met. His last words were— I'm being for real, now—'Lemme show you my dick.' Okay? So, he had lots of… if not enemies, detractors. Besides, if Urs killed him, why would he hire me to investigate?"

"Because it's something an innocent person would do, and he wants to look innocent. And exploit your confirmation bias."

"Sounds like maybe the police have a little confirmation bias too though, yeah?"

"Oh, hell yeah. Like I said, most of them."

"And you?"

Tameka held Ellis's eye contact for a moment. "Personally, I think Urs Schreiber is an arrogant, over-privileged nepo baby, but also a pretty good actor. And definitely not a killer."

Ellis nodded. "One hundred percent. Same here. So, who do you think killed Larry Price?"

"The Southland Sniper. I mean, if it walks like a duck and quacks like a duck…"

"But he said he specifically *didn't* shoot Larry."

"But he's also psychotic. We're just supposed to take the word of a psychotic killer?"

Before Ellis could respond, a baby-faced man with a tiny goatee, wearing a Bullseye Props polo shirt, stepped halfway outside: Ramsey Skillern—the guy Terry Montero paid sixty thousand dollars to (via Ellis) on behalf of "a colleague".

"Hey, Aunt Cheryl says to—" He clocked Ellis and faltered. He licked his lips and spoke again with more bass in his voice. "What the hell's this? What's going on?"

Tameka frowned. "Pardon me? What the hell does it look like, motherfucker? I'm having a conversation with a friend of Uncle Court's." To Ellis, she said, "This is my little cousin Ramsey."

Ellis smiled as if he didn't feel the tension and understood the dialogue to be all in fun. He approached Ramsey with his open hand extended and a look on his face that he hoped read, *I come in peace.*

"Hi. I'm Ellis Dunaway. Your uncle and I go way back."

Ramsey scowled and licked his lips like a dog about to bite, but then shook Ellis's hand, a damp, single pump. Then he cocked his chin at Tameka.

"Aunt Cheryl says to c'mon inside. It's time to say grace. Everybody's hungry."

Tameka exhaled smoke and ground her cigarette out with her heel. "I'm coming."

"You know, you're going to break Aunt Cheryl's heart with those cigarettes."

"Aunt Cheryl better not find out."

Ramsey shot Ellis another evil eye and went inside.

"Sorry about that," said Tameka as she led the way into the almost too-warm house packed with Hollender's family and friends.

The Christmas tree was real. The ornaments reflected decades of togetherness—an etched glass angel dated 1974, Snoopy and Garfield in Santa hats, the 7 Up spot dangling from a candy cane, a satin ball commemorating Barack Obama's inauguration… The lights blinked. Plastic garland swagged the mantle from which Courtland and Cheryl's oversized felt stockings hung. Votives flickered in red and green glass holders. Red electric candles burned in all the windows.

After Hollender's rote but robust blessing, The Jackson 5's "Santa Claus is Comin' to Town" jumped from the stereo, and everyone swarmed the buffet. Seating was catch as catch can, and Ellis broke bread with a pair of sheriff's deputies whose conversation lurched back and forth between their pensions and the sorry condition of the Rams' defensive line. He excused himself to sit beside Cheryl's elderly, bald aunt, who just stared through rheumy eyes when her children, grandchildren, and great-grandchildren stopped by her cracked Barcalounger to ask, loudly, if she wanted anything—"I said, *'More punch, Grammy?!'*" And yet somehow, Hollender's dentist was even less interesting.

"Great teeth—the whole family. Incredible enamel. I see all the Hollenders. Not a cavity in the bunch. I tell them, 'If all my patients were like you, I'd have to give up golf.' Haha!"

"I'm playing the best golf of my life," said Ellis. He immediately regretted it when Dr. Felix Tolbert didn't get the reference and asked Ellis's handicap.

Except for bumping Tameka's elbow at the buffet while they were both talking to other people, he couldn't get next to her. On the other hand, he and Ramsey easily and happily avoided each other.

The party was in full swing—a quartet of cousins singing along to Marvin Gaye's "Purple Snowflakes"—when Ellis overheard Hollender say, "You can't leave now. They're gonna do 'Someday at Christmas' next."

"I have to," said Tameka. "Everybody's working overtime because of the Sniper."

"You didn't have any coconut cake. Let me get you some to take with you."

"No thanks, Uncle Court. Really, I'm too full. I gotta go."

"Okay. Well, be careful out there, baby girl."

"I will."

"Listen, I'm not judging you for smoking. I know what it's like out there. I just love you. I worry about you."

"I know. I love you too."

Hollender and Tameka hugged, but there was no twisting or growling this time.

"Congratulations on your career and your retirement," she said, getting on tiptoe to kiss his cheek. "You're a good example for me and all police."

He hugged her again, tenderly kissed the crown of her head, and let her go.

Ellis stepped into the empty space and thanked Hollender for a good time. Hollender thanked him for coming and didn't put up any resistance to his leaving. There was no offer of coconut cake to go.

Outside, coming around the huge inflatable Rudolph the Red-Nosed Reindeer lawn ornament, Ellis waved to Tameka as she pulled away in her black-and-white. She didn't see him. He lowered his arm and ordered an Uber.

Heading east on Nordhoff Street, in the back seat of a Prius that smelled like lemon air freshener and French fries, Ellis searched for Tameka Settles on his phone.

The first link was a two-year-old news item from San Angelo, Texas: *Police Chief Fred Catron confirmed that SAPD Det. Tameka Settles has been placed on "administrative reassignment," meaning she is no longer patrolling the streets. Settles was caught on video saying, "Homie's gonna need a closed casket," and laughing, about Dashaun Stewart, who was fatally shot by another officer, following a high-speed chase on September 3. Settles's remarks were recorded on a Facebook Live stream Stewart began during the chase.*

A picture accompanying the article confirmed she was the same Tameka Settles Ellis had just met. He swiped the article away and opened the next one…*outrage*…the next…*demanding her resignation*…and the next…*death threats*…

Ellis figured that Tameka had transferred to the LAPD to flee the hostility in San Angelo, and Hollender hadn't mentioned it because of the ignoble circumstances. Transferring to another police department meant starting back at square one. Ellis was sympathetic to the challenges of living down past mistakes and starting over.

Waiting at a stoplight to merge onto the 405, his phone buzzed. It was Reshma. He let the call go to voicemail. He knew what she was going to say: his deposit check for the apartment in North Hollywood had bounced. His shame was tempered by relief. He had hated that apartment and the depressing little pool. He didn't want to move to North Hollywood or anywhere else, and now he could pretend, at least for another day or two, that it wasn't inevitable. Booze would help. As he was about to request a stop, a mechanical snarl cut him off.

A motorcycle, splitting the lane, pulled next to the Prius. The rider was wearing a yellow leather jacket. Ellis felt his eyes burning through the iridium face shield of his helmet. When the light changed and traffic started to move, the bike rocketed up the onramp with an ear-splitting howl.

# CHAPTER 10

THE NEXT DAY, SITTING IN THE BACK of Mr. Singh's cab, caught by the third red light in a row on Santa Monica Boulevard, Ellis bounced his knee and considered blowing off his AA meeting. It started in half an hour, and even if traffic were moving on the northbound 5, he would be cutting it close. On his best day, he hated the conspicuousness of coming in late, and today wasn't his best day. His nerves were shot from being screamed at and counter-counter hexed.

Ellis and Mr. Singh's first trip had been to the Order of Divine Light Research Center, which took three times longer than it should have, thanks to a pile-up on the southbound 5 that had it closed down to one lane. Ellis was looking for answers about what happened to him and his car, but when he arrived, he found the mansion closed until the solstice, still a couple of weeks away. No one was answering the phone.

Their next stop was Spellbound Spiritual Emporium, which, according to the website, was *a new age metaphysical shoppe and crystalarium located in super-magical East Hollywood!!!* Situated in a pigeon-flocked two-story strip mall, less than a mile from the Century Club and the site of Larry Price's murder, the area struck Ellis as very unmagical. But, for its part, the store displayed the strength of its conviction. The shelves were stocked with divination and ritual supplies like jars and vials of herbs and oils, feathered dream catchers, prisms, and pendants bearing pentagrams and runes. Every few feet stood an altar-like display of candles, incense, crystals, stones, and statuettes of Buddha, Vishnu, Baphomet, Osiris, and other fantastic characters Ellis didn't recognize. Ten minutes of internet sleuthing that morning told him this was where he might find Everleigh Sullivan. He acted like it was a coincidence.

"Rapunzel…? Hey!"

She looked up from the pile of polished stones she was organizing into color order. "I'm sorry?"

"I almost didn't recognize you without the wig. My name is Ellis. You gave me a tour at the ODLRC a couple nights ago, remember?"

"Oh, right," she said with a blasé smile. "How'd you like the films?"

"I didn't see them. I got lost and ended up in some strange… bedroom, I guess it was, in the basement, where Krampus threw a bag over my head and assaulted me."

Everleigh frowned. "The mansion doesn't have a basement. And, the guy in the Krampus costume was my friend Zander. He's in my kundalini yoga class, and he's a total sweetheart. He spent a fortune on that costume, and he is, fer shur, one hundred percent committed to the role, but he would never actually attack anyone. Especially not a grown man. Krampus comes after children."

It was hard for Ellis to accept that what he'd encountered was a person in a costume, but the supernatural alternative was too ludicrous to countenance. Even while huffing sage in a crystalarium.

"I passed out and woke up under a bush across the street from the mansion. My car was stolen."

Everleigh rolled her eyes and resumed sorting rocks. "That sucks, but I'm not really surprised. The unhoused community has a strong presence there at night. I'm not saying that they're all dangerous car thieves. I mean, obviously, late-stage capitalism forces us all to make hard choices—" Ellis rolled his hand in a *get-on-with-it* gesture. "Plus, you were clearly really stoned. Your aura was a total mess. I thought you were tripping on DMT or Two C-B or something."

"I have no idea what that is, and I wasn't tripping."

He had considered the possibility and dismissed it because he couldn't fathom when he would have been dosed. He had declined to drink at the ODLRC, and as far as he remembered, he hadn't even made physical contact with anyone.

"What's more likely is that you guys are running some kind of human-trafficking-car-theft-ring, drugging people somehow, maybe with some kind of gas, or—"

"Stop, stop. Wait. What is going on right now? You're accusing me of gassing people and trafficking them?"

"Not you necessarily, but the ODLRC maybe, I don't know, but something very weird happened to me, and I want answers. At the very least, I want my car back."

"You're insane."

"I considered that, too, but I really don't think so. In fact, I'm saner than I've been in a long time, but that's a lot of personal stuff. That's not germane to what I'm—"

"Coming here wasn't a coincidence, was it?" Everleigh asked, squinting. "You think I had something to do with your misogynist-pig pal Larry Price's death, don't you? You think I hexed him, and you're here to counter-hex me. Is that it?"

"What the—? Now who's tripping? Listen, Larry Price was not my pig pal. I had no idea you were the cunt he—"

Everleigh's eyes flamed at the word.

"Sorry. That came out wrong."

"You have no idea who and what you're messing with," she waved a bundle of smoldering herbs in his face, "Now *I* am counter-*counter*-hexing *you!* Out, devil, out! *Get the fuck OUT!*"

As much as Ellis wanted to tell Mr. Singh to take him to Hi-Hat Discount Liquor to pick up a handle of Old Grand-Dad, he accepted that that impulse meant he needed to go to a meeting right away.

When he walked in, three minutes to the good—"You're a miracle worker, Singh."—Sanya, the former meth head, flashed her new choppers and hugged him, "I'm glad you're here," then drew back. Softly, but with an elementary schoolteacher's strict tone, she said, "Sobriety is like gender, right? It's fluid. It's a journey that's different for everybody. So, that makes it even more important to respect each other's journeys and help if we can. If we can't do that, we should at least try not to make anyone's journey harder. Y'know?"

"Yeah, totally. I agree. What makes you say that?"

Sanya stiffened. "You smell like weed. *I'm* not judging you, but some people in the group are struggling with—"

"It's not weed. It's sage or something. Somebody hexed me."

"I'm not judging you, Ellis, but I am asking you to be respectful to—"

"It was a counter-counter-hex, actually. Why are you frowning…? I swear."

"Uh-huh. Whatever. Just please try not to *get hexed*," she made air quotes, "before any more meetings, okay? And if you have to, maybe use a vape pen."

"I'll definitely try."

"I know you will." Sanya squeezed his shoulder. "That's the best any of us can do. Now, grab a muffin. They're gluten free, and the coffee is a medium-dark roast Sumatran blend. Everything is fair trade and organic."

Ellis scooped some raw sugar into his coffee but passed on the muffins, which looked like golf balls made of sawdust. He took a seat in the circle of metal folding chairs as far from everyone else as he could get, demonstrating his respect for their sobriety journeys.

Just as the meeting was getting underway, a woman walked in whom Ellis had never seen before. She had blonde hair, whitened teeth, an even tan, and breasts that had the geometry of fakes.

"Welcome," said Sanya. "Help yourself to a cup of organic fair-trade coffee—it's a medium-dark roast Sumatran blend—and a gluten-free vegan muffin, and sit anywhere."

The woman got a coffee and took a seat opposite Ellis. Her manicured hands betrayed middle age, but her Botox-smooth and expertly made-up face made it hard to get a fix on her age within ten or twelve years. Almost anywhere else in Los Angeles, she would have melted into the mass of generically pretty blondes, but in the Fellowship Room of the Pathways Church, she might as well have been Claudia Schiffer.

Antonio shared first. "I've watched all the YouTube videos on how to pass the GED test. So, I'm not too worried."

Ricky had a bandage on the side of his neck where he'd had the *LUSH* tattoo removed. "It hurt like a motherfucker. I think I'ma just leave LIFE on there."

Lucinda was having second-act problems with her screenplay. "I'm getting feedback that my journey of sobriety and self-discovery is kind of repetitive."

Darren took a phone call. "I can't talk right now. I'm in a meeting… Uh-huh… Huh…? Hell no! No. Not for that price… Fuck that shit!"

"Reese Witherspoon bought some of my beeswax candles from my Etsy store," said Shereé, "and posted them in an Instagram story! She forgot to tag me, but still."

Ellis had intended to pass on his turn to share. He didn't always speak, but when he did, unlike most of the group, he kept his remarks on topic and impersonal. He had never even mentioned the name of the television show he had written, nor with whom he had written it, because he had never cared to impress anyone in the Fellowship Room. Until today.

He cut his eyes at the pretty new face across the circle and introduced himself. "I've had a pretty crazy couple of days." Larry Price's exploding head and Krampus's yellow fangs and forked tongue flashed through his mind. "Um, yeah, so, I'm writing a new show that Kent Moran is producing." A ripple of interest ran through the circle. "I've worked with him before, so… Anyway, I can't say too much about the new show at this point because we're still in development and we've hit a couple of snags making a network deal," another flash of Larry's brains on the pavement, "but that's to be expected. So, yeah, things are looking good. We're optimistic." He hadn't planned to say any more, but the new lady's attentive green eyes compelled him. "I guess, if I'm being honest, I'm a little nervous, too—not that we won't make a deal; I'm confident of that—but because like, when things go wrong, it makes me want to drink, and when things go right, I also want to drink. Sometimes, even more. Success can be disorienting, and for most of my life, getting wasted was like, my true north, y'know, my default setting. So, now, all of a sudden, all this shit is going on and… I dunno, it's good shit, but I'm feeling a little extra tempted."

"What's the show about?" asked Antonio.

"I can't say. We're still in development."

"Is it finna be about zombies?" asked Ricky.

"No. *That* I *can* tell you, it's not about zombies."

"Is Kent Moran as handsome in real life as he is in pictures?" asked Shereé.

"Not really."

"Will you give him my screenplay?" asked Lucinda.

"Sure." No chance.

"Make it quick. I'm in a meeting," Darrell said into his phone.

The new lady's name was Deena. A wannabe actress turned jewelry designer, she had been sober for twelve years.

"My story isn't too exciting. I did some modelling and booked a few commercials, but things never really clicked, and at a point, I had to admit they were never going to. But instead of making peace with that, or maybe finding another way to be involved in the industry, I got really bitter, and I started drinking. It cost me all my relationships, including my marriage. But I didn't stop until I started gaining weight. I know that makes me sound shallow and terrible, but there it is. I was afraid of losing my looks. Not that they were doing me much good. At this point, I don't feel tempted to drink anymore. I just like to come to meetings now and then as just kind of a tune-up." She shrugged as if there was nothing more to say, but then added, "Also, I'm always on the lookout for cool stones and beads for my jewelry, so if anybody knows of a source, let me know. Thanks."

After the meeting, Ellis caught up to Deena in the parking lot. "Hey, I know where you might find some beads and stuff."

# CHAPTER 11

SCREAMING AND MACHINE-GUN FIRE echoed under the twenty-foot beamed ceilings of the eighteen-room Spanish Colonial mansion Urs Schreiber was renting in the Hollywood Hills.

"The place was designed by a famous architect a long time ago," Urs said, giving Ellis a tour. "Errol Flynn used to live here. He was an actor in the early twentieth century."

"Uh-huh," said Ellis, almost tripping over a wrecked remote-control car in the Tunisian tile hallway.

The only piece of furniture in the only bedroom, besides the master, that had any furniture in it was a glass cabinet housing what looked to Ellis like common junk.

"It's my collection," said Urs. "That's a packet of Flavor Aid from Jonestown. Have you heard of the Jonestown massacre?"

"Yeah, I remember it."

"Very cool. And that's one of David Berkowitz's pay stubs from the Bronx Post Office. He was the Son of Sam serial killer."

"I know. I remember that too."

"And I got this from a guy on the dark web. It's Dennis Rader's Boy Scout manual. He called himself BTK, which stands for bind, torture, kill. He used to take his victims and—"

Ellis held up his hand. "I'm familiar."

"But man, my favorite piece was that IBET Saturn medallion. It's one of only like, two or three known to still exist. In retrospect, it was pretty stupid to actually wear it around. I'm sure whoever stole it traded it for crack or something. Now, there's no telling where it is."

The only thing in the library was a pinball machine. The built-in shelves held only a few empty liquor bottles and beer cans. A framed Italian one sheet for *Brass Hearts* (*Cuori in Ottone*) was propped against the wall in the empty dining room, which could have accommodated twenty guests. In the middle of the hardwood floor was a single flip-flop, a glass bong, and a drum set. Urs picked up a drumstick and twirled it between his fingers.

"These are the same kind of sticks Lars Ulrich uses. You know who he is?"

"Of course."

"Yeah, you look like a classic-rock-type of guy."

"Metallica isn't classic rock."

Ellis's voice was drowned out by Urs bashing cymbals. When he stopped, explosions and anguished cries filtered through the ringing in Ellis's ears.

The violence was coming from a wall-mounted 120-inch television in the living room. A couple of guys who looked just like Urs—handsome and thin, wearing designer T-shirts and sweatpants—were slouched on the leather sofa, smoking weed and playing the *Graveyardland* video game.

Urs opened arched French doors onto a stone terrace with views of the Griffith Observatory and the city lights that dwindled toward the ocean. He kicked back in a deck chair and lit a joint.

"Man, you should have been there yesterday. Zuke was amazing."

"There" was the police station. "Zuke" was Urs's attorney, Andrew Zucco.

"It was like an episode of *Southland HEAT*. Zuke was all, 'My client has answered and re-answered all your questions. He's been more than cooperative. So, if you don't have any real evidence to charge him with, we're outta here.' And we left! All the cops have is an anonymous tip from somebody saying they saw me running up Hollywood Boulevard with a rifle, which is ridiculous. The field investigators say the gunshot came from a high angle, like on top of a building or something. So, it's impossible that I could have left the club, got up on top of a building with a gun, shot Larry, and got back down and run off in the time the witness says they saw me."

Ellis didn't think it was impossible but agreed it was unlikely.

"And what's my motive? Me and Larry had an argument? We argued all the time. That doesn't mean I wanted him dead. It's all bullshit. Anyway, the cops are," Urs deepened his voice to a mock-authoritative register, "changing the focus of the investigation."

"See? I told you. It was just a matter of time. There are plenty of other people for the police to investigate. Seems like Larry was unpopular with almost everybody, especially female subordinates."

Ellis handed Urs a manila envelope containing his investigation report. Urs traded Ellis the joint and started reading.

"Kendra is such a bitch," he said when he got to Ellis's interview with Larry's assistant. "No doubt Larry could be a pain in the ass. That's what made him a good agent. Her talking shit on him now that he's dead is so fucking typical. Everything with her is trauma this and trauma that. She was a terrible assistant. She couldn't get a lunch order right to save her life." He waved the joint back over. "You think she might be the anonymous tipster?"

"Obviously, there's no love lost between you two, but she didn't strike me as the vindictive type. You never know, though."

Urs toked and read on.

"What the fuck? Christian Cooper is pissed because I *stole* the part in *Brass Hearts* out from under him? He was never up for that part. He's so fucking delusional. Like he could have played it anyway."

Ellis clarified. "Brandii Bunnz said Christian is pissed, but he denied having any hard feelings about you or Larry. He was kind of hard to read, though. He was a little guarded."

There was something else that seemed off about Christian… the way he offered an alibi for the night of Larry's murder without being asked: celebrating his stepfather's birthday. And the bruise on his neck. At first, Ellis guessed it was a hickey, but now it came back to him how edgy Christian became when the AD mentioned it.

Urs tossed the report aside. "That," he pointed at it, "right there, is why I don't fuck with those losers anymore. When we were in high school in Costa Mesa, they were like this cool, popular, power couple—I know it's hard to believe—and I wasn't cool enough to be in their little clique. Also hard to believe, I know, but back then I was just the dork whose uncle produced all those lame reality shows. Never mind that he also created *Southland HEAT*, one of the most successful shows ever. He was the King of Cable, for fuck's sake! But anyway, when I got *Graveyardland*, they crawled out from under their rocks, all like, 'Wassup, Urs? It's all love. Let's kick it.' And I'm like, 'Uh, yeah, okay, sure, whatever. Let's kick it,' right? Like, I'm trying to be the bigger person and let the past be the past. But they didn't want to be friends. All they wanted was for me introduce them to people and get them jobs and shit. And I'm like, 'Jobs doing what?' They don't fucking *do* anything. *I* took an acting class. *I* put in the work. Now, everybody's saying I got where I am because of Uncle Aaron. But if he was just this washed-up producer, how did he still have clout?" He looked at Ellis like he expected an answer. Ellis shrugged. "You can't have it both ways. No, I got here," he opened his arms to the 9,000-square-foot house, to Hollywood, to the sky, "because I'm talented. If I wasn't, it wouldn't matter who my uncle was."

"It would matter a little," said Ellis, "but I take your point."

"It didn't matter to Christian, though, did it? Not even a little. If being a nepo baby is supposed to be some magic bullet, why didn't it work for him?"

"What do you mean?"

"Oh, he didn't tell you Larry was *his* uncle? …No? Imagine that. I'd be embarrassed too."

"Wait, Larry Price was Christian's uncle?"

"Yup. His mom's brother. That's how I met Larry in the first place. Next thing I know, he's representing me, but not Christian, his own flesh and blood. That sounds cold blooded, and it pretty much is, but it just goes to show you how bad Christian sucks as an actor. He literally has no talent at anything but being a whiny little bitch. And get this, his mom is his manager. So, don't you think if Christian could even just walk and chew gum at the same time, he'd be famous? Of course he would, but he can't, so he's not."

"What's his mom's name?"

"Belinda."

"Cooper?"

"Ferris. Actually, I think she goes by Ferris-Stafford now. Christian and his mom, their whole… relationship is completely fucked up."

"How so?"

"It just is. They've always been kind of like, too close, or something. She's supposed to be his manager, but honestly, it's hard to tell who works for who."

"What about Christian's stepdad? Who's he?"

"Anton Stafford. He's like this self-help-guru-influencer or some shit. His YouTube channel has like, a million subscribers."

Ellis took in the view along with the new information.

"So, you think Christian and Brandii are trying to frame me?" asked Urs.

"Anybody could have called in a bogus tip to the police, including them. But I doubt either of them did it. It was probably just some troll, messing with you or the cops. Or both."

Urs leaned his head back, shut his eyes, and exhaled a plume of smoke. "…gotta be above it…gotta be above it…"

"You're a Gemini, aren't you?"

"Yeah. Why?"

"No reason. I am too."

In his report, Ellis gave an abbreviated account of his trip to the Order of Divine Light Research Center and conversation with Rapunzel, omitting Krampus, and Larry Price's Death Café premonition that a Gemini who had squandered his nepotistic advantage and was desperate to redeem himself would cause Price's death. Urs and Ellis both fit the bill, and while Ellis put no stock in astrology, he couldn't help being disconcerted.

"Did you see today's horoscope?" asked Urs. Ellis hadn't. "It said now that a personal challenge has been overcome, it's a good time to start a new project."

That didn't change Ellis's mind about magical thinking, but good news was good news. An opening was an opening. "Great," he said. "I had some thoughts about the show. A *Miami Vice* reboot is a good idea, for sure, but what if we pivot slightly to an original story about a rookie detective in Texas who—?"

"I dunno, man. I think everybody might be right." Urs stood and leaned on the balustrade, looking into the night with his back to Ellis. A motorcycle revved in the canyon. A dog barked. Another one answered. "Maybe I should probably just lay low for a while."

"Absolutely, lay low. I've been thinking about re-writing the third act anyway, and if we go with something more original—"

"Nah. I'm talking about taking some real time off. Not working on anything. Maybe Larry was right."

"Larry was wrong. You're just having a crisis of confidence. His murder shook you up. I get that. It shook me up, too, to say the least. But the best way through the tra—" he started to say *trauma*—"bullshit is to get back to work. Like our horoscope said, now's the best time."

"Not working *is* the new project," said Urs. "Maybe I'll start a band like, just for fun. I'm getting pretty good on the drums."

"Cool. Lots of actors are musicians on the side. Johnny Depp, Keanu Reev—"

Ellis was interrupted by the French doors popping open. "Hey, man," said one of Urs's friends. "Can you call your coke dealer?"

Urs sighed. "Really, dude? I'm on parole."

"Please." The guy drained the glass in his hand. "Also, you're out of Patrón."

"Gimme a minute," said Urs, shooing him back inside. "You can't see I'm in a meeting? Damn."

When they were alone again, Ellis sighed and said, "So, who's your favorite drummer?"

# CHAPTER 12

ELLIS SPENT THE MORNING at the official police garage beside the 405 in West L.A., picking up his car. The Porsche had been recovered on 4th Street below Santa Monica Boulevard, twenty miles west of the Order of Divine Light Research Center. Besides the pre-existing crumpled fender, the only damage was to the ignition system and steering column from being hotwired. Nevertheless, the car was drivable, and Ellis was so shocked and relieved to have it back, he drove straight to a car wash on West Olympic where he ponied up for the Tsunami Special, which included applications of triple-foam conditioner, Max-Glow LusterWax, TireBright, and RainX. The latter was an absurd extravagance in a city that only got thirty days of rain a year, but it was an affordable atonement for taking such a cool car for granted for so long. But no more.

He arrived early at Starbucks in Sun Valley, where he was to meet Kaitlynn Arliss, who had hired him to follow her cheating husband, Jay, the import car salesman with the mean right hook. The bruise on Ellis's cheek had faded to a sickly yellow-green. When he declined to try a "seasonal creation" like an Eggnog Latte or a Toasted White Chocolate Mocha and ordered a plain black coffee, the pierced and tattooed barista gave him a shrug that said, *spoilsport.* She sniffed when he only tipped a dollar. To a light-jazz rendition of "All I Want for Christmas is You", he took a seat near the window and started to text Reshma, but then decided it was nobler to call.

He pumped his fist when it went to voicemail. Merciful voicemail.

"Hey, Reshma," he said, upbeat. "Sorry, I've been out of touch. I've been crazy—I mean, busy—crazy busy, the last couple of days... Uh, so, anyway, if the apartment in North Hollywood is still available, I'm still interested. I got paid last night, and I'm waiting to settle up with another client now. So, I promise, I can cover the deposit." He gave a contrite chuckle. "But, um, seriously though, I, uh... I'm sorry about before, with the check. Some bill payments went through, and I didn't realize— Well, anyway, give me a call whenever you can... Uh, yeah... Hope you're well. Tell Prashanth I said hi. Okay. Bye."

He hung up, opened Safari, and scrolled for information on Belinda Ferris-Stafford. There was none, including social media accounts. On the other hand, her husband, Anton Stafford, was everywhere radiating chill vibes.

Blue-eyed and deeply tan, he had a head full of wavy steel-gray hair, a whitish beard of manicured stubble, and a physique that suggested hot yoga, funyaking, and climbing coconut trees. His website bio called him a "spiritual teacher, holistic healer, soul revivalist, and author of *The Dancing Soul: Unlocking Humanity's Spiritual Potential*, forthcoming from Simon & Schuster."

*LA Weekly* called him a "self-help guru"; *New York Post*, a "New-Age quack."

Ellis searched Anton's Instagram followers and Facebook friends, which included Oprah Winfrey, Drew Barrymore, and Tony Robbins, but not Belinda Ferris. The videos on his YouTube channel had titles like "Cultivating Astral Empathy", "Energizing Emotional Awareness", "Unleashing Harmonic Biofeedback", and "Harnessing Compassionate Intentionality". In every one of them, Anton was wearing a turquoise mala and beige linen pajamas.

Unimpressed, Ellis opened the L.A. Times app and started scrolling:

*Climate activists vandalize Museum of Tolerance*

*Southland Sniper continues to taunt and evade police*

*LAPD warns of crime wave after*

*recent smash-and-grab robberies*

*Khloe's latest plastic surgery stuns fans*

*Cardi B sings empowerment anthems for Zillennials*

*Deadly crash shuts down westbound 10 Freeway for hours*

That last one triggered something. He dug a notebook out of the hip pocket of his Levi's and flipped it open. Only the first page had anything written on it:

*SHOW IDEAS:*

- ~~*Navy SEALS*~~
- *Rookie detective gets caught on a hot mic making insensitive remarks about a suspect shot by the police and has to transfer to L.A., and...?*

He uncapped a ballpoint pen and wrote,

- *Something about cars*

He drummed the pen against the page, at a loss for more. He hoped not to have to refer to the notebook anytime soon, anyway, but he sensed that it would be wise to prepare for *Miami Vice* getting stuck in development hell, if it even made it that far. Urs was losing interest, his agent was dead, and Kent had his pick of shows to produce.

His coffee was cold by the time Kaitlyn walked in. For a split second, he thought she was Deena, the lady he had just met in AA. They had the same blonde streaks, clear skin, perfect teeth, and likely fake breasts on a thin frame. Ellis deflated when he realized his mistake. Kaitlyn apologized for being late but made him wait another five minutes while she went to order a drink.

"Ugh. I asked for six scoops of matcha," she said, frowning into her candy-cane striped cup. "This is like, maybe four. At the most." Ellis waited some more while she returned to the counter and got it straightened out. "I have to go to Culver City after this, and I'm not going to make it on four scoops."

Without opening the manila envelope that held her report, she pushed it back across the table to Ellis. "You can keep that. Jay and I reconciled." She inhaled sharply. "I have forgiven him. In fact, we've invited Kirra into our marriage. We're going to be a throuple."

"Isn't she your cousin?" asked Ellis.

"By marriage. Mm-hmm."

"So, she's... *Jay's* cousin?"

"It's complicated. The bottom line is we're not getting divorced." For this, Kaitlyn expected a discount. Ellis said he was happy for her, but that wasn't how things worked. "But, also, Jay knew you were following him. So, there must be some wiggle room there." Ellis disagreed. "If I wanted him to know he was being followed, I could have done it myself."

In the spirit of the season, Ellis relented. "Okay, um… I'll knock off ten percent."

"How about twelve?"

"Fine, twelve."

Kaitlyn started tapping her phone screen. "Do you take Apple Pay?" Ellis didn't. "Venmo?" Uh-uh. "Oh. Okay, weird. So, what do we do here?"

"Cash? Or you could write me a check, as stipulated in our contract?"

After convincing her he was serious, she stood to leave. She picked up her report and winked. "Just in case."

SITTING AT A STOPLIGHT at Burbank Boulevard and Cahuenga, no longer in the mood for Christmas music, Ellis flipped through radio commercials, searching for classic rock solace. *…spending the holidays alone? …financing as low as zero-point-nine percent APR! …deep-dish bacon-wrapped pizza for just ten bucks… no interest until next year!* When he got to KT102, "Blackhole Sun" by Soundgarden was playing. Disgusted, he snapped the radio off and cursed.

Instead of having enough money to cover the deposit for a new apartment, he would have to wait until he got a check from a woman whose husband had punched Ellis in the face. He wouldn't be holding his breath. Maybe there was something to karma after all… Mentally rehearsing his next excuse to Reshma, he was startled by pops of gunfire.

To his right, two men in black hoodies burst from a liquor store, carrying armloads of bottles against their chests. They scrambled into a waiting Ford Fusion, which reversed out of the parking lot just as the light turned green and smashed into the car in front of Ellis. No time to brake, he swerved left, cutting off a pickup truck with giant tires, while the store owner stood in the parking lot, shooting. Ellis took the first left out of harm's way, slowed down, and loosened his sweaty grip on the steering wheel.

On the passenger seat, his phone buzzed: *No Caller ID.*

Ellis let it go to voicemail, figuring it was spam.

# CHAPTER 13

TUCKED IN THE CORNER of a Van Nuys shopping center, Royal Tiger Tae Kwon Do Studio was familiar to Ellis as a location in action movies and *Southland HEAT* episodes, but this was the first time he'd been inside.

Standing beside a heavy bag hanging by chains from the ceiling, he watched Mark Redondo finish his private after-hours workout with two young Asian women. He was middle-aged, muscular, and couldn't have been much taller than five feet. His hair was buzzed, but it was clear it was graying at the temples and thinning on top. Not the kind of guy Ellis would expect to be so flexible, fleet of foot, or have such a powerful roundhouse kick.

Redondo and his sparring partners attacked and blocked each other with balletic precision and speed. Mark took a kick to the gut but stayed upright and flipped the woman to the mat. He ducked a flying kick from the other woman, spun, and landed two blows to her head and midsection. Before the first woman was back in a ready position, Mark swung the blade of his hand toward her unguarded face.

"Heee-*yaahhh!*"

Ellis winced, waiting for the crunch of a broken nose, but Mark stopped within an inch of making contact.

"Gotcha," he said, delighted.

He helped the woman to her feet, and all three combatants bowed to one another. Then, they began unpeeling the Velcro straps of their pads.

"Thanks for coming on such short notice," Mark said to Ellis, "but with me, there's no other kind, right?" He toweled the sweat off his face and extended a damp, stubby hand.

Ellis shook it and smiled. "No problem."

"Girls!" Mark called to the women. "Come meet Ellis Dunaway." They approached and nodded hello. "They're helping me train for my black belt."

The taller of the pair had a mole on her cheek and long ponytail; the shorter one had short hair and a tattoo of a koi fish on her forearm. The women looked familiar to Ellis, but he couldn't recall where from. Maybe an AA meeting, or any number of dispensaries, Starbucks, or fast-food joints he frequented. He didn't think so, though. They didn't look like they allowed themselves many indulgences.

Ellis's focus snapped back to Mark when he told the women, "Ellis is going to get my money back for me."

"Ellis doesn't know what he's talking about," Ellis said to them. To Mark, he said, "Wanna fill me in?"

"I started taking martial arts classes four years ago. It takes most people at least five years to earn a black belt, and that's if they're extremely dedicated and focused. See, my whole life, people have disrespected and underestimated me because of my height. They think because—"

"Sorry," said Ellis. "I was talking about the money you mentioned."

"See there? You're proving my point. If I was tall, you woulda let me finish." Ellis thought it better not to argue. "I'm getting to the money. It's all connected. Anyway, like I was saying, I've always been disrespected and underestimated. In school, I was always the smallest kid in the class, plus I got a late birthday, so I was always the youngest, too. My parents were going to hold me back a year to give me time to *catch up*," he made air quotes, "but I begged them not to. I didn't need that humiliation on top of being a runt. And besides, I'm really fuckin' smart—if anything, I shoulda skipped *ahead* a grade or two—so, because I'm such an intelligent student of human nature, I developed a sense of humor as a defense mechanism. By making a joke outta myself, I showed the other kids I knew my place. I filled a position in the hierarchy, not at the absolute bottom, but nowhere near the top where I deserved to be. Eventually, I became pretty popular as the funny guy, y'know, the class clown. I even managed to get laid a few times. The girls weren't winning any prizes, but what the hell? I was grateful for whatever action I could get. So anyway, the bullying kinda let up, but still nobody took me seriously. I played my role too well, and everything I said—no matter what it was or how I said it—it was treated like a joke. Or even worse, totally fuckin' ignored… You have no idea what I'm talking about, do you?"

"I think I do," said Ellis.

"How tall are you? Six feet? Six two?"

"I don't know. Something like that."

"Tall people never know how tall they are. I know within a fraction of an inch. Five foot two and five eighths. That's on a good day. Among its other benefits, tae kwon do showed me that power has nothing to do with size. A low center of gravity can be an asset when the shit goes down. When I got my green belt, that was the defining moment of my new life. I saw myself as someone else, someone that I liked and admired. It was a whole new feeling and I thought, 'Shit. This is it. This is me now. I'm a new person!' And the past just…" he waved his hand, "blew away. Now, I respect myself. I'm confident in my mind and my power, and people can tell. And I get respect. I don't have to make noise to get attention. I carry myself with the dignity of a warrior." Ellis wondered if that was another example of Mark's intelligent sense of humor. "But every now and then, people challenge me. Like you did before, when you interrupted me. And when people challenge me, I have to step up, right?"

Careful not to interrupt, Ellis nodded.

"Now, about the money. I did a job for a friend of mine—at least I thought he was my friend—and he never paid me. You know him, too." Ellis raised his eyebrows, waiting for Mark to go on. "Ramsey Skillern." Ellis frowned. "Ramsey subcontracted with me, so my payment was coming from a third party," Ellis's stomach tightened as something dawned on him, "and I don't know if Ramsey ever got it, because when I called him about it, he never called me back. I couldn't find him at home, at work, anywhere. Then I find out, he's fuckin' dead. So now, I'm asking you, did you deliver the fifty thousand dollars that sleazy nightclub-owner-wannabe-actor-motherfucker Terry Montero gave you to give Ramsey?"

As he spoke, Mark had moved imperceptibly into Ellis's personal space.

"Wait," Ellis backed up and bumped into the heavy bag, "Ramsey is dead?"

"Answer my question first."

"Yes. I delivered the money."

Mark squinted. "All of it?"

"Yes."

"You sure?"

"Yes! Actually, I delivered *sixty* thousand dollars."

"Ten off the top was Ramsey's commission. I only care about the fifty grand that's due me for services rendered. Maybe you killed Ramsey—"

"Get serious."

"—and now you got my money squirreled away somewhere."

"I don't."

"Well, whether you're lying or not, you—"

"I'm not lying!"

"Ah. But you keep interrupting me. I told you about that."

Before Ellis knew what was happening, the taller woman, with the mole on her cheek, kicked him in the stomach. He doubled over, breathless, and stumbled backward. The shorter woman punched him squarely in the mouth and he went down on his ass.

Mark loomed over him. "Interrupt me again and you're really gonna get hurt. Understand?" Ellis rubbed his jaw and glared. "You look like you understand. Good. Anyway, if what you say is true, and you delivered the money, then Ramsey took it—*my money*—to Texas, where somebody killed him, execution style," Mark made a finger gun and put it to his temple, "two in the head, point blank, and stole it. And you're gonna get it back."

Ellis scoffed. "You think I'd work for you after this?" he said, getting to his feet, tasting blood.

"No, you'll be working for yourself. Lemme remind you, I'm two days away from getting my black belt. If you haven't brought me my fifty thousand bucks by then, I'm going to kill you with my bare fucking hands. Then, I'm going to kill Montero. I already warned him, which is how I got your number."

AFTER BEING DISMISSED, Ellis moved the Porsche deeper into the parking lot, where it would be camouflaged by other vehicles. The pain in his abdomen had spread down to the top of his head. His top lip was split. Using the side view mirror, he kept an eye on Royal Tiger, waiting for Mark Redondo to leave.

When he finally did, Ellis tailed his black Volvo S90 east on Saticoy Street, then right on Hayvenhurst, and left on Sherman Way. At the Taco Bell, he merged onto the 405 South and picked up speed. If Ellis hadn't already known Mark suffered from a raging Napoleon complex, he could have guessed it from the pointlessly aggressive way he drove—tailgating, cutting in and out between cars, passing on the left and right without signaling, and getting no further than three or four car lengths from Ellis who maintained his 65mph speed in the right lane.

Mark exited, again no signal, and took a left onto Sepulveda, then a right on Valley Vista, and another right onto Woodcliff Road in an upscale neighborhood north of Mulholland in Sherman Oaks. With no more traffic to cover him, Ellis stayed as far back as he dared. On Lynnwood Court, he pulled to the curb a few houses down from the one where Mark's Volvo was parked.

Set into a hillside at the apex of a cul-de-sac, the place was a case study in mid-century modern architecture: a steel and glass shoebox stacked on top of a carport. The yellow front door was on a covered terrace accessible only by a curving set of stairs. Houses like it had appreciated vastly in the last seventy years, especially ones this well-maintained and in this zip code. So expensive a house was likely to be outfitted with a security system that included motion lights and cameras. Ellis lowered his head and risked it.

Crouched among the bougainvillea and jasmine, he had a narrow view through the floor-to-ceiling windows of an open living room. A fake, flocked Christmas tree stood adjacent to a roaring stone fireplace. Mark Redondo was pacing in and out of Ellis's field of vision, talking to someone unseen. Judging by the red of Mark's face and how he occasionally cracked his knuckles and flexed his neck, whoever it was had disrespected him. A prickly pear prevented Ellis from scooting over for a better look.

Eventually, Mark stepped out of frame, and for a few minutes, there was nothing to see except the fire and the Christmas tree. With his knee beginning to ache along with his stomach and face, Ellis was about to slink away when a man with wavy steel-gray hair, wearing beige pajamas and a turquoise mala, backed into view.

Anton Stafford. He was holding a drink in a lowball glass.

Mark squared up to him, crowding him like he had done Ellis, pointing his stubby finger in Anton's face. Anton held up his free hand, palm out, in a gesture of surrender. Mark grabbed the offered hand and twisted. Anton dropped his drink, his face a rictus of agony. Mark's bicep bulged as he twisted harder. Anton collapsed to his knees in the puddle of booze and glass shards, crying. Mark shouted something Ellis didn't make out, released Anton, and vanished from sight.

Ellis's heart leapt into his throat when the yellow front door flew open. He flattened to the ground just as Mark stormed past him and down the curving steps to the dark street. Ellis stayed still, holding his breath, until he heard the Volvo zoom away, then he checked the window of the house to make sure the coast was clear. His knee popped and twinged as he got to his feet and ran down the steps two at a time.

By the time he got the Porsche turned around, his odds of catching up to Mark were fifty-fifty. Ellis turned left but guessed wrong.

The street was deserted.

# CHAPTER 14

THE ONLY REASON THE TV in Terry Montero's office wasn't turned all the way up like always was that it was smashed on the floor, along with the stereo, computer monitor, and framed *Night Street* poster. Sitting behind his desk, Terry was also in bad shape.

"Look what they did to my fuckin' face," he said. "I'm still paying for the damn thing, and it's fuckin' ruined!"

He was right. The sockets of both surgically lifted eyes were black. A line of stitches crossed his bruised purple jaw. Both lips were swollen and split. A wad of bandages hid his reshaped nose.

"They broke my fuckin' nose. Six thousand bucks, down the fuckin' drain."

Ellis repeated the question: "Who are *they?*"

"I'm tellin' you, I never heard the name Mark Redondo in my life before he showed up here with those ninja chicks, talking about how I owe him fifty grand, and kicked my ass and broke all my electronics and shit. Look at that shit."

"You gave him my name."

"What the hell else could I do? I tried not to. Look at me for fuck's sake. I thought they were gonna kill me."

"They are, right after they kill *me!*"

"I'm sorry, really. I didn't know this would happen. I didn't know Ramsey was supposed to give the money to this Redondo guy, whoever the hell he is."

"When you gave me the money, you said you were the middleman between a *colleague*," Ellis put the word in air quotes, "who utilized Ramsey's *services*," more air quotes, "leading my dumb ass to think it had something to do with renting movie props. But that wasn't it, was it?" Terry shook his head. "What then? Who is the colleague, and what was the service Ramsey subcontracted to Redondo?"

Terry's eyes were cast down. He was gingerly touching his nose and whining to himself. "Six thousand bucks… down the drain."

Ellis slammed the flat of his hand on the desk. "Answer me!"

"Okay, okay. Jesus. An actress I knew from *Night Street*, thirty years ago, came to see me. We've kept in touch a little bit, y'know.

I hook her up now and then. But anyway, she wanted a hit man. I don't know why. I mean, I know why, but I don't know who she wanted killed. I didn't ask. The less I know, the better."

"Who's the actress?"

Terry hesitated like he was trying to make up his mind about something and sighed.

"Annalee Gentry. All I did was connect her and Ramsey. He's a reformed gang banger who's not all that reformed. I figured if he didn't want the job, he'd know somebody who did, and he'd get to keep a percentage. I don't know, that's for him to work out. Anyway, I passed along Annalee's money. That's it."

"Wrong," said Ellis. "*I* passed along the money. And you *did* know Ramsey was going to give the money to somebody else."

"I didn't."

"You knew it was a possibility. Why the fuck didn't you tell me all that, instead of all that shit about how you aren't just my drug dealer, you're my friend? I guess that's just another meaningless thing people say, huh?"

"What are you talking about? We're friends."

"Not anymore."

"Babe, listen—"

"What does Anton Stafford have to do with all this?"

"The guy who played the Asian detective on season four of *Southland HEAT*?"

"Don't play dumb, Terry."

"I'm not playing. I never heard of him."

"What about Christian Cooper? He's friends with Brandii Bunnz."

"I-I don't know, maybe."

"You used me, man. You fucked me! That's not friendship, that's bullshit."

"W-well… how do I know you delivered that money to Ramsey like you were supposed to, huh? How do I know *you* didn't fuck *me*?"

Ellis grabbed the edges of the desk and leaned down close to Terry's battered face. "Is that a joke? Are you fucking kidding, asking me that? If you're calling me a thief, it better be a joke or Mark Redondo and his ninjas aren't gonna get a chance to kill you, I'll do it my-fucking-self!"

"W-whaddya want me to say? I'm sorry. I shoulda told y— …Aww *fuck!* My fuckin' tooth fell out." Terry pushed back from the desk and scanned the floor. "These things cost a fortune. Do you see it?"

"Yeah, it's right here." Ellis stomped on it and ground the porcelain veneer against the concrete floor.

"I'm s-sorry, Ellis-s! Pleas-s-se…" The words came with a whistle because of the missing tooth. Tears leaked out of his puffy, bloodshot eyes. "I was-s a bad friend. I'm s-sorry. I'm a bad pers-s-son."

Ellis knew the apology was sincere because Terry was also a bad actor.

HER BIO ON IMDB revealed nothing useful: *Annalee Gentry was born on 19 September 1966 in the USA. She is an actress known for the TV show* Night Street *(1989).*

The only picture of her was a still from the show. In it, she was wearing sunglasses. All Ellis could see for sure was that she was white, thin, and brunette. She had no social media presence, and there were no clips of her on YouTube. *Night Street* was a mid-season replacement series that only ran twelve episodes. It was never rerun; no streaming service carried it.

Ellis lit a joint and stared at Annalee Gentry's pixelated image. Zooming in only made it less clear. He zoomed out and sat back. Annalee's tenuous connection to the entertainment industry heightened Ellis's suspicion that Larry Price's murder was the one she contracted. The timing of the payment to Ramsey was too perfect.

Catalyzed by the weed, other sympathies emerged. Like Annalee, Ellis was also a Gen-Xer born in the USA. And he knew the resentment of watching others succeed where he had failed—

one measly credit from thirty years ago. As embarrassing as it was, thirty years was a long time to hold a grudge. Ellis was an expert on the subject. But maybe Annalee Gentry's grievance ran deeper and was more immediate than just a stalled career.

A search for Mark Redondo turned up nothing at all.

*More trouble for actor Urs Schreiber,* said Tayleigh Tompkins on MaxxNEWS. Ellis shut his laptop and turned the TV up. *He was arrested again tonight at his Hollywood Hills home. This time, the star of* Brass Hearts *and the hit TV series* Graveyardland *is being charged with the first-degree murder of his agent, Larry Price, who was shot and killed on Hollywood Boulevard after leaving a nightclub around eleven p.m. on the night of December second. Police say they found a necklace like the one Schreiber had been wearing that night on a rooftop near the scene of Price's murder, where police allege the fatal shot was fired from. The troubled star was on probation for a DUI conviction in October.*

CUT TO: footage of that arrest, the Saturn medallion glinting in the paparazzi flashbulbs. Tayleigh, VO: *He is seen here wearing the necklace in question.*

CUT TO: Tayleigh in the studio: *Tonight, Schreiber is back in jail. His attorney released a statement saying that, quote, 'Urs is the victim of a witch hunt, and he will be totally exonerated.' But many in Hollywood aren't so sure.*

The yellow bobtail cat with the broken fang jumped into Ellis's lap, hollering for her dinner.

# CHAPTER 15

RUDOLPH THE RED-NOSED REINDEER was slumped over, knees buckled, antlers drooping like he was drunk, or dying. Courtland Hollender, wearing Bollé Eagle Vision sunglasses and a black suit and tie, was in a battle to get the lawn ornament reinflated and upright.

"Why're you so dressed up?" asked Ellis.

"Just got back from my nephew Ramsey's memorial service."

"My condolences."

"Thanks. What happened to your lip?"

"A couple of Mark Redondo's ninjas beat me up."

"Who's Mark Redondo?" asked Hollender, searching Rudolph's seams for the air leak.

"A hit man who's gonna kill me in approximately thirty-two hours unless I give him fifty thousand dollars." Hollender paused, giving Ellis his full attention. "A couple days before your retirement-slash-Christmas party, Terry Montero asked me to deliver some money to Ramsey's prop house. He said it was from a *colleague*," air quotes, "who had utilized Ramsey's services. I naturally assumed it was for renting props to a porn shoot or something. But apparently, it was payment for a contract murder."

Hollender let Rudolph crumple. "What the hell are you talking about?"

"An actress friend of Terry's, named Annalee Gentry, asked Terry to get her a hit man… and he went to Ramsey."

"Bullshit!"

"But Ramsey didn't do the hit."

"Of course he didn't."

"He subcontracted it to this guy, Mark Redondo. The money I delivered to Ramsey was supposed to go to him—Redondo— minus ten off the top that was Ramsey's cut for making the connection. But Redondo says Ramsey never paid him anything. And now Ramsey is dead, and I'm on the hook for fifty grand. If I can somehow buy some more time… Like, maybe there's a way to find some suspicious overages in Bullseye Props' accounts. I'm just spitballing here, but if Ramsey was laundering money or—"

"No, uh-uh. I don't believe it. Ramsey left all that gangster bullshit behind a long time ago."

"The fact that he was killed in the Texas desert days after I handed him an envelope full of cash for," air quotes again, "*services rendered* doesn't make you question how reformed he really was? You seriously don't see any red flags?"

Hollender whipped off his Eagle Visions. His eyes were pink and rimmed with tears.

"You better watch your tone and get those stupid air quotes outta my face. Today is not the day for this shit!"

"Today is the *only* day for it! I'm fucking freaking out here, man. I need to know what to do. I don't have anywhere close to fifty thousand dollars. I can't pay, so I have to give Redondo something he'll take instead. Information or something. Anything! Please, man. If there's anything you know—anything you even *think*—about Ramsey that could buy me some time, please—"

"You want me to sell out my nephew's memory to get your ass out of trouble you got yourself into with Terry Montero? I warned you again and again about that shady motherfucker. You wanna know what to do? Go to the police. I'm retired."

"I don't have time to go to the police. And I don't have any proof of anything anyway."

"Sounds like you're fucked then. If you don't wanna listen to me, I don't know why you came over here. Today of all days."

"I came because I thought maybe you'd help me."

Just then, Hollender's wife Cheryl popped her top half out of the front door. "Court— Oh, hi, Ellis. How you doin', sweetie?"

"Hey, Cheryl. Not great."

"Y'all quit playin' with Rudolph and come in the house. Tameka's on TV!"


THE HOLLYWOOD AREA JAIL stank of BO and hot garbage. Ellis could only imagine how bad it was on Urs Schreiber's side of the thick plastic window.

"I tried breathing through my mouth," he said into the landline-style phone receiver, "but then I could literally taste it. It's like… spoiled milk and onions."

"Uh-huh. I don't have a lot of time," said Ellis. Just nine hours, twenty-two minutes and counting. "Have you ever heard of—?"

"You've gotta help me, man! I shouldn't be here. This is a witch hunt, plain and simple. Have you seen this bitch cop who found my chain, acting like she's some kind of fucking hero, running her mouth about how nobody is above the law and how my white, nepo baby privilege can't save me now? I mean, what the actual fuck? That's racism, dude. That's hate speech."

Although Ellis would have picked different words, it was true that LAPD officer Tameka Settles had been on TV an awful lot since yesterday, reveling in the telling and re-telling of how she chased a man whom she caught breaking into cars, and how he climbed on top of a dumpster and from there pulled himself onto a terrace and then onto the roof of a building on Hollywood Boulevard. Ultimately, he got away, but Tameka found a gold chain with a Saturn-shaped IBET medallion. The spot where she found it had a direct sightline to where Larry Price was gunned down.

At a press conference, Chief Davies commended Officer Settles's bravery and sharp eye and reiterated her point that no one, not even "Hollywood elites," was above the law. It was a resounding PR win for the LAPD, which sorely needed one for the lack of progress in the Southland Sniper killings. Discovering the key piece of evidence in a high-profile arrest would certainly help Tameka reclaim in Los Angeles the rank she blew in Texas.

"She can't prove the necklace she found is even mine," said Urs. "Do I look like somebody who would climb up on a fucking roof?"

"But there are only two or three of those medallions known to exist, right? It's pretty damning evidence."

"*Known* to exist. All I know is what the guy who sold it to me said. He coulda been lying. Maybe there are lots of 'em out there. Nah, this bitch just wants to be famous. She saw an opportunity to use me and took it. Just like everybody else. Watch and see if she doesn't get a Netflix deal outta this."

"Be sure to mention Netflix at your arraignment. I'm sure that'll make just the right impression," said Ellis.

Aware that his visit with Urs was being recorded, he picked his next words carefully. He wasn't about to admit that he delivered fifty thousand dollars of Annalee Gentry's money to Ramsey Skillern—cousin of the police officer who put Urs away—for a murder that Mark Redondo committed but was never paid for, and now that Ramsey was dead, he—Ellis—was responsible for the money.

"Have you ever heard of an actress named Annalee Gentry?" he asked.

"Is she the skinny chick on *Stranger Things*?" asked Urs.

"No. No, she was in a couple episodes of *Night Street* back in 1989."

"Never heard of it. Christian's mom was on a show called something like that, though. *Crime Street* or *Heat Street*... Something like that."

"*Night Street*?"

"I dunno. I think it was maybe like... *Street Beat*? They had a poster of it in their house in Costa Mesa. It had like, some cops' faces on it and stuff."

Ellis knew what it looked like. Terry Montero had one in his office, and long ago, there had been one in the hallway outside the writers' room at Maxx Studios.

"Well, there never was a show called *Street Beat*, but there was one called *Night Street*. So, that's probably what you're thinking of."

Urs shook his head. "I don't think so, dude."

"Dude, I'm telling you, there was never a show called—" Ellis cut himself off, thinking: Christian said he was with his parents the night of Larry's murder. His mother was on the same obscure show as Annalee Gentry, and his stepfather… "What's Anton Stafford's connection to Mark Redondo?"

"I follow Anton on Instagram, but I've never met him in person. And who was the other guy?"

"Mark Redondo."

Urs shook his head. "Was he also on *Street Beat*?"

"No, he's…" It didn't seem wise to say "hit man" out loud in the police station… "a karate expert."

"Never heard of him."

"What about Ramsey Skillern, the guy who runs Bullseye Props?"

"Uh-uh. Bullseye made some props for *Graveyardland*, though." Urs leaned forward, almost touching his forehead to the plexiglass. "Listen, man, I'm not very liquid right now. All my money is tied up with Zuke, but you gotta help me. It sucks in here, bro. I can't do prison. Everybody in here wants to either fuck me or kill or me, or both, in reverse order. Please, you gotta—"

Ellis hung up and bolted from the visitor's room.

Eight hours, forty-three minutes and counting.

SUN BEAT DOWN on the Porsche parked on North Wilcox Avenue, a block from Hollywood Station. A parking ticket pinned under the windshield wiper fluttered in the grimy wind. In a sweat, Ellis rolled down the window and stuck the key in the busted ignition. Before he could turn it, the sudden appearance of an obese woman in a soiled bathrobe, pushing a shopping cart full of junk up the sidewalk, startled him.

"Shit. Where did you come from?" he asked in a rhetorical mumble.

"Got a message for you, from the boy," she said, reaching into a crumpled Carl's Jr. sack and withdrawing a folded piece of paper.

Ellis started rolling up the window.

"Message for you," the homeless woman hooked her gnarled thumb behind her, "from the boy." She slipped the paper in the car just before Ellis got the window all the way up.

He looked over his shoulder. Up the block was a kid on a Schwinn Tornado—black with yellow and orange trim, just like the one Ellis had—wearing a *Star Wars* iron-on T-shirt with blue ringers, also like Ellis used to have. Same rangy build and shaggy brown hair, too.

Like déjà vu or a waking dream, a woozy feeling came over him.

The homeless woman broke the spell, rapping on the window. "Gimme few bucks?"

Ellis shook his head. "I don't have any cash." He showed his open palms as if to prove it.

The woman flipped him off and shuffled away, and Ellis looked back behind him. The kid was gone. He started rolling down the car window to call to the homeless woman, but she was gone too. He looked over both shoulders twice. Nobody anywhere. He unfolded the paper.

It was a page from a porn magazine. A woman with hot-pink lips, ice-blue eyeshadow, and blonde Farrah Fawcett waves belied by lush brown pubic hair was reclining on a zebra-striped bedspread. The uninspired photography combined with the model's exposed inner labia suggested to Ellis that the picture came from a late-seventies *Hustler*, *Club*, or *Genesis*—magazines he used to sneak peeks at in 7-Eleven on Saticoy Street after school.

In the margin was written in smeared ballpoint cursive, *Will history blame me, or the bees?*

Ellis had heard the question twice before: once in the summer of 1978 at the Baronet Theatre and again fifteen years later, in his apartment, on a rented VHS tape of *The Swarm*.

# CHAPTER 16

THE WINDOWS OF BULLSEYE PROPS were smashed. Inside, the grid of autographed headshots on the front office wall was askew. The glass was broken in some of the frames. There were blank spots where Sylvester Stallone, Jason Statham, and Charlie's Angels (2000) had hung. Behind the reception desk, a girlishly thin Latina with long, straight hair was talking on the phone.

"…three bazookas, four uzis, ten M-16s, six MK-48s, six AK-47s… No, they're machine guns… A dozen RPGs… It stands for rocket-propelled grenade… No, none of this stuff is real. I mean, it exists, so it's real like that, but they're all props for movies and TV shows. You see what I'm sayin'?" She flipped the page of the clipboard she was reading from. "Okay, so, they also stole eight muskets, fourteen laser guns, and a sidewinder missile. And that's it… Okay… I'll email pictures of the damage in a minute, but it'll take until tomorrow to get all the receipts together… No! I keep telling you, they're not functioning weapons! There's literally no such thing as a laser gun. They're *props*… Right. Yes, exactly… Okay. Bye."

She hung up and forced a smile at Ellis. "Are you here from *SEAL Team?*"

"Uh, yeah," said Ellis, surprised. "How did you know?"

"You made an appointment for three o'clock."

Ellis's delight crumbled with the realization: "You must be talking about the new *SEAL Team* with David Boreanaz."

The look on her face said, *Of course; what else?*

"I was a writer on *SEAL Team Trident* in the nineties. Anyway, forget it. What happened here? You were robbed?"

She sighed. "Yeah, last night. They smashed their way in and got into the warehouse and took all kinds of stuff. The cops said it must have been a gang of robbers to have gotten away with so much stuff so fast. I've been on the phone with the insurance company all day."

A pudgy, bearded guy entered from the warehouse. The keypad door lock was dangling by wires.

"Uh, hey, Yolanda? Sorry to interrupt, but the helmets and night-vision goggles the people from *SEAL Team* wanted to look at were stolen."

"What the fuck, Dylan?" Yolanda started flipping through the clipboard. "I don't see helmets and night-vision goggles on the list."

"I know. I just found out." He backed away. "Sorry."

Yolanda shut her eyes and rubbed her temples.

"Do you think the robbery has anything to do with Ramsey's death?" asked Ellis.

"I don't know," said Yolanda. "Probably not. The police said six other businesses in the neighborhood were robbed last night. This is the second time we've been hit in the last six months. So…"

"I'm kind of surprised you're still open after he was killed. I'm a family friend, by the way."

"There are some silent partners that want to stay open for now. But they've also been talking about selling off the inventory. So, who knows? I'm only the office manager. Why tell me anything?"

Ellis smiled. Time to play the hunch that had brought him to the prop house in the first place.

"I can see you have your hands full, so I'll keep it short. My name is Ellis Dunaway. I'm writing and producing a docu-series with Kent Moran—"

Yolanda lit up. "Oh, we love Kent around here." She pointed to the wall of crooked and damaged headshots. Kent's was the only one still hanging straight.

"Yeah, he's quite a guy. Anyway, the show is about the Iapetusian Brotherhood of Eternal Tranquility, that doomsday cult that committed mass suicide in 1988, and we heard a rumor that Bullseye fabricated some replicas of the Saturn-shaped medallions they used to wear. So, we're wondering if somebody has maybe beaten us to the punch."

"Yeah, we did make one of those," said Yolanda.

"Just one? Who commissioned it?"

"I think there was only one, and I wouldn't tell you who it was for, even if I knew. It's against company policy. I do know it was a rush order Ramsey was handling himself, though, so it must have been pretty important."

"Did Ramsey ever mention a guy named Mark Redondo?"

Yolanda squinted. "Not that I remember."

"That's cool." He put his hands in his jeans' pockets, hoping to put Yolanda at ease with his nonchalance. "So—I'm just curious—how do you go about making a replica of something like that medallion? I mean, did you work from photographs or what?"

"I don't know anything about the fabrication side of the business, but I do know that they cast it from an original. Ramsey showed it to me. The one we made was an exact copy, except for an engraved serial number we put on there. All our props have serial numbers."

She held up the clipboard for Ellis to see.

"Where'd Ramsey get an original medallion? Aren't they like, super rare?"

"No, I'm pretty sure he just bought it off eBay. Somebody found a box of them in an abandoned storage unit in San Bernardino back in the early 2000s. It's a good thing, too, because the original we had and the replica were stolen last night."

It's also good news for Urs's legal team, thought Ellis.

"And there was only one replica?"

"I honestly don't know, you'd have to ask one of the fabricators."

"Can I—?"

Just then, a woman in tight designer jeans, a flannel scarf piled around her shoulders, and a ball cap pulled down low entered. A middle-aged hipster guy in checkerboard Vans and a sport coat over a vintage Harley-Davidson T-shirt followed her.

"Hey," said the woman. "We have an appointment today to look at some props for *SEAL Team*."

Yolanda hopped to her feet and came around the desk with the clipboard. "Of course. Hi. I'm Yolanda. Pardon the mess. We were robbed last night."

The stylish man and woman looked around, just noticing the disarray.

"Follow me, and I'll connect you with Dylan, who'll show you around," said Yolanda.

Now that the only television creatives who mattered were here, Yolanda was finished with Ellis. Without a glance in his direction, she opened the busted warehouse door for her clients.

"Unfortunately, some of the props you were interested in were stolen. The night-vision goggles and—"

The door closed behind them, leaving Ellis alone in the office.

He darted behind the desk and rifled it, hoping to find anything that might impress Mark Redondo enough to spare his life. But the papers on top of the desk meant nothing. He was tugging at the locked desk drawers when Yolanda's angry voice spun him around.

"What the fuck do you think you're doing?!"

"Nothing. I, uh… just wanted to take a closer look at this picture of Kent."

"I knew there was something off about you. You're one of the robbers come back to finish the job."

Ellis put his hands up. "I'm not. I swear."

The only way out from behind the desk was toward Yolanda.

As soon as he took the first step, she screamed, "Dylan, call the police!" and threw her clipboard like a Frisbee. It chopped Ellis across the bridge of his nose.

With blood dripping down his shirtfront, he bolted from the office.


ZERO HOUR.

Ellis stood in the doorway of Royal Tiger Tae Kwon Do Studio, sweating and weak-kneed, while the taller of Mark Redondo's Asian-lady goons, the one with a mole on her cheek, patted him down for weapons. He had none. He didn't have Mark Redondo's money either, or any reason Mark shouldn't kill him. All Ellis could do was argue that if he were allowed to live, at least a little while longer, maybe he could figure out where the fifty thousand dollars went. He was hoping for, but not expecting, mercy. Or a miracle.

The woman concluded her pat down by squeezing Ellis's balls. When he jumped, she snorted a laugh and thumped his swollen nose right where the clipboard had cut him. Pain sang through his skull. Tears sprang to his eyes.

With a flick of her ponytail, she bade Ellis to follow her to the back of the darkened dojo. The shorter woman, with the koi fish tattoo on her arm, followed so close she stepped on his heels twice. She shoved him through the doorway of a windowless, wood-paneled office. The only furniture was a desk, a filing cabinet, and a pair of straight-back chairs. Crossed katanas were mounted on the wall. The floor was carpeted, giving Ellis cold comfort that he probably wouldn't be cut to pieces with the swords, leaving telltale stains.

Mark Redondo was leaning against the desk with his arms crossed, wearing a karategi cinched with a black belt. Koi Fish left the room, closing the door behind her; Ponytail, the crotch grabber, remained.

"Right on time," said Mark. "I like that. Punctuality is a sign of respect. But enough making out. It's time to fuck. Where's my money?"

"I have no idea. But if you give me—"

From behind, Ponytail chopped Ellis on the neck below the jaw. "*Fuck!*" He stumbled, instantly dizzy, but stayed on his feet.

Mark tsk-tsked and stood away from the desk. "You've got balls. I gotta give you that—you've got some balls. I never thought you were gonna come up with the money. I was always pretty sure I was gonna have to kill you. But I thought I'd have to track you down first. I figured you'd run and hide like a little bitch."

"If you'll just listen, I—"

Mark cut off Ellis's plea with a punch to the solar plexus and another to the side of his head. This time, his vision foggy, Ellis fell back against one of the chairs, toppling it and himself.

Ponytail kicked him in the ribs. Once. Twice…

"That's enough, that's enough," said Mark. "Okay, on your feet, asshole. It's gonna be a long night." He cinched his black belt, bent down, and grabbed a fistful of Ellis's hair. "Stand up, motherfucker."

Ellis struggled to get his feet under him and at the same time pry Mark's vice-tight fingers out of his hair when the office door popped open and Koi came in.

Mark let go of Ellis. "What?!"

She whispered in his ear and slipped him a manila envelope.

He looked inside. "I'll be damned." To Ellis he said, "Who woulda thought a little bitch like you would have a fairy godmother?"

"H-huh?"

Mark held the envelope out to Ellis, who was still kneeling, gasping on the carpet. It was the same one Terry Montero had given him, with Ramsey Skillern's name and the address of Bullseye Props written on it.

Ellis was dumbfounded.

"Wh—? Who…?"

Mark's focus was back on the envelope full of cash. "Get up and get the fuck outta here, you fuckin' sack of shit."

"B-but how…? Who…?"

"I said, get the fuck *outta here!*" Mark drew back his fist. Ellis flinched. "Go buy a lottery ticket before your fuckin' luck runs out and I change my mind about killing you."

Stumbling out the door of Royal Tiger, Ellis stopped and took a gasping breath of night air. The asphalt and fast-food grease were an invigorating potpourri, if only because he was alive to smell it. His head spun with relief and confusion as he scanned the empty parking lot for some sign of his fairy godmother, but there was nothing and no one stirring.

A miracle on Saticoy Street.

# CHAPTER 17

ANOTHER DAY, another miracle.

The mariachi Christmas music playing in Don Miguel Cocina Mexicana on West Riverside Drive in Burbank was a little too loud. But Ellis appreciated how it fit the festive atmosphere. He had suggested the restaurant when Deena, the bottle-blonde bombshell who had detonated the homely status quo of Ellis's regular AA meetings asked if he wanted to get something to eat afterward. Don Miguel was close—less than a mile from Pathways Church—parking was easy enough, and the food far outclassed the taco shops that also sold pizza and hamburgers but wasn't as outré (or expensive) as the nouveau fusion places. Piñatas of Santa Claus, Frosty the Snowman, the Grinch, and, inexplicably, Garfield had replaced the usual burros, cacti, and sombreros. The red bulbs in the fake gas lantern sconces and the strings of multi-colored lights swagged over the bar glowed year-round.

Seated under a brick arch, sipping iced teas and picking at the bowls of chips and salsa, Ellis and Deena laughed about the foibles of the people in the AA group. To keep the mood positive, Ellis pretended to be more charmed by them than he was, which was not at all. Antonio and the GED test; Sanya and her rigid diet and flexible definitions; Ricky and his tattoo removal; Lucinda and her screenplay that was probably bad enough actually to sell; Shereé and her celebrity candle clientele. Ellis even gave Darren and his antisocial refusal to comply with the no-cell-phone policy a rueful laugh. "He's, uh… something else, that guy."

Deena agreed, with an exaggerated eye roll. The moment stretched out—a couple more chips and sips of tea—but before it turned awkward, Ellis said, "I was surprised you approached me after the meeting."

"Oh yeah? How come?"

"Well, I mean, on one hand, I get it. I'm cool, I'm stylish as hell, and I look exactly like Chris Hemsworth. But you strike me as somebody with better sense than to ask a middle-aged alcoholic, especially one with a face full of cuts and bruises, out on a date."

"Oh, sorry, did you think this was a date? Dinner isn't necessarily a date. And I asked you to dinner. I know because I rehearsed it in my head all through the meeting." She batted her eyelashes.

It had been at least a decade since a woman expressed anything like romantic interest in Ellis. The recommended ways a poor man in his early fifties might meet women were unappealing, especially now that bars were no longer an option. Dating apps, social media, yoga and acting classes, gym membership—no, gracias. He hadn't flirted or been flirted with in so long that it came across like a foreign language. Wanting for a witty rejoinder, his cheeks and ears burned. Hopefully, the dim red lighting hid the blush.

"No, yeah. For sure," he said. "This isn't a date. I was just, uh—"

"Not *necessarily* a date."

Another flush rose up Ellis's neck. Deena's pace was dizzying.

"Anyway, I'm a middle-aged alcoholic too, you know." She circled her finger around her face, meaning Ellis's. "What happened, by the way?"

"I'm packing up my apartment, and there are boxes everywhere, and the furniture's all out of place, and I bent down to pick something up and *bam*. Right into a bookshelf."

"Ouch. Got you on the lip and the nose."

Ellis wondered if she was letting him know she detected his lie.

She went on, "Moving is such a pain."

"Yeah, literally. I've lived in the apartment a long time, too. So, I keep finding all this stuff that I should have gotten rid of years ago, but—"

"But now, it's like, impossible to let go of because you have some sort of misplaced sentimentality attached to this stupid thing that you forgot you had in the first place."

"Exactly."

"I hate moving. And I have a sentimental streak too. I'm in Sherman Oaks now, and I love it. It's more walkable than people think."

"I looked at a place in North Hollywood," said Ellis, still ashamed of writing Reshma a bad check, "but I dunno…"

"North Hollywood is evolving. And it's really walkable, too. My acupuncturist is there. She's amazing. She looks just like Rosamund Pike. My friends are all like, 'Why would you go to a white acupuncturist?' and I see their point, but she's really good."

"When I was a kid, my orthodontist looked like Larry Manetti," said Ellis. He was impressed that Deena knew who that was.

"Are you kidding? I love *Magnum P.I.!* I literally had a poster of Tom Selleck in my bedroom when I was twelve. Are you watching *True Detective?*"

"Not the new season." True. "But it's on my watchlist." False.

They had both liked *Breaking Bad* but lost interest in *Better Call Saul.* "Michael McKean was good, though." "He always is." Deena couldn't remember the last movie she saw in a theatre. Ellis could: "*Aquaman*, opening day, last Christmas. I don't care anything about Aquaman, but I always go to the movies on Christmas Day. I don't have family here"—or anywhere at all that he knew of—"so I usually go to a matinee, get Chinese food, and just enjoy the way the city slows down and empties out for a couple days."

Deena said she liked that too. "The only time I think I've gone to the movies on Christmas was seeing *A Star Is Born* at the Fox in Westwood Village when I was seven. Barbara Streisand made me want to be an actress."

Ellis couldn't believe she had never seen *The Lost Boys*—"I saw it five times at the Cineplex Odeon in Universal City."

She couldn't believe he had never seen *The Princess Bride*—"I've got the whole thing memorized." She quoted a line, but Ellis didn't catch it.

The names and places of their youths churned a wave that washed Ellis back to the bedroom of his high school girlfriend, Kara Castillo. *When Doves Cry*, she said, dipping the key to her hand-me-down yellow Audi into a vial of cocaine she stole from her dad; *Material Girl*, Ellis said, aligning the strings of his tennis racket, after-school sun streaming through the windows.

Maybe if Kara hadn't moved over the hill to the city, and he hadn't been so immature... Maybe then... Maybe a lot of things. Ellis forced himself to zone back in on what Deena was saying.

"Okay. Before this goes any further, I have a confession to make, and if this is a dealbreaker, I understand, but..."

"But what? You're making me nervous."

"I know you're friends with Kent Moran and everything, but..." Deena inhaled, "I just can't get into *Graveyardland*. I'm sorry. I know it's supposed to be like, this work of genius and everything, but I just don't get it."

Ellis dropped his shoulders and grinned. "That doesn't offend me at all. I feel the exact same way. Seriously. I hate that show. And believe me, Kent is no genius. I love him like a brother," not true, "and he's a super-talented guy," sort of true, "and, while I appreciate *Graveyardland*," bald-faced lie, "I don't actually *like* it." Very true. "Does that make sense?"

"Wow. Yes. What a relief." Deena pretended to wipe sweat off her brow. "I thought I was the only person in the world who doesn't watch it."

"Same here."

"So, what's happening with the new show you're working on? Can you give me any details?"

"There aren't a lot to give." Ellis ran his finger through a ring of condensation on the table. "It was meant to be a vehicle for

Urs Schreiber. So, obviously, now that he's in jail, things are, um… in flux."

"Yeah, I guess they would be. But look at it this way, maybe this is an opportunity to get somebody good."

"Not an Urs fan, huh?"

"Yeah, no, I like him fine. I mean, I did before he had his meltdown and everything. Plus, he kind of reminds me of a wet cigarette. Y'know, just like, how… wan he is."

Ellis laughed. "I can see that."

"Think he killed his agent?"

"Not really. I've gotten to know him a little bit, and he's got his faults, for sure, but climbing up on a rooftop and shooting his agent with a sniper rifle… that's another level. I don't see that."

"But what about the police finding his necklace up there?"

"How do they know it's *his* necklace? You can buy those medallions on eBay, and then there are replicas. Plus, like you said, he's a wan, wet cigarette. He's not climbing up on anything higher than a pool float. I think the eagerness to convict him and the claims that it's all a witch hunt because of his white-male-nepo-baby privilege are a bit overheated. But then again, I dunno. I'd almost believe anything at this point." Even the existence of monsters.

"If you don't think Urs did it, who do you think did?"

Ellis didn't know who pulled the trigger, but he knew who was responsible: Annalee Gentry by way of Ramsey Skillern and Mark Redondo, with Ellis himself unwittingly assisting them. He cleared his throat and took a drink of tea. "I have no idea. Maybe the Southland Sniper, even though he denied it. Or a copycat?"

"So, just totally random?"

"Maybe. Anyway, I think there are people out there who had more beef with Larry Price than Urs."

"Oh yeah?" Deena leaned in. "Spill the tea."

"Yeah, so, apparently, Price was a real asshole. I've heard consistent accounts of him sexually harassing the women he worked with. I only met him once, and that was the night he got killed, so I can't—"

"Wait. Really?"

"Yeah, I was standing right next to him when he got shot. He wanted me to get in his car so he could show me his dick."

Deena sat back, stunned. "Pardon me?"

"Uh-huh." Ellis told the story. Just as he was finishing—"…he goes, 'Lemme show you my dick,' and then bang, his head exploded"—the teenage waiter walked up, prompting Ellis and Deena to consider their menus for the first time.

On her insistence, he ordered first.

"I'll have the burrito ranchero with chicken and refried beans, please."

Deena's turn. "Um… Does the achiote sauce in the cochinita pibil have a lot of coriander in it?" The waiter said he thought it was the normal amount. "Hmm… Can I switch it for the tomatillo sauce?" He guessed so. "And instead of the creamy black beans, I want the beans de la olla, okay?" Okay. "And instead of fried bananas, can I get grilled nopales? Do you have nopales?" Si, nopales. "Cool. I want that, but on the side. And Spanish rice instead of white rice, and no cilantro… I think it tastes like dirt," she said to Ellis as the waiter departed, scribbling on his order pad.

"So, anyway, that is a crazy story." Deena dipped another chip into the salsa, which Ellis refrained from pointing out had cilantro in it. "I wish I could have seen the look on his face."

"On Larry's face, when he was shot? You'd have had to look quick. It wasn't there for long."

"Oh, shit. I'm sorry. That was weird, wasn't it? Ugh. I wasn't trying to make light of your trauma or whatever—I mean, I'm sure witnessing that was terrible—but I can just imagine how a moment like that would energize your emotional awareness."

Ellis got a flash of Larry Price's pooling blood reflecting the streetlights. "I was energized, alright."

A beat, then Deena drifted the conversation back to the shallower end of the pool. "So, what all shows have you written?"

Giving himself a second to change gears, he ate some chips, washed them down, and dabbed his sore lips with a napkin. "Just a few short-lived shows in the nineties. Mostly action-adventure, cop shows, military dramas... *SEAL Team Trident?*" It was the only show he had written, and the title sparked no glimmer of recognition in Deena's eyes. He rushed the attention off himself.

"What about you? You were in some commercials?"

Deena reached for the chips and repeated Ellis's stalling-for-time routine.

"Yeah. Let's see," she counted on her fingers, "Bartles and Jaymes wine coolers, Tresemmé shampoo, Folger's coffee singles, and, um, Preparation H." She blushed. "It's so embarrassing now. But y'know, at the time, I thought, wow, this is it, I'm really on my way. Some big-time CAA agent is going to see how excited I can get over instant coffee and how earnest and sympathetic I am talking about hemorrhoid relief, and sign me up. And it almost happened." Deena lowered her eyes. "Except I refused to sleep with him," she prodded the lemon wedge floating in her tea with her straw, "so then... he raped me."

The words hung on the brassy strains of "Silent Night".

"Oh... Shit..." said Ellis, again out of his depth. "That sucks. I, uh— I'm so sorry. It's so gross how the industry draws sensitive artists and psychopathic assholes into this... I dunno, web of co-dependence and exploitation. I-I don't know what to say."

"Ugh. I killed the vibe. I'm so sorry. I don't know why I dropped that on you. I guess it's because I feel comfortable with you. I'm sorry. Let's— Let's move on."

"No, please. Don't apologize. You didn't kill any vibe." She kind of did, though. "*I'm* sorry that happened to you. Is that why you quit acting? Because of… that?" Deena nodded. "Man, that sucks. Being in a Bartles and Jaymes commercial is nothing to sniff at. I used to drink that shit by the case. It's delicious. You have a lot to be proud of. I mean, with your, uh—… I'm sure you would have had no trouble booking TV, movies, whatever you wanted."

"Thanks," said Deena, "but what were you about to say? I feel like you started to say something else there."

Now it was Ellis's turn to worry his lemon wedge. "I guess I was just gonna say with your looks and charisma, I'm sure you could have been a star. I'm sorry some asshole took that from you. That really sucks."

Deena reached across the table and touched his hand. "Thank you, Ellis. You're sweet."

The last woman who had told Ellis he was sweet he watched shoot herself in the head on the deck of a burned-out seafood restaurant. Even so, he swooned at the words and the heat of Deena's fingertips.

But when the food arrived, the vibe took another minor hit.

Deena was miffed that the grilled nopales weren't on the side like she had requested, but she balked at sending back her order.

"No," she said, reigniting her smile. "It's cool. I can deal."

# CHAPTER 18

FANCY FEAST was the most ironic cat food brand on the market, which Ellis appreciated, and one of the costliest, which he didn't. Holding his breath, he scooped the rank glop onto a plate. He had tried cheaper brands, but Stevie Nicks would only sniff them and then go back to complaining. So, he worked his way up the price ladder until he got to the Fancy Feast Gravy Lovers Poultry & Beef Collection, which she devoured. Naming the yellow bobtail cat was another journey. After striking out with Squeaky, Vanna, Charo, and Elle McFierce, Stevie Nicks finally stuck.

Meowing her hoarse meow, she hopped onto the kitchen counter, nudged Ellis out of the way, and dug in.

"Slow down. Y'know, you shouldn't be so greedy. I remember when you used to eat roadkill." Already licking the plate clean, she ignored him. "Is that how you broke your fang? Huh? Eating roadkill, or was it a fight?"

Ellis scratched her behind the ear, went into the living room, and resumed packing his CD collection. Many of the discs he'd had since the technology was brand new.

In 1987, his father, a successful entrepreneur and newly minted author, bought a Sony CD player, the first one Ellis had ever seen outside of Radio Shack. His copy of *Appetite for Destruction* still had a receipt stuck in the jewel case—$12.99 from Tower Records on Sunset. He remembered buying U2's *Rattle and Hum* at Wherehouse on Ventura. *Green* by R.E.M. came from Sam Goody in Fallbrook Mall.

*I'm playing the best golf of my life, thanks to Zyx—*

Ellis muted the television. Watching Terry Montero mouth his lines, he pictured his face the way it looked when Ellis saw it last: broken, bandaged, and missing one of those giant capped teeth. Part of Ellis thought he should call Terry and compare notes on the fairy godmother who had saved them from Mark Redondo. But the greater part of him, the part that trapped grievances like prey and kept them alive for sport, was happy to ghost Terry, maybe forever.

When a commercial for magnesium supplements came on, featuring a professional skateboarder who'd been a big deal when Ellis was buying R.E.M. CDs at the mall, he turned his attention back to last night with Deena. Under the sodium lights in the Don Miguel parking lot, she touched his hand a second time.

"This was fun." He thought so too and suggested they "do it again sometime." Whether "it" was a date or just another dinner, and when it might occur, he was content to leave open for now. Though he was out of practice, he at least knew better than to be too eager. He had to be cool.

As soon as he got home, though, sitting cross-legged on the floor, with Stevie Nicks in his lap (an honor she had begun extending in the last day or two), he opened his laptop and scoured YouTube for Deena's commercials.

After an hour of scrolling and cat scratching, he found her 1992 Folger's coffee ad. In it, she dunked a sachet of instant coffee into a steaming mug, took a sip, and flashed a high-watt smile. Ellis replayed it until he had, or more likely, had created a memory of seeing the commercial during an episode of *SEAL Team Trident*. Ellis was excited to see Deena again whenever and in whatever real-life context he could. Maybe he would learn her last name and why she attended AA meetings in Burbank while living in Sherman Oaks.

A man like him, lucky enough to attract a woman so far out of his league, didn't have any right to look for red flags. Still, her use of the phrase "energize your emotional awareness," which Ellis recognized from one Anton Stafford's YouTube videos, discomfited him—less that Deena was among Stafford's legion of dupes than the coincidences of Stafford being Christian Cooper's stepfather, that they were celebrating his birthday the night of Larry Price's murder, and Mark Redondo bringing Stafford to his knees in agony right after brutalizing Terry and threatening Ellis.

As an investigator and an existentialist, Ellis accepted that coincidences didn't mean anything. Until they did.

His phone buzzed. Prashanth.

"What's up, man?"

"Hey. Um, I need your help." The boy was breathless. "You, uh… You know that house where you dropped me off before? For band practice?"

"Yeah. What's up?"

"I, uh— I need you to come pick me up there."

"No can do. I have a meeting at Maxx Studios in Culver City in an hour."

"Me and the drummer got into a fight, and I like, really messed him up. I think he has to go to the hospital."

"The hospital? What's the matter with him?"

"He's all fucked up. He-he— He's just like, laying there. Can you come pick us up? Please? Like, right now?"

"Is he conscious?"

"I don't know. There's blood everywhere. Please, man!"

"Call an ambulance."

"I'll get in trouble." He was crying. "I'm n-not even supposed to b-b-be here. I'm grounded. Please!"

Ellis rubbed his suddenly aching forehead and sighed. "Shit. Okay. Sit tight. I'm leaving right now."

He hung up. "Motherfucker." As he gathered his keys, wallet, and sunglasses, his apartment door opened, and a man in a dress shirt, stone-washed jeans, and gleaming basketball shoes strolled in.

"What the—? Who the fuck are you?!" asked Ellis.

"Holy shit! You scared me. I, uh— I'm Wayne Duggan."

"What the fuck are you doing in my apartment, Wayne? Where'd you get a key?"

He looked down at the keys in his hand and back at Ellis, befuddled. "I work for Hyperlocal Integrations Group, the new owners of the property. The landlord told me all the units were vacated." He scanned the half-packed living room.

"Well, that's obviously not the case. So, get the fuck outta here, and close my door before you let the cat out."

"I don't know if you're a squatter or what, but the bulldozers are coming in a couple weeks, and you better be out of here—"

Ellis threw his keys at Wayne's head, but Wayne ducked, and the keys went flying through the door.

Wayne and Stevie Nicks ran out after them.

SINCE THE LAST TIME Ellis saw it, the house in Canoga Park where Unholy Sodomy held their band practices had been decorated with a plastic holly wreath on the front door and icicle lights along the eaves. As Ellis pulled into the driveway, the garage door rose.

"Where have you been?" asked Prashanth, ducking under.

"I had to find my keys."

In addition to the usual garage stuff—trash cans, tools, bikes, beach umbrellas, bulk packages of paper and canned goods—there was a drum set, a guitar amplifier, and a teenage boy in a blood-soaked Cannibal Corpse T-shirt wallowing on the ground. Everything was splattered with blue paint, the same shade as the house shutters.

"What the hell did you do?" asked Ellis. "What's with the paint?"

"I hit him with a paint can, and the lid came off," said Prashanth.

"Why?"

"I guess because it wasn't on tight enough."

"I mean, why did you hit him with a paint can?"

Between the blood, blue paint, and bruises, the wounded kid's face was a purple Halloween mask. One eye was swollen shut. The other was rolled back. His nose and front teeth were broken.

The gash running from his left temple to his jaw was going to need stitches. Lots of them.

Prashanth looked away. "He, uh… He said… He…"

"Never mind. You can tell me on the way to the hospital. Let's get him in the car. Grab his legs."

As Ellis sped south on Fallbrook Avenue, gunning it through yellow lights and weaving in and out between cars, Prashanth, relieved of the pressure of eye contact, opened up. The moaning boy ruining the upholstery in the back seat was Zayne, the drummer for Prashanth's grindcore band, Doom Scroll.

"I thought it was a black metal band," said Ellis.

"It was, but our bass player quit. So, we decided to just be a grindcore duo."

Prashanth went on to say that after his mom, Reshma, dropped him off at Zayne's house, he—Zayne—said he had a wet dream last night about tit fucking her and blowing his load in her face. Ellis, who'd had similar fantasies, agreed that it was a fucked-up thing to say but hardly worth bashing the kid's head in with a paint can.

"But he says shit like that all the time," said Prashanth. "Lots of guys at school do. But Zayne is the worst. He calls me on the phone and says he's jerking off to her Instagram and makes all these gross noises. And he makes fun of my dad for being gay, like, all the time. I know he's just messing around and trying to piss me off, but I'm so fucking sick of it. I mean, he's supposed to be my friend, right? I told him to stop a million times, but he won't. He just laughs."

Slumped semi-conscious in the backseat, Zayne made a gurgling noise. Definitely not a laugh.

"So, this time I hit him. And… I don't know, it's like… something inside me snapped, and I hit him again and again. He fell down, and I got on top of him and kept hitting him." A tear dropped onto Prashanth's scraped knuckles, but his voice stayed low and even. "I don't remember picking it up, but all of a sudden, I was pounding his face with a can of paint. Then, he quit fighting back, and the lid flew off and paint went all over the place… And then I called you."

Ellis sighed and gave the Porsche more gas.

In the five years he had known Reshma and Prashanth, he had seen the boy go from a taciturn adolescent to a metalhead delinquent. The transformation accelerated when his father moved back east to teach physics at Yale, a job that was supposed to have been temporary. Instead, Amartya had a homosexual affair, divorced Reshma, and hadn't been back to California since.

Ellis sympathized with the pain of being ignored by a father enthralled by his exciting new life. Teenage doper Ellis was never able to win Hank's attention away from his business, book sales, and gigs as a technical advisor in Hollywood. Recognizing the decline of Prashanth's self-esteem activated a paternal instinct in Ellis that he didn't know he had. At first, unfortunately, his expression of it was to hang out and get stoned with Prashanth while Reshma worked her second job. Now, as a sober person, Ellis was appalled at how irresponsibly he'd enacted a worthy impulse.

After turning left against a red light onto Burbank Boulevard, a motorcycle appeared in the rearview mirror. Zayne's battered head blocked the view, making it impossible to discern the color of the rider's jacket. Michael Bublé was singing "It's Beginning to Look a Lot Like Christmas" on Sunny96 as Ellis squealed to a stop in front of the emergency entrance of Kaiser Permanente hospital in Woodland Hills.

SWEATING AND BREATHLESS from his jog across the Maxx Studios visitor's parking lot and up and down the corridors of the main building to Kent Moran's office, Ellis fanned his shirt front and chugged the bottle of water Kent's assistant gave him and took in the shrine to Kent's achievements and ego.

Framed *Graveyardland* promo posters and magazine covers bearing Kent's image lined the walls. *All Hail the King of Streaming… The Dostoevsky of the Undead… Kent Kills It Again… New Moran Rising…*

"Sorry I'm late," said Ellis. "I had to—"

"I know. You told me on the phone. You had to look for your keys. But why do you have blue paint all over you?"

"I—" Ellis looked down at his ruined clothes. "I, uh— I was helping a friend paint his shutters, and the ladder— Y'know, the ground was uneven and, uh…" He let the lie trail away, correct in his assumption that Kent wouldn't pursue such a plebian subject.

"Is that blood? On your sleeve?"

"No. No, that's paint too."

"Uh-huh." Kent wasn't buying it, but mercifully, moved on. "I don't have a lot of time, now. I have a meeting with Blumhouse in a few minutes," he looked at his giant wristwatch, swirled and clicked the computer mouse, frowned at the 30-inch monitor, then, still frowning, looked at Ellis, "but, yeah, let's talk. You had some questions or concerns or something?"

"Uh, yeah. I mean, no, not really concerns but…" It wasn't just the blood and paint spattered scramble of the last hour that had Ellis discombobulated. Squirming in a straight-back guest chair while Kent reclined in his black leather executive chair behind a steel desk the size of an aircraft carrier, emphasized the power dynamic that had always existed in their friendship. Even when they were both rookie staff writers on *SEAL Team Trident*, they were never quite equals. Kent and his ideas were always favored by the show's producer, Aaron Grant. And now, Kent, the King of Streaming, occupied the one-time King of Cable's old office, and Ellis was again the pitiful supplicant.

He cleared his throat and started over. "Yeah, so, I, uh, just wanted to, y'know, see where we are with the show?" Ellis himself wasn't sure if it was a real question or just California English.

"The show? You mean *Graveyardland?*"

"No, dude, *Miami Vice.*"

"Oh. Right." Kent paused to scroll through his phone. "Well, we're not anywhere with it."

"But now that Urs is out on bail, I'm sure we can get him back on board."

"I'm not on board, though. I don't want to work with Urs. Nobody does. His brand is…" Kent puckered his face like he smelled dog shit, "dog shit."

"Fair enough. We'll get somebody else. Check this out—this came to me as I was falling asleep last night—what if Crockett is a woman? That's pretty cool, right? I was thinking somebody like Priyanka what's-her-name. I'll rewrite the part—"

"Chopra."

"Sorry?"

"Priyanka *Chopra* is the actor's name you were looking for."

"Oh. Okay. Right, so, I'll just rewrite the part for a woman and—"

"Stop, stop, stop. I see where you're going, and it's not the worst idea in the world."

"Thanks."

"Your script is pretty tight. I mean, there are some dull spots in the second act, and the turning point is predictable and comes way too soon. My advice is rewrite it, make Crockett a woman— hell, make Tubbs a woman too, lesbians maybe—give it a real ending, and I think, y'know, then you might have something. But, not for me." Kent checked his phone and leaned forward like he was about to stand. "So, anyway, I have to prep for my next meeting."

Ellis tipped up the water bottle but found it empty. "Okay. I have a couple of other ideas." He dug his notebook out of his hip pocket and flipped it open. "Um, let's see… How 'bout this? A rookie detective in Texas gets caught on a hot mic making insensitive remarks about the victim of a police shooting and she has to start her life and career over again in L.A.—and again, I'm thinking she's a woman of color, maybe like you were saying, a lesbian—a lesbian of color…" Kent had his head down, texting. "Or, if you're not into that, I was thinking something about cars maybe?"

"Sorry, man, but I don't have time to hear a pitch right now." Kent put his phone down, placed his palms flat on his desk, and leaned forward. "Like I said, I have a meeting with Blumhouse," a beat, "and I don't want to be late."

Ellis got it but refused to take his exit cue.

"You were never serious, were you?"

"Huh?"

"About *Miami Vice*. You never really intended to do it, did you?"

"I was serious enough to pay you out of my own fucking pocket and take a meeting at the Century Club, of all places. I'm actually offended you think I have time to waste on anything I'm not serious about."

"Be straight up with me, man. You hired me to write a screenplay you never intended to produce, just to fulfill your promise of working with me again, didn't you? It was a way of getting off cheap."

"Dude, what the fuck are you talking about? What promise?"

"Are you serious? *What promise?* The promise you made that we would work together again after *SEAL Team Trident* got canned."

"I literally have no idea what you're talking about."

"You don't remember sitting in the Good Time doing shots and promising we would write another show together someday? That's what you're telling me?"

"That's what I'm telling you. I don't remember making any promise. It sounds like the kind of bullshit people say when they're drinking, though, so maybe I did. Even so—"

"You don't think I'm a genius at all, do you?"

"*Huh?*"

"You said you wanted me to write *Miami Vice* for Urs because I was a genius. But that was bullshit too, wasn't it?"

"Holy shit, dude. Wow. I don't know where this is coming from, if you're back on drugs or what, but—"

"Fuck you. I'm not on drugs."

"Well, you sound fucking nuts. Why are you being so literal? You've heard of metaphors. Genius? It's just a thing people say. You're a genius. That's genius. I love you, man. I wish you were dead. Let's get drinks soon. I promise we'll work together someday."

"Metaphors."

"Only words. Look around this office," Kent pointed to the slush piles of scripts, the bulletin boards covered with pastel notecards, the dry erase board crowded with scribbled ideas. "I'm neck deep in ideas for shows. Good ideas—great ones, a lot of times—by hugely successful writers. I said no to Vince Gilligan the other day. *Breaking Bad…?*"

"I know who he is."

"Of course you do. Everybody does. I had to say no to Vince fucking Gilligan. Look, dude, I'll be straight with you. I know you think you wanna be a writer, and for a minute, a long fucking time ago, you had potential. But, at this point, if you were gonna be a writer, you'd be one. You never would have quit. When *SEAL Team Trident* got canned, I was out of work, too, same as you. But I'm a writer. So, I kept writing. I got another job, and another, and another. Nothing was ever going to stop me from being exactly where I am now. I know you were counting on this, and I wish it had worked out, but it's just not in the cards. I mean, the world needs private investigators, too, right? Probably even more than it needs yet another gender-swap reboot of a classic IP that doesn't need fixing. Know what I mean?"

Ellis started to tell Kent to fuck himself. But why bother? After all, a man who thought "I love you" and "I promise" were metaphors—only words—would probably take it as a compliment. Too late to save face, Ellis could at least save his breath. He stood and left the office.

"Good talk," Kent called after him. "Let's get drinks soon!"

BACK AT HIS APARTMENT, Ellis was stunned to find a check from Kaitlyn Arliss in the mail. Ellis had been sure he was going to have to follow up, probably multiple times, before he got paid for exposing the affair her husband was having with his cousin. Now, Ellis could afford the deposit on a new apartment he didn't want. Looking around at all there was still to pack, he sighed. Maybe he could live in the storage unit he would have to rent if he didn't secure a place soon.

Instead of sorting his clothes—what to pack, what to donate—he flopped into the orange bamboo chair and flipped TV channels. There was yellow cat hair on his pants. Though he only had Stevie Nicks for a little while, he missed her now that she was gone. Maybe he would eat the rest of the Fancy Feast when he was living in the storage unit.

Re-watching an episode of *Cheers* for the millionth time, Ellis struggled to digest the psychological comfort food. The day kept intruding: Stevie Nicks running off; Prashanth's tears; Zayne's smashed face; Kent's brutal honesty—*if you were gonna be a writer, you'd be one.* Before Krampus Night at the One Divine Light Research Center, Ellis had relied on marijuana, like *Cheers*, to settle him in the present moment and round off the edges of anxiety, regret, and self-loathing. But ever since, he'd been afraid that the terror he experienced in the bowels of the mansion was symptomatic of some latent psychosis that weed had finally triggered. The roach of the joint Ellis had smoked that night before leaving for the ODLRC was still in the ashtray. He plucked it from the ashes. Tonight, he would almost welcome being dragged to hell by a mythical monster. Instead, chemical peace flooded his nervous system, and the old *Cheers* magic shone through.

After only a couple of enchanting minutes, his buzzing phone broke the spell.

Reshma.

Ellis's fledgling high iced over into paranoia. He doubted she was calling to thank him for helping her son out of a jam. Probably because dropping Zayne in the ER and racing away was a cowardly way to do it. Ellis should have called Reshma; he could see that now, staring at her name on the screen. If Zayne slipped into a coma or died, was Ellis an accessory? Why had he not considered that until now? "Shit." Ellis thought about letting the call go to voicemail, but then decided that stoned and short-term-memory impaired was the best way to face the music, rancorous as it was likely to be.

"Hey, Reshma." He stood and started pacing.

Her voice was unexpectedly bright. "Hey. You busy?"

"Um, no. No, just packing. What's up?"

"I found the perfect apartment for you… Hello…? Ellis?"

"Sorry, yeah. I'm here. The perfect apartment?"

"Yes. In a vibrant, open-courtyard-style community in the heart of the NoHo Arts District. It's a little more expensive than the last place we looked at—fifteen-seventy-five a month—but it's *a lot* more spacious. Four hundred and *fifty* square feet."

"Oh… Um, okay."

"Everywhere you look, there are pops of color, upscale finishes, and cinematic accents that give the apartment a vibe all its own. It is so you."

Was this real? Had getting stoned been a mistake after all? All the other times Reshma had contacted him about an apartment, she had just texted him a listing and saved the effusive realtor-speak for when they met at the address. "Cinematic accents?"

"And classic details with a modern twist to make you feel right at home."

"Uh… awesome."

"It's walking distance from cafes, art galleries, theatres, and shops. It's the best of North Hollywood living."

"Yeah, yeah, I hear it's really walkable."

"It is! NoHo is a whole lifestyle. The apartment is not officially listed yet, so I can't show it to you until next week, but I'll text you the address. This place is going to go fast."

Reshma wasn't the kind to play head games. She wasn't mentioning Prashanth either because she didn't know what had happened that day, or she knew, but Prashanth had kept Ellis's name out of it. Either way, relief warmed away the cold dread he'd answered the call with.

In a bubbly lilt, she told Ellis all about the amenities: pool, jacuzzi, fitness center, on-site parking, and laundry facilities.

Part of him knew he should interrupt and tell her that her son put another kid in the hospital, even though it would betray Prashanth's confidence. This was Ellis's chance to accept the responsibility he had refused before. But Reshma sounded so happy, he couldn't bring himself to bum her out. So, again, making an excuse for the gutless way he was protecting her and himself, he stayed mute and let her enjoy her spiel.

"The gourmet kitchenette has been renovated with designer tile flooring, quartz countertops, and a beautiful breakfast bar overlooking the dining area and living room. The stainless-steel appliances are all brand new. Gated entry points with intercom and surveillance cameras provide security."

Terry's Zyxeltra commercial pulled Ellis's attention away from Reshma's monologue. Watching Terry brag about playing the best golf of his life—*I shot an eighty-six, and no soreness!*—and afforded empathy by the weed, Ellis was unable to conjure any more anger over Terry's giving him up to Mark Redondo.

"…ceiling fan with an elegant light fixture and dimmer switch…"

Ellis's ribs still ached where the Asian woman with the long ponytail had kicked him. If he'd had a name to give up in that moment, he might have done just like Terry.

"…energy-efficient double-pane windows with wooden blinds…"

But luckily, he'd never know. A miracle had occurred: the money Terry gave Ellis to give to Ramsey Skillern that he—Ramsey—owed to Mark Redondo for carrying out a hit contracted by Annalee Gentry appeared. But who delivered it?

"…minutes from the One-Oh-One, the One-Thirty-Four, and the One-Seventy…"

Redondo said it was Ellis's fairy godmother.

*Do not use Zyxeltra if you are pregnant or plan on becoming pregnant.*

Suddenly, he knew who she was.

# CHAPTER 19

*LAKE HOLLYWOOD PARK WELCOMES YOU*, read the sign
at the entrance. The signs dictating where, when, for how long,
and on what days you could park on Canyon Lake Drive, which
circled the park, were as confusing as any in the city, but the
reminders to hide your valuables and lock your car were plenty
clear. Other signs warned of rattlesnakes and prohibited smoking,
drones, soccer, fence sitting, and letting dogs go unleashed.

In the middle of the grassy field, a guy in a unitard and his
hair in a bun was running through a sequence of motions
somewhere between tai chi and break dancing while a drone
hovered above. Dogs—mostly pit bulls, mostly off leash—
romped while their owners stared at their phones. Hot moms in
Lululemon yoga pants pushed baby strollers. Locals picnicked
while tourist families and influencers posed for pictures under the
Hollywood sign, the only sign anyone paid attention to. After

most people embraced the photo op, they split, and traffic crept by steadily as parking spots changed hands.

Ellis circled for almost ten minutes before he found a spot a dozen car lengths down the hill from a photoshoot in which two models in string bikinis were washing a red Camaro and splashing each other with sudsy sponges.

Reaching the entrance to the park, Ellis caught his breath and said, "You saved my life. Why didn't you tell me?"

"I didn't want you to know," said LAPD Officer Tameka Settles. Her dress and demeanor were the opposite of what they'd been when Ellis met her at her uncle Courtland Hollender's Christmas/retirement party. That night, in her uniform, her posture was commanding. Today, on her day off, she was slumped in oversized gray sweats, resting her forearms on the fence. "And I didn't do it for you."

Ellis was unsure whether or not he should be offended. "Um, okay. So then, who'd you do it for?"

"Me. Who the fuck you think?"

"I don't get it."

"I've never met him personally, but based on what I know about Mark Redondo, he's a cop magnet. He's the kind of guy whose luck runs out. He's temperamental and reckless—"

"You can say that again."

"—and that's dangerous. If he was to kill you and get caught, he might talk about Ramsey, which could blow back on me. And that can't happen, especially not now that the mayor and the commissioner are pushing me as the face of the all-new, diverse, and equitable LAPD." She rolled her eyes. "No, at this point, Redondo just needs to go away—the happier the better."

"How did you get the money?"

Tameka shook an American Spirit from the pack and stuck it between her lips. Then she eyed the *NO SMOKING* sign, huffed, and returned the cigarette.

"Ramsey owed money to a South American cartel called the Black Fist."

"I'm familiar," said Ellis.

"So, his stupid ass took the money he was supposed to give Redondo and was gonna pay the narcos with it. He asked me to go to Texas with him and guard him and the money. But," she stuck out her bottom lip and shrugged, "I failed, and Ramsey got himself killed before he could make the payment. I found him dead in the bathroom of the Deluxe Inn Motel where we were staying. Two in the back of the head."

Ellis noted that, like Christian Cooper had done, Tameka proffered details to give her story credence.

"Why did they kill him if he had the money?"

"How the fuck do I know? I told you I wasn't there."

"I thought Ramsey was shot in the desert."

"The Deluxe Inn Motel is in the desert."

"And how did you know I was in trouble with Redondo?"

"Uncle Courtland told me. He's the other reason I saved your ass. You mean a lot to him, and he means a lot to me. Sixty thousand dollars a lot. It's not like I couldn't have used the money, too. But I got to keep Ramsey's cut. So, I still came out ahead."

She turned her steely gaze on the people in the park and their violations of the posted rules: the teenagers sitting on the fence, passing a blunt; two men in flip-flops and ballcaps trying feebly to break up a dog fight; some kids throwing rocks at a snake; a soccer ball landing in a bowl of potato salad; a homeless man pissing in the bushes.

"Larry Price was the target of the hit Annalee Gentry contracted with Ramsey, wasn't he?" asked Ellis.

The squeaky-clean red Camaro rumbled up the hill. A white Tesla with tinted windows passed going the opposite direction.

"I have no idea," said Tameka. "I didn't ask."

"But the timing of the contract, Price's murder, and Ramsey's payment is too perfect. It can't be a coincidence."

"Why not? Sure it can."

Ellis almost walked away, but he had already gone this far. He inhaled deeply and exhaled, "Ramsey fabricated the necklace you found on that rooftop, didn't he?"

Tameka glared at him with a fury that made his heart rate spike and temples sweat.

He swallowed and went on. "I went to Bullseye Props and learned Ramsey bought a Saturn-shaped medallion like Urs's online—apparently, they're pretty common—and he made a copy of it. Now, they're both missing."

"And?"

"And, so there are multiple medallions floating around out there, at least one of them fabricated by your cousin."

"What the fuck is this?" Tameka backed away from the rail and squared up to Ellis. "You're not gonna stand there and accuse me. I saved your fuckin' life, motherfucker! I don't have to justify myself to you."

Ellis raised his hands and backed up a step. "I know, and I'm forever grateful. Believe me, I'm not asking you to confirm or deny my theory. That's all it is, a theory. Only words. But if I'm right about any of it, please, all I'm asking…"

The white Tesla came around again, slower this time. A glint on the windshield pulled Ellis's attention for a second. He blinked and looked back at Tameka.

"All I'm asking is that you clear Urs as a suspect. Don't scapegoat him just to—"

Ellis was cut off by the crack of gunfire, two quick shots, from the lowered window of the Tesla. The first bullet shattered the windshield of the SUV Ellis and Tameka were standing beside; the second pierced the fender with a metallic *plunk!* They dropped to the ground and covered their heads as the Tesla sped away and the park erupted with people screaming and running in all directions, diving for cover wherever they could find it, behind trees, cars, trash cans, and each other.

Tameka darted across the street to her silver Toyota Camry. Ellis followed and jumped into the passenger side as she started the engine.

"The fuck you think you're doing?" she asked.

"I— I, uh…" He had acted without thinking. Was it a sense of duty, curiosity, a death wish? Or the basic survival instinct to follow the alpha dog?

Tameka didn't wait for Ellis to articulate.

She set her jaw and peeled away from the curb, chasing the white Tesla down Canyon Lake Drive and through the twists of the Mulholland Highway to Durand Drive—basically an alley snaking through craggy hills peppered with Mediterranean estates, Modern erector sets, and Spanish haciendas, all costing millions upon millions.

The hairpin turns would have been treacherous even if Tameka were going the posted ten-mile-per-hour speed limit, but she was pushing the Camry two and three times faster. On a sloping lane of blind corners, it felt like warp speed. Ellis clutched the seat belt, fearing the car would flip when Tameka jerked the wheel to make the sharp S curve onto Heather Drive.

Around the next bend, they came within a breath of sideswiping a Lincoln Navigator coming in the opposite direction. Blowing through a stop sign onto Ledgerwood, they nearly T-boned a UPS truck.

Ellis finally took a breath when the Tesla veered onto North Beachwood Drive, which was wider and straighter. The other side of the coin was that the pursuit jumped into a higher gear.

The Tesla was ten car lengths ahead and gaining distance fast. Now able to take a hand off the wheel, Tameka tossed her phone to Ellis, told him to call 911, and put it on speaker.

In a torrent, she identified herself to the dispatcher as a police officer, giving her name and badge number. "I'm headed south on North Beachwood in pursuit of a white Tesla. Four doors, tinted windows. Can't see the license number. The driver fired two shots at me at Lake Hollywood Park. Didn't get a look at the shooter. I'm driving a silver Toyota Camry, and I have a civilian with me."

The dispatcher asked if they were injured.

"No. We just turned right onto Franklin Avenue, heading west."

The Tesla weaved in and out of traffic, twice crossing the double yellow line into oncoming traffic.

"Tesla just turned left onto Highland," Tameka said, "headed south, speeding, driving recklessly."

They were still several yards away from the six-lane intersection when the light turned yellow. Ellis stomped on the floorboard, wishing there was a brake pedal. Tameka hit the accelerator.

The light turned red, but she was too committed. Without lights or a siren, there was no way to warn advancing cars to stop. Ellis shut his eyes and braced for impact as Tameka skidded between vehicles coming from both directions. But she made it.

Southbound Highland was jammed. There wasn't much the Tesla could do to get away. Except become camouflaged in the tourist-trap heart of Hollywood.

Ellis and Tameka craned their necks to find the Tesla in the crush of nearly identical, neutral-colored vehicles.

"There!" said Ellis. "Turning right onto Hollywood Boulevard."

Tameka repeated it to the dispatcher. Sirens rose in the distance. She turned right, leaning over the wheel, scanning the street for the Tesla. She didn't have to look far. It was pulled to the curb in front of the Chinese Theatre, half a block ahead.

She pulled over, too, between the Dolby Theatre and the Hard Rock Cafe, relaying her and the Tesla's positions to the dispatcher.

"What the fuck is this?" she asked.

Ellis knew the question was rhetorical but said, "Maybe the battery died?"

To the left, traffic poked along. To the right, so did the gawkers on the sidewalk—taking pictures of the littered Walk of Fame, fitting their hands and feet into the famous prints in the concrete. People dressed in unconvincing Batman, Spider-Man, Captain Jack Sparrow, and Marilyn Monroe costumes extorted rubes to take pictures with them. If whoever was in the Tesla fired again, there was no way there wouldn't be a victim in the throng.

An LAPD chopper circled overhead. Keeping her eyes locked on the Tesla, Tameka slid her hand under her car seat and withdrew her nine-millimeter semi-automatic Glock service pistol.

Ellis's mind raced as quickly as his pulse: Who was in the Tesla? And who had they been shooting at, him or Tameka? Both? Neither? Had it been random? Was this the Southland Sniper?

Ellis had a flash of Larry Price's head exploding just inches from his own. Maybe the gunshots at the park had been the *second* botched attempt on *Ellis's* life. Maybe in retribution for killing Black Fist cartel initiate Nazario Sanchez. Ellis wiped the sweat off his upper lip with the back of his trembling hand.

Marked patrol cars with flashing lights and blaring sirens appeared in the rearview mirror.

"That's the cavalry, motherfucker," said Tameka to herself and the driver of the Tesla. "What's your move?"

As if in answer, the driver's side door of the Tesla came open. Tameka unlatched her seatbelt and opened her door, too. Police cars were now visible ahead, coming up Hollywood Boulevard from the west. Like the ones in the rearview, they were slowed by the traffic that could only do so much to make way.

A pair of stubby legs extended from the Tesla. Tameka adjusted her grip on the pistol and slid from her seat, taking cover behind the car door.

"Don't be stupid…" she said. "Don't… be… fucking… stupid."

Tameka described the person emerging from the Tesla to the dispatcher: "Male Caucasian, wearing a black T-shirt, gray sweatpants, and running shoes. He's short, maybe five-three. Short gray hair."

Ellis gasped. It was Mark Redondo.

When Tameka delivered his fifty thousand dollars, she had only dealt with one of his lady ninjas and had maybe never seen him before. Tameka tensed, like a sprinter anticipating the starting gun. But then, she dropped her shoulders and leaned back—"Fuck!"—and Ellis knew why.

Per *Get 'Em*, Chapter 19: Stay in Your Own Lane: "You're a PI, not a police officer. Never chase the subject of your investigation. Nobody will know you're the good guy. All they'll see is one person running after another, and the real cops might mistake you for the bad guy."

Of course, Tameka was a real cop, but off duty and out of uniform, the same rules applied. Uniformed patrolmen were swarming the street now anyway, to the delight of the tourists recording the commotion on their phones, blissfully unaware of the killer hiding among them.

# CHAPTER 20

ELLIS WASN'T SURE, but he thought the mariachi renditions of Christmas standards playing inside Tres Brazos Mexican Cantina in Woodland Hills were the same ones he had heard in Don Miguel when he was on his date (or dinner or whatever it was) with Deena. However, the music and a small fiber-optic Christmas tree beside the cash register were the only concessions Tres Brazos made to the holiday season.

Ellis and Hollender had been meeting at the no-frills establishment for lunch every month or so for the last five years. In all that time, the women who ran the place—an older woman who sat behind the counter and her adult daughters—regarded Ellis with total indifference, bordering on outright contempt. Hollender, they adored.

"Algo mas?" the waitress asked, serving his usual order of Nachos Volcanicos.

"No. Gracias."

"Tu ves muy informal hoy."

"Ahora, soy informal todos los días," he said. He was wearing a Dodgers sweatshirt instead of the Oxford shirt, khakis, and repp tie he wore every day when he was still on the job. "Estoy jubilado."

"Ah! Muy bien. Felicidades."

Ellis guessed the ladies preferred Hollender because he spoke Spanish with them. Ellis tried, but though he had lived in Los Angeles his whole life, he hadn't picked up much of the language beyond the basics. He took French in high school, every bit of which he had long forgotten.

"Gracias," he said when the waitress shoved his à la carte beef burrito in front of him. "Muy bien. Muchas gra—"

She was already walking away.

"You see this?" Hollender asked, already chewing. He held his phone out. The *Los Angeles Times* homepage was on the screen.

*Arrest made in Southland Sniper killings; hero cop promoted*, read the headline. Below was Mark Redondo's mugshot. His expression was hangdog, but with a glare Ellis recognized as Redondo's anger at being disrespected.

The article, which Ellis had already read, detailed Redondo's pursuit and apprehension within minutes of his Tesla running out of power, just as Ellis had figured. Police found Redondo hiding in the back of a souvenir shop disguised as best he could in what was available: cheap sunglasses, a Route 66 ballcap, and an *I* ♥ *L.A.* hoodie. The Ruger Super Redhawk .44 Magnum he used to shoot at Ellis and/or Tameka was recovered from a nearby trash can. An investigation was ongoing with city and county detectives and forensic services working together to determine whether or not it was the same weapon used in the Southland Sniper shootings. Redondo hadn't spoken since his arrest, except to his lawyer, who maintained the evidence would prove his client was not the Sniper.

Hollender took another bite of his nachos and said, with his mouth full, "And check this out."

He started a video of LAPD Chief Malcom Davies, a stocky man in his mid-fifties with a gray buzzcut, reading a prepared statement at a press conference.

"Yeah, I saw it," said Ellis.

Hollender paid no mind. He tilted his phone sideways, so that the video filled the screen, and propped it against a Tapatio hot sauce bottle.

*The fearless tenacity of Officer Tameka Settles's police work—*

"She gets that fearless tenacity from her grandmother," Hollender said with his mouth full.

*—resulted in the quick arrest of a violent criminal offender. She is truly a guardian of our community and deeply committed to the cause of justice. Her courage is matched by her empathy and commitment to equal justice for*

*all Angelenos. I am proud to announce her promotion to the rank of Detective, effective immediately.*

The chief didn't mention that Tameka had been off duty when she gave chase or that Ellis, a civilian, had been with her. Such reckless protocol violations would have tarnished the victory the LAPD needed.

"That's great," said Ellis. The idea that Tameka had exploited Larry Price's murder, by fabricating and planting evidence to frame an unpopular and thus vulnerable actor, to reclaim her rank as a detective—and that it *worked*, however indirectly—put a knot in Ellis's stomach.

"I know how proud you must be."

You didn't have to be a trained investigator to see that. Hollender hadn't stopped smiling since he sat down. His chest was literally puffed out as he washed down his nachos with gulps of black coffee, a preference Ellis understood almost less than Tameka's skewed moral compass.

Hollender wiped his mouth with the napkin tucked into his collar. "I still can't get over what an amazing coincidence it is that Tameka just happened to be in the park when this Redondo asshole caught up with you."

"I know," said Ellis. Unable to meet Hollender's twinkling eyes, he looked out the window at a barefoot homeless guy digging through a dumpster, throwing garbage on the ground. "It's really crazy."

Ellis regretted having smoked weed on the way over. His tolerance was still low from the break he took after Krampus Night, and he was starting to draw connections between unrelated things—the bubbles in his Diet Coke, the guy in the dumpster, the mournful "Silent Night" trumpets: paranoia rising…

TC was too savvy a detective to believe Ellis and Tameka's meeting at Hollywood Lake Park yesterday was a coincidence. Did he suspect Ellis was keeping something from him, lying by omission? Starting to perspire, he shifted in his seat and sipped his soda. It cooled him off and eased the tension in his stomach somewhat. Then a new perspective dawned on him: emotion was inhibiting TC's instincts—pride for Tameka; sorrow for Ramsey.

"No question," said Ellis, "Tameka is my fairy godmother. If I hadn't met her at your party, if she hadn't been at the park and stepped in, Redondo would still be out there trying to kill me, if he hadn't already."

All true, and all Hollender needed to know to keep his proud illusions intact.

Ellis's mind drifted to the nagging question of why Redondo had tried to kill him and/or Tameka after he had gotten his money. To keep them quiet was the easiest answer. But why take such a risk in broad daylight at a public park full of witnesses? Ellis didn't believe it was because Redondo was the Southland Sniper, driven by a demonic compulsion to execute random strangers. Besides that, Ellis wasn't a stranger to him.

"You not hungry?" asked Hollender. He had already leveled half his nacho volcano. "Now that you don't smoke weed anymore, you don't have an appetite?"

The question was another blow to Ellis's conscience. There was a time when he would have been happy for Hollender not to know he was stoned. But Hollender always did, and would break Ellis's balls over it. Not Ellis's favorite aspect of their dynamic, true, but a consistent one. Now, it was more deception. Then again, maybe the question *was* the ball breaking, and Hollender *did* know he was stoned… The bum in the parking lot was hopping on one foot.

"No, yeah," Ellis forked a hunk of burrito, "I uh— I was just thinking about everything, I guess."

"You've been through a lot lately, haven't you?" said Hollender.

"Nah, not really. I mean, not like other people, y'know. Like, Tameka risked her life, y'know, I mean, that's… that's… huge."

"That's her job. She knew what she was signing up for."

Ellis watched his fork push the burrito around the plate and nodded.

"Being shot at sucks," said Hollender.

Ellis felt the compassion in the understatement and responded in kind. "A little."

"You know you can always talk to me about how you're feeling. You know that, right?"

"Yeah, man, I know. And it means a lot, but— Yeah, no, I'm good. I don't feel any—… No, I'm good."

Again, Ellis had to look away. Crows were flocking to the mess left by the homeless guy. Ellis could hear them cawing under the brassy strains of "White Christmas".

Hollender polished off his nachos, stifled a burp, and wiped his lips. "I owe you an apology," he said, wadding the napkin.

"For what?"

"The last time we talked, after Ramsey's funeral, when you came to me for help, I'm sorry I turned you away. I wasn't mad at you—I mean, I was—I don't know how many times I've told you not to fuck around with Terry Montero," he shook his head, "but that's not the point. I was heartbroken over Ramsey. I really wanted that kid to succeed. I really wanted to believe his gang banging was in the past. But I guess it's like that line from *Casablanca*, 'We might be through with the past, but the past ain't through with us.'"

"That's from *Magnolia*," said Ellis, "not *Casablanca*."

Hollender frowned. "*Steel Magnolias*?"

"No, *Magnolia*. The Paul Thomas Anderson movie."

Hollender considered it. "I'm pretty sure it's from *Casablanca*."

"Dude, it's not. Believe me. When have you ever been right about something like this?"

"All the time. Anyway, listen, I was in denial. That's the first stage of grief."

"I'm sorry too. You just lost your nephew, and I was only thinking about myself."

"Of course you were. You thought you were about to die. I shoulda been there for you."

"Nah, man, you were there for me. It was just bad timing. It was a terrible day. Let's just..." Such emotionalism made Ellis want to pound a beer, or six. "Let's just forget it."

"I'm proud of you, Ellis. I know your dad would be, too."

"Thanks." It didn't express his feelings, but he didn't know what else to add.

Relieving the burden, the waitress appeared and refilled Hollender's coffee.

"Te gustaron los nachos?" she asked, smiling.

Hollender pointed to the empty plate and smiled back. "No. Terrible."

She giggled and slapped his shoulder. Ellis's plate still had more than half a burrito on it, but without asking or even looking at him, she picked it up along with Hollender's and took it away. Ellis started to protest but then, fuck it. Whatever.

"Why do they hate me so much?" he asked.

"They don't hate you. They're just a stoic people."

Right on cue, the waitress, her two sisters, and even the old lady from behind the counter approached the table, applauding. The waitress was carrying an enormous wedge of flan with a burning candle in it.

"Felicidades!" they said. "Muchas felicidades por tu jubilación!"

The waitress put the dessert in front of Hollender.

With only one fork.

# CHAPTER 21

THE MOTORCYCLE RIDER in the yellow leather jacket had been following Ellis for the last ten minutes. When he sped through a yellow light at the intersection of West Olive and Victory, the bike ran the red and stayed on his tail. Ellis lost him, merging onto the 134, and tried to relax. The biker had never threatened him or made any attempt at contact, but it was unsettling to keep seeing him. In a city of fourteen million drivers, could it be a coincidence?

Ellis took the 101, which was moving, to the 405, which wasn't. Sunny 96 FM told him why: *All lanes of the southbound 405 are closed due to a deadly collision at Sunset Boulevard, involving six cars and a semi-truck.* Ellis heaved a sigh and put the Porsche in neutral. He dug a roach out of the ashtray, lit it, and flipped through the radio stations: KT102 …*what are you waiting for?* Power 106 …*pay no interest until next year…* KROQ …*for a thinner, younger-looking you, call today…* KLOS …*spending the holidays alone?* When he circled back to Sunny 96, Melissa Etheridge's cover of "Happy Xmas (War Is Over)" was on. Not ideal, but better than commercials. By the second chorus, though, he was over it and reached for the radio dial when a motion in the rearview mirror caught his eye.

The biker in the yellow jacket was back. He was splitting the lanes, coming up on Ellis's left. When the bike shot past, Ellis exhaled, rolled his shoulders, and popped his neck. So far, the drive to Santa Monica reaffirmed his prejudice against the place. There was just something about it…

An hour-and-a-half later, the freeway started to flow, and Ellis continued on his way to 22nd Street, north of Montana Avenue, and Bettina Grant's 7,500-square-foot home. Built in the late 1980s, it was a coked-up dream of a Mediterranean mansion in pink: six bedrooms, eight bathrooms, bespoke chef's kitchen, and a wine cellar. There was also an outdoor kitchen, pool, and spa. The arched front door was hung with a wreath the size of a truck tire, tied with a pink velvet bow.

Ellis had known Bettina since 1991, when he and Kent Moran were staff writers on *SEAL Team Trident,* and she was a hotshot casting director at the Maxx Network. Back then, they all bowed and scraped before the King of Cable Television, Aaron Grant. But almost from the moment they met, their fortunes split. Bettina married Aaron, Kent began his run at the throne, and Ellis lost his father and, in a depressed, drunken fog, took over his investigation agency.

Sometime around 2015, Bettina started hiring Ellis to keep tabs on Aaron, who had an appetite for hard drugs and underage girls. Eventually, documenting his former boss's downward spiral was the only thing keeping Ellis afloat. And only barely. He was also spiraling. The night he watched Aaron get blown apart by a shotgun blast from Nazario Sanchez, he earned about a thousand bucks. Not even enough to cover his rent. For passing along Aaron and Bettina's nephew, Urs's, headshot to Kent, who made the kid a star, Ellis didn't get paid at all. Not even a thank you text from anyone involved.

Surely—*surely!*—it would be different if he could definitively clear Urs's name in the killing of Larry Price. Maybe then Ellis would be rewarded not just monetarily but also with another bite at the apple—a second chance to work in television. It felt good, if a little delusional, to hold out hope.

As he raised his hand to ring the bell, a woman's agonized screams pealed behind the door. He tried the handle. It was unlocked. Inside the vaulted entryway, the screaming was amplified and echoey. Wishing he were armed, he ran to the living room, where the cries came from.

There, seated in the lotus position on facing yoga mats, were Bettina and Anton Stafford. They were flanked by a ten-foot Christmas tree and a floor-standing Buddha statue Bettina bought from a Thai restaurant that closed during the pandemic. The tree lights were on but pointless in the flood of natural light pouring through the picture windows.

"What the fuck?" Ellis and Bettina said at the same time.

"You don't know how to ring a goddamn doorbell?"

"Yeah, I know how to ring a goddamn doorbell. I was about to, but I heard you screaming. I thought you were in trouble."

"I am." In her blue-gray Lululemon athleisure wear, she sure didn't look it. "My spirit and consciousness are in total disharmony."

Ellis's adrenaline ebbed, but his annoyance at Bettina's characteristic self-centeredness spiked. "That's what you were screaming about?"

"Primal screaming, yes… Don't look at me like that. My chakras have been completely fucked since Amedeo quit."

"Who's Amedeo?"

"My chef. He quit because his father is dying or some bullshit. Right here at the holidays, too, the sonofabitch." She gritted her whitened teeth and began to growl. Just as the sound reached a tortured crescendo, Anton touched her shoulder.

"Excellent," he said. "You're really accessing a wellspring of power. Now, rest. Remember…" he inhaled theatrically, "breath is the key to the balance of astral empathy."

Bettina shut her eyes and took a slow, deep breath in… swelling her silicone chest… and out, through her chemically filled lips. "You're right. You're right, as always." She took another, shallower breath.

"This is Ellis. He's… I don't know, a friend." To Ellis, she said, "This is Anton Stafford, my new healer, life coach, and guru. His TikToks all get over, like, two million impressions. Oprah Winfrey follows him."

"I know who you are," Ellis said to Anton. "I've seen your YouTube videos."

He had also seen Mark Redondo knock him to the floor of his Mid-Mod pad in Sherman Oaks and twist his wrist until he cried.

"*You've* seen Anton's videos?" asked Bettina, unfolding her shapely legs. "Really?"

In her early sixties, she had been lifted, tucked, sucked, tanned, peeled, dyed, and dermabrased by the best. If Ellis didn't know better, he might have guessed she was his age.

"Why are you surprised?" he asked. "I really like the one about compassionate intentionality."

Anton got to his bare feet and bowed to Ellis. "Pleased to meet you. Namaste. I'm honored that you found the videos helpful."

"Oh yeah. Definitely, definitely. I'd shake your hand, but…" He nodded to the brace on Anton's wrist.

Anton smiled. "Ah. Pain and healing are essential parts of the life cycle."

"What happened?" Ellis was curious what lie Anton would tell.

"I slipped on the steps outside my house."

"Ouch."

Bettina cleared her throat at Ellis. "We're in the middle of a very expensive session here. What do you want?"

"Sorry to interrupt, I just—Anton, you might have some perspective on this—I just wanted to talk to you about Urs."

"Urs? What for?" asked Bettina.

"Because he's been charged with murder?" Ellis said in California English.

"And why would Anton have perspective on that?"

"Well, it's a high-profile case, and he's Christian Cooper's stepfather." Bettina squinted and shook her head as if to say, *What the fuck are you talking about?* "Urs and Christian are old friends from Costa Mesa. So, maybe," nodding toward Anton, "he has some, y'know, karmic perspective."

Anton cocked his head. "You know Christian?"

"Yeah, no. Not really. I met him once through Urs. I'm writing his next show. Kent Moran is producing it."

Bettina scoffed. "Really."

"Unfortunately, I've never met Urs," said Anton. "I married Christian's mother after he and Urs were already travelling divergent paths. And all I know about his murder case is what little I've seen on the news. So, I don't know how much *karmic perspective* I can offer. But," he tucked his able fist under his chin in a classic Thinking Man pose, "at the risk of sounding glib—"

"Not you."

"—fame has gone to Urs's head. I work with a lot of celebrities, and there's certainly a chicken-and-egg factor at play. Meaning, are damaged people more likely to become famous, or does fame damage people? Of course, there's no pat answer. But it holds true across the board that the ego, inorganically stimulated by fame, is a distorting lens that refracts light away from the soul. And in the darkness, monsters are born. Like I said, I don't know him. But maybe Urs has some unresolved trauma in his background. There are myriad ways the psyche can mutate. Either way, he's manipulated his way into a spiritual orientation where he forestalls consequences for the disruptions he creates in the unified field of consciousness."

"So, you think Urs killed his agent?"

Anton chuckled like he was indulging a special-needs kid. "All I'm saying is, for someone lost in the maze of the ego, there are no limits to the depths of depravity. Nothing would surprise me."

"Bettina, you know Urs better than any of us," said Ellis. "What do you think?"

"I think this is costing me a hundred dollars a minute, my chakras are fucked, and you're making it worse."

Ellis turned from her to Anton. "Urs is Bettina's nephew. I don't know if she mentioned that."

Anton blushed and forced a smile. "No, no. Wow. What a… a small, amazing world we inhabit, huh? No, I, uh— I didn't mean that Urs was damaged or depraved—"

"Sounded like it."

"Okay, okay. But allow me to complete my point—Urs is obviously a bright, talented young man," a glance at Bettina, "with unlimited potential. But everyone—you, Urs, even me— we're all susceptible to illnesses of the mind, body, and spirit. Fortunately, we also have the miraculous power to heal. I pray that Urs finds the courage and character to turn his current challenges into the first steps of a healing journey."

"Wow. It's not for nothing you have all those followers and subscribers and everything." Ellis wanted to ask what that did for a person's ego, but instead went with, "Personally, I like Mark Redondo for the murder of Larry Price. If I had anything to bet, I'd bet it was him."

"Pardon me," said Anton.

"Mark Redondo. The guy they arrested yesterday in front of the Chinese Theatre after he shot at a cop at Hollywood Lake Park? He's a suspect in the Southland Sniper killings. It's been all over the news."

"No, yes. I, uh—I did hear about that. I just forgot the name." Anton stooped and started rolling his yoga mat. "Yes, hopefully, he's the killer and Urs will be exonerated. I was celebrating my birthday with my family that night." Ellis knew he meant the night of Larry's murder. It was the same unsolicited alibi Christian offered on the set of *Stop! Or My Mom Will Squirt*.

"You're married to Belinda Ferris, aren't you?"

He squinted, cagey. "That's right."

"And she was on *Night Street*? Back in 1989?"

"Um… What, uh—? How do you—?"

"I'm a big fan of the show."

"I'm surprised you've heard of it. It didn't last very long."

"Ellis has a special talent for living in the past," said Bettina.

He ignored the remark and stayed intent on Anton. "By any chance, has Belinda ever mentioned working with an actress named Annalee Gentry?"

"I uh— No, the name doesn't ring a bell." Anton put his yoga mat in a sling and looped it over his shoulder. "Maybe, though. I don't know, sorry. It, uh— It was nice to meet you."

"What are you doing? You're leaving?" Bettina looked at her Fitbit. "Our session isn't over for another eleven minutes."

"This session is on me."

"Please, stay," said Ellis. "Finish your session. I'll get out of your way."

But Anton was already out the door.

Bettina rounded on Ellis. "What the fuck? Thanks a lot! Do you know how hard it is to book a private session with him?"

"He's hiding something."

"What do you mean?"

"Where do I start?" Ellis plopped down on the white leather sofa. "So... whether or not Mark Redondo is the Southland Sniper—and I don't think he is—he's definitely a killer. A hit man. Last week, he got stiffed on a job and went to Anton's house to rough him up. That's the real reason he has a brace on his wrist. Redondo is little but he's also an ass kicker. He's a black belt."

"You've finally lost your mind," said Bettina. "I knew it as soon as you came barging in here, reeking of weed."

"I don't reek of weed... Do I?" He sniffed the front of his shirt.

"Anton Stafford is the most compassionate, enlightened person on earth. He's practically freakin' Gandhi. He would never hire a hit man. And if he did, he would pay him."

"Anton didn't hire Redondo. Annalee Gentry did. Well, she gave money to a middleman who hired a guy named Ramsey. Ramsey farmed the job out to Redondo but kept the money to pay an old debt to some narcos in Texas. I'm pretty sure the hit was on Larry Price. And now, Urs is being framed for it, however clumsily."

"Stop-stop-stop. Why are you telling me this?"

"Because Urs didn't kill Larry. At least, I'm like, ninety-nine-point-nine percent sure he didn't."

"So, what the hell do you want from me that you had to come running in here like a crazy person and interrupt the most expensive, exclusive therapy session I've ever had?"

A fair question. Ellis squinted and chewed the inside of his cheek.

"I don't know really. I just had a feeling that if I came to see you, it would pay off. And it did. You saw how rattled Anton got when I mentioned *Night Street*. Did you catch his reaction when I—?"

"Yeah, I sure as shit did catch his reaction. He fucking left and it'll be a miracle if I ever get him back. Right now, when I need him most, too. I have to find a chef for Christmas Eve and I am fucking freaking out!"

"Maybe your chakras *are* fucked. Something sure is."

Bettina pointed a French-manicured finger at Ellis's face. "Don't you fucking chakra shame me. I've done all I can for Urs. You know, that little shit never even thanked me for recommending him to Kent?"

"He never thanked me either."

"Why would he thank you?"

"Because I gave Kent his headshot."

"What are you talking about?"

"I gave Urs's headshot to Kent, as a favor *to you*... You seriously don't remember?"

Bettina shrugged and rolled her eyes. "Well, I've done all I'm going to do for selfish, self-destructive men. And that includes you, buddy boy. The best way I can bring truth and light to this moment is to just breathe," she inhaled... and exhaled... "and focus on myself."

"Yes, definitely. Focus on yourself for a change."

Ellis showed himself out. As he was shutting the door behind him, Bettina started screaming again.

# CHAPTER 22

IN A MINI-MALL PARKING LOT on Ventura Boulevard, a homeless man was on his knees, smoking crack and barking like a dog. Watching, Ellis whistled the Randy Newman tune "I Love L.A."

Ellis got out of the Porsche when Christian Cooper walked out of Eco Clean dry cleaner with an armload of clothes in slick (presumably biodegradable) plastic bags. Eyeing the homeless guy, Ellis made sure the car door was locked, then jogged over to where Christian was unlocking his Ford Explorer.

"Christian? Hey, man. I thought that was you."

Christian frowned over the top of his sunglasses. "Um… hey?"

"I'm Ellis Dunaway. We met on the set of *Stop! Or My Mom Will Squirt*. Remember? I'm friends with Urs?"

Christian pushed his wavy hair out of his eyes. "I remember."

"It's a crazy coincidence running into you like this. I just met your stepdad yesterday." Ellis waited for him to ask for details, but he didn't. "Anton said your mom used to be an actor on a show called *Night Street*." Technically, he didn't, but maybe Christian would.

"He mentioned that?" asked Christian, skeptical.

"Mm-hmm."

"She was only in a couple of episodes, as an extra."

Aha! "That's crazy. It's a pretty obscure show—"

"Yeah, kind of," Christian said sardonically.

"—and I know somebody else who was on it. Terry Montero."

"Okay…?"

"He owns the Century Club. Your mom ever mention him?"

Christian's hair flopped back in his face. "I don't know, dude, maybe. She talks about the past all the time. It's pathetic. I mostly just tune it out, y'know."

In turning away, one of the dry-cleaning bags slid to the pavement. Ellis picked it up—a beige sleeveless blouse with a scoop neck. The label read, *DKNY*. He held it while Christian got the SUV open.

"All this shit is my mom's," he said, tossing the clothes into the backseat, letting them scatter and crumple on the floorboard. He snatched the blouse from Ellis and held it loosely. His index finger was in a splint.

"This is the third fucking time I've brought this thing to the cleaners because of some microscopic stain. It's obviously not coming out, but you can barely even see it anyway." He stripped the plastic bag off, letting it flutter across the parking lot, and held the blouse out to Ellis. "See?"

Ellis squinted and found a faint discoloration on the left shoulder of the blouse, about the size of a dime.

"Yeah, if you hadn't pointed it out, I would never have noticed it."

"No shit, right? But she keeps sending it back, and the cleaner keeps saying they can't do anything else about it without damaging the material. But I guarantee you, she'll send me back here with it again. She's so fucking—...ugh!"

He threw the blouse in the backseat with the rest of the clothes.

Ellis thought back to Urs, in jail, saying, that Christian's mom was his manager, and their relationship was "fucked up" because they were "too close," and that it "was hard to tell who worked for who."

"What happened to your finger?"

"My mother broke it when I reached for the remote while she was watching *Real Housewives of Dallas*. She hate-watches it because she went to high school with one of the housewives. D'Andra, I think. Or maybe Kameron."

"Still, that's a pretty extreme reaction."

"When she found out Uncle Larry got killed, the heartless bitch actually *laughed* about it. Her own brother. How fucked up is that?"

"Larry Price is your uncle?"

"Not anymore."

"Right, but why didn't you mention that when I asked you about him when we first met?"

"You asked how I felt about him, and I told you. I barely knew him. He and my mom always hated each other, going back to when they were kids. All I ever heard was what an asshole he was, that he resented her for being born—stupid sibling shit like that. Because she can't let go of a grudge, I missed my chance to be represented by him. I had to sit there while Urs took my spot. It should have been me on *Graveyardland*!"

He took a breath and lowered his voice. "But whatever, man. I'm above it. I'm not like my mom. I'm moving forward."

Emphasizing the point, he got in the SUV and reached to close the door. Ellis grabbed it.

"Hang on. I think you know something about Larry's murder."

"Like what, my mom did it?"

"Did she?"

"Of course not. Look, man, I know you're a private eye. I know what this is."

"What what is?"

"This…" Christian twirled his splinted finger like he was dialing a rotary phone. "This little cat-and-mouse routine. Your being here isn't a coincidence."

He tried again to close the door, but Ellis held on.

"Annalee Gentry was your mom's stage name, wasn't it?"

Christian tugged harder on the car door.

"Or vice-versa?"

He yanked the door out of Ellis's grip and slammed it.

"Christian, wait!" Ellis knocked on the tinted window, but Christian started the engine and peeled out of the parking lot.

The barking homeless guy had the plastic dry-cleaning bag tucked into his sweaty collar, where it flapped like a cape in the Santa Ana wind. Glinting on his chest, bobbing with his herky-jerky gait, was a gold Saturn-shaped medallion.

# CHAPTER 23

TRAFFIC ON THE 5 was sluggish enough that Ellis could guide the Porsche with his knee while he got a joint rolled and sparked. He took a couple of tokes before having to engage first gear and drive instead of drift.

As Josh Groban's soulless rendition of "I'll Be Home for Christmas" faded on the radio, Ellis decided to save some for the party and roached the joint in the dashboard ashtray. After a barrage of commercials—*Why wait? Call today! ...for a thinner, younger-looking you ...no interest until next year... spending the holidays alone?*—the news, traffic, and weather report came on.

*The Southland Sniper strikes again. Los Angeles police confirm another case has been tied to a string of shootings in the L.A. area. A total of nine shootings have occurred so far, in different neighborhoods. Seven of those have been deadly. The latest, a twenty-two-year-old man and his companion, were killed last night in West Hollywood. As in all the other cases, the Sniper sent a letter to the police, taking credit for the killings. He promises to continue his rampage until the demons in his head tell him to stop. The reward for any information leading to an arrest and a conviction has been increased to fifty thousand dollars.*

So, as Ellis suspected, the incarcerated Mark Redondo wasn't the Southland Sniper. Did that mean the attack on Ellis and/or Tameka had been Redondo covering his tracks, or had it been contracted? Ellis got a cold trembling in his gut, thinking somebody out there still had it in for him.

An angry buzz rose in the distance and drilled through Ellis's skunky fog of worry. In the rearview mirror, a motorcycle was racing up on his left, splitting the lanes. He cut his eyes up at the sun visor where he had tucked the picture of the naked woman torn from an old porn magazine, a message from a kid who looked just like he used to: *Will history blame me, or the bees?* His pulse spiked when he saw that the motorcycle rider was wearing a yellow jacket. There was no way the connection didn't spell Ellis's doom. His whole life, he considered the universe mute, but it had been sending him omens he hadn't taken seriously until now, when it was too late. Somebody wanted him dead, and all signs pointed to this being his killer. The conditions were perfect—the cover of blue-hour shadows, traffic moving enough for the noisy but nimble bike to zip into obscurity.

Ellis shut his eyes and braced for a bullet in the brain.

But again, the motorcycle sped past. Then, an identical bike driven by a rider in a matching yellow leather jacket raced by on the right. Now, they were streaming along both sides of the

Porsche, a dozen or more of them, vanishing into the curving river of taillights.

HIP-HOP THUNDERED throughout Urs Schreiber's rented Spanish mansion in the Hills. For a "cancelled" celebrity, he had managed to pack the place with guests. Bella Thorne and Julia Garner stood beside the drum set in the dining room, talking to an actor Ellis recognized but couldn't name. In the book-free library, four guys with dreadlocks and tattoos on their faces were passing a blunt. Down to their neon sneakers, sagging jeans, haute couture T-shirts, and enormous wristwatches, they were dressed exactly alike. A pink-haired girl in a silver mini dress was sitting on the pinball machine, which was flashing and squawking as if in protest. Cheers erupted from the knot of people watching the muted Lakers game on the movie-screen-sized television in the living room. Shards of a broken champagne bottle crunched under the feet of people freshening their drinks and snorting coke off the marble island in the kitchen. But no sign of Urs.

Angling his way to the terrace doors, Ellis spotted Kent a few feet away by the carved stone fireplace, rapt in animated conversation with a man and two women.

"…good word-of-mouth and four-quadrant appeal…"

"…low-hanging fruit…"

"…percentage of the adjusted gross…"

"…circle back after the holidays…"

Ellis forced down his bitterness, pressed his lips into a smile, and raised his hand just as Kent threw his head back, laughing. Playing off his unseen and abortive wave, Ellis ran his fingers through his hair while his cheeks burned with embarrassment. Head down, he pushed his way outside, where a guy who looked like, but probably wasn't, Ryan Seacrest was taking selfies with two women who looked like, and definitely weren't, Kim Kardashian and Miley Cyrus.

Ellis dug the joint he started in the car out of his shirt pocket and lit it. Inhaling, he leaned on the balustrade and took in the twinkling view of the city. Just then, a hand clapped him on the shoulder from behind. He startled and swallowed the roach. Seized by a coughing fit, he spun around to see Urs grinning.

"You okay, man?" His right nostril was rimmed with cocaine.

At least, Ellis assumed it was coke, but who knew anymore? "You scared the shit outta me."

Urs laughed and pulled Ellis into a hug, sloshing brown liquor down his collar. "I'm sorry, bro."

Ellis disengaged and stepped back. "Ack. No problem. Anyway, congratulations."

"Thanks, man. Thank you. It's been rough, but it's all behind me."

The party was a celebration of the news that all charges against Urs had been dropped after ballistic evidence revealed that the gun Mark Redondo used to shoot at Ellis and Tameka

Settles was the same one that had killed Larry Price. Redondo still hadn't confessed, not that it mattered much.

"I got you a present," said Ellis. He pulled a gold chain with a Saturn-shaped medallion from the hip pocket of his jeans. No engraved serial number from Bullseye Props. An original.

Urs's eyes bugged. "My chain! Holy shit. Where'd you get it?"

"I saw a crackhead wearing it. I traded him forty bucks and a handle of vodka for it."

"Seriously? That's fucking amazing." Urs gave Ellis another back-slapping, drink-spilling hug. "So, the one that bitch cop found was planted to frame me. I knew it!"

Ellis wiped the booze off the back of his neck. "Or it was just a coincidence."

"A coincidence? In what way?"

"Because it, uh…" Ellis didn't want to disabuse Urs of the idea that his necklace was rare. He wanted him to enjoy his party. "Let's just… not worry about it."

"Of course, I'm fuckin' worried about it. Somebody was out there trying to frame me, bro. Obviously." Urs hung the chain around his neck. "This proves there's something shady about that fuckin' bitch cop. I knew it. I want you to investigate her."

Ellis shivered. "Huh?"

"Yeah. I'm hiring you to investigate that bitch cop and prove she tried to frame me."

Ellis held up his hand. "Whoa. Let's, uh—" He hoped never to cross paths with Tameka Settles again. If she killed her cousin Ramsey, like Ellis suspected, what was there to keep her from doing likewise to him if she thought he crossed her? Her uncle Courtland's affection for Ellis would only deter her so far.

"Let's talk about it later, okay? Tonight, let's just, y'know, celebrate you being in the clear."

Urs snorted and *ha-a-a-awked* to clear the cocaine drip out of his throat, then said, "We have something else to celebrate, too."

"What's that?"

"The show is back on." He threw his hand up for a high five.

Ellis complied. "What show?"

"*Miami Vice*. It's happening."

"Wh—?" Ellis shook his head. "For real?"

"For real. Only, I'm playing a drug dealer now, and Crockett and Tubbs are gonna be women. Lesbians, actually. Lesbians of color. So, since they went with my idea of making Crockett black, I get a producer credit."

"That's fucking awesome!" said Ellis. This time, he initiated the hug. "Since it was my idea to make him a woman, I wonder if

I'll get a producer credit too." Urs shrugged. "It doesn't matter, either way. I just— I-I'm stunned. I gotta talk to Kent."

Shouldering his way through the party, Ellis's head spun with euphoria, relief, and gratitude. His heart raced, and his smile was so wide it hurt.

Kent was still by the fireplace, but now he was talking to a black lady with a pierced septum and a pink mohawk.

"Urs just told me the show is back on," said Ellis, "with lesbians of color."

"Yep," said Kent. "That's right. We," he nodded at the lady who didn't look old enough to be drinking the red wine in her hand, "were just talking about it."

"Awesome." Ellis hugged Kent. "So fucking awesome."

"Thanks, man." To the young woman, he said, "Tasha Stargin, this is Ellis Dunaway, an old friend of mine. We started out together as staff writers on a show called *SEAL Team Trident* back in the nineties."

Tasha shook Ellis's hand. "Sounds jingoistic as fuck."

It wasn't, but for some reason, "Oh, it was," popped out of his mouth.

"Tasha is our new writer," said Kent.

"Our, uh…? You mean on *Graveyardland?*"

"No," Kent looked down into the fireplace. "*Miami Vice.*"

Ellis's breath caught like he'd been punched in the chest. "Wait... Sorry. You mean, she...?"

"*They*," said Tasha. "I'm non-binary."

"They wrote a graphic novel about a teddy bear that comes out as transgender and runs for President as a communist," said Kent, "called *Teddy Equity*—it's brilliant—and we've been trying to find the right project to work on together, and—"

"And it's *Miami Vice*?" asked Ellis. "Gender swapping Crockett and Tubbs was my idea."

"Well," said Kent, "honestly, that's pretty low-hanging fruit."

"Spare me the fucking jargon, okay."

"Anybody can come up with a gender swap, but Tasha brings an empathy that goes beyond the surface. Her—I mean, *their*—voice needs to be heard, especially in this climate."

"Southern California?"

"Come on, man. Don't be obtuse. You know what I mean. A story about lesbians of color should be told by a lesbian of color. That's just common sense."

"I would argue that a show about detectives should be written by a detective," said Ellis.

"But I'm not interested in detectives," said Tasha. "I'm interested in uplifting marginalized voices. I'm interested in telling my story."

"How in the world is *Miami Vice* your story?" asked Ellis. "Why not stick to comic books if you——?"

"What the fuck?" Tasha stiffened. Her eyes and nostrils flared. "I know you're not trying to tell me my place. You're out of your fuckin' mind if you think I'm gonna let you bully me. Lemme tell you something, everything I write, if it's TV shows or graphic novels or my fuckin' grocery list, it's pitched at a frequency that old-ass white men like you can't even hear."

"I wish," said Ellis.

Back in the kitchen, a different group was gathered around the marble island, doing blow—or whatever it was. The broken glass on the floor had been ground into small pieces. Ellis found a red Solo cup, filled it half full of Absolut, and drained it in one long gulp. Unaccustomed to the burn, he shivered as it spread through his blood to his boiling brain. For a terrible moment, he feared he would pass out or vomit, or both. But the sensation passed, and left a familiar numbness. He poured some more, emptying the bottle, and again polished it off in one go. He gasped, grabbed the counter's edge for stability, and waited for the room to stop spinning. When it levelled off, a guy in a vintage Judas Priest T-shirt looked up from the island, pinched his nose, freshly packed with powder, and extended a rolled-up twenty.

"Want some?"

# CHAPTER 24

ON LYNNWOOD COURT, in the hills of Sherman Oaks above Mulholland, strands of Christmas lights traced the angular contours of the multi-million-dollar mid-century homes and wound around the trunks of palms and jacarandas in their sloping front lawns. Blue LED icicles dangled from the carport at the end of the cul-de-sac.

Ellis pulled to the curb and cut the Porsche's engine, shutting down "All I Want for Christmas Is My Two Front Teeth" along with it. He took a deep breath, and then another, but couldn't steady his pulse or hands. Despite the chill in the air, he was sweating as he reached under the seat for his gun. The day Mark Redondo shot at him and Tameka Settles, Ellis ripped open the box his .38 Smith & Wesson revolver was packed in and started carrying it again.

Two hours ago, Ellis arrived excitedly early for his second date with Deena at Bhairavi Market, a new "Indian-inspired" restaurant on Sherman Way in Reseda. Sitting in a booth, under webs of multi-colored Christmas lights and plastic flower garlands so dense Ellis assumed they were part of the permanent décor, sipping ice water and gazing at the wine list, he was relieved he hadn't woken up that morning with too much of a hangover. Just a scratchy throat and a woozy headache. Six cups of coffee, a half-gallon of water, a microwavable breakfast burrito, a joint of Bubblegum Kush, and back-to-back reruns of *Southland HEAT* had cleared up everything but his conscience. Luckily, the powder he snorted in Urs's kitchen had been plain old mid-grade cocaine, not fentanyl or some sketchy research chemical that might have had longer-lasting effects or killed him outright. Although last night, he wouldn't have cared if it had.

"Sorry, I'm late," said Deena.

"No problem." Ellis stood, being gentlemanly, and she hugged him. And just like that, the pangs of regret at allowing Kent Moran to reawaken his up-to-then more-or-less dormant death wish wafted away on a gust of floral perfume and blushing nerves.

They sat opposite each other and smiled.

"I— Uh…"

Now that Deena was at a distance and he could take her in, he was struck equally by her beauty and her beige, sleeveless, scoop-neck blouse. It was exactly the same as the one Christian

Cooper picked up from the dry cleaner yesterday for his mother. Ellis squinted, but the restaurant was too dark to make out whether or not there was a faint, dime-sized discoloration on the left shoulder. In a city of two million women, he told himself, obviously, many of them would have the same clothes. And when you narrowed the numbers down by demographics, it was a wonder you didn't see more people walking around in the same outfits. Still, the coincidence made Ellis wipe his palms on his knees.

"Yeah?" said Deena.

"Sorry, what?"

"I thought you started to say something… Wh—?" She looked down her front. "Is there something on my blouse?"

"Oh," he couldn't remember what he had started to say when the blouse distracted him, "no. No, it uh… It's nice. DKNY?"

"Yeah." Deena smiled like Ellis had just correctly guessed which card she picked from a deck. "How did you know?"

"It's the craziest coincidence. I bumped into an actor friend of mine at the dry cleaner the other day, and he was picking up a blouse just like that for his mother."

"Really? That *is* crazy. What actor picks up his mother's dry cleaning?"

"Christian Cooper." Deena shook her head: *name's not familiar.* "He's a young guy, trying to break in."

"Ah. That old song."

"Exactly."

"What are his chances? Does he have the goods?"

Ellis shrugged. "According to him, he was up for Urs Schreiber's role in *Brass Hearts*. He seems to have a lot of personal baggage. That could help or hurt. Maybe he's the next Montgomery Clift. But honestly, I doubt it."

"What do you mean about personal baggage?"

"I dunno. It's just a feeling I get. His mother is his manager, and he does porn. I mean, I'm a liberal dude and everything, but that's kinda odd, right? And he told me she broke his finger when he reached for the remote while she was hate-watching *Real Housewives of Dallas*."

"Wow."

"No kidding. And on top of that, his stepfather is Anton Stafford, the new-age guru guy."

"Oh yeah?" Deena perked up. "I know who he is."

"Seems like it could be a… fraught situation for Christian."

"I was totally skeptical of Anton Stafford at first. I thought, this guy's just another new-age snake oil salesman, but then I actually watched his YouTube videos, and I have to admit, he won me over. He's really not that kooky. A lot of what he says makes sense."

Ellis disagreed, but said, "Oh, totally. I've seen a couple of his videos too, and yeah, he's interesting, for sure."

The ensuing small talk followed the radio format: news—"…the Southland Sniper's latest letter…" "…cops with machine guns at the Beverly Center…"—traffic—"…wreck on the 405 North at the 105 interchange…" "…*two hours* to get from Westwood to the Marina…"—and weather—"…*fifty-two* degrees this morning…" "*Literally* freezing!"

The waiter arrived, and Ellis ordered tandoori chicken. Silence expanded while Deena scrutinized the menu.

"Take your time," said the waiter, shuffling his feet. "Any questions?"

"Um… Can I do like, a shrimp masala?"

"Tandoori shrimp?"

"Shrimp masala."

The waiter furrowed his brow. "We have tandoori shrimp, or you can substitute shrimp in the fish moilee." He pointed to it on the menu. "It's the cat's pajamas. Yum yum! It has a coconut milk sauce with turmeric and cori—"

"Thanks. I can read," said Deena. "I hate coriander. Last time I was here, you made me shrimp masala. I know it's not on the menu, but the chef said it was no problem."

"You can substitute shrimp for—"

"I don't want coconut-coriander soup with shrimp floating in it. I want shrimp masala. What's the big deal? You have shrimp. You have everything to make eggplant masala, tikka masala, chana masala…" She pointed to each one on the menu. "Look, okay, let's do it this way—make it easy—I'll have the eggplant masala with shrimp instead of eggplant. Okay?"

The waiter was scribbling on his order pad. "Um, I'll try but—"

"Does that come with makhani sauce?"

"Does…? You want makhani sauce?" The waiter's voice cracked.

"Yeah. So, like, eggplant masala, with shrimp instead of eggplant, and *light* makhani sauce. Like I said, I don't want it too saucy. I don't want soup." She handed over the menu. "Thanks."

Relieved that was finally over, Ellis broke his middle-distance stare and re-entered the moment with a smile. While he and Deena bullshitted about TV shows he had never seen or outright hated—"…slow burn until season three…" "…*Big Little Lies* meets *Black Mirror*…"—he wondered how many more of Deena's food orders he cared to endure, no matter how symmetrical her features, pert her (probably fake) breasts, disarming her smile, and bewitching her eyes.

When the food arrived, Deena was describing her last trip to the acupuncturist, the one in North Hollywood who looked like Rosamund Pike, in a self-deprecating and genuinely funny way.

"So, I keep blurting stuff out to cover the sound of my stomach growling. It's all like, peaceful and chill, and she's sticking these needles in me, and I go like, 'I saw Jake Gyllenhaal at Whole Foods!' I was so embarrassed."

It was reassuring for Ellis to know she was capable of the emotion. But then, her shrimp had too much makhani sauce on it.

"I specifically said *light* sauce." She dragged Ellis in. "Didn't I?"

His stomach twisting with hunger and tension, he nodded, making eye contact with no one. "It does look a little saucy."

"Yeah, no, I'm sorry," Deena pushed the plate away. "I can't eat that."

"You, uh— You want to send it back?" asked the waiter.

"It's not what I ordered. I asked for *light sauce*. So, yes, I'm sending it back."

The waiter took the plate and slunk away.

Deena smiled at Ellis as if she were having fun. "Please, go ahead and eat."

Taking another opportunity to be a gentleman, he refused. "I'd rather wait for you."

"You're sweet." The magic words. He swooned, but not as deeply as last time. "You seem a little, I don't know... distracted. Everything okay?"

"No, yeah, sorry. No, everything's great. It's just—" He was staring at Deena's blouse again, thinking about how Christian Cooper said he had brought an identical one back to the cleaners three times because his mother couldn't be satisfied. There was no advantage in bringing that up again, though, so he said, "I, uh... relapsed last night."

He took a long drink of ice water and looked out into the bustling, colorful dining room, searching for a cue card that would tell him what to say next.

Deena spared him. "Oh no," she said, taking his hand. "That sucks. But it's okay, y'know. It happens. You wanna talk about it?"

Her gaze was intent in a way nobody ever looked at anyone else in the Fellowship Room of Pathways Church, where relapse stories were clichés. But here in Bhairavi Market, Ellis felt seen and heard, like he mattered, like his pain wasn't just garnish to free-trade coffee and gluten-free muffins.

While his chicken's heat and savory aroma dissipated, he opened up, telling Deena all about Urs's party and the humiliating whipsaw of learning his comeback show was greenlit, but that he had been replaced as the writer.

"I felt like lashing out at myself and everyone else. And I did it the way I do best—booze and drugs. After all this time, too… So fucking stupid."

"It's not stupid. It's a symptom of a cruel disease. I've relapsed plenty of times, and bad too, believe me. Beating yourself up just makes it worse. You don't heal that way."

She squeezed his hand, and he felt the warmth all the way up his arm, around his heart, and down to his groin. "Addicts have it worse than other people when it comes to recognizing our own value. We either have no capacity for self-love or we have wa-*a-a-ay* too much."

"Funny how it's kind of the same thing. Know what I mean?"

"Yeah. It's easy to forget that compassionate intentionality is a two-way street. It's like, I know that sometimes I forget to check in with myself, and I end up making a big power-play out of a simple thing like ordering dinner. I mean, makhani sauce and masala sauce are basically the same thing. I hear myself, and I'm like, 'Deena, shut the fuck up. What's the matter with you? You're gonna blow it again.' But it's like I can't keep from being a bitch and all because I'm insecure and I don't want the cool guy I'm with to sense it. But rather than intend compassion for myself and my egotistical desires, I make other people feel as locked up and awkward as I do. If that makes sense…?"

Cool guy? Did she mean him, Ellis? Was she kidding? That was the weirdest thing Deena had said all night, even weirder than the Anton Staffordisms and the obsessive food order. But then, maybe thinking so exposed the heart of what he thought Deena was saying about self-love and Ellis's diminished capacity for it. Maybe, despite himself, he *did* come across as a cool guy.

"Yeah, no, that makes total sense. And you're not a bitch. You're right, substituting shrimp should be no prob—"

"Please, stop." Deena shook her head. "I didn't say that just so you would say I wasn't a bitch. I know I'm not. Not really. I just act like one sometimes, and I hate it, but I have to accept it, because then maybe, over time, I can catch myself quicker and correct course. I'm proud to say, I'm better than I used to be, believe it or not."

Unsure whether it was better to say he believed it or didn't, Ellis just smiled.

"And, P.S.," said Deena, "a screenwriter who loses a job to some young asshole—that's like, almost a good thing. It means you're in the game. Losing is part of it. Most people never get a job to lose. Most people don't even get that close."

"Good point. Thanks. I needed to hear that."

Deena accepted her remade entrée gracefully, clapping her hands and saying it looked "just perfect! The cat's pajamas!" Ellis agreed, trying not to think about all the spit and other body fluids it was assuredly steeped in. If there were no kiss goodnight tonight, that might be a blessing. Deena even apologized to the waiter, who pretended it was no big deal, but still looked gun-shy.

As Ellis finally tucked into his cold chicken tandoori and Deena her steaming shrimp whatever-it-was, she paused.

"After this, let's go to my place. I mean," she looked down, but even in the dim light, Ellis spotted a reddening of her cheeks, "I know how that sounds, but just to talk. After my last relapse, my sponsor literally saved my life by staying up with me all night, just being there, listening and talking and distracting me from feeling sorry for myself, which is why I relapsed in the first place." Her eyes widened, and she reached across the table as if out the window of a leaving train. "I'm not saying you're feeling sorry for yourself. I just mean—"

"It's cool," said Ellis, bowled over by his good luck. "I know what you mean. And I accept your invitation. That sounds awesome. Thanks."

While they ate, Ellis with gusto, Deena like the proverbial bird, they cemented their bond over the main thing they had in common: addiction. He told her about his days of coke-and-booze-induced hallucinations, and she told him about going to a job interview at an insurance firm, totally blacked out. Rueful though it was, it was the first time Ellis had laughed in he-didn't-know-how-long. It soothed him like a hot bath and a double bourbon. And what a smile Deena had.

It blinded him to all warning signs until he was following her BMW SUV south on the 405, and she exited at Valley Vista Boulevard. How did a jewelry maker and part-time yoga teacher afford a car like that? Ellis's suspicion became dread when she took Woodcliff Road to Stonewood Drive. The turn onto

Lynnwood couldn't have been a coincidence; Deena's parking under the carport of Anton Stafford's house confirmed it wasn't.

Ellis looked at the .38 in his lap, then up to the house, and back at the gun. He took a deep breath and put the revolver back under the seat. Then he got out of the car, but fear wouldn't let him advance. He re-opened the Porsche, grabbed the gun, and put it in his pocket.

Trudging up the front steps, he tried to block all gallows metaphors from his mind. He knocked on the yellow door.

Deena's voice beckoned him to enter.

Inside, the air was spiced with evergreen potpourri.

"Deena…? Hello?"

"Make yourself at home," she called from down the hall. "I'll just be a second."

The open floor plan had a hotel-lobby-like sterility, with Modern furniture expertly coordinated in high-end neutrality. No junk mail cluttered the Danish credenza, and no tchotchkes or family photos blemished the slate mantel. The white walls were bare of art that wasn't a print of a Warhol Marilyn, a Hockney swimming pool, or the kind of black-and-white stock photo of waves and palm trees that comes with the frames.

The flocked artificial Christmas tree was decorated with glass icicles that amplified the cold, clear, energy-efficient LED twinkle lights and defied the heat of the blazing gas fireplace. The exception that proved the house's generic rule, the single inelegant touch of quasi-individuality, was a framed *Night Street* promo poster.

Ellis congratulated himself on his instincts, yet wished the poster were another seascape. Deena padded into the room barefoot, wearing a bathrobe. Her hair was loose and brushed out as if she were ready for bed. Now that they were somewhere bright enough to tell whether or not her blouse had a faint discoloration on the shoulder, she wasn't wearing it. But now he knew the answer.

"I hope you don't mind," she said. "I had been in those clothes all day. You know how it is."

Ellis cleared his throat. "Totally." He looked back at the poster.

"*Night Street.* For such an obscure show, it's been coming up a lot lately."

Deena, who was close enough to him that he could smell the almond-scented soap she had used to wash off her makeup. "Oh yeah?"

"Yeah. I've seen one of these posters twice before—in the hall across from the writer's room at Maxx Studios, back when I worked there, and in Terry Montero's office at the Century Club."

He looked back at Deena. Her eyes revealed nothing but open interest, so he went on. "He was a featured extra on a three-episode arc. He played a chauffeur. But you know that."

That remark triggered an inquisitive squint and head tilt.

"And Urs Schreiber told me there was also a *Night Street* poster in Christian Cooper's house in Costa Mesa because his mother, Belinda Ferris-Stafford, was also on a couple episodes. And Terry told me yet *another* featured extra on the show, Annalee Gentry, came to him looking for a hit man days before Larry Price was killed. And by crazy coincidence, when I bumped into Christian yesterday, he said Larry Price was his uncle—his mom's brother—and that she had always hated him. Christian said she laughed about his death. But you knew that too, because by another, *even crazier* coincidence—this is her house."

An amused, relieved look spread over Deena's face.

"It's too bad you're not as good a screenwriter as you are a private investigator," she said. "You might not be broke. I mean, I don't know, but I'm guessing even a below-average screenwriter does better than an average PI?"

"Probably."

"So, how'd you figure it out?"

"The night Mark Redondo beat me up and threatened to kill me over fifty thousand dollars he never received for committing a contract murder, I followed him here and watched him break Anton's wrist."

"It's just a sprain."

"*Night Street* only ran twelve episodes. How many featured extras could there be out there arranging murders with one another? So, which is your real name—Deena, Belinda, or Annalee?"

She half-sat on the arm of the cream-colored chenille sofa and gazed into the fire. "It's Baby Sue Scoggins. Baby is my given name. Since I didn't want to do sex work, you can see why I changed it to Annalee Gentry, and then, after she bottomed out, I upgraded to Belinda Ferris, not that she performed much better. Deena, I just made up on the spot because I thought it sounded believable for an AA meeting in Burbank."

"It totally does."

"So, who paid Mark his fifty thousand? He wouldn't say."

"My fairy godmother."

"Cute."

"That's what Mark Redondo told me," said Ellis, staring at the gas flames emanating from the fake logs. "I don't know if he knew who she was at the time. One minute he's beating the shit out of me, the next minute, one of his henchmen, or henchwomen—henchpersons?—hands him an envelope full of cash and he turns me loose. So, I was really confused when he tried to kill me later."

"I don't believe you. You're lying. You know who saved you. In addition to being a failed screenwriter and a so-so private eye, you're a bad actor."

"Well, you're an excellent actor. You really disappeared into the role of Deena."

She waved the ironic compliment away with ironic modesty. "I just gave my audience what I knew he wanted."

"Well, I gotta hand it to you, you fuckin' nailed it." He started pacing, but kept an eye on Baby. "How'd you track me to AA? And why?"

"When Christian came home and told me you came to the set of *Stop! Or My Mom Will Squirt* asking about Larry Price's murder, I went back to Mark Redondo and had him find you."

Ellis remembered thinking the Asian women who beat him up looked familiar. Now he knew it was because, at some point, he must have seen them without seeing them.

"I wanted to gauge for myself how much of a threat you were before shelling out for another hit." Baby was on her feet now, running her finger along the slate mantle. "Your AA meeting seemed like a good place to find you at your most open and easy to read. When we went to dinner and you said you didn't think Urs killed Larry, that there were people out there with bigger beefs against him, you were right. Of course, you couldn't have known it then, but you were talking about me. And I knew, because you're so desperately eager to please, I knew you would just keep sniffing around, doing your witless best to prove your worth to sleazy pimps like Kent Moran and my brother Larry. You're just another one of their whores. Maybe, not so deep down, you know that, too—but you'd be surprised at just how cheap you really are."

"I doubt it."

"Hey, I get it. I hate myself too. One thing that made Deena easy to play is that I really am an alcoholic, albeit a very, *very* high-functioning one. I've been drunk every single time you've ever seen me. And you never knew it."

"I suspected." He hadn't.

"Liar. I'm drunk right now."

"Dee— Baby, sit down."

"Having a Hollywood pimp like Larry Price killed is one thing, but losers like you are worth so little, I could afford to have Mark Redondo kill you, too. Obviously, he fucked it up that day in the park—and I'm out my deposit—but, like I said," she winked, "it wasn't much."

Ellis was interested in the monetary value of his life on the murder market, but not as much as proving the speculators wrong. Now, it was apparent that Baby was drunk. Her posture was slack; her gestures exaggerated. Probably there was a pistol in the pocket of her bathrobe. She kept sticking her hand in there, making it hard for Ellis to tell if it carried any tell-tale weight. If he could keep her talking—usually pretty easy with drunks—he might be able to defuse the situation enough to get out of the house alive.

"C'mon," he said, "let's sit down. Tell me what your brother did that was so bad you had him killed."

"Larry was the CAA agent I told you about who raped me."

Ellis didn't trust her, but he wanted her placated. Lying or not, the more she talked, the better. "That's awful."

"No shit. Larry resented me from the minute I was born. He told me so and proceeded to make it obvious. But still, he was my big brother, and I worshiped him. If he paid me any attention at all—if he so much as glared at me across the dinner table, I would swell up with... I don't know what... pride, I guess? Love? How fucked up is that? Anyway, he would ignore me for weeks and then all of a sudden call me down to the den like he wanted to share something really special with me, and I would run in there, so excited, and he would knock me down and jump on my back and pull my arm out of the socket, like he was trying to tear it off. He did it all the time. And I kept falling for it. He got home from school earlier than I did, and he would hide in the coat closet until I came home. Then, he would jump out wearing this hairy werewolf mask and scare the shit out of me. He would jump out of the closet in my bedroom in the middle of the night, too. It scared me so bad I literally pissed the bed. He would wait in there *for hours* just to terrorize me.

"Years later, after he came home from college back east and was working as an assistant at CAA, I was just getting started—or so I thought—modelling and acting, and he told me he could get Phaedra Sutton to represent me. She was like, *the* agent du jour for hot young TV actresses. She handled Robin Givens, Alyssa

Milano, Lisa Bonet, and the girl from *Growing Pains*, the anorexic one…?"

"Tracey Gold," said Ellis.

"Right. So, Larry set up a meeting at Phaedra's house, and when I got there, we had a glass of wine, and I didn't even finish mine before I was lightheaded, and my vision was all blurry. I remember saying I felt dizzy, and then," Baby snapped her fingers, "I woke up on the floor of a hotel somewhere and Larry was on top of me, like when we were kids, but this time he was raping me. Phaedra was on the bed, masturbating and snarling like an animal, watching the whole thing, wearing a werewolf mask."

"What the fuck?"

"The next morning, I shot my Preparation H commercial. There I was, happily extolling its benefits—*relieves burning and itch on contact*—while my own asshole was burning and itching because my brother…" A tear crested her lashes and rolled down her cheek to the corner of her lips. She took a deep breath. "He had to die… Since then, I've just been biding my time." She stepped away from the hearth. "There's no way I'm the only woman he did this to, and didn't you say he wanted to show you his dick? It's a long way from rape but it's still pretty fucked up."

"Most definitely."

"Larry was a monster. He would have just kept hurting people."

Baby took another step toward Ellis. He backed toward the door, thinking that maybe he would have to just bolt, leap down the steps, run to the Porsche, and get the hell out of Dodge before she shot him in the back. He was too far away for that yet. He took another step back.

"But why all the stuff between you and me? The dinner dates and flirting? Why not just shoot me in my car some night? Why make it so personal?"

"Because *I'm* not a killer. And because making it personal is fun! I'm an actress. I don't need the industry's or anybody else's permission. I work all the time. Twenty-four seven. I told my friend I ran over a coyote on Figueroa. I was crying and everything. I FaceTimed her so she could see the tears. It was all acting. Yesterday, I made Anton jealous by telling him about a guy who made a pass at me in Erewhon. I didn't even go to Erewhon yesterday. I was acting when I told you Barbara Streisand in *A Star is Born* made me want to be an actress. That movie bored me to death. I slept through most of it."

"If you're doing all that and nobody else is acting, you're just lying."

"But everybody *is* acting. All the time. Only some of us realize it. It's Deena who hates *Graveyardland*. Belinda loves it. Belinda thinks Kent Moran is a total genius."

"How does Baby Sue Scoggins feel?"

She took another step toward, holding Ellis's gaze. "I knew by the self-deprecating, humble-bragging way you dropped Kent's name in AA, scoring easy clout in a room full of losers where it makes no difference except to your open wound of an ego, I knew then that you would be defenseless against a pretty lady who didn't like Kent, who liked you for you, and not your tenuous connection to a creative genius you only happen to know by dumb luck."

She breathed in through her nose like she was taking in the view from a mountain summit. "It was a rush getting you up here. I just want to stay in the moment, before the next part, which…" inhale… exhale… "is going to hurt."

Before he had time to wonder, she slapped Ellis so hard his ears rang and his vision clouded with stars. He was trying to shake his head clear when she raked his face and neck with her fingernails. Then another dizzying slap. He staggered, his face on fire.

She threw herself down on a walnut end table, toppling it and smashing a ceramic lamp. She twisted the cord around her neck twice and pulled hard. *"RA-A-A-APE!"* She rolled her face in the shards, breaking them smaller and smaller. "…*r-rape… p-p-please s-s-stop…*"

Getting to her feet, she cried as her pink soles were impacted with ceramic splinters. Once steady, she hopped backward, as if attempting a flip, and struck her head against the portrait of Marilyn Monroe. The glass shattered and rained down on her as she wallowed, banging her heels and elbows against the floor, screaming for help. Her robe fell open. In total commitment to the role, she was nude underneath. Struggling to her knees, she clawed the wall and beat her head against it.

*Go!* a voice in Ellis's head screamed. *Now!*

He broke for the door but only got a few feet before Christian blocked his way, holding a small, black semi-automatic pistol. His grip was sloppy because of the splint on his finger, and his stance was too narrow. He took one shaking hand off the weapon and pushed his hair out of his eyes.

"Christian," Ellis put his hands up, "Put the gun down, man. This situation doesn't have to get any worse, okay? Just put the gun down and—"

"What the f-f-fuck are you waiting f-f-for?" said the boy's mother. Her nose poured blood. Her swollen purple lips sparkled in the firelight with slivers of glass. "Def-f-f-fend me, idiot! Sh-h-hoot him!"

Christian spun and pointed the gun at her. "Shut the fuck up!"

"What are y—?"

"I said, shut. *The fuck.* UP!" Christian wiped away tears and pushed his hair back. "I'm done listening to you. I'm done. I'm done lying, and covering for you, and being your little fucking bitch boy. You're fucking sick!"

"I'm your mot-t-ther."

"What kind of mother pushes her kid into porn?"

"I'm als-s-so you're manager. I never push-h-hed you into anything! You have a gif-f-ft. You begged me to introduc-c-ce you to—"

Christian turned the quaking gun back on Ellis. "She's been lying since you got here. She's never seen an episode of *Graveyardland* from beginning to end. She doesn't love it or hate it. She doesn't love or hate anything except *A Star is Born*. She loves that. She plays the soundtrack all the time. She was lying about lying, for fuck's sake. And her real name is Brenda Jarvis, not Baby Jane Whatever-the-fuck."

He pushed his hair back and aimed at his mother. "You're lying about Uncle Larry raping you, too, aren't you?"

"Christian… s-s-sweetie… you're having another epis-s-sode. I can s-s-see it in your eyes-s. You haven't taken your meds-s."

"Stop it! Just…" he was panting, "stop…"

He vomited, right in Ellis's path to the door.

"S-s-sweetie, lis-s-sten to me, he's-s-s the problem," she pointed at Ellis. "He did this-s-s. This-s-s sh-h-hould have been a family matter. S-s-sweetie, I love you."

Christian shot his mother in the cheek. Blood spattered the wall where Marilyn used to hang.

Sweat, tears, snot, and vomit ran down Christian's face. He turned the gun on Ellis.

"Why did you come here? I tried to warn you."

"You did?"

"I was trying to be cool about it. I didn't know she was calling herself Deena until just now. So, even if I said, flat out, my mom, Belinda, had her brother Larry killed and she's gonna kill you too, you still would have ended up here, thinking you were gonna get to fuck Deena, right?"

Right. "Well, I mean, not necessarily. She said she just wanted to talk. Christian, please, put the gun down. Come on, man, really... Come on... I can help you. I'm on your side. I'll say you had no choice. Listen, man, framing me for rape was never gonna work. DNA evidence will prove I never touched—"

"Have you been living under a rock? Of course, it'll work. You stalked me to the set of my movie, you stalked Anton to a private session in Beverly Hills, then you broke in here and assaulted my mom. I freaked out and shot her by accident."

"Christian, don't! Think—"

*KA-BANG!!*

Something sharp struck Ellis's ear. Certain he'd been shot, he dropped to the floor and scrambled behind the sofa, where he realized Christian had missed; the bullet hit the stone accent wall behind Ellis, and a chunk of it had hit him. He clawed the .38 out of his pocket.

The camera zoomed out.

LONG SHOT: the King of Cable, Aaron Grant eviscerated by a shotgun blast from Nazario Sanchez. SMASH CUT: the Porsche crashed on San Fernando Boulevard; Sanchez shooting out the rear windshield. DOLLY IN: blood running down Ellis's face, returning fire. FULL SHOT: Nazario's knee exploding; him dropping the shotgun. CRANE SHOT: Ellis shooting the boy in the throat as he grasps for the shotgun. SMASH CUT: Ellis sprayed in the face with Larry Price's blood and skull fragments. SMASH CUT: bullets piercing the sofa inches from Ellis's face.

Back in the present moment, Ellis heard Christian's approaching footsteps crunching the glass and ceramic debris. He wouldn't miss again. Ellis's mouth was dry and tasted metallic. His voice wouldn't come. Christian was close enough now that Ellis could smell his cologne through the tang of gunpowder and vomit.

Adjusting his sweaty grip on the .38, he wondered if dying by the gun wasn't the most cosmically balanced outcome. Maybe this was his irreversible fate, to reap precisely as he had sown. Maybe he should surrender to karma. But then, he flashed to Double-Double value meals, reruns, the smell of Kara Castillo's shampoo, Reshma's crooked tooth that showed when she laughed... Fuck the cosmic balance. The gun was his salvation.

He took a deep breath, held it, and in one motion, popped up and threw the pistol overhand like a baseball. It nailed Christian in the face. Blood spurted from his nose. He yelped and pulled the trigger of his semi-auto. The round cut the Christmas tree in half, dousing the lights and raining glass icicles to the floor.

Stumbling backward, he hit his head on the mantle, fired again, shattering a window, before dropping the gun and falling into the fireplace. His luxuriant hair ignited. Howling, he got to his knees and beat himself on the head to smother the flames that had spread to his sweater. The smoke alarm blared.

Ellis flung a vase of cut flowers at Christian. But there was no water. The flowers were fake, and they melted while the boy writhed.

# CHAPTER 25

FOR THE NEXT TWO DAYS, high winds blew smoke from a wildfire in Sunland-Tujunga down onto North Hollywood, where Ellis was touring a 450-square-foot studio apartment in a newly renovated building called The Moxie. Despite the "energy-saving, double-pane windows," the bouquet of fresh paint and Clorox was polluted.

"Wood-inspired laminate flooring in the living-dining space," said Reshma, her voice muffled by the N95 respirator mask she was wearing on the recommendation of the county Department of Public Health. "Subway tile backsplash and new, stainless-steel appliances in the gourmet kitchenette."

The mask made breathing even more unpleasant for Ellis, so he went without. He oohed and ahhed at the "stylish light fixtures" and "modern ceiling fan," but he kept seeing Christian Cooper in the ICU, bandaged like a mummy, intubated and mute, plugged into beeping machines that were keeping him alive and numb. All he could do was blink when Ellis apologized to him. Hurting Christian was the second-to-last thing he had wanted to do. The very last thing was to kill the boy. At least he hadn't done that, though the prognosis was bleak.

"…designer tile in the bathroom," Reshma said, "and a spacious closet…"

Before going to the hospital, Ellis had eaten a 25-mg. Dr. Zonker's Sunrise Sativa Strawberry Granola Bar—the first edible he had dared since Krampus Night—but it didn't kick in until after he left and was headed to The Foxwood Room, where he downed a double bourbon and a Corona before meeting Reshma here at The Moxie. Apart from being late, so far, so good.

"…just a few blocks from the Arts District, with a walkability index of eighty-nine."

"Eighty-nine? That's all I needed to hear," said Ellis. "I'll take it."

He wasn't too buzzed to realize it would take nothing short of a miracle to make the $1,575 rent every month, but he *was* buzzed enough to sign the lease anyway.

While he made out the check for the deposit, Reshma said, "If you're thinking of getting a pet, cats and small dogs are welcome at The Moxie for a one-time, non-refundable fee of two hundred dollars."

He thought of Stevie Nicks, the yellow bobtail cat, out there in the flaming streets, eating roadkill. Alas. "Nah, I'm not thinking of getting a pet." He handed Reshma the check.

"This one's not going to bounce, is it?" Her smile was wry and her tone was playful, but Ellis saw through it. She had every right to be concerned, and he told her so, with a promise that the check would clear. Next month, there was no guarantee, but that wouldn't be her problem.

She took off her mask and suggested they take a commemorative selfie. The bad air made the light coming through the Venetian blinds blood-orange and soft. Reshma's breast touched Ellis's arm when they leaned into frame. He wasn't sure whether it was more awkward to move it away or pretend he didn't notice. He went with the latter. Reshma didn't seem to notice either as she clicked away, calibrating the angles of her chin and decolletage and finetuning her smile—sometimes coy, sometimes wide enough to expose her crooked canine tooth. Her bosom, still rubbing his arm, was firmer than Ellis had guessed. Probably because it took thick, sturdy material to make an effective bra that big.

Satisfied with the coverage, Reshma stepped back and scrolled through the pictures.

"Great," she said. "They look really real."

She showed Ellis her favorite. Her crooked tooth showed, and the copper light accentuated the swell of her breasts. Ellis asked her to send it to him.

"It does look really real," he said when it came through, not quite knowing what he meant.

"So, what's happening with your show?" she asked. "Did you make a deal with Netflix?"

"No. No, not yet." Ellis looked out the window where, if the sky weren't full of ash, he would have had an unobstructed view of the 170 freeway. "But we, uh… we're optimistic."

"What's it like working with Kent Moran again?"

"It's okay."

"He's a genius."

Ellis rubbed his chin. "Mm-hmm."

"Can you give me *any* details? I'm dying to know what it's about. I won't tell anyone, I promise."

"Well, I can tell you it's a reboot of a popular IP."

"Oh." A hitch in her smile. "I thought you said it was something new."

"It is. It's a new take—actually, yet another, *even newer*, take on *Miami Vice*, but replacing Crockett and Tubbs, the characters you know and love, with—hang onto your hat—lesbians of color. No shit. Finally, right? *Miami Vice* for the," air quotes, "*modern audience.*"

Reshma was deadpan. "You're making fun of me." She swept the lease and Ellis's check into her fake Louis Vuitton handbag and looped the strap over her shoulder.

"Wait, don't— Reshma, wait. I'm sorry." His stomach turned. Without trying, he had hurt Reshma and ruined the moment again. "I wasn't making fun of you, I swear. It's just…" She turned and faced him, still impassive. "The show is off. I mean, it's still happening, but not for me. Kent hired another writer. A twenty-year-old smartass with an axe to grind—" Getting mad all over again, he cut himself off and took a breath… "Sorry. Anyway, I'm just really… bummed out about it."

He looked down and away from Reshma's hard stare. A door slammed in another apartment. A car stereo thumped in the parking lot. Sirens cried on the 170.

"Yesterday, Prashanth went back east to spend the holidays with his father and stepfather," said Reshma. "We needed a break from each other, but I miss him."

"Did, uh, something happen?"

"Last week, he got into a fight with another boy and put him in the hospital. The police got involved."

Ellis started to sweat. Both times he called Prashanth to follow up, the calls went to voicemail and weren't returned. It hadn't occurred to Ellis that it might be because the boy was in Juvenile Hall.

"No charges were filed. Not yet anyway."

Ellis swallowed hard and licked his lips. "I should have told you sooner, but I took Prashanth and Zayne to the hospital that day. Prashanth called me after the fight."

"When he refused to tell me who gave them a ride, I figured it was you. Anybody else he would have told on."

"I didn't want to tell on him either, but still, you had a right to know. I should have handled the whole thing differently. I see that now. I was just—" kicked off the show he thought would be his ticket to a new life and almost killed by a hit man— "occupied with my own shit at the time. It's not an excuse, it's—"

"It's okay. You were being loyal."

"I was being a coward."

"How so?"

"I was afraid if you knew I was an aid and accomplice to another one of Prashanth's screw ups, I'd never see you again."

"I'm glad you were there for him."

"Me too, but somehow, I always manage to let you down. I'm late, my check bounces, I say the wrong thing or do the right thing the wrong way… It's exhausting for me; I can only imagine what a trip it is for you. I don't know, I just can't seem to get it right. And that sucks because you're the person in the world I most want to impress—even more than Hollender, and I've known him since I was a kid. But you… I feel like you really see who I am and still believe in me."

"I do."

"I wish I knew why."

Reshma took a deep, bosom-swelling breath. "Let's go celebrate, and I'll show you."

"Celebrate?"

"Christmas Eve eve. New beginnings."

"Okay, yeah. That'd be great. I know a place to get a drink right over on Magnolia, The Foxwood Room. It's dark, old school, low key."

"I was thinking dinner at Bhairavi Market on Sherman Way. It's colorful, new, and upbeat. Plus, it's in Reseda, and the air is better there."

"Perfect. I hear it's the cat's pajamas."

Turning to the door, they were stopped by a high-pitched squall. For a second, Ellis thought it was a baby. But then, a yellow bobtail cat sprang onto the quartz breakfast bar.

Reshma's mouth popped open. Her eyes bugged. "How in the world—? When did a cat get in here? How…?"

Ellis approached the cat, who started pacing and meowing in a familiar scratchy voice. Sure enough, one of her fangs was broken. Stevie Nicks had found him again.

"What did you say the pet fee was?" He asked Reshma, withdrawing his checkbook.

They left Stevie with a stopped-up sink of water and a promise to return with some leftover tandoori shrimp.

Walking to their cars, Reshma said, "If you're interested, I think I might have a job for you. It's not a TV-writing job, though, so don't get too excited."

Ellis could tell she was smiling under her N95. He smiled too. "What is it?"

"A friend of mine manages an apartment building in West Hollywood, and someone has been stealing fixtures and vandalizing the empty apartments. He doesn't want to call the police because some of the tenants used to be sort of famous, and they're touchy about their privacy."

"Well, I've got a wide-open schedule and an expensive new apartment," said Ellis. "I can't wait to hear more."

## Acknowledgements

My thanks to Melissa McMurtrie, T.E. Vaughn, Howard Michael Gould, Joseph Schneider, Denise Salhany, Daniel D. Smith, Sr., and Elise Lewis

## About the Author

Keith Edward Vaughn is the author of essays, art criticism, and fiction. His debut novel, *The Loneliest Places*, was published in 2023 by Blondie Street Publishing. This is his second novel.